Arrow
to
the
Heart

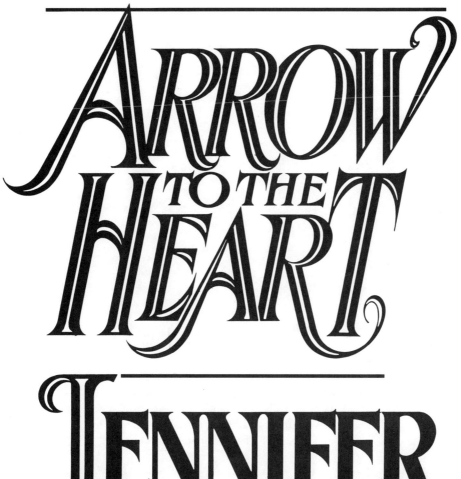

ARROW TO THE HEART

JENNIFER BLAKE

FAWCETT COLUMBINE • NEW YORK

*Bla
C3*

A Fawcett Columbine Book
Published by Ballantine Books
Copyright © 1993 by Patricia Maxwell

Library of Congress Cataloging-in-Publication Data
Blake, Jennifer, 1942–
    Arrow to the heart / Jennifer Blake. — 1st ed.
    p. cm.
    ISBN 0-449-90824-0
    1. Louisiana—History—Fiction. I. Title.
PS3563.A923A89 1993
813'.54—dc20   92-55000
                                                          CIP

Design by Holly Johnson

Manufactured in the United States of America

First Edition: July 1993
10 9 8 7 6 5 4 3 2 1

Arrow TO THE HEART

CHAPTER ONE

The dance, a quadrille, was ending as the man entered the ballroom. Katrine Castlereagh saw him at once from her vantage point on the dais. She drew a sudden, sharp breath, then stood perfectly still.

The new arrival paused in the doorway, glancing around him with quiet assurance. The butler had left his post as the evening advanced; there was no one to announce this late-coming guest, no one to take his high evening hat of black silk or the rain-spotted cloak that hung in heavy folds reaching from his broad shoulders to his heels.

The dance floor cleared, leaving an open stretch of gleaming parquet between the door and the dais. The man turned his head, gazing down the aislelike stretch of space.

His gaze narrowed as it fastened upon Katrine. He allowed himself a slow and complete inspection of her person from her shining curls to the hem of her ball gown. His expression was hard, stringently assessing, before it smoothed into polite, social blandness. Removing his hat, he tucked it under his arm and began to walk toward her.

He moved with long-limbed grace and a total lack of self-consciousness. His stride was neither too fast nor too slow, but held enough controlled power to cause his cloak to expose its red silk lining as it dipped and swirled around him.

His evening clothes were perfectly tailored to his tall, solid-muscled frame and correctly somber, yet the rich cream-on-white paisley of his waistcoat hinted at exuberance. The dark waves of his hair were close-cropped; the soft rain of a Louisiana autumn falling beyond the ballroom's long windows had spangled them with droplets that caught the light from the wax tapers in the chandeliers overhead. Smile lines were set around his mouth and eyes, burned there by the same hot winds and strong suns that had weathered his skin to the golden brown of the polished oak floor. The green of his eyes was the muted, reflective shade of a woodland pool, a dark color that hinted at deep and private thoughts.

Katrine's husband, Giles Castlereagh, standing at her left hand, turned from his nephew to whom he had been talking as he noticed the approach of the new guest. An odd excitement came and went across his puffy features. He shifted with ponderous deliberation and descended a single step from the dais, putting out his hand to grasp that of the other man.

"Rowan de Blanc, I believe?" Giles said in smooth satisfaction. "Welcome to Arcadia. Permit me to present you to my wife, sir. Katrine, my dear, you will have heard a great deal in the past about M'sieur de Blanc."

Katrine turned from signaling for the butler to come forward and take their guest's hat and cloak. Her greeting was given automatically, as a matter of training, though she was not sure what she said as she surveyed the man at close quarters.

Rowan de Blanc inclined his dark head in a bow. The movement, she saw, was just as it should be, low enough to show respect, not so low as to suggest undue humility. His voice as he made his salutation was deep and even in timbre and his choice of phrase gallant without being flirtatious. If he noticed the tremor in her hand as she gave it to him, he was considerate enough to give no sign of it. His grasp was firm yet gentle and the brush of his lips on the gloved back impersonal in spite of its heat.

His brow was broad, his nose straight; his lashes a thick ambush from which to view the world. There was generosity in the molded shape of his mouth and his chin was aggressive in its firmness. He would have been devastating if there had been any warmth in his expression, Katrine thought. As it was, he was too handsome, too well-bred, too strong, too discerning, too experienced. Rowan de Blanc was much too near perfect for comfort. And because of it, he terrified her.

"You will forgive my tardy arrival, I hope," the newcomer said, nodding his thanks at the same time to the butler who relieved him of his outer wear. "The *St. Louis Belle* was late in landing at St. Francisville this evening. Though I received your invitation to the tournament while in New Orleans, I only learned of the ball to open the festivities after I reached my rooms here."

"Think nothing of it," Giles answered with an expansive gesture. "The gathering was an impulse arranged because several of the gentlemen arrived ahead of time. In any case, Katrine and I had only just begun to think of deserting our post."

"You're very generous," the other man said, his gaze resting on Katrine's face once more as she stood in regal stiffness before him.

The lady was not, Rowan had to admit, precisely what he had expected. There was no hardness in the warm coffee brown of her eyes, no evasion in her gaze. The delicate flush that overlaid her cream-satin skin gave her finely drawn features a look of freshness, while the moist and sweetly curving lines of her parted lips drew his gaze like a magnet. There was fascination in her hair that fell in thick, shining coils from a diamond pin at the crown of her head. The color was elusive, now russet and gold with shadings of rich brown, now warm brown with a red-gold sheen. Her gown of sea-green brocade draped the gently rounded curves of her breasts, hugged the narrow span of her rigidly corseted waist, then billowed into the enormous, shimmering bell of her skirt.

There was a certain medieval appearance to the long, flowing cuffed sleeves of her gown. It was appropriate for the occasion, and also the setting. The gilded paper of the ballroom's walls was half-hidden by age-darkened tapestries and the banners of kings long dead; the musicians playing pianoforte, violins, French horn, and harp were dressed like court fools, while through the open doorway of the supper room could be seen a long trestle table. There was no torchlight or rushes on the floor, however. Giles Castlereagh had been wise enough not to become too carried away by the present vogue for the literary excesses of Sir Walter Scott.

Quietly on the air came the first strains of the old English air "Greensleeves" played to a gentle waltz tempo. Rowan took instant advantage of the music. "If you have indeed finished receiving your guests, Madam Castlereagh, may I have the honor of this dance?"

Dismay congealed upon Katrine's features. "No. Oh, no, really—that is, I believe I am already engaged for it."

Her husband turned his head to stare at her with a lifted brow. "Are you, my dear? To whom?"

"To you, naturally," Katrine said with color rising to her cheeks, "as it will be the first of the evening."

"Nonsense. We won't stand on ceremony, not when my gout is near crippling me."

"I will sit the dance out with you then." Her words were decided. Giles was a man of many ailments, most of them highly convenient, for him. They were also useful to her on occasion.

"No, no. Go along with M'sieur de Blanc. I will not have you deprived, and you know I like watching you enjoy yourself. Besides, I think I hear the siren call of the card room."

"Really, Giles—" she began in protest.

"To please me?"

The request was mild, but the look in his eyes was adamant. She could press the matter no further without giving offense to Rowan de Blanc.

"As you wish." Lowering her lashes, Katrine placed her hand upon the stiffly held arm of the dark-haired man, permitting him to lead her onto the floor.

They circled gently, with the correct distance separating them and the correct formal restraint in their movements together. In spite of that, there was an uncomfortable intensity in the gaze he bent upon her. The freshness of the damp night clung to him, mingling with the warm male scent of well-ironed linen and bay rum. His grasp at her waist, firmly guiding her into the turns, seemed to burn the imprint of his fingers into her skin. The movements of his thighs with their well-defined horseman's muscles were disturbing as his legs pressed against the silken fullness of her hooped skirts.

Katrine drew a deep but discreet breath to steady her nerves. There was no point in sulking; it was not going to help. She gave Rowan a swift upward glance as she said, "I would not have expected someone of your repute to be amused by our annual games."

"I wasn't aware I had a reputation, Madam Castlereagh," he returned.

"Your brother spoke of you at length. He was proud of your exploits, you know."

"I know." The words were abrupt.

Her gaze flickered away, then back again. "I only meant that our archery competitions and jousting at brass rings must seem tame. They can hardly be compared to hunting with the Indians of the Amazon forests, riding with Arabs with blue faces, or trekking into the heart of Africa."

"You think I require an element of risk to ensure my amusement? Your tournament can supply that, surely."

The lethal softness of his voice sent a tremor down the length of Katrine's spine, but she refused to acknowledge it. "I doubt the small dangers of competition can equal those in your travels."

He smiled down at her, a superficial movement of his lips. "Such ventures can be expensive, and you forget the prize for the winner."

"A purse of gold? What do you care for that? Your father's estate was more than adequate, so I understand, to permit you to follow whatever whim may move you."

His smile faded. The words abrupt, with a slicing rapier's edge, he said, "Terence told you a great deal."

Katrine looked away from his direct gaze. "We spent much time talking."

"Did you?" He paused, then went on deliberately, "And did my brother tell you how much he loved you before he died? Did he, perhaps, die of love for you?"

Her gasp was so ragged that it tore at her throat. She missed a step, and he caught her close for an instant to aid her recovery. His arms were taut with muscle under the smooth broadcloth of his coat sleeves; the hard closeness of their hold was like a prison. Something stirred, fluttering in panic, at the center of her being.

She pushed away from him as she answered in sibilant tones. "No, he did not! There was never any hint of such a thing."

"Are you quite certain? Did he, perhaps, offend with his calflike adoration, so that he was forced to appear on the field of honor?"

"It wasn't like that at all. No one knows why he shot himself. He was only found beside the lake with the pistol in his hand."

"Then why," he said deliberately, "did my brother call you *la belle dame sans merci*, the beautiful lady without mercy?"

For a dreadful instant, Katrine saw the candlelight dim, heard a rushing in her ears. There was a constriction in her chest that could have been from remembered pain, from the press of her corset, or from the iron firmness of his grasp. She drew a difficult breath against it. She would not swoon, she would not.

"Terence, your brother—" she began.

"My half brother."

"Yes, I know," she said in distress. "He—those words were a jest of his, just a title he gave me."

"Was it indeed? Is that why he said you were most merciless of all with yourself?" His voice was low, almost intimate.

"I have no idea. I never knew he thought it—never knew he spoke of me."

"He wrote that and much more in his only letter home to his mother, our mother. He thought of you often, apparently. You intrigued him, the beautiful young woman married to a sickly and doting older man, smiling yet forlorn as you held your Court of Love—I do have that last right, do I not?"

"Yes, yes," she said almost at random. "It was a game we invented for the week of the tournament, Musetta, my sister-in-law, and I. Terence—played it well."

"He had imagination, if that's what you mean. He saw you as some bartered bride, traded by your father for an ideal, showered with riches by your husband while being kept imprisoned here at Arcadia like some medieval princess in a tower. It appealed to his sense of the romantic to think of rescuing you, though he knew you were well guarded."

"Don't be ridiculous," she said in a sudden surge of annoyance. "That isn't the way it is at all!"

"No?"

"Furthermore, I don't believe that your brother saw me as an object of pity."

"Not pity, but knight-errantry, perhaps. My mother, who is much like him, wondered if he tried to rescue you and was killed for his pains."

Katrine could hear the undertone of scorn in his voice. "But you think it unlikely? You are right. I can't imagine what he can have said to give her such an idea; it's far too fanciful."

"Terence had more sympathetic feeling than was good for him, but he was not known for being fanciful."

"Just what are you suggesting, then?" she demanded as the reviving effects of anger swept along her veins. "A sordid liaison? The revenge of a wronged husband?"

"It seems a possibility."

She lifted her chin with the lightning of wrath flashing in her dark brown eyes. "If you think so, then you know nothing of your brother."

"You know more?" There was a twist to his lips.

"Why not, when you have scarcely been near Louisiana in years. Even if that were not true, I fail to see how a man who spends his time adventuring in the wilds of Arabia can speak of another man's romantic impulses."

"My reasons for preferring other climes have nothing to do with romanticism." The words were stiff.

"No, your nose was totally out of joint because your mother remarried after your father died, because she left you with her father in England and traveled to this country to raise a second family, including another son to supplant you." It gave Katrine immense satisfaction to see his look of surprise and dislike at her knowledge of his background.

"It's true I was a misfit in my mother's new family and new life," he said evenly. "The reason had more to do with being of French and English blood and born in Europe than it did with jealousy of a younger brother."

"Half brother," she said in biting imitation of his earlier correction.

"He was no less to me for having a Louisiana Frenchman for a father. We were both my mother's sons. As for what I knew of him, I saw him every year or two in England, when he and my mother visited her father's family. And I understood him well enough to know that he would not have willingly left this earth and its joys."

Pain struck deep inside her, turning her gaze black as she stared up at him. Memories swept across her mind, memories she could never share with anyone, least of all this man who held her as they swayed and circled in time to the music. The song was winding down toward its end. She moistened her lips. Finally she said, "You did not come for the tournament."

"Did you think it for even a moment? No. I came to see you, madam, to discover what you can tell me about my brother's death."

"Nothing. I can tell you nothing." Her voice was a raveled thread of sound.

"I don't believe you," he returned without hesitation as the music died away and he was forced to release her. "I suppose that means I will have to stay for these games. What is the award for the first contest? The honor of escorting you in to dinner tomorrow night and sitting at your right hand? You will at least not be able to escape my questions then."

"You first have to win," she rejoined as she turned with her hand resting as lightly as possible on his arm, moving toward where her husband, Giles, stood talking to a neighbor.

"Oh, I believe that may be arranged," he answered.

The confidence in his voice was like the scraping of a fingernail on glass. "What arrogance," she said, "when you have not seen the other contestants."

"The event is fencing, I believe?" He lifted a brow as he spoke.

"Yes." Her voice was chill in its remoteness.

"There is no arrogance involved when you are able to do as you say."

They were too near Giles for her to form an answer, and he gave her no opportunity in any case. Expressing his gratitude for the dance with punctilious manners, he inclined his head in a curt bow, then left her.

Katrine stared after him, at his straight back, his wide shoulders emphasized by his dark coat, and the easy swing of his long legs. She thought she should have been relieved that Rowan de Blanc was using the tournament only as an excuse to visit Arcadia. Somehow, she was not. He had entered the lists, after all. That still made him dangerous.

Suddenly she hated this annual event, the round of fencing and archery and jousting at rings that always ended with a race staged with horses from Giles's beloved breeding stables. She despised the pageantry based on Scott's novels that Giles insisted upon, abhorred the false medieval pomp and pretense. It was her husband's show, all of it; it had nothing to do with her. She had wanted to cancel it this year, but he would not hear of it. If her wishes had been followed, then Rowan de Blanc would have had no excuse for coming here.

"What did the man do to make you so furious?"

Her husband's nephew asked the question with sly insinuation as he paused beside her. The son of an older brother, Lewis Castlereagh was a young man near her own age. Katrine barely glanced at his slender form as she answered. "Nothing whatever. What makes you think so?"

"You are frowning at him as if you would like to put a knife in his back."

She lifted a hand to touch the pucker between her eyes. "I must be getting a headache."

"My dear Katrine, don't be coy. I saw you having words with the man." A smile remarkably like a sneer curled Lewis's thin lips. He watched her intently, his pale blue eyes as silvery as mirrors reflecting an empty room.

"Did you?"

"Terence's older brother, is he not? I wonder why he came."

"For the obvious reason, I would suppose," she said shortly.

"Oh, do you think so? You should know if anyone does. He appears a formidable competitor and very sure of himself."

"He is certainly that," Katrine answered with a trace of quiet bitterness.

"Ah, well, perhaps we can hope for a defeat for him tomorrow. A nice little sword cut perhaps, right between the eyes."

Katrine was loath to agree with Lewis about anything. He was not her favorite person, a feeling that was mutual. Vain, grasping, with a gift for active malice, he had, from the day he arrived from England six years ago, just before she was wed to his uncle, set himself to annoy her. He resented the marriage and lived in constant anxiety that she would conceive a child who might inherit all of Giles's considerable estate. He need not have worried, though Katrine had no intention of explaining the matter to him.

Lewis smoothed a hand over his fine, silver-blond hair, pushing back the straight, metallic strands on his forehead in a quick gesture of irritation. "You know," he said acidly, "you really should warn Giles if de Blanc means to make trouble."

"I expect Giles is able to judge that for himself. He did invite the man."

"So he did. One is forced to wonder why, given the circumstances."

Katrine gave him a stabbing glance. "What do you mean by that?"

"Why, the untimely end of young Terence last fall, what else?" He opened his eyes wide while he waited, scarcely breathing, for her reply.

She should have known he was angling for information. He

dearly loved secrets, especially those of other people. She was saved from having to reply, however, by the arrival of another man. She turned, thankfully, to give Alan Delaney a welcoming smile.

"Did I hear you mention Terence?" Alan said. "I've been thinking of him often of late—natural, I suppose, with the tournament at hand. I miss him. He was one of the few who understood when I talked of books."

Giles's nephew gave the other man a cynical smile. "We were speaking also of his older brother. Rowan de Blanc has been annoying our Katrine. We can't have that now, can we?"

Alan was of average height and solidly built. Dressed with neatness and circumspection, he had the ruddy complexion of an outdoorsman in spite of his serious manner and bookish turn. He was also no one's fool; he knew well enough when he was being baited. He frowned at Lewis with color rising under his skin before he turned to Katrine. "Is this true, madam?"

"Not in the way Lewis suggests," she said shortly.

"Did I mention in what way?" Lewis protested.

Alan ignored the other man as he insisted, "But de Blanc was giving you trouble?"

"I was irritated with him, that's all," Katrine answered. "He seems to think I was in some way to blame for Terence's death."

"Ridiculous," Alan said with a shake of his head. "He should know you are the most blameless of women; he has only to look at you to tell. Shall I speak to him?"

"I beg you won't do anything of the kind!"

"No, no," Lewis thrust in, "I doubt he would listen anyway. But you have some skill at fencing, as I recall, and the Delaneys never lack for courage. It would be a fine thing if you could give him a scratch or two to remind him of his manners."

Alan met Lewis's calculating gaze with a steady regard. "The sabers will be blunted, you know."

"The points only, not the edges."

"True, but there are still rules a man cannot break and be called honorable."

Lewis shrugged. "Well, then, let him know he has been in a fight. If you can."

"What of you?"

"I? Cunning is my forte. I leave real swordsmanship to stalwarts like yourself."

"I will try my best, as always." Alan's words were dry.

"That," Lewis said with matching irony, "should do the trick." Dividing a sour smile between Alan and Katrine, he nodded and walked away.

"Coxcomb," Alan muttered under his breath.

Katrine was inclined to agree, though she pretended not to hear.

It was later, as supper was ending, that Musetta drifted to Katrine's side in a swirl of golden yellow gauze. Giles's half sister, born of his mother's second marriage and some twenty years younger than he, was holding a plate of ivory china trimmed in gold and eating the last crumbs of a buttery-yellow coconut macaroon. With her soft, golden blond curls cascading around piquant features and over her ivory-tinted shoulders, she made an exquisite picture. It was the kind of artless artistry that was typical of Musetta.

"Tell me quickly, Katrine," she said in soft, suggestive tones, "is he worthy of our court?"

"You mean Rowan de Blanc?" Katrine gave her sister-in-law an innocent look.

"You know I do; the rest we have taken apart and put back together a dozen times over."

"Have we?"

"You especially. Don't be mean. I have done everything except dangle my dance card in front of his nose, but he has asked no one to stand up with him except you. Answer me."

"Very well," Katrine said, her voice abrupt. "I don't think he will do."

Musetta drew back a little, her cerulean-blue eyes widening. "But he seems such a valuable candidate. Think of the European polish he can bring, think of the knowledge of women and love he must have gained during his travels. You can't tell me you don't want to hear what he has to say?"

"I don't think he will be interested in word games. And I don't think you would care for his answers to your questions."

Musetta tilted her head, her eyes narrowing. "You intrigue me, yes, you do. Is that what you intended?"

"Not at all," Katrine said with a shake of her head that brought a shining auburn curl rolling over her shoulder. "I just think it would be a mistake to treat this man lightly. He is here about Terence."

"What of it? If he asks questions, there will be no answers, for we have none. His name is entered for the tournament; he will compete with the others. While he rests with the others, perhaps he will play, like the others."

A moist wind lifted the lace curtains at the window near where they stood. Its cool breath brushed Katrine's shoulders. She folded her arms at the waist, rubbing at the gooseflesh that roughened her skin. Frowning a little, Katrine told her sister-in-law of Rowan de Blanc's threat to win the next day's contest in order to question her at his leisure.

"You are taking it all too seriously, as usual," Musetta said with a shrug.

"I still wish Giles had settled for a simple house party," Katrine replied in moody tones.

"And spoil our fun? Don't be silly. I swear, if I didn't know better, I'd think you wanted to keep Rowan de Blanc to yourself. I saw the way you hung on to him when you stumbled."

"I didn't." Delicate color rose in Katrine's cheeks in spite of the denial.

Musetta gave her a wicked smile. "I wouldn't mind clutching a handful or two of him myself. I can't wait to see him stripped for the fencing. Dear me, the way his pantaloons will stretch across the backs of his legs. It makes me feel quite warm to think of it."

Watching Musetta unfurl her fan and ply it hard enough to make her curls fly around her face, Katrine asked, "What would Brantley say if he could hear you?"

The other woman shrugged. "He would pull his beard, frown his disapproval, and go back to counting cotton bales. If he won't dance with me himself, or amuse me with a little conversation, then he can hardly complain if I look elsewhere."

Musetta's marriage had been arranged by her brother after her arrival from England trailing the scent of scandal from an aborted elopement to Gretna Green, apparently not her first such escapade. That the match was a mistake was accepted by everyone except Giles.

Katrine said, "And Perry?" The music was beginning again as the musicians answered a signal from Giles, who had appeared at the far end of the room. She had to raise her voice to be heard over the strains of a Strauss waltz.

"Dear Peregrine," Musetta said with warmth rising in her eyes for the young man who had been entertaining her of late. "I might consider his thoughts, if he asked me."

There was the sound of a step behind them, then a quiet voice made rough with emotion asked, "My thoughts on what?"

Musetta turned in a yellow swirl of skirts. "Perry, my love, there you are. I've been waiting for you. You must tell me what you think of our new arrival as we dance. Will he best all of you as easily as he boasts?"

A moment later they were gone. Katrine stood watching as the two blended with the other dancers, the laughing blond woman and the slim dark-haired young man with the serious face, dark, fiery eyes, and moist red lips. Perry, it appeared, was denying with vehement emphasis that he would be bested by anyone. His flamboyant gestures were in keeping with the flowing polka-dotted cravat and overly long hair of the romantic style he favored.

Katrine sighed a little and tightened her arms around herself. Musetta was so capricious. She could be honey sweet one moment and a witch the next. She lived from moment to moment, swayed by the least emotion that touched her, with little care for the consequences of the things she said and did under its influence. In the two days since young Peregrine Blackstone had arrived, he had hardly left her side. Flattered by his obvious passion for her, she had little discretion.

But perhaps her husband wouldn't notice. Giles's brother-in-law was a busy man; the responsibility for the prosperity of Arcadia rested on his sturdy shoulders. Acting as Giles's man of business, he kept a careful accounting of every acre of cotton put into production, every mule, breeding mare, piece of furniture and knickknack bought, every item used from the storehouse, and every bite of food consumed at every table. He attended to the sale of the cotton and watched over Giles's fortune in gold that increased with every growing season.

Heavyset, several years older than his wife, bearded in the style recently made popular by Napoléon III, he could be officious at times. It was Brantley Hennen who parceled out Katrine's monthly household allowance and her personal pin money. It was only natural that she should resent him for the careful way he counted it out coin by coin each time, as if it came from his own pocket. That did not, however, keep her from feeling just a little sorry for him.

On the far side of the room, beyond the shifting kaleidoscope of dancers, Rowan de Blanc was standing with his broad shoulders propped against the wall. He was watching her, his dark brows drawn into a single line over his eyes.

Katrine had known he was there. She had felt his gaze upon

her from the moment he settled into position. There was something about the intensity of it that made her feel vulnerable, stripped bare of defenses. She didn't like it.

She had armored herself with hard-won resolution and dignity as the chatelaine of Arcadia and wife of its owner. She could not bear that anything should disturb her precarious balance in that role. She would not permit it. Not from Rowan de Blanc. No, and not even from Giles himself.

Turning her back on the man against the far wall, she lowered her hands, letting her left rest lightly on the bell of her skirt. She lifted the heavy satin brocade of her hem in the front with the other, then raised her chin to a proud tilt and walked slowly from the room.

Rowan de Blanc frowned as he watched that majestic departure. The provocative swing of Katrine Castlereagh's full skirts caused an ache in his groin that was as unexpected as it was uncomfortable. The way the candlelight gleamed on her shoulders, the shimmering silk of her hair made his fingers tingle with the need to touch, to hold. The urge to peel away the layers of heavy clothing she wore, to discover and explore the feminine mystery underneath, was so strong that he clenched his hands into fists in his effort to subdue it.

He was beginning to see why Terence had been bewitched.

Terence, so young and idealistic, had been no match for this woman, a married lady of wealth and position as well as unusual beauty. But he was. This he knew without conceit.

He would counter her every evasion, strip away her pretenses one by one. He would discover how his brother had come to die for her sake. He would know the truth, no matter how long it took, or what he had to do to force an answer.

He would not be denied. Nor would he be bewitched.

CHAPTER TWO

"Well, my dear, what do you think of the field?"

It was Giles who asked the question as he seated himself with care in the armchair beside the one where Katrine was ensconced. There was no one near them at the moment. A few other guests were climbing the wooden steps of the canvas-protected grandstand at the far end, but most were still straggling down from the great house or from the carriages lining the circular drive. The men shouted and called to each other, their voices ringing back in thin echoes from the dense woods that surrounded Arcadia. The women cried out greetings while trying to hold their parasols against the warm afternoon sun with one hand and keep their skirts from being stained as they trailed over the newly shorn grass with the other.

Beyond them, looming against the rich, Indian-summer blue of the sky, was the great Gothic pile of a house that Giles called his Arcadia, named for the Greek ideal of pastoral contentment. With its pale gray plastered walls, its angles inset with balconies, its pointed-arch window openings filled with stained glass and tall gable ends emphasized by quatrefoil carving, there was nothing either Greek or pastoral about it. Nor was there much contentment within its thick walls.

The lake, a still, brown pool with a glaze of blue on its surface from sky reflection, lay in a slight depression behind and to the side of the house. On the far bank, its entire height repeated in mirror image in the water, stood the tall, crenellated stone tower topped by a cupola that Giles had built as his retreat. It was designated as his folly, by his neighbors, in part because it served as a rather unique conservatory, but also because it was the fashion for plantations to have such a purposeless edifice. From the lake's edge, the lawn over which the guests moved made a perfect fan-shaped sweep down to the similar bowl-shaped hollow, like a natural arena, where the grandstand had been constructed.

"The field?" Katrine said in answer to her husband's question, allowing her gaze to rest on the stretch of greensward that lay stretched out before them. "It appears to be groomed to a nicety, every blade of grass cut just so, like a cloak of emerald velvet."

"You know very well I spoke of the field of contestants." Giles's voice was testy as he jerked his head in the direction of the men lining the open area.

She pursed her lips in a pretense of consideration. "Yes, well, they seem to be a remarkably hardy lot this year. I can't think when I've seen so much brawn all together in one place."

"Strength is important, and endurance."

The words were in the parlance of her husband's hobby and private passion, his breeding stables. She turned to give him a straight look as she answered. "So it is, for a stallion."

"Don't, please, make the matter more crude than it need be," he said with a heavy frown. "Is there none who finds favor, none you would put down money for to win?"

Her lips curved in a smile touched with irony. "Since strength is the criterion, then yes, there is. I rather like the looks of Satchel Godwin."

The man she spoke of was a giant, the most brawny of the lot. Bluff and hearty, he had sandy hair so rough it appeared he must wash it with lye, reddened skin that no amount of sun would ever tan, and a manner as coarse and irreverent as it was humorous. He loved sport of any kind, from fencing to fishing, and never missed one of the tournaments Giles arranged.

Her husband stared at her with censure in his faded blue eyes. "This is not a game, Katrine, it never was. I prefer that it not be treated lightly."

She looked down at her hands, worrying the edge of a flounce on her muslin gown. "I think it is a game, Giles. Only it's yours, not mine."

"You gave your word."

"Only because you would allow me no peace otherwise."

He drew a deep breath, letting it out in a heavy sigh. "Whatever the reason, I intend to hold you to it, one way or another."

Looking up in naked appeal, she said, "Giles, please—"

"No. You could have arranged this matter differently, with discretion and simple feminine wiles, if you had so chosen. You did not."

Distress sounded in her voice as she heard the finality in his words. "It isn't as easy as you seem to think."

"You are afraid, and that I count my fault, at least in part. You have been too long an innocent wife. You are wary of trusting yourself to another, have never developed those responses which—"

"That isn't it," she broke in with hot color flaming across her cheekbones. "It's just—it's wrong."

"I salute your principles, my dear, but they are a foolish impediment. Time is growing short."

"You are not going to die," she said shortly. She had spoken that reassurance so many times in the five years of their marriage that she had lost count, though usually it was expressed with more concern. That he had but a few short years to live was a morbid fancy of Giles's that he could not seem to shake.

"But I am, in due time. And due time for me is so much sooner than for you. You are young, Katrine, as I am not. It will be years before you follow me to the grave, years in which you may do as you please. But for now, I want this, want it with all my heart and soul. You must give it to me, or I—" He stopped abruptly, drawing himself up with his unseeing gaze fastened on the men on the field. Finally he gave himself a shake and reached to touch her hand. In a low voice of supplication, he said, "You will do the right thing, my dear. I know you will."

He pushed to his feet, then, and walked away. Katrine watched him go, watched his slow progress back down to ground level and along the edge of the cleared field toward where the contestants were choosing their fencing weapons.

Giles would like to be one of the combatants, she knew. That his days of vigorous, manly activity were over was a constant irritation. It was, perhaps, a part of his obsession. Just as he was unable to perform on the field, he was unable to perform in the bedroom, unable to render her the service he felt was her due. Just as he was reduced to watching other men compete in the tournaments he arranged, he also needed to watch—

No. She would not think such things of him. He was her husband and he loved her in his way. Though she had married him from duty and deference to her father's wishes, she had come to have a fondness for him.

He was unfailingly thoughtful and generous; hardly a day went by when he did not do something to show his consideration for her welfare. He was a kind master to his servants, a host who dispensed Arcadia's bountiful hospitality as a joy rather than a duty. He was an honorable man, one of high standing in the nearby town of St. Francisville and in the entire area of Louisiana that had once been known as British West Florida. How could she complain of anything he might ask of her?

There was a light step behind her. Katrine turned her head,

smiling as she saw her maid, Delphia. The other woman carried a pair of fans dangling from their silk cords.

"So has anything interesting happened?" Delphia said as she handed Katrine one fan, keeping the other for herself.

"Not really," Katrine answered.

"There is no one who catches your eye, none who stands out above the rest?"

Katrine lifted a brow as she surveyed her maid's arch smile. "Is there supposed to be?"

"They are saying in the quarters that there is a giant with the new man, de Blanc. They say this manservant of his is a heathen in a turban with a great sword at his side that has a hilt of pure gold."

"I haven't noticed," Katrine said. She had wronged her maid; she had thought she was teasing her about Rowan de Blanc himself. There was a good reason why she had not seen his manservant. She had been deliberately avoiding looking in that direction.

The other woman made no reply as she turned to scan the ever-increasing crowd of men below. Squinting a little against the bright light, she put her hands on her hips.

Delphia was a quadroon. Her skin was the color of toffee candy and her eyes dark and liquid, while her hair curled in loose, tobacco-brown abundance to her shoulders. Beautiful in an exotic fashion, she was as vain as she was good-natured. Since she laughed at herself for it and cared not a whit who else did, few faulted her. She had a decided appreciation for men of all sizes, ages, and colors. Delphia had been Katrine's maid-companion since she had arrived as a bride at Arcadia. As was usual between maid and mistress, the woman was well aware of the situation with Katrine.

"They say," the maid went on after a moment, "that this barbarian wished the use of the copper bathing tub for his master last night. Instead of asking, he simply walked over to it, picked it up, and went off with it—a tub which needs two strong men to carry it. This morning he ate two whole plates of Cook's biscuits, then left without so much as a word of thanks."

"Perhaps he doesn't speak English," Katrine suggested.

"Maybe," Delphia agreed. Abruptly her eyes widened. "There he is. Gracious me, but he is a big one. I wonder if the rest of him is to size."

The awe in the maid's voice was enough to make Katrine crane her neck to look. The other woman was indicating a knot of people just across the field. It was a moment before the old men, young boys, and other contestants shifted enough for her to see.

Delphia had not exaggerated; the manservant was built on a mountainous scale. Standing head and shoulders above most of the men around him, he was dressed in a voluminous white shirt open to the waist and wide-legged pantaloons caught at the midsection with a sash striped in vermilion and green from which swung the curved sword Delphia had mentioned. With his arms akimbo and a forbidding look on his aquiline brown features, he was standing guard over the velvet-lined saber case that lay open at his feet.

His sensibilities and his eyesight were keen, apparently, for it seemed he felt their regard and turned to stare in the direction of the grandstand. His gaze skimmed over Delphia to meet Katrine's across the space that divided them. He did not open his mouth, but somehow drew the attention of his master, nodding toward where Katrine sat.

Rowan de Blanc turned from speaking to Giles, perhaps discussing the merits of the personal saber he held compared with those provided by his host. As he met Katrine's gaze he swept his blade upward, bringing the basket hilt even with his chin in the traditional duelist's, or fencer's, salute. Sweeping it back down, he spread his other arm outward while inclining his upper body in a graceful bow.

"My," Delphia said. "Wasn't that pretty."

"More likely he was mocking me." Katrine's answer was curt.

"Then you must pretend not to notice while you raise one hand in a regal wave," her maid instructed.

"You know who he is?"

"Of course. Quick, before he looks away."

Katrine did as Delphia suggested, though her wave was more grudging than gracious.

"There now, you see? He thinks you are all admiration."

"I hope not!"

"At least he will not guess that you despise him."

"I don't despise him," Katrine said shortly.

"What then?"

"I wish he had never come."

The maid held her gaze for a long moment, her own sober, before she said, "But he is here. And he is everything you told me."

"I knew you wouldn't be able to resist getting a look at him."

The maid tilted her head with a rueful smile. "He never looked at me," she said, "he or his giant."

Katrine and Delphia were joined a short time later by Musetta and her husband, Brantley. The grandstand was filling up, becoming noisy with the hum of voices. Four musicians with French horns appeared, aligning themselves in pairs on either side of the viewing area. Katrine's husband returned to his chair. The buzz of conversation began to die down as the crowd realized that the time was approaching for the games to begin.

It was then that Alan Delaney detached himself from the group of contestants and walked to stand just below where Katrine sat.

"Madam Katrine," he said, with a small bow, "it was suggested last evening that I be your champion today. If you are still of the same mind, perhaps I may request a token of your favor?"

He was referring to Lewis's stupid challenge. Her smile took on a wry twist. "You seem to be getting into the spirit of the meeting."

"I have read my Scott," he answered, grinning up at her, "Not to mention Tennyson's new *Idylls of the King* about Arthur and his knights. I considered the matter, and decided I might as well be as gallant as possible."

Was it possible Alan could best Rowan? There was no way to tell; certainly Rowan did not appear to think so. And yet, if a favor from her could give the younger man encouragement, then she would not withhold it.

She had no convenient head scarf about her, no hair ribbon, no parasol with decorative trailing bits. However, the skirt of her gown of coral muslin had tiers of ruffles, each outlined in ribbon of a different pastel color and looped up with bow-knotted ribbon streamers of these varying shades. Her searching gaze lighted on the matching knot of ribbon at her corsage. Its streamers were extra long, and perfectly suited to the purpose.

Katrine stripped off the fluttering knot in colors of cream and pale rose, aqua blue and yellow. Leaning down, she handed the collection of ribbons to Alan, who stretched up to receive them.

He waved them back and forth a little, looking a bit uneasy at their feminine softness. There was appeal in his voice as he said, "Now that I've got them, what do you think I should do with them?"

It was Delphia who answered, though her manner was much more subdued than that she used with Katrine. She said, "Tie them to the arm?"

"I'm no hand at that at the best of times," he answered with a shake of his head.

"Allow me," Katrine said.

She took back the ribbons and rose to descend halfway down the short flight of steps built for her ease in awarding the prize for the day to the victor. Bending a little, she quickly tied the long streamers about the upper part of Alan's left arm, being careful not to pull them so tight that they would constrict movement, but making them snug enough so that they would not work loose and become a handicap.

"There, Sir Knight," she said when she was done, "you have my favor and my blessing."

"With those, how can I lose?" he said, an earnest sound in his voice. Ducking his head once more in a bow, he backed away, then turned and sprinted to his place.

Giles, who had watched the byplay in silence, spoke in a low undertone as she settled back in her seat. "Was that wise, my dear?"

"As wise as any of this," she answered without looking at him.

Giles frowned, but said no more. A moment later he gave the signal for the horns to sound, then rose to his feet to bid the games begin.

Sabre fencing, fencing with sabers rather than foils, was an Italian sport that had come into vogue of late. Giles felt that the longer and heavier weapons made for an exciting contest, one that had more in common with true duels fought with swords than did ordinary fencing. He disliked duels with pistols, contests that were gradually taking the place of swordplay. In meetings with blades, he said, the elements of endurance, intelligence, and intuitive perception were much more in evidence, leaving plenty of room for the divine intervention that was supposed to be on the side of right. There were enough men of like mind in Louisiana to keep the *salles d'armes* busy, the establishments where men practiced with foils against the possibility of facing an opponent with sword in hand. And because of this practice, there was every reason to suppose the fencing matches today would be exciting.

The matches would be fought simultaneously in round-robin style, best two rounds out of three, with three touchés per round. As there were sixteen men on the field, there would be four rounds fought. The losers of each previous round would be eliminated and the winners paired off again until only two contestants were left. The winner of the final round would then be the winner for the day.

As Alan had pointed out the night before, the points of the sabers were blunted, but the edges were not. Thrust and parry was the usual style of play, but cuts were permitted. The target zone was the body trunk only, from below the collarbone to just above the thighs, an area protected by body padding. The honor system would be used to acknowledge a touch, with each man calling out as he was hit. In case of a double hit—each man hitting the other at the same time—the player who was in the offensive position as the touch was made would be awarded it.

Katrine hated the swordplay. She hated the wire-mesh masks and quilted padding that turned the men into strange, faceless warriors. She hated the scrape and clang of steel blades in opposition. She hated the fearful watch for the uncontrolled cut that spilled blood. Most of all she hated the soft vulnerability she felt in her vitals as she watched the sabers flash in and out.

And yet, at the same time, it fascinated her. She admired the courage of the men who fought as well as the lightning action and gritty striving amidst the interplay of surprise and ingenious tactics. More than that, these matches, conducted with exact rules and ceremony yet with an ever-present element of danger, were as close as she would ever come to seeing a duel. Such meetings on the field of honor were, of course, forbidden to females.

It was odd to see the men without their coats in public. That item of apparel was never discarded, even on the hottest of days, except in dire emergencies and with profuse apologies. To watch them all shrug from the confinement of frock coats and cravats, standing exposed in their shirtsleeves so that their true physiques were shown without the help of a tailor's darts or padding, was a secret excitement shared by every female present. Katrine saw Musetta sitting forward on her seat, staring without pretense, while the other women flung quick, sidelong glances toward the arena, or else looked at the sky, the grass, the banners snapping in the wind, anywhere except at the men in their shirtsleeves.

The first round did not take long, as the less experienced swordsmen were weeded out. In the second, Giles's nephew, Lewis, was eliminated by the burly Satchel Godwin. This left Satchel, Rowan, Alan, and Musetta's Perry for the third round. After a short rest, the contest began again with Alan matched against Satchel, and Perry opposing Rowan.

The manner in which the fencing matches were set up, one following the other in fairly quick succession, made them a supreme test of endurance as well as skill and guile. It had not mattered so much with the first two rounds, but now it began to tell.

Earlier in the day, Satchel's size and strength had been an advantage, allowing him to overreach his opponents and beat them down with the weight of his wrist-numbing blows. His physical condition, however, did not match his first show of power; he had drunk too deep of wine and corn whiskey, eaten too well. As the third round began it was easy to see that he was flagging. Alan, lithe, quick, and tireless, kept beyond his long reach for the most part, moving in and out in fast attacks that the larger man parried only with wrenching, gasping effort. The first touch was made, and the second, one to each man. The third touch was to Alan's credit. They settled, then, to a series of feints, thrusting attacks, and ripostes that gained nothing, went nowhere.

Rowan and Perry were better matched for strength and agility, though Rowan had the slightly longer reach. Rowan's main advantage, however, was skill; it soon became evident that Perry had advanced this far because of poor opponents. The first touch, scored to Rowan, came seconds after the match began. The second, to the same man, followed on its heels. The third was delayed, it seemed, only because Rowan was prolonging the contest out of consideration for the pride of the other man.

That Perry was aware of the act of mercy was also plain. His movements grew stiff with rage and chagrin, and the small portion of his face visible at the edges of his mask turned dark red. He parried time after time, backing in retreat, unable to initiate a sustained offense.

Meanwhile, in the first contest, Alan made his final touch, a swift, beautifully timed redoublement, a second attack after the first has been parried. It slid through Satchel's guard like a hot knife through butter, so that Alan's blade bent almost double against the bigger man's chest padding.

Satchel let out a roar as he acknowledged the touch. In that moment of distraction, Perry launched a running attack upon Rowan, beating, binding, swirling his blade free, and slashing downward with vicious strength in a cut designed to slice to the bone.

Rowan leaped back as he deflected the illegal blow. Still the edge of the other man's saber caught him above the knee. It split the fabric of his pantaloons, showing a welling of bright red.

Women cried out. Men shouted. Giles surged to his feet with a barked order to halt the match.

It was too late.

The light gleamed like a silver-blue flash of lightning along Rowan's blade as, ignoring both his injury and his host, he engaged Perry once more. There was a flurry of action far too fast to follow, but which sent Perry stumbling backward, desperately parrying. Blades shrieked in a long, excruciating glide of metal on metal, there was a sudden, blinding whirl of steel. Then Perry was on the ground and Rowan standing over him with his saber point dimpling the padding directly over the younger man's heart.

"Touché, I think," Rowan said quietly, then reached up to strip off the mask he wore.

Perry looked at the saber blade that held him to the ground and the trenchant gaze of the man who wielded it. He turned his head then to stare toward the grandstand where Musetta sat. The blond-haired woman, on Giles's far side, looked away from the man under the sword.

Perry lay back. His whispered acknowledgment was loud in the quiet. He added, in louder tones, "Forgive the cut, if you can. The heat of the contest—I lost my head."

Rowan whipped aside the saber and reached to extend his hand to help the younger man rise. His voice deep and quiet in approval, he said, "I can."

The bout between Rowan and Alan that came next was almost an anticlimax after that. Technically correct, rigorous in execution, meticulous as to form and manner, it was a neat, well-fought contest that left both men winded and bathed in perspiration.

Regardless, the outcome was never in doubt.

Katrine had tried not to watch Rowan during the long afternoon, but she could not help hearing the comments around her on his finely honed skill, his precision of movement, and his punctilious conduct. The way he had allowed his cut to be bound, then insisted on continuing with the next round had gained him the admiration of all.

Perfect, he was perfect. It wasn't fair.

Her resentment rose hotly as she allowed herself to follow his movements now. His form was precise, with his saber held in exact guard position and his left fist resting on his hip. The white bandage against the black broadcloth of his pantaloons drew attention to the flexing of the well-defined muscles in his thighs and lean flanks, especially as he lunged. The dampness of his shirt clung to the sculpting of his broad back, emphasizing the smooth glide of the bands of muscle that enwrapped his upper body. He had folded his sleeves back to the elbow at some time, leaving his hard, sinewy wrists and forearms exposed. His exertions had caused his hair to curl in a tight pelt over his head, giving him the look of an ancient Roman gladiator.

There was something in his utter concentration on the point of his opponent's saber, something in the contained way he moved, that made him seem different from the other men around him. It was as if there was a machinelike ruthlessness inside him that would expend the last measure of his own strength and will to bring him what he wanted, or else extract every vestige of life from anyone who opposed his need.

Alan threw up his left hand as he acknowledged the last touch of the match. The two men bowed at the waist, then removed their masks and placed them under their arms as they turned to face the grandstand. They stood side by side, breathing hard, their saber points buried in the grass at their feet.

A cheer went up as the applauding crowd surged to its feet. The horns blasted out a sonorous chorus of victory. The pennons and flags decorating the grandstand waved gently in the breeze while young boys, black and white, capered out onto the field, mingling with their elders, who surged forward to congratulate the winner of the day.

"Well done, Rowan de Blanc!" Giles called out from where he stood leaning on the grandstand railing. "Come forward and receive your prize."

Katrine watched Rowan hand his mask and saber to his manservant, who had stepped forward with his hands held out for them, watched him advance step by firm step until he stood below her. Only then did she rise and take in her hands the crown of laurel leaves that Delphia brought from its storage box and held ready.

As Katrine moved forward to the steps she met the dark, considering gaze of Rowan de Blanc. She paused an instant, as if she had hit an invisible barrier, before she forced herself to descend toward him.

Rowan, hot and sweaty and tired in every bone, stood and watched the lady Katrine come down the steps that led from the grandstand. She looked so cool and untouchable, yet so delicious in her gown the color of a ripe peach. He wanted, suddenly, to taste her, to wipe away the cool disdain and the reluctance he saw in her face and have her sweet and succulent, warm and pliant in his arms. Amazement for the strength of that desire held him still. So strong was it that he was not sure he could move without reaching out for her.

Katrine stopped on the last step. Her voice melodious but not quite steady, she said, "I present you, Rowan de Blanc, with this laurel wreath as a symbol of the victory you have won by right of arms, and also in token of the high standard of play you have displayed today. I will, if you permit, place the wreath on your brow with the Roman kiss of good fortune."

She lifted the wreath. He bent his head to receive it. When the circlet of greenery had been settled on his dark waves just above his broad brow, she placed her hands on his shoulders and leaned toward him.

She meant to kiss the hard planes of his face, first one side then the other. He permitted her to salute one lean cheek, but at the last possible moment, as she touched her lips to the other cheek, he turned his head.

The smooth, firm surfaces of his lips were hot and tasted of salt and honeyed desire. They burned with a jolting, consuming fire that seemed to penetrate, pouring like heated oil along her veins. Thought fled, while a slow, sweet yearning invaded her senses. She clenched her fingers on the firm muscles under her hands, unable to move.

He shifted a fraction, lifting one hand as if he would reach out for her. She drew a swift breath and pushed away from him. With her lashes lowered so she would not have to look at him, she swung away.

She mounted the steps with her head held high. And left him standing there crowned with laurel, with his feet planted in the grass.

CHAPTER THREE

"Your wound was not serious?"

The question Katrine asked was the kind of polite conversational gambit she had been using since she and Rowan had taken their places at the head of the long banquet table. She did not feel polite.

Her nerves were on edge and her skin prickled with the feeling that every person at the board stretching before them was watching the two of them. The memory of the meeting of her lips with those of the man beside her lay like a white-hot coal in the forefront of her mind. It constrained her speech, her manner, her every movement, leaving it more impossible than ever for her to behave naturally toward him. His own relaxed manner struck her as an additional affront.

"It was nothing," Rowan replied as he lounged back in his chair.

Katrine had known how he would answer. For one thing, it was the kind of man he was. For another, Delphia, who had it through the servants' grapevine, had told her that Rowan had re-fused all offers to send for a doctor. He preferred the services of his manservant, who had some skill in caring for minor ills.

"You are certain?" she said with some asperity. "The archery contest tomorrow will be strenuous, and the other men will not spare you."

"Your concern is balm enough for any wound. In any case, I must be ready if I am to be tournament king for the evening once more, with the privilege of sitting at your side."

There was a silken undertone to his voice that Katrine did not like. She said, "Actually the prize is to serve as my escort for an al fresco outing. That is a prospect I'm sure you would be devastated to miss."

He gazed at her a long considering moment. "And you would prefer that I did."

Katrine made no answer as she looked away from the board. Shaped like a letter *T*, it was laden with silver and crystal, with individual saltcellars, knife rests, and wreaths of laurel twined with asters and ivy. The flickering light from the crystal and ormolu chandelier overhead cast a golden glow over the assembly. In that soft sheen Giles, at the far end of the table, appeared more healthy and more benevolent than usual, the male guests all seemed to have a heroic air, and all the women appeared fair. The light was deceiving.

The subject under general conversation at the moment was the recent raid on an armory in Virginia by some lunatic named John Brown. Katrine would have liked an excuse for joining it, avoiding her tête-à-tête with Rowan, but none presented itself.

"Perhaps there was another man you would rather took my place?" Rowan suggested. "Possibly the one who wore your ribbons? Or maybe the young hothead who wanted so badly to win that he forgot himself?"

"Either would do," Katrine said in goaded tones.

"It's my presence that bothers you then, since you have no preference. Why should that be if you are innocent of blame in my brother's death?"

Halfway down the board, Lewis made some low-voiced remark while turning his malicious gaze toward the head of the table. The young woman seated on his left, a pale, dark-haired girl with enormous black eyes, turned scarlet and bent her head over her plate. His other neighbor on the right threw back her ginger-colored head and gave a gravel-voiced shout of laughter. The two young women, Charlotte Martinez and Georgette Lowrey, were cousins from downriver, below St. Francisville.

Katrine compressed her lips before turning to vent her annoyance on the man beside her. "Do you think I should be overjoyed at your success, which gives you the opportunity to torment me in public?"

"Torment? A strong word, surely, for the little that has passed between us."

"You warned me how it would be, did you not?" she said, ignoring his comment. "How gratified you must be to have been proven right."

"That's what is bothering you, the fact that I won?"

"Everything about you—" she began, then stopped, aghast at how close she had come to giving herself away.

"Now, this is encouraging," Rowan said, his mouth curving in lines of mockery. "Your dislike is personal. Can that be because I remind you of Terence, and of things you would rather forget?"

She gave him a long look. "I cannot imagine a man more unlike Terence. Your brother was unfailingly kind and considerate, a gentle soul. He had his moments of high spirit, but there was nothing mean about him."

Rowan's lips thinned. It was a long moment before he said, "You loved him for these qualities?"

Katrine stared at him, at the pain etched in the strong lines of his face and the sudden grief rising in the hypnotic depths of his green eyes. A vagrant impulse drifted through her mind to give in, to stop fighting and let Giles have his way.

She drew a startled breath, wrenching back in her chair as

far as its high back allowed. She moistened lips gone suddenly dry as she cast about in her mind for something to say. His question, echoing in her ears, gave her sudden inspiration.

"For those things, yes, and much more," she said with a husky note in her voice. "But Terence was so young, he didn't understand the—the game."

"The game," Rowan repeated, his gaze narrowing.

"Yes, of course. What else? I am a married woman." Where had the inspiration for the pretense come from? From Musetta, Katrine thought, who was always rattling on about the love games among the upper-crust families of England, where marriages based on wealth made love something to be sought outside of matrimonial bonds.

"My brother wanted something more than you were willing to give?"

"I'm afraid I laughed at his suggestion that we run away together," Katrine went on, embroidering with verve. "It was so wildly impractical, so hopelessly romantic. I didn't know how serious he was, or how desperate. It was only after he was gone that I realized how much I cared for him."

He watched her a long moment. Finally he gave a slow shake of his head. "There is only one thing in what you just said that I believe. Terence was far too young for you."

She blinked a little as she raised her chin. "You want to know how your brother came to kill himself, and I have told you. I'm sorry you don't like the answer, but there it is."

"And now I can go away and leave you alone. Is that it?"

"If it pleases you," Katrine said, her tone sharp with her anger that he had seen through her so easily.

"It doesn't. I think I frighten you for some reason, that I'm a threat to your rich, safe world. I'm not sure why that is, but there is one thing of which I have no doubt." He hesitated an instant. When he went on, his voice was soft with insinuation. "I am not too young to play any game of your choosing."

In the quiet that fell between them, the voices of the other diners, the clink of silver and china seemed far away.

Did he, could he, mean what she thought? Katrine, watching him with her breath suspended in her throat, could not decide. Nor was she sure she wanted to know.

"What, no answer?" he said. "No curiosity to discover in what ways Terence and I may be alike? We were thought to be very similar, I give you my word."

Rowan waited for her answer with his heart like an iron fist inside his chest. Would she agree and play up to him, thereby convicting herself of being a heartless flirt, or would she reject him out of hand, proving that she cared for Terence and was not interested in a substitute? Either way, he feared, would be a loss for him.

He was angry with himself for caring, angry for allowing himself to be attracted to the woman beside him, angry that he was allowing himself to be distracted from his purpose. That anger was familiar; he had been carrying it for all the long months since he had heard that Terence was dead, but especially since he had reached Arcadia. He had used it this evening to shade his every utterance with self-indulgent, and self-protective, sarcasm.

As she stared at him the color drained away from Katrine's face. Her voice only a trace of sound, she said, "You know, don't you?"

He didn't, but he would like very much to understand whatever it was that could change the vibrant woman who had been sitting beside him into a pale, defensive female with the eyes of a wounded doe. He said in tentative agreement, "I may, then again—"

"You don't have to be discreet; I am well aware of the situation since it has been going on for years. There can be no reason for not being honest with me."

"I would prefer that as well," he said, feeling his way with care. "And yet—you will admit there are difficulties."

"Oh yes," she said, a crooked smile touching her pallid lips, "that much I will concede."

"Perhaps if you told me your feeling on the subject?"

"Opposed! Forever and inalterably opposed."

"Now why?" His dark gaze was penetrating.

"Decency, honor, a personal dislike for submitting to the direction of another in so private a matter. As well as every other objection you might suppose given the extraordinary nature of the agreement." Katrine, speaking with some heat, came to a halt as she saw frowning puzzlement growing in his face.

"And you are telling me," he said in slow disbelief, "that my brother was once involved in this matter without decency or honor?"

Rich color rose in her face. She said abruptly, "You deceived me. That was unforgivable."

"Was it indeed?" he said in hard tones. "There is no means so low that I won't use it to discover what happened to Terence. I can't believe he was willingly a part of anything that might be the opposite of the terms you used, but if he was, then I must know it."

"The problem I spoke of has nothing to do with him, at least . . ."

"You were going to say?"

She looked away from his hard, searching gaze. "I have said more than enough, none of it having any bearing on the reason you came here. It will be best if you forget it. Forget everything, and just go away."

"You won't be rid of me that easily."

She turned back to him. "You will listen to me, if you are wise."

"I've never pretended to wisdom," he said, his gaze meeting hers squarely.

A shiver of combined dread and excitement moved over Katrine at his words with their bold hint of determination. He didn't know what he was saying, of course; how could he? She had been mad to think even for an instant he might. Terence had never been informed, not directly, of the reason he had been invited to Arcadia. How could he have told his older brother?

No. No one knew except her, her maid, and Giles. She sometimes thought Lewis suspected, but it could be no more than that. He was not the kind of man to allow such knowledge to pass unchallenged if he was sure. He would have acted on it even if it meant offending his uncle and jeopardizing his position at Arcadia; he would not have been able to help himself.

"Katrine, my dear, give us the answer to a question of importance!"

The call came from Musetta, who sat halfway down the long table with her husband, Brantley, across from her and Perry on her right.

"Now?" Katrine asked. Such questions as she knew Musetta meant were usually discussed in the parlor after dinner, or else when everyone was gathered on the front gallery, out on the lawn, or some other such informal setting.

"What better time, since it has just arisen?" Musetta, luminous in cream satin overlaid with blond lace, sent Perry a laughing glance before she went on. "It is this: What primary duty does a man owe the woman to whom he has pledged his heart?"

"Love, of course," Katrine answered almost at random.

"Yes, certainly, and undying devotion, that goes without saying. But after that."

It was a relief for Katrine to be able to turn her thoughts to this mental exercise. That was the way she viewed such questions, as matters of philosophical interest and mental escape, though she was aware they were something entirely different to Musetta. Her sister-in-law treated the debates as a form of flirtation.

"I submit," Perry said with high color in his face, "that the first duty is honor in all its forms. Every outward show of courtesy and respect should be observed, regardless of what may occur in private."

"And I maintain," Musetta argued with audacious laughter in her dark blue eyes, "that it is obedience to the wishes of the lady. Hers is the greatest danger, therefore it is her right to determine every move of the romance, every change of direction that it may take."

The hum of conversation had died away as the interest of the other diners turned toward the small drama being played out before them. Georgette, the big, red-haired girl next to Lewis, leaned to whisper something to him that made him give a snicker of laughter, instantly smothered. Two older women put their heads together, their gazes stern yet avid as they watched Musetta while speaking in low voices.

Everyone, it seemed, suspected an amorous intrigue. Katrine was doubtful. Musetta liked to raise eyebrows, enjoyed flirtation, but she was more careful of the proprieties than she pretended. Katrine sometimes thought her sister-in-law behaved as she did to punish her husband for his indifference.

"What you say, both of you, is valid," Katrine said, tilting her head as she considered. "I would suggest, however, that the greatest duty a man owes a woman in this situation is protection, both physical and mental."

"Protection?" Musetta wrinkled her nose. "How dull."

"I don't find it so," Katrine answered. "The devoted lover must never do anything which will cause his lady grief, never allow anyone else to harm her by word or deed. The honor and obedience the two of you have mentioned are embodied in this concept: If a man has a care for the woman's good name and social standing as well as her personal good, then he must honor her in public and in private. If he would keep her safe and free from needless worry, then he must be obedient to her wishes, expressed and unexpressed. For as long as love lasts, his life is dedicated to her. For a man, this is his sole purpose in living, to protect the woman he has honored with his love. In a perfect world this would also be the woman who carries his name, bears his children, and thereby provides immortality for them both. Ours is not a perfect world, but can, if we are lucky, come close."

Musetta wrinkled her tip-tilted nose at Katrine. "Well-spoken, as always, and right, as always. How provoking."

"I didn't mean to be," Katrine said, smiling a little.

"I know," the other girl said. "That only makes it worse." She shrugged a rounded shoulder with a moue of mock anger that dissolved in a smile before she turned away.

"It seems a subject to which you have given much thought," Rowan suggested in quiet tones as the others lost interest and resumed their interrupted conversations.

Katrine faced him with reluctance. She searched his gaze, wondering if he had meant to suggest that she must be experienced in affairs of love. At last she said, "Living as we do, in this small community, there is plenty of time for such philosophical exercises."

"I see. Is there nothing more practical to occupy you?"

Katrine spent much of every single day at the tasks she had been trained for from birth: supervising the cleaning and repairing of the great house, planning meals; training the house servants and solving problems and settling disputes between them; being certain her husband's frequent guests were comfortable; checking on the health and well-being of the field hands, children, and old people in the servants' quarters—all while being a competent and attentive hostess.

Quietly she answered, "Nothing to occupy the mind."

"I thought perhaps it was simply that you enjoyed playing the queen, giving the prizes and accepting homage as your due."

Her lips tightened before she spoke. "You are insulting, but then I suspect that you meant to be."

"Now, why should I do that?"

"You are determined to dislike me, I think, determined to see me as a villainess capable of anything."

"If I am wrong, show me how and where."

"I can't do that," she said with a firm shake of her head. "You must think what you will."

"Suppose I told you that I think you the most desirable woman I've ever seen. What then?"

Her gaze widened a fraction before she lowered her lashes. "I would suspect you of trying to persuade me to do your will by a means as unfair as it must be unavailing."

"You might be right," he said on a short laugh, "but then again, you might not. Have you thought of that?"

"I would remind you that—"

"Yes, I know, you are a married woman," he finished for her with an impatient gesture. "What has that to do with anything, especially for one who talks so easily of lovers and their ladies?"

"I spoke, as you must know, in theory only," she said, goaded into the explanation by the skepticism she saw in his eyes.

"What? No imagination, no fantasy? You can hardly expect me to believe it when your husband is so much older."

"Giles has nothing to do with it."

"No?" He shook his head, his eyes dark. "Don't you think he should have a part?"

She drew a deep breath, but the calm she sought was not forthcoming. Through her teeth, she said, "My relationship with my husband is no concern of yours. You will oblige me by not speaking of it further."

"Will I?" he asked, as if asking the question of himself. Then he moved a wide shoulder in dismissal. "Perhaps I will, if you can introduce a subject of greater interest."

"Or," she said with a flash in her eyes, "we can cease to talk at all."

"That might look as if we had quarreled, and I'm sure you

would not want that. The only people who quarrel in public are enemies and lovers."

"Then, by all means let us be enemies."

Katrine thought her words were a shade too emphatic for good manners, but she would not retract them. From the frown on his darkly handsome face it certainly seemed that the arrangement was not to Rowan's liking. He said no more, however, and at last, mercifully, the meal came to its end.

The morning that followed was not the best for archery. The blue-gray darkness of the sky along the horizon to the south promised rain. Dirty-looking clouds drifted across the heavens, creating a constant haze that muted the sun's glare but made visibility uncertain. The light wind that flapped the canvas roof of the grandstand and rippled the grass of the bowl-like arena could well affect accuracy. Smoke from the barbecue pit fires that had been set at dawn hung low, its smell making everyone feel that true autumn could not be far away. It had even turned a little cooler in the night, though it was nothing that could not be warded off with a light cashmere shawl.

Katrine had armed herself with a small scarf in soft ivory silk chiffon as a signal of her favor today. She had presented the scarf to Satchel just after breakfast. He seemed a likely champion since she knew that he often hunted deer with bow and arrow in the manner of the woodland Indians who had once roamed the area.

He had been more affected by the gesture than she had expected. His face turkey red and his voice gruff, he said, "I'll not fail you, ma'am."

"Your best will be good enough, I'm sure," she answered as she tied the scarf around his upper arm.

"I'll best them all so bad they'll leave with their tails between their legs, especially the foreigner."

She gave the big man a brief upward glance. "You don't like Rowan de Blanc?"

"Too sure of himself by half, you ask me," Satchel said with a brooding look in his eyes.

"My thoughts exactly," Katrine said softly.

"Don't you worry, I'll see to him." Satchel gave a ponderous nod.

"Good," she answered. "Good."

Now as she took her place in the grandstand, Katrine saw the burly giant striding up and down on the field. He was flapping his arm to make the silk scarf wave like a flag and beaming with all the pride and pleasure of a child with a new toy.

There came a step behind her, and Lewis bent over her chair to whisper in her ear. "I understand your choice for today, my dear," he said, "but don't you think you should have counseled him to be less obvious?"

"Now, why?" she asked with only the barest upward glance at his thin face topped by silver-gilt hair.

"So you need not be so humiliated when he goes down in defeat."

"What makes you think he will be defeated?" Her tone was incisive.

"Private information. I am told on the best of authority that our Rowan grew up with a long bow in his fist, that he was taught its many fine points by his grandfather's gamekeeper, who was a converted poacher."

"I might have known." Katrine closed her eyes, pressing the lids tightly together.

"So you might, if you had asked me. I'm so certain of his superior prowess that I've put my money on him."

"Rather than testing your skill against him?" she asked as his lofty tone scraped on her overstrained nerves.

"Oh, no one ever directed any gamekeeper to teach me; the

sport, you know, smacked too much of the lower classes for my father's taste. Besides, I don't waste my time with useless endeavors."

"Meaning," she said astringently, "that you admit to being no match for Rowan de Blanc?"

"If you like. There is more to being a man than mere physical achievement."

"Ah, you feel his mental equal," she suggested.

A pained expression erased his supercilious smile. "At the very least."

"I wonder," she said, her tone pensive as she allowed her gaze to seek out and find the man of whom they spoke.

"You wound me," Lewis complained. "I had not thought you had so little opinion of my intellect."

"It isn't that," she said, her gaze limpid as she turned back to him.

"You have so great an opinion of de Blanc's then? Now, this is interesting."

"I have a certain respect for him, yes. Were I you, I would take care not to underestimate him."

The thin man's smile was waspish. "Bested you in an argument, has he? That isn't a guarantee of his acumen."

She accepted the insult without a flicker of expression. "He isn't here for the games, you were right about that. He thinks there is something odd in Terence's death."

"That's hardly my affair," her husband's nephew said, though a tiny frown drew his brows together as he, in his turn, sought out the tall figure of Rowan.

"I only thought you should know," Katrine said, lowering her voice and speaking quickly as she saw Brantley Hennen coming toward her.

Musetta's husband was smiling with his usual distracted affability, as if he was totting up figures in his mind. When he spoke, his tone was offhand. "Have either of you seen Musetta?"

"Not this morning," Katrine answered. Musetta did not make a habit of coming down to breakfast, preferring a tray in her room before she put her feet on the floor. She would dress at her leisure and put in an appearance when it pleased her.

"We agreed last night that we would sit together. Now I can't find her."

"I expect it slipped her mind."

"I'm sure of it," Musetta's husband said on a sigh. Turning his head this way and that, he moved away from them.

Katrine turned to search the field with her eyes. Perry Blackstone was nowhere in sight. It was indiscreet of Musetta to be absent at the same time, and so publicly.

Lewis, his gaze on the field below them also, clicked his tongue in a mockery of scandalized disapproval. After a moment he wandered away, perhaps to search for the truant.

The games began in good time. The first target of the morning was a common bull's-eye set at a distance of a hundred paces. Satchel, shooting first, sent all three of his arrows through the target, so they hung with their fletching feathers barely protruding on the marked side. They were not, however, and regrettably, in the high-scoring center.

Alan had two arrows in the bull's-eye, though by a whisker only. None of the others came so close. That was, until Rowan shot. His three arrows lodged so closely in the exact center that they appeared as one.

The remainder of the morning passed in the same depressing fashion.

Rowan hit the swinging pendulum target with each of his three tries.

He placed every arrow in his quiver in the array of sitting targets long before the sand in the glass had run away.

Shooting from horseback like an Indian of the western plains, he hit the stuffed dummy that was the target five times in five tries, each arrow squarely in the red heart marker.

At last, there came the final contest, the papingo shoot. Derived from a medieval test of archery skill, the target for the event was supposed to be a live bird of bright plumage, traditionally a rare and valuable parrot. At Arcadia, a dove was substituted. Katrine disliked this event nearly as much as the fencing, though in truth it was seldom fatal for the dove. She tried never to watch the live bird being tied by one leg to its long braided leather line and then the line fixed to the top of the pole. She did her best to look elsewhere as bird and pole were hoisted high into the air and the pole set in the ground. The year before, she had made an excuse to leave the grandstand while the arrows flew toward the poor papingo that struggled, wings wildly flapping, to escape into the sky. She could not do that every year, however, not without attracting notice.

The pole was set, the arrows were checked, the men stood ready. The members of the audience who had wandered away during the intermission returned to their seats. The laughing and chattering, the wagers and discussions of form and style and tales of past contests died away.

It was then that there came a mournful call, the two-note dirge of a mating dove. The flitting shadow of another gray bird swept over the green arena. It swooped around the pole holding the shrieking prey, then winged away again. A moment later it was back. It lit for a moment atop the pole beside the tethered female dove, then dived away, circling with the soft golden glow of the fading light on its wings, calling as it went.

Katrine sat forward in her chair, her gaze fastened on the swooping bird. It was a male dove colored the same soft gray as the clouds beginning to gather overhead and marked with a dark ring around its neck. Behind her, there were questions and quiet murmurs as the other guests took note of what was happening.

Giles, seated beside her, leaned in her direction as he spoke in low tones. "There's been some kind of mix-up. The female on the pole must be one of a mated pair."

"But that's terrible," she said. "Have them take it down."

"It's only a bird, my dear. If it tries to fly after the male, its struggles will make for much better sport."

"What does that matter? No, really; it's so pathetic, Giles."

There was something tragic in the frantic circling of the male with his cries mingling now with those of the trapped female. It made Katrine's chest feel as if it were compressed in a vise. She clenched one hand in her lap while the fingertips of the other turned white from the force of her grip on the chair arm.

"I don't think the men on the field would thank me for interfering," her husband said.

"Tell them it's at my request." Her voice was constricted in her throat.

"You don't want me to do that. You wouldn't want to cause dissension here in the midst of the games, I know. Besides—ah, it's too late."

The first contestant, a young man from a neighboring plantation, had stepped up to the mark, notched his arrow, and let it fly. It sped wide to the right of the target. His second try came no closer. Even so, the sound of the dove's wings beating the air was loud as it tried to take off in the opposite direction.

"Now," Katrine said to Giles as the young man stepped away from the mark. "Tell them to stop it now."

Giles gave a slight shake of his head. "It would not be fair to change the target after the shooting has begun. Every man should have the same chance, face the same degree of difficulty."

"What of the dove's chances?"

Giles, his attention on the field, made no answer.

One by one, the archers took their turns. Perry came closer to the free dove than to the tied one. Alan's arrows passed underneath the fluttering bird. Satchel put his first shot in the pole. On his second, the arrow sped straight toward the dove, so straight that Katrine surged to her feet with her hand to her mouth. The dove squawked. The arrow arched away while a trio of pale gray feathers drifted earthward, swirling in the vagrant breeze.

Katrine sank slowly back into her seat. She looked toward the last man waiting his turn. Rowan was watching her with his brows drawn together over his eyes. She met his gaze for a brief moment, then looked away out over the treetops. Behind her, the noise of the crowd died away into a waiting silence.

There was no possible way on earth that the trapped female dove could live. Rowan was too accomplished, too disciplined, too perfect. The poor little thing was doomed, Katrine knew it. Its mate, so faithful, so helpless in its distress, could not save her. Death would come on a speeding arrow thrusting into her heart. Bloodstained, she would fall. She would swing, lifeless, at the end of the leather line that she had twisted around the pole in her terror. All joy, all memories of devotion and passionate pairing would be over.

Katrine felt an odd identification with the bird held fast to the pole. It almost seemed that it was her own heart that would feel the arrow, her own life that would be over before it had well begun. She ached inside with the anticipation of it, felt the same frantic need to fly from the fate bearing down on her. She couldn't stand it. She couldn't bear to watch. And yet, neither could she find the will and the strength to leave the small drama.

As if drawn, she looked once more toward where Rowan stood. He had stepped to the mark and was notching his arrow with absorbed care. Holding it in place, he looked up at the target, then glanced once more toward where Katrine sat. His eyes narrowed.

Katrine felt impaled by his stare, caught in its stringent concentration, its consummate assessment. The impending storm gray of the sky, she thought, was reflected there, as was the tempered steel of his determination.

A puff of wind fluttered the ends of her shawl. She shivered in its coolness. "No," she whispered in unconscious entreaty as she gave a small shake of her head. "Please, no."

Rowan returned his gaze to the target. He took his stance. He drew his bow. He glanced up at the heavens once more, as if judging the wind, then fastened his sight on the crying dove.

Straight and tall he stood, with the breeze ruffling his hair and molding the folds of his linen shirt against the sculpted form of his upper body. His booted feet were planted, his dark pantaloons clinging to the taut muscles of his calves and thighs. Still, he stood so still, yet there was no strain in the set of his shoulders as he held the heavy bow, no sense of hurry or doubt.

He let the arrow fly.

The arrow sang as it sped fast and high, singing a faint, deadly tune. The gathered guests drew breath with a ragged, gasping sound. The circling male dove shrieked. The men on the field turned their faces skyward.

Katrine squeezed her eyes shut and covered her ears. She could not look, would not see or hear the slaughter.

There was a shout, a yell, a chorus of wonder from a dozen throats. Then a cheer rang out. Katrine opened her eyes.

The first thing she saw was the doves. They were a pair again; the female was free. They circled each other, barely grazing in flight, swooping in graceful arabesques, silent in the delirium of their gladness as they climbed higher and higher into the air above the arena. In a final, sweeping turn, they heeled westward and winged slowly out of sight.

Rowan stood leaning on his bow, watching the departure. There was a rueful smile fading from his lips. He turned away as Alan came forward and clapped him on the shoulder.

At the pole centered on the field, an arrow quivered into stillness with the barb buried in the wood near the top. The line that had held the dove dangled free, waving in the wind. It had been sliced cleanly in two by the arrow's barb.

No, not just one arrow. Two. Two arrows had been shot into the leather line.

It was no accident that the line was cut.

Rowan had freed the dove. He had sacrificed his chance to win the day for the sake of a show of mercy toward a dumb creature.

He had not objected to drawing his bow at a live animal, so it hardly seemed it could have been done from compassion. There had been no reason of honor that might require him to refrain from killing the dove simply because the others had not been able to accomplish it.

The question, then, was why had he done it. Why?

CHAPTER FOUR

Giles rose to his feet and turned to face the people with his hands held at shoulder level, motioning for silence. As his guests began to mute their expressions of wonder over Rowan's skill with a bow and arrow, he raised his voice to speak.

"My friends," he said in deep and solemn tones. "Seldom have I been permitted the privilege of witnessing such a display of marksmanship as that just presented for our edification. But never, I repeat, never, have I seen such a fine example of gallantry and compassion. It takes a great man to throw away the chance to win when it is firmly in his grasp. It requires an extraordinary one to do this for no reason except a care for the sensibilities of a lady."

Katrine gave her husband a swift upward frown. He smiled down at her before he went on. "I saw, my friends, the look of appeal my own dear wife cast the man who would have been victor here today. I saw, too, the moment when Rowan de Blanc took the decision that the appeal from her rare and tender heart should not be in vain."

Katrine lowered her lashes, then sent a quick glance through them at Rowan, still standing in the arena. Was it true? she wondered. Then the question went out of her head as she heard her husband's next words.

"In reward for this superior manifestation of sportsmanship, on my own recognizance and with your gracious permission," Giles went on in sonorous tones, "I herewith extend to Rowan de Blanc the title of tournament king for this day, with all the honors and privileges which pertain to the position."

The crowd signaled its approval with applause and huzzas. Giles joined them, turning toward Rowan as he did so. The noise went on for endless moments. When quiet began to descend again, he held out his hand to the man with the bow and arrow, calling, "Come forward and be recognized!"

Alan leaned to take Rowan's weapons, making some laughing comment at the same time. There was dark color staining Rowan's cheekbones and his neck as he turned away and began to walk toward the grandstand.

It almost seemed to Katrine that he was reluctant to accept the honor being offered. She wondered if he truly felt undeserving, if possibly he objected to having his weakness of bowing to a woman's whim exposed in public, or if he only preferred his triumphs to be more fairly won.

It made no difference. It was still necessary for her to rise and take up the laurel wreath laid ready, then move to meet him. She would have descended the steps, but Giles put his hand on her arm to stop her, then motioned to Rowan to climb up to meet them.

Rowan mounted the steps with wary treads. There was a heaviness inside him, and more than a little puzzlement. He was not sure where the impulse to spare the dove had come from. He had looked at Katrine Castlereagh, had seen the pain and distress in her face, and the next thing he knew the deed was done. It seemed there had been no need for thought between the moment he had sensed how she felt and the instant he had acted to remedy it.

He didn't like it. He didn't want the damned laurel wreath, didn't want to be close to her, not now, not like this, and not until he had worked out in his mind what had happened to him. He wanted a bath and a massage from Omar's capable hands to work the kinks out of his neck and, hopefully, the foolishness from his brain.

She was moving toward him with the wreath in her hands. He was too tall, she was not going to be able to reach his head to place the twice-damned wreath, not while he stood there gawking at her like a country clod.

On a soundless sigh, he went to one knee. It was, perhaps, the position he deserved. At her feet.

"I must thank you," she said as she reached to press the leaves into the crisp waves of his hair. "It truly was a gallant thing to have done—whether it was for my sake, or for some reason of your own."

He lifted his gaze to her face. "It was nothing, Madam Castlereagh. There is no obligation."

"You risked your crown as tournament king for it; I believe that means something to you. As it turns out, the sacrifice cost you nothing. The winds of fortune, it seems, are with you."

"I can only agree," he said, his mouth curving in a crooked smile. "To do otherwise would be too discourteous."

"And you could never be that, could you?" She made as if to turn away.

"What?" Rowan said softly, his gaze resting on her mouth. "No kiss of victory?"

He did not move from where he knelt as she turned back to him, so that she was forced to stoop to his level. It restored a measure of his self-possession to see the reluctance in her movements, the combination of resentment and dutiful compliance in her eyes. And yet, there flickered through his mind a yearning curiosity to know how she might look if the kiss was of her own will and desire.

The touch of her lips on his face did nothing to banish his wayward thoughts. They were cold, as cold as slivers of pond ice brought south by steamboat from the north, and yet they sent tingling warmth flooding through him. He wanted to warm them, to pull her to her knees in front of him and—

He was mad. She was a lady and another man's wife. She was the woman who had, somehow, caused his brother's death. He would not be caught in her dangerous spell. Not if he could help it.

The clouds that had threatened scattered with hardly a rumble of thunder and not so much as a drop of rain. A few low-lying swaths remained, but the sun sailed through them with alternating brightness and shadows. The gathering straggled up to the house to freshen up before the noon barbecue was served. Afterward they spread out over the lawn, trailed by servants carrying their plates of food and glasses of cider and wine. They finally arranged themselves in small groups according to age and interest, reclining in chairs set under the trees.

The smell of roasted beef and pork, of spiced beans, potato salad, egg salad, stewed apples, pears, pickles and relishes, and of coconut cake and fried apple turnovers mingled with the tang of wood smoke and the spicelike scent of leaves beginning to turn color. At the edge of the woods, the tall stems of goldenrod, low masses of blue ageratum, black-eyed Susans, and lavender asters, all tangled with binding vines of pink morning glory just closing its flowers. Mockingbirds called in bell-like clarity and cardinals flitted from tree to tree. Yellow and orange butterflies drifted over the grass and fence rows with fragile wings and tenacious inclinations.

Giles was seated with some of the Barrows, neighbors from the surrounding area who were often referred to as the richest family in the parish. Since he shared many of the same predilections as the older male Barrows, such as horse racing, cards for high stakes, and extended house parties, he called them good friends.

Katrine had her own conclave some distance away under the spreading branches of a pin oak tree. Musetta was there with Perry at her side; Alan was escorting shy Charlotte, an act of charity that seemed to give him pleasure, while Georgette had attached herself to Satchel. Rowan was also there, lounging at his ease, accepting the congratulations that came his way with easy grace and a touch of self-deprecating modesty. He seemed oblivious to the glances he attracted from the females wandering by, just as he paid no attention to the worshipful fashion in which Charlotte hung on his every utterance, to Musetta's flirtatious airs aimed in his direction, or Georgette's candid appraisal.

The women were not the only ones who seemed impressed. The men showed him a certain respect that had not been there before, and they deferred to the opinions expressed by Rowan de Blanc with embarrassing frequency.

It would have been funny, Katrine thought as she watched the byplay, if it had not been so irritating. Why should a skill with weapons, one of them of no earthly use to a gentleman, suddenly raise a man's stature? Oh, she understood the appeal of excellence combined with rare sportsmanship—she even felt it herself—but it was still ridiculous.

The worst of it was that the advantage he had gained might be more than she could surmount. That fear hovered always at the back of her mind like a headache that would not be assuaged. It did not make her a congenial hostess, though she tried to join in the banter and listen to the analysis of the morning's events that went on around her. When Alan and Rowan began a discussion of the insurrection in Haiti that had ended with the suicide of the black ruler, the Emperor Christophe, she listened for a moment, then allowed her mind to wander.

They were an attractive group, she thought; a near-perfect representation for West Florida, which was now becoming known again by its old name of Feliciana, the happy land. Perry, whose mother had been French, had the longest family background in the area; his people had arrived shortly after the settlement by the French in the early 1700s. Satchel's family had owned their land since the British acquired this section of Louisiana by treaty after the Spanish took over Louisiana some ninety odd years ago; his great-grandfather had been granted his three thousand acres because of his service as a captain in the British army, an inducement to settle what had then been wild country. Georgette's great-grandfather had arrived after the Revolutionary War, as a Tory in flight from the young United States who hoped to find friends in British-held territory, and had not been disappointed. Charlotte's Spanish grandfather had arrived from New Orleans with the Spanish governor, Galvez, when he had taken advantage of British preoccupation with the insurrection on the eastern seaboard to lead a campaign to end British occupation.

Katrine herself owed her present place to a grandfather who had pulled up stakes in the Carolinas during the War of 1812 and arrived in Feliciana in time to join the group who ousted the Spanish and declared the section an independent republic. For seventy-four whole days they had been self-governing, complete with army, flag, and anthem, until federal forces from the United States came to annex the small new country.

He had been quite a man, her grandfather. His son, Katrine's father, had not been quite so hardy or resourceful or lucky. If he had been, then she might never have been persuaded to marry Giles.

There was no point in thinking such things, of course. She set her plate with its serving of food aside untasted. She was, abruptly, not at all hungry.

"I swear, Katrine," Musetta said in tart tones, "you grow more absentminded every day. Stop woolgathering and attend to me. This is a question in vital need of an answer."

"I'm sorry, I didn't hear."

"I know you didn't. I asked if a man who sacrifices his own

good for the sake of his mistress has any right to expect a reward?"

Katrine saw at once where the question had come from, saw, too, that Musetta was using it as a way to attract Rowan's notice. Her voice was flat as she said, "No."

Her sister-in-law lifted a brow. "Dear me, but you are definite. Only consider: If a man gives up what he most desires out of selfless motives, and his mistress has it in her power to compensate him for the loss, should he not have the comfort she can give?"

"Put that way, yes, of course," Katrine answered. She paused, then continued as her thoughts clarified. "But you asked if he had a right to expect this reward. If he expects it, that indicates an ulterior motive for his action. There is no sacrifice. The man has proven himself base by trying to trade an appearance of selflessness for a prize. He should be given nothing, should not even hope to retain the regard of his mistress."

Rowan sat forward in his chair as he spoke. "A harsh judgment, surely? Can a man not hope for comfort, or at least some sign that his mistress recognizes his deed?"

She gave him a straight look. "Hope is another thing entirely; anyone can have hope. The point here is that what a woman may offer is entirely different from what a man may expect by right. Or even what he may be granted by another person."

"Oh, that's it, is it?" he asked, the words soft with insinuation.

Katrine came to her feet with a movement so abrupt that the hoop of her gown caught her chair and overturned it behind her. She barely noticed. The verbal fencing, the polite insults and hidden meanings suddenly set her teeth on edge. She had to get away.

"You—you must excuse me," she said. "I have a few errands to run in St. Francisville before dark."

She whirled from them all, moving as quickly as the swinging bell of her skirt would allow. She had gone no more than a half-dozen steps when she heard the quiet sound of cloth brushing cloth, felt a presence at her side.

Black boots, highly polished. Fine broadcloth pantaloons in a subdued gray striped in black.

Halting, she spun to face Rowan. She demanded in goaded tones, "Where are you going?"

"It is, if you remember, my hard-earned privilege to escort you wherever you wish to go."

"I have a groom for that."

"Dismiss him," he suggested.

"I don't need an escort, and I don't want one." Surely he could understand such plain speaking as that.

"The point here is," he said in deliberate parody of her word earlier, "that I have the right to be with you."

"Not against my wishes." She was proud of the evenness of her voice.

"As to that, I don't recall the mention of anyone's wishes."

He smiled down at her as he spoke, a pleasant smile, but one so laden with calm power that she felt a fierce desire to be male and tall and strong, if only for a single, annihilating second.

She tried another tack. "You will be bored; I expect to match embroidery silks, buy a new pair of gloves, and bring back the crate of pineapples destined to be tonight's dessert that came on the steamer this morning."

"Then you will be in your carriage. It will be an honor to drive you."

She stared at him a long moment. Finally she said, "Why?"

He tilted his head. "Why would you think? I have designs on your virtue and your pineapples."

"You think you can persuade me to talk about Terence," she said with a scathing glance before she turned from him and began to walk again.

He kept pace beside her. "And you are just as determined to say nothing. It's possible we can find some other topic."

Katrine thought of canceling her plan, sending Delphia and one of the hands for the things she needed. The outing was no more than an excuse to be alone, and if she could not achieve that, then it had lost its purpose. She would not, however, allow him to control her actions. Besides, if she remained at Arcadia, he would still be there to hound her.

"You will not drive me," she said. "If you prefer not to be driven by a woman, then you may remain behind."

"Agreed," he said at once, adding in dry tones, "it will be a novelty."

"You'll also have to wait while I change into something more suitable."

"I can use the time to change also."

She stared at him a long moment, suspicion for his determination to be pleased strong in her mind. There seemed nothing to be done, however, except to allow him to have his way.

The errands were accomplished with a minimum of fuss. Rowan proved surprisingly useful in the task of matching silk colors and choosing good-fitting gloves. At the dock, rather than waiting for a hand to come and load the pineapples, he himself hoisted the heavy crate into the space behind the carriage seat.

He proved himself an agreeable companion also; not once did he mention his brother or the situation at Arcadia. He talked instead of the cotton harvest just past and the six hundred bales of white gold that had been taken from the fields that stretched for miles beyond the wooded area surrounding Arcadia. He spoke of Paris fashions and foibles, the sights of London, and a villa he owned in Rome. When she mentioned friends in St. Francisville, he followed her lead by recalling people he had met during the annual New Orleans *saison des visites*, when everyone who was anyone went downriver for the latest in opera and theater.

It was as they drove away from the steamboat dock that they noticed how dark the sky had grown. There was a gray-purple cloud looming up from the northwest. Katrine elected to try to make it back to Arcadia before it began to rain. That was the first mistake. The second came when they were well out of town, bowling along with grit and blown leaves flying in their faces in the rising wind, and the tree limbs of the great oaks and beeches that overlapped the roadway like a tunnel creaking overhead.

"Maybe it would be best if I took the reins," Rowan suggested.

"I can manage." Katrine's answer was short. She needed all her strength and attention to control the bay mare between the shafts as she shied at a vine that had blown free to dangle in the road. She could feel the strain of it in her back and shoulders, and in the pulled stitching of her chestnut leather driving gloves.

"I expect you can, but why should you make the effort when it would be much easier for me?"

There was no time for a reply. A great owl, disturbed by the early darkness, came sailing toward them. The mare threw up her head in whinnying terror, then bolted in the harness.

The carriage careened across the road. Katrine's glove split as she fought the reins. Rowan leaned to clamp his hands over hers in a grasp that came near to crushing the bones. The carriage skidded in a cloud of windblown dust.

Katrine tried to release her hold on the reins, giving them up to Rowan. Even as she made the transfer there was a loud and ominous cracking noise. The carriage lurched, then fell onto one axle with a teeth-jarring thud. In a hail of dirt and leaves, it slid, shuddering, tipping toward a ditch.

She felt herself slipping from the seat, felt the carriage heaving under her. She saw the tree trunks rushing toward them. Then a steel band clamped around her waist, cutting off her breath. She was flung into thin air, tumbling, falling. Something glanced across her head and shoulder with blinding pain. Held fast, she sank into sharp-edged darkness.

She awoke by minute degrees; it seemed she could feel before she could hear, and hear long before she could find the will to open her eyes. She lay on something warm and firm. She had a slight headache, but she was wonderfully comfortable and her breathing was free and unrestrained. There was a rattling, drumming sound somewhere in the distance, but she was safe from it, safe from everything. The air was cool and damp, and smelled of old wood ashes, dust, and mice.

She frowned a little, as it occurred to her that nothing was as it should be. Slowly, conscious of the necessity and her own reluctance, she opened her eyes.

She was cradled in Rowan's arms. Their hard strength surrounded her along with his scent that was compounded of warm rain, well-pressed linen, and leather. His face was set in stern lines and his manner had an edge of fierce competence, though there was concern in the shadowed depths of his eyes.

They were in a cabin, one empty of furnishings that she recognized as being on a worked-out piece of land where a family had pulled up stakes, leaving a sign on the door saying GONE TO TEXAS. Close by was a smoke-blackened fireplace with the hearth caked with old ashes. The rain drummed on the roof overhead, pouring through in a steady stream in a far corner. Rowan sat in his shirt sleeves with his back against a rough wall. She was covered by his coat. Under it, the bodice of her tailored driving costume was open to the waist and her corset had been loosened.

Katrine lay perfectly still as it was borne in upon her that Rowan de Blanc had brought her to the cabin while she was unconscious, had unbuttoned her clothing, unfastened her corset cover, exposing her breasts, and unhooked her corset. Then he had sat himself down and taken her into his arms.

What else had he done?

Hot color rose from somewhere deep inside her to flood her shoulders and neck and burn in her face. Her breathing deepened. Her hands, stripped of their gloves, curled into fists.

Rowan watched the signs of agitation. He knew their cause, had been expecting no less; still, he was incensed by them. He had done what he had to do while half afraid she was dying. The terror of it had shocked him; he could not believe that he could care so much. When he had discovered her heart still beating, found that she could breathe once freed of her corset's cruel bite, his fear had eased. It was then that he saw the sweet, swelling perfection of what he had uncovered, the pearl-like luminosity of her naked skin, the delicacy of the bones underneath it.

His hands had started to shake. For a brief instant he had reached to touch, his hands hovering over the slender waist that he could span so easily. His fingers had cupped for the perfect fit of breasts shadowed by a fragile tracery of blue veins and tipped with rose coral above their lovely globelike contours.

He had drawn back, though the effort brought a cramp to his arms and knots to the pit of his stomach. He had covered her, then sat in an exercise of iron will, forbidding thought, beseeching forgetfulness, commanding the quickening of his body and the devout lust inside him to subside.

He had won that bout with temptation. He had sat perfectly still, watching the contours of her face and the blue shadows of fatigue and strain under her eyes. Yet for what? To see accusation in her steady gaze, regardless. Or was it only in his own mind?

"I'm sorry," he said, the words abrupt, harsh. "Your breathing was too shallow, and there was no one else to help you."

Something inside Katrine responded to the baffled anger she saw in his face, to the controlled tension she sensed in his arms. He desired her, she knew. Never in her life had she felt so vulnerable, not even in those moments on her wedding night when

Giles had lain beside her and opened her nightgown, before he had turned from her in shame at his inability to do more.

She wondered, suddenly, how it would have felt if she had been awake to know Rowan's intimate touch as he worked to release her, wondered what it would have been like if he not stopped there. She wished, in sudden longing, that she was the kind of woman who could reach out to him, saying, "Do what you will. Hold me close. Take me, show me all those things Musetta hints at but never explains. Make me feel something, anything. Love me in that desire that is the counterfeit of love, if you cannot love me forever."

Such thoughts were so foreign to her nature, so beyond anything she had ever considered possible, that they seemed to drain her will, making it impossible to draw away from him. The most she could do was lower her gaze. It lighted on the firm shape of his lips, so precisely molded yet with sensuous tucks at the corners. The memory of their heated smoothness against her own mouth was so vivid that it almost seemed she could feel the tingling pressure still. The need to know it again, to savor it, was so strong that her mouth throbbed with it. She wondered what he would do if she reached up and put her hand behind his neck, drawing his head down until—

No.

She closed her eyes tight. The blow to her skull must have affected her mind. She was light-headed with its effects. She could not think where such wanton impulses had come from otherwise.

The man who held her was her greatest danger. What hope had she of retaining her chastity, her integrity, her self-respect, if she allowed her defenses against him to be weakened in this way?

"Are you all right?" he asked, a trace of anxiety in his low voice. "The bump to the back of your head didn't seem serious; I've often seen men regain their senses and go about their business when hit just there. But I can ride for a doctor if need be. The mare was not hurt; she's tied up outside."

Katrine mustered a brief smile. "I'm well enough, I think. You seem to have—managed everything nicely. Now, if you will allow me to get up?"

"Of course," he said, the words clipped, his concern vanishing as if it had never been.

He exerted a minimum amount of pressure and lift, and she was upright. She grabbed with both hands for the fine, soft wool of his coat covering her as it began to slip. Pushing farther away from him, she scrambled to her knees then struggled to stand. He was on his feet in an instant, his arm at her waist to support her as she untangled her feet from her skirts and gained her balance.

"Thank you," she said in stilted tones.

He made no reply, only stepped away from her and turned his back, moving toward the open door. Leaning one shoulder against the frame, he stood staring out at the falling rain.

He was giving her the privacy to attend to her open bodice, Katrine realized. She was grateful to him, both for the deed and the understanding. It made no sense to be annoyed with him also, and yet she was. He need not have made it so obvious that he had no interest in watching the spectacle.

He spoke over his shoulder after a moment. "The rain seems to be slackening. I don't like the idea of leaving you here while I ride to Arcadia for another carriage. You can take the mare, if you like, and I'll follow on foot."

She glanced at his stiff back. "There's no sidesaddle or bridle. I'm not sure I can control the mare without them, not if she catches sight of a flapping skirt."

"I'll undertake to hold her in, then, if you don't mind riding pinion."

He was reminding her of her insistence on driving that had

landed them in their present predicament. Her tone astringent, she said, "Why should I mind?"

It was not a comfortable ride. Katrine had been forced to jettison her small daytime hoop and petticoats, and still there was an uncomfortable amount of skirt to be held down to prevent the mare from taking fright.

She did not actually ride pinion, but rather was seated in front of Rowan with his arms encircling her. Without the protection of her usual underclothing, she was painfully aware of the hard muscles of his thighs under her and the movements of the horse, which nudged her own soft curves against him with rhythmic regularity. It was as well that the distance they had to cover was not great.

They were cantering up the drive to Arcadia when Rowan spoke. "There is something you should know," he said. "It's about your carriage."

Katrine made a sound of inquiry, though her attention was distracted by the stir of unusual activity around the front door of the great house ahead of them. Their return, it appeared, had been delayed long enough to cause concern.

"The vehicle is actually yours? You make a habit of driving yourself?"

She gave him a swift upward glance. "I've always done so, since I was old enough to hold the reins. Giles doesn't mind; the carriage was a birthday gift from him."

"It was a broken wheel that caused it to overturn. Several spokes of that wheel had been sawn halfway through."

She was silent as she considered the possibility he was suggesting, that someone had damaged the wheel in order to cause an accident that might injure her. Her voice was taut as she said, "You must be mistaken."

"Maybe. But you might have your groom or the man in charge of the stables keep watch from now on."

There was no time for more. As they neared the house a half-dozen people came to meet them: Alan and Satchel, Musetta and Perry, the butler Cato, and Delphia. Giles stood waiting at the top of the steps, beneath the Gothic portico.

The exclaiming, the demands for explanations and comments on their lucky escape carried them inside. Giles permitted it to go on for some minutes more, though a frown settled over his lined face from the instant he heard about Katrine's head injury. Finally he broke in on the eager spate of questions.

"That's enough, everyone. I'm sure Katrine and Rowan will tell us about the adventure in detail at dinner, but for now I think Katrine should lie down and rest."

"I'm quite well, really," she said with a mechanical smile, "and there are things I must do. I should send someone after the pineapples if we are to have them tonight, and then a wheelwright needs to be instructed to repair the carriage and bring—"

"It will be attended to, never fear. You should attend to yourself. I'm sure you would like to change your clothing, at the very least." Giles turned her in the direction of a pier mirror as he spoke.

Katrine did not care for the reprimand in her husband's tone; still, she saw what he meant. Her hair was falling down and flecked with bits of tree bark, there was a streak of dirt on her face, and her skirts sagged, trailing over the floor, without her petticoats. She said no more, but signaled to Delphia and went with her up the stairs and along the hallway that led to her bedchamber.

Giles followed after them. He entered the room with her and, waiting until Delphia was inside, closed the door behind him. His gaze was intent on Katrine's pale face as he turned to her once more. In abrupt tones, he said, "I was worried about you."

"I'm sorry, but it could not be helped." She moved to seat herself at her dressing table, where Delphia began at once to pull the pins from her hair.

"I thought at first, when you did not appear at the expected time, that perhaps you had changed your mind." His voice was suggestive. He waited expectantly for her answer.

"You mean . . ." she began, then started again. "No, I had not done that."

"That is fortunate, as it happens. There was some comment about de Blanc going off with you. It would be a great pity if everything should be spoiled by a moment of indiscretion."

"I should have thought," she said bitingly, "that you would have been happy no matter how the affair was arranged."

"You would have been wrong, my dear. It was never my intention to look the fool, or to be a public cuckold. You must know that would negate the entire reason for the charade."

Katrine met the gaze of her maid in the mirror and saw her own weary anger reflected there. She said to him, "You need not have worried; there was no danger."

"So I apprehend. You might keep the thought in mind, however, for the future."

She turned her head to give him a long, direct look. "I doubt there will be a need."

He rocked a moment on his heels before he moved toward her, stopping at her shoulder. "You are tired and sore from your fall, and so I won't press you. But I will remind you for the last time that you gave your word. I have told you that I will hold you to it, and I intend to, no matter how much it distresses you. It will be much better if you do not force me to measures we may both regret."

There was something in his voice that sent alarm skittering along her nerves. "What are you saying?"

"There are ways of being certain that a reluctant filly stands still for the stallion's mount. You might strive to remember that."

He turned as he finished speaking and walked away from her. She sprang to her feet, calling after him. His face as he swung back to face her was flushed reddish purple, but implacable.

The protests and pleas that crowded in her mind died away inside her, leaving only bleak despair. Tightness closed her throat, so it was impossible to speak.

"Yes, my dearest Katrine?"

The endearment gave her courage. "Tell me something, Giles, just one small thing. Do you care for me at all?"

"I love you dearly, in my fashion. Haven't I told you so many times?"

"What fashion can it be if you can do this?" The words were a cry from the heart.

"You must know that this is also best for you. I am trying, Katrine, to be unselfish, though it is difficult." He swung away once more. The bedchamber door closed behind him.

He didn't mean it, he couldn't. He was trying to frighten her into submission. Giles had never treated her with anything except consideration bordering on indulgence. He had never raised his hand or even his voice to her. He was, she would have said, kindness itself.

And yet, she could not forget the day he had taken her to the stable yard to see a fine young mare of excellent bloodlines he had bought. She was to be covered by his prize stallion, Katrine knew, for he had told her, but she had not known it was to take place that morning.

The mare, for all that she was physically ready to be mated, was terrified of the rampant ardor, the plunging and shrill neighing and hard love nips of the stallion. She had raced around the paddock wild-eyed, kicking and biting. Her evasion was successful, until Giles ordered her roped and tied, snubbed to the fence so she could hardly move. Katrine's husband had watched in smiling satisfaction as the eager stallion had been released upon the helpless, trembling mare.

Surely he had not meant to suggest that he would offer her

that humiliation. He couldn't; only a madman would consider it. She was his wife. It was impossible.

Wasn't it?

Katrine lifted a hand to her forehead, rubbing it. Looking at the maid in the mirror once more, she said, "What am I going to do?"

"Oh, madam," Delphia said softly, "you will do what must be done, like all of us."

CHAPTER FIVE

The jousting the following morning was held in much the same style as the fencing competition, though choosing the winner was somewhat more simple.

A series of a dozen tall poles had been erected at intervals down the length of the field, with bars attached at right angles at the top of each pole. From the bars hung chains with brass rings attached to the lowest links. Beginning from the right of the run of poles, the first ring was the approximate size of a full harvest moon seen on the horizon. Each ring grew progressively smaller and more difficult to spear until the last was no larger than a small woman's wrist.

The horsemen were required to collect as many of the rings as they could on a lance held under one arm while riding at a dead gallop. The man who collected the most rings won. In case of a tie, the two contestants involved must run the field a second time, competing only against each other.

It was a contest of skill, coordination, steady nerves, and horsemanship without equal, short of an actual joust with man pitted against man. It called on every resource a man who considered himself any kind of sportsman or horseman could muster. The only outside factor was the mount the man chose to ride.

Rowan's manservant led out a gray stallion, all nerves and

quivering muscles and sinews, with arched neck and perfectly brushed hide gleaming like polished steel in the morning sun. The horse was a thoroughbred with Arabian lines. Word from the stables said he was called Saladin. From the moment Katrine saw him, she knew a bleak fatalism. She also felt a frisson of trepidation, one that brought a flush to her face that was a long time in fading.

The day was bright and clear, the sky a transcendent blue against the green of the enclosing trees. It had turned cooler in the night after the rain and there were more leaves drifting down here and there. A cloak was required to ward off the wafting chill in the morning air, though it would be warmer by noon. The long Indian summer of a Southern fall was nearing its end.

Katrine took a certain sensual pleasure in the pure warm light, and also in the sight of the men thundering down the field with lances held at the ready and concentration in their faces. She cheered the number of rings speared by the others, and groaned as, too often, they struck a ring on the edge and sent it leaping, crazily swinging, into the air. She had given her favor to Perry on this day. Musetta, she thought, regarded the fluttering scarf with annoyance in her light blue eyes, but it could not be helped. Of all the men from around Arcadia who were on the field, Perry had the keenest eyes and best seat in the saddle.

Katrine sprang to her feet with hope thudding in her breast as Perry took the rings one after the other, without a miss—until he came to the last and smallest ring. That one he did not catch. She suspected the outcome of the match then, and it was as well she was prepared.

Rowan rode harder, faster, with more vigor and élan. He held the heavy lance as if it were no more weighty or cumbersome than a walking stick, and rode as if directing the stallion with his heart and mind instead of the reins. And he speared every ring, from largest to smallest, as though picking apples or peaches at his leisure.

It was infuriating. It was dismal. Katrine wanted to leave her place in the grandstand, to turn her back and walk away without awarding the prize, without having to look into the eyes of Rowan de Blanc and see the expression of victory there.

She could not. She had her duty. It was expected of her, and none would understand a refusal. Giles, undoubtedly, would not permit it.

So she sat where she was while Rowan rode down the length of the field with the rings shining on his upturned lance. She remained in her seat while he drew his stallion to a stop in front of her and dipped the lance slowly toward her. She sat quite still as he allowed the collected rings to slide down the lance and cascade in a clanging, ringing mass into her lap.

She hated him, hated the fact that there was no gloating but only calm assurance in his face, hated that he made her feel he deserved his award, hated the way he sat his horse on her own level and waited for what he knew must come.

She thought of pretending the weight of the rings held her captive in her chair, so that someone else was forced to take her place. She thought of standing and letting them fall around her feet while she swooned away in an artistic faint. She thought of throwing the brass rings one by one at the head of the man on the horse.

Then from the corner of her eye, she saw Musetta start to rise from where she sat. Her sister-in-law meant to usurp her rightful place; Katrine could tell. She would, no doubt, delight in giving the kiss of victory to Rowan. Suddenly that, too, was intolerable.

Katrine lifted the rings and transferred them to Giles's lap, where he sat beside her. She rose to her feet and descended to the bottom step as Rowan dismounted and moved to meet her. The placing of the crown of laurel, the delicate touching of lips, first to one hard cheek, then to the other, was quickly over. He kept his eyes lowered, stood motionless, though his face was flushed with exertion and his heartbeat jarred the smooth broadcloth of his coat.

She didn't trust him. She began to turn in a hasty retreat. The low heel of her slipper caught the hem of her stiff, full skirts of Balmoral tartan. She staggered, off balance.

He shot out his hands to catch her, snatching her against him. For an instant she felt the hard muscles of his shoulders under her hands, the press of her breasts against the firm planes of his chest, the bend of her hoops around his spread legs and the bite of his strong fingers into the flesh of her upper arms. She was surrounded by the aura of overweening masculinity and leashed power, by the aroma of horse and bay rum, starched linen and hot male. She felt, rather than heard, his sudden, sharp-drawn breath.

He stepped back, steadying her an instant before he released her and dropped his hands to his sides. "Take care," he said in somber tones. "You'll hurt yourself."

"And you," she answered, her voice tight in her throat.

A whimsical smile came and went across his face, though there were shadows in his eyes as somber green as the underside of a white oak leaf. "Nothing could be more likely," he answered.

Short hours later they were waltzing, the two of them, moving in perfect synchronization and physical accord to the strains of the "Moonbeam" waltz. It was in the double parlor, rather than the ballroom, that everyone had gathered, pushing the chairs and tables against the walls to make room.

They had eaten dinner, after which they had been favored by Musetta at the piano. She was not only lovely sitting before the keys, but something more than competent as she gave them a Chopin sonata. Afterward, quiet, dark-haired Charlotte was urged to perform. She would have refused, but her cousin Georgette insisted, pressing her forward. She gazed around the company, her face as pale as her white dress and her eyes as blank as if they had asked her to commit a crime. That was until Rowan strolled forward to take up the guitar lying on top of the piano. With his support and encouraging smile, Charlotte gathered herself together enough to sing "Maiden's Dream" and "Scarborough Fair." She had hardly taken her worshipful gaze from Rowan since.

It was a simple evening of the kind that Katrine preferred. Only the twenty-odd houseguests were on hand. The company was subdued; the gentlemen were tired after their strenuous three days, while the ladies were saving their energies for the great ball that would be held after the races tomorrow.

The tournament was over, for all rights and purposes. Rowan as king would reign tomorrow night. The purse of gold promised as a final prize would be presented in private. And that would be the end of it for another year.

Regardless, it was unlikely that Giles would permit everyone to leave so soon. He had arranged for a hunting expedition the day after the races, one that would require a trip downriver on his own steamboat. He preferred that his house parties last at least a week, and often two or three.

Katrine had thought that she would have until after the races at least to find a way out of her dilemma. As the evening wore on she began to wonder. Giles had looked grim all day; now he stood watching her and Rowan circle the floor with his eyes narrowed and his mouth set in lines of tight resolve.

"Your husband," Rowan said as he swung her easily in the waltz, "was generous in sharing your company until last evening. Now I don't believe he is quite so pleased to see you in another man's arms."

"He has no cause for jealousy," she said.

"For most husbands, no real cause is needed; it's the appearance of the thing that matters. I confess that it's his attitude now that seems most reasonable to me."

"You don't understand," Katrine said, though she frowned

as the memory of Giles's objections the night before moved through her mind.

"Possibly not," he answered. "Did Terence?"

Rowan steeled himself against the pained reproach he saw in her face as she looked up at him. He had been in danger of forgetting why he had come here, in his involvement with the games and with his hostess.

He had, in the past few days, made opportunities to talk to Alan and Perry and even Brantley Hennen and the charming Musetta. For what good it did him.

Time was passing and he was no nearer to knowing what had happened to his brother than he had been the evening he arrived.

It had occurred to him the night before, as he lay in bed trying not to think about the way Giles Castlereagh had taken Katrine away to her bedchamber, that it was possible there had been a deliberate attempt to divert his attention. It would not be the first time a woman had been used for such a purpose. The question was how far Katrine would go to achieve it. Also, whether she was a willing tool.

She had her scruples, he knew, or thought he did; it might be no more than pretense. He didn't want to think she was less than she pretended.

He had known many women, though few had been able to hold him beyond a night or a day. This one fascinated him, though it galled him to admit it. She was all soft seduction and elusive guile. She was also forthright anger and repudiation. She advanced and retreated, beckoned and ran away until he wanted nothing so much as to catch and hold her, then slowly strip her bare to see what she was hiding.

He had very nearly done that, and what had it brought him? A night of throbbing and uncomfortable desire. When it had passed, he was still fascinated.

Dancing with her, feeling her pliant in his arms, obedient to his guidance, was a perilous pleasure. She moved with such grace and accord, as if reading his mind and instincts. The brush of her hoop against his shins and thighs was like feeling the delicacy of her bones through her skin, a prelude to intimacy. The scent that rose from her skin and hair hinted of a moonlit garden, with lavender and roses and jasmine in full flower. The luster of her skin in the candlelight, the sheen of her hair, held him in thrall. He blessed the tradition that said it was his right as king to solicit as many dances as he chose. He would take all he could get, and never mind the stiff soreness of the cut on his leg.

Katrine didn't like it, he knew. She refused to meet his eyes for more than a second at a time, and she kept a strict distance between them. It troubled him, but he had no intention of letting it keep him from what he had to do.

He spoke into the small silence that had fallen between them. "You were avoiding me earlier, I think. Have I done something to displease you?"

"Of course not," she said. "I was simply busy with my duties."

He ignored the excuse. "There is no need for embarrassment between us, if that is the problem. What happened yesterday afternoon, at least between us, was unavoidable."

She gave him a glance of acute irritation. "I am aware."

"Good. Then why are you blushing?"

There was a rich note in his voice that sent a vibration through some long-unused chord inside her. Katrine looked at him from under her lashes. His face was softened by a smile of such charm that her voice was constricted as she answered him. "I'm not blushing; it's the exertion."

"Yes, of course," he said, and whirled her into a series of spins that left her dizzy and clinging to his hard arms. In the midst of them, he said, "Your husband is signaling, though I'm not sure whether he wants to speak to you or to me."

Katrine's stomach knotted inside her, but she made no answer.

Giles was perfectly affable as they came to a halt in front of him with the end of the music. "Forgive me, my dear," he said to Katrine, "but I fear I must take your partner from you for a short while. There is a matter I must discuss with him in my study."

The matter might well be the prize purse of gold, but she was afraid that was not the whole of it. Meeting her husband's faded blue gaze, she said, "Perhaps I should join you?"

"Oh, I think not. It will be better if we speak man to man."

Katrine saw Rowan's frown from the corners of her eyes. She ignored it as she concentrated on her husband. "Are you quite sure about this?"

"Yes, yes, my dear. You must not worry if I don't return here; I believe I'll have an early night, afterward."

"Are you ill?" There was a blue tinge to his lips, and his color was pale. There were other strains that could also contribute their part.

"I'm not feeling my best, something I ate at dinner, no doubt."

"Shall I send Cato to you?"

Her husband gave her an impatient look. "Don't fuss, please, Katrine; I'll ring for him when I need him. For now, you must see to our guests."

"I suppose I must," she said almost at random. She did not move as she watched the two men walk away in the direction of the study.

The evening did not last much more than a half hour past the time Giles and the guest of honor deserted the company. One by one, the others wandered away to their separate bedchambers. Katrine gave a few directions to Cato and the two maids who were setting the double parlor to rights, then she went swiftly along the hall and past the winding stairs to the combined library and study that was Giles's preferred retreat.

Outside the door, she paused. She lifted her hand to knock, then brought it back down again, clasping her fingers together in front of her. She stared unseeing at the door panel, then her lips tightened. Lifting her hand again, she rapped on the wood. She reached for the chased silver doorknob, pushed the door open, and stepped inside.

Giles sat at his desk with a glass of brandy at his elbow. He looked ghastly, his skin pallid and his shirt collar soaked with perspiration. He pressed his hands into his stomach, as if it pained him.

Rowan was on the far side of the study. He stood with his back to the room and one hand gripping the heavy window draperies as he stared out into the darkness. He turned slightly as Katrine entered. He met her gaze over the red Turkish carpet that centered the room, though the look in his eyes was unreadable.

Her husband turned to face Katrine with a feverish light in his eyes and a smile of satisfaction on his trembling mouth. "Come in, my dear," he said. "You will be happy to know the outcome of our talk. Rowan has agreed."

Katrine stopped so suddenly that the swing of her full skirts sent the back of her hoop against the calves of her legs. It was a long moment before she could force sound through the clamped tightness of her throat.

"No," she whispered.

"I assure you it is so. You must not think it was an acceptance easily won, for it was not. Still, I claim this victory."

She swallowed hard, grasping at a measure of control. Her voice was strained, toneless, as she said, "Congratulations."

"Thank you. Now I am quite fatigued. I feel the need to lie down. In any case, there is nothing more to be done except leave the two of you together."

She opened her lips to protest, but no sound came. A moment later she abandoned the attempt. It might be best if what must be said came now.

Giles heaved himself to his feet and moved toward the door. With the knob in his hand he paused and looked back. "Good night, my dear," he said.

Katrine did not answer. After a moment the door closed behind him.

She turned slowly to face the man at the window. In the stillness that lay between them she could hear the ticking of the mantel clock and the sputter of the candles in the brass chandelier overhead. She could see them both reflected in the window glass, two people as rigid as statues, and as lifeless. There was such pressure inside her that she felt it constricting her heart, aching in her throat. She wanted to scream, to cover her face, to run and hide, anything to escape the next humiliating moments. It was impossible.

She drew a breath so deep her corset made a small creaking sound in protest. At last she said, "I had begun to think that I could depend on your refusal as a man of honor."

"You were wrong." The words were rough.

"Why?" she cried, the word torn from her. "Dear God, why?"

He dropped the curtain and turned to face her. "Several reasons, some of them involving questions of honor."

"Oh, please!" Her grimace was disdainful.

"Foremost among the reasons was an impression that you were not entirely opposed, not if I was the chosen man." The words were stark, without inflection.

She drew a sharp breath. "If Giles said that to you, he was mistaken. You will remember that I told you myself—"

"Yes, I do," Rowan said, inclining his head, "though I was not aware just what you were talking about at the time and there was a small possibility that you had changed your mind."

"No, I have not." Her voice was abrupt.

"So I see." He paused, raking a hand through his hair. "We were speaking of my reasons, I think. Curiosity was also among them. I could not resist the chance to discover if my brother was made the same offer. And if he took it."

"No again, to both questions," she said, clenching her hands together so tightly that her rings cut into her fingers. "Since you have your answers, you are now free to withdraw."

"Am I? What of my vow to discover the cause of my brother's death? Can I afford to refuse an opportunity that would permit me to remain here for another few weeks, weeks that might reveal the truth?"

A chill smile touched her lips. "Is this the place where your honor is supposed to be engaged? How can you reconcile it with your principles to do a base thing in order to satisfy this vow?"

"It isn't completely base if there is a benefit." The words were firm, though he removed his gaze to the pattern of the carpet at their feet.

"Oh, your consideration knows no end. The benefit, I would remind you, isn't mine. It's my husband's!"

"The benefit is yours," he said softly, "if by refusing, I expose you to pain and danger."

He met her gaze then, his own clear and dark emerald in the candlelight. There was, she would have sworn, not a trace of guile or salacious consideration in it. The words clipped, she demanded, "What are you saying?"

"I was given to understand, by your husband, that if I refused his request, there would be no more competitions held to fill my place. He would apply directly to the man he should, perhaps, have chosen from the first, his only male blood relation."

"Lewis?"

"Just so. Your husband is aware you don't care for his nephew. Lewis would be instructed—though with great regret—that force would be an acceptable means of assuring your cooperation."

The color drained from her face. She swayed a little where she stood. At the same time she recalled vividly the warning

Giles had given her about nervous mares. It was a moment before she could steel herself to look at Rowan again. "And you," she whispered, "were you granted the use of—this means?"

The expression in his eyes was steady, though his lips curled with contempt. "What I may have been granted, and what I will do, are two different things."

"You were," she said, her eyes enormous in her face.

"I have never forced a woman in my life, and I see no reason to start now," he said in tones that grated like steel against steel.

Katrine hardly heard him. How could Giles do this to her? How could he, and claim to love her? She couldn't believe it, even now.

Her husband was mad; there was no other explanation. His illness must have affected his mind.

But what difference did that make, so long as she was required to live by his dictates? He wanted an heir and would go to any lengths to gain one; that much had been made abundantly clear. She had avoided the issue for months, even years. She could do so no longer.

"No," she said, crossing her forearms around her, rubbing her chilled flesh with the palms of her hands. "I can't. It's wrong, all wrong. I hardly know you, or you me. It offends every sense of decency. Most important of all, the vows I made as a wife forbid it."

"You also promised to obey, and this is your husband's request."

She shook her head so hard her high-piled curls danced. "He has no right to make it."

"Right no longer matters. It's been made."

She gave him a look of scorn. "What of you? Doesn't it trouble you to know Giles has put you through your paces like a prize stallion chosen for stud?"

An expression that might have been self-contempt crossed his features and was gone.

"It did when I realized it, when I was told that I was chosen because of my supposed prowess. It still does, in all truth. Regardless, I came here for my own reasons and can hardly complain if others have theirs."

"You could refuse, even now." There was appeal behind the coolness in her eyes as she stared at him.

"So could you. You could leave your husband and return to your family."

"Don't you think I've considered that?" she cried. "I have no family. My father died within a year after my marriage. My mother has been dead since I was a few days old. I have no one, no place to go, no way to live."

"What will you do if I withdraw? Submit to Lewis?"

"Never," she said in tones of loathing.

"Then what other choice is there for you except to follow your husband's arrangement?"

Her eyes were dark as she met his eyes. "No. I will never allow—I won't permit—I can't—"

"Can you not put it in plain words even now?" he said in grim irony. "Never mind; I understand. You will never willingly allow me in your bed, never lie in my arms to make love, never carry my child."

There was something in his voice that sent a sharp shaft of distress deep inside her. It also brought images to the forefront of her mind that made her feel dizzy and not quite herself. She banished them with some difficulty as she thought she saw a way out.

"Then you accept that it's impossible?"

It was a long time before he answered, then his voice was quiet with finality. "No, Madam Castlereagh, I do not. I can't. It is your vows against mine, your well-being against my benefit, your doubts and fears against my word. I made an agreement with your husband, and I will use every means at my disposal to carry it out." He added, "Short, of course, of force."

Bitter anger boiled up inside her as he blasted the tenuous hope inside her. "You give your word so easily and are so good at finding points of honor to suit your purpose. You will forgive me if I wonder how important a little matter of force can be to you? I also have to question how I can be expected to trust you when your word of honor is so changeable?"

A muscle stood out in his jaw as he watched her. His chest rose and fell with the deep breath he took. When he answered, his voice was hard and without compunction. "We will see, won't we? Your husband suggested there was no reason for delay, and every reason to begin at once."

"At once," she repeated, her voice faltering.

"Tonight, this moment, if I so choose; he left the decision in my hands."

"No," she whispered.

"Yes. He also gave me leave to visit your bedchamber through the connecting door leading from his room. That way, he said, would be more discreet."

"It can't be." She was aware of an extra undercurrent of savagery in his voice directed at Giles and, perhaps, himself. She thought of the rabbit warren of rooms and halls in the house, the double parlors, the various sitting rooms; the card room, billiard room, ballroom, and the great, curving central stair leading to the fifteen bedchambers with their connecting dressing rooms. There was only a slight chance of anyone being seen coming and going.

A chill smile curved Rowan's mouth. "I assure you the matter is arranged. Your part in it is to be accommodating. Oh. And fertile."

Katrine felt as if she was being pummeled by his words. That Giles had said such things to him, that they had discussed the details of this perfidious seduction so openly, was beyond her comprehension. A sick and empty feeling gathered inside, adding to her rage.

She lifted her chin with the chill of revulsion in her eyes. "No," she said. "Never!"

"Yes," he returned softly as he moved toward her. "Now. Are you ready?"

CHAPTER SIX

Katrine stood her ground until Rowan was close enough to reach out for her. Her nerve broke then. She backed away in haste. "Don't touch me!"

"What is your objection?" he asked, taking another step after her. "Are you afraid of love, as Giles seems to think? Or is it me?"

"What difference does it make? Just leave me alone." She came up against Giles's leather-topped desk and slid along the edge.

"Call it a whim, call it vanity even, but I'd like to know."

He moved with tempered grace and the sudden glide of smooth muscles. Abruptly she was captured with her back to the desk and her wrists manacled by his iron hands. His grasp was neither tight nor hurtful, but was inescapable. She struggled for an instant, but it only caused her to be drawn closer to him. He carried her arms to the small of her back, holding them there as he slowly increased the pressure of his hold until only thin satin and linen and broadcloth separated her breasts from the ridged hardness of his chest.

"Is this the way you keep your word?" she asked in sudden breathlessness that had nothing to do with her fury.

"Yes," he answered on a deep-drawn breath, "I think it is."

He lowered his lips to hers by degrees, watching the fleeting expressions on her face through narrowed eyes. She stood as if mesmerized, wanting to protest, yet caught in the sudden assault on her senses of his vital masculinity and her own amorous curiosity. Then his lashes swept down and she felt the heated touch of his mouth.

Sweet, his kiss was sweet and gentle in its persuasion, a delicate yet thorough invasion. The surfaces of his lips were silken smooth, edged with a slight prickle of beard stubble. The infinitesimal movements of them upon hers was a tender incitement, a seeking of permission for further intimacy.

While her will wavered her lips parted. He took instant advantage, his tongue abrading the gentle corners, probing the honeyed moisture, sweeping over the fragile and pulsing lining within to entice her own explorations. Grainy surface on grainy surface, they tasted each other in sinuous twining.

It was shocking, yet infinitely familiar, like happening while awake upon caresses felt only in dreams. With it came the rise of a slow, sweet yearning that could become an ache in need of fulfillment. Katrine wanted it, wanted him, wanted to revel in the onslaught of emotion that she could feel hovering, half-aroused, half-acknowledged, somewhere in the most secret recesses of her mind and body.

She raised her hands to his shoulders, sliding them to touch the strong column of his neck, reaching to clasp him closer. His skin was warm, as if it held the touch of the sun that had browned it.

Abruptly she realized she was free. He no longer held her imprisoned in his grasp. His own hands were at her waist and the center of her back.

Angry chagrin swept through her. She clenched her hands on his shoulders and pushed him from her with all her strength. He stepped backward, letting her go so quickly that she stumbled against the desk.

There was a bemused look in his eyes as he surveyed her flushed face and the quick rise and fall of her breasts. His voice low and a little thick, he said, "It isn't that you're afraid."

What he did not say, from innate courtesy, Katrine thought, was that her objection was also not with him. She was grateful for that show of consideration. It not only saved her blushes, but gave her some small reason to think that there might be a way out.

"No," she said with a lift of her chin. "It's only that I despise being treated like a brood mare with no will or wishes of my own. I sympathize with my husband's goals, but I cannot meekly accept the man of his choosing because of them."

He absorbed that in silence a moment. "What will you do?"

Looking away from him toward the reflective surface of the window, she said, "I thought—that is, I have a suggestion, if you are agreeable."

"I'm listening."

His reply was quiet, without anger. It gave her the courage to continue. "If you—that is, if we were to only pretend . . ."

He came to her rescue as she paused to search for words. "You want to fool your husband, make him think that we are lovers, but without there being actual intimate contact between us."

"That's it," she said in relief at his ready understanding.

He tilted his head as he considered her. "And how would this be accomplished?"

"You would come to my room as arranged, through Giles's bedchamber. After a—suitable length of time, you could leave again."

"Your husband suggested," he said in dry tones, "that it would be best if I stay until morning, when it would appear more natural that I might have been paying an early visit to my host in his rooms."

Katrine thought rapidly. "Well, then, my maid could sleep with me and you could have her cot in my dressing room. Perhaps your man could leave a nightshirt and dressing gown there for you."

"That should make me comfortable," he said with a shading of irony.

"I'm sorry," she said with defensive sharpness, "but at least you would still be able to stay on here as you wanted."

"There is that," he agreed. "I have to ask, however, just what you hope to gain by this subterfuge. When no child results, won't your husband only turn to his nephew to accomplish what he wants?"

"Perhaps not. If you have had other children by other women, then he may blame me, may think that I'm barren."

"I've left no by-blows behind me to my knowledge." The denial was hard and instant.

"Oh," she said, and was only marginally aware of the reluctant amusement that sprang into his eyes as he heard the disappointment in her voice. "Then I suppose I'll have to think of something when that time comes. For now, this moment is all I can worry about."

"There is something else you may not have taken into account. What happens if Giles decides to come into your bedchamber?"

"Why would he do that?" she asked, a frown pleating her forehead.

"To check on your welfare at my hands, if nothing else. I know I would be concerned if I were in his shoes."

"Would you?" She stared at him in closer consideration before she went on. "I don't believe he will intrude, for fear of antagonizing you, if nothing else."

He gave a small nod, though he did not look convinced. "You would expect me to come to you tonight?"

She hesitated only a moment. "If that's what Giles intended."

There was a thoughtful look in his eyes as he watched her.

Katrine waited for his decision with her heart beating high in her throat. So much depended on the kind of man he was, and on precisely what he wanted at Arcadia.

Rowan's mind was clouded by a dozen ideas and doubts, all of them clamoring for his attention. What Katrine Castlereagh was suggesting would not be easy. To spend endless nights so close to her—knowing she slept unguarded, knowing that he had been given leave to make love to her—would try a saint, and he had never pretended to be that. To see her dressed for bed, to spend time with her in the intimacy of her bedchamber and never encroach beyond the limits she had set would be torture.

He should never have kissed her. He was not sure where the impulse had come from. It was all very well to tell himself that she had impugned his honor, something he would force a man to account for on the dueling field. No, it was more than that, and he knew it. He had wanted to know how she felt about him, had needed to know what moved her to reject him. Most of all, however, he had wanted desperately to touch her, had been able to think of little else since the moment Giles Castlereagh had raised the possibility of bedding her. Seeing that tantalizing prospect slipping away, he had reached out to take a small recompense. As reprehensible as it might be, that was the truth of it.

He had accepted the proposal put to him by Katrine's husband, not just for the reasons he had given her, but because he wanted her. That was the final, unacceptable truth. It was the one that made it a kind of twisted justice that he be forced to remain near her and never touch her again.

What she was suggesting would be best for both of them. Given free rein to take her to bed, he might forget his purpose, forget his brother, forget ever leaving Arcadia. Terence's memory deserved more.

"Very well," he said abruptly. "In an hour, then. Will that give you enough time?"

Katrine realized he was offering her the opportunity to undress and make ready for bed. It was an aspect to which she had not given much thought. She was grateful that he had done so. Her voice was husky as she let him know an hour would be more than sufficient. Swinging from him, she walked to the door. She paused as he reached it ahead of her and held it open for her.

"Until later," he said.

"Yes, until then." The words were only a thread of sound.

Rowan came to her precisely on time. He tapped on the door and, when bidden to enter, stepped inside and closed it behind him.

Katrine was alone. Delphia had asked permission to attend a gathering in the servants' quarters. Katrine had let her go, but not before warning her that she must return early and telling her why. She had thought it might be easier to face Rowan without Delphia hovering on guard. She wished now that she had kept her with her; a guard would have been a comfort.

She was wearing a nightgown and peignoir of white batiste that was convent-made, with a scooped neck edged with heavy lace and long sleeves with lace cuffs that fell over her hands. Her hair hung down her back, shining from Delphia's brush strokes, drifting about her with every movement.

She had gotten into the high bed when Delphia left her. She had lain still only a moment before sliding out again; she didn't want it to look as if she were waiting for him there. She arranged herself then in the slipper chair with a book, but that had seemed too studied. She thought of sitting at the dressing table, brushing the ends of her hair around her fingers, but that, too, appeared unnatural. She had perched on the edge of the bed while she tried to think. As the knock fell on the door she had jumped to her feet.

She moistened her lips, as Rowan advanced into the room, saying the first thing that came into her head. "Was Giles in his room? Did you see him?"

"Cato let me in. Your husband appeared to be sleeping; there was the dregs of a draft of some medicine in clouded water beside the bed."

"He takes such sleeping drafts often."

A crooked smile touched his mouth. "Did you think I was suggesting that he may have ordered it as a special concession to tonight?"

"It seemed possible." Her words were stiff.

"Perhaps he did, and who can blame him? Or it may be that he was feigning sleep to avoid having to see me." His gaze as he spoke drifted over her, coming to rest on the hem of the nightgown that flowed around her slippered feet.

Katrine caught the edges of the peignoir, drawing it closer over her breasts with one hand while she waved in the direction of the connecting dressing room with the other. "If you would like to retire, the other bed is in there."

He glanced in the direction she indicated, but said, "It might be best to remain together at least a short time. Giles, if he is awake, might expect there to be a little conversation before we blow out the candles."

Katrine could feel the heat rise in her face. She wished that Rowan did not have quite so much power to disconcert her. In an effort to appear more at ease, she climbed back up the bed steps to sit on the bed, reaching to drag a pillow behind her back.

In tart tones, she said, "I'm sure you're right. I expect you have had more experience than I."

"Not," he answered deliberately, "in a situation quite like this one." He shrugged out of his coat and tossed it across the walnut footboard of the bed with its four fluted posts and silk-lined tester, then began to loosen his cravat. It followed the coat, Putting the jet cravat pin he had removed in the pocket of his pantaloons, he began to slip the matching studs from his shirt.

"What are you doing?" she said, sitting up straighter against her pillows.

He paused. His gaze was steady, measuring. "I didn't mean to alarm you. I thought it might be better if I was less formally dressed."

Her eyes narrowed a little as she remembered the smooth manner in which he had approached before he kissed her earlier. Surely he would not—

No. If she let such thoughts disturb her every time he made a move, she would soon be a blathering idiot. She closed her eyes an instant, looking away from him. "As you like."

Rowan limited himself to two studs taken from his shirt before removing the links from his cuffs. He slipped these in his pocket also, and began to roll up his sleeves. His gaze was on the lock of hair that lay across Katrine's breast, shimmering with every rise and fall of her quick breathing.

She didn't trust him. But then, why should she? He wasn't sure he trusted himself.

There was, however, a painful pleasure for him in being there with her, in slowly insinuating himself into her private domain. He wondered how far she would allow him to advance. It might be interesting to see. Not that he intended to go too far. It was just that he required something to distract him from what might have been.

She was safer than she knew, in spite of his lapse earlier. His scruples had been tempered by many trials, and had never failed him. They were, however, dependent on her continued resistance. He was not sure they could withstand a surrender.

Stepping to the bed steps, he used the lower tread to mount to the mattress. Settling himself well away from her, near the footboard, he crossed one ankle over his knee and waited to see if she would object.

Katrine clenched her hand in the lace at her throat. To have the man she had so feared for these three long days actually seated on the bed where she had lain alone all her married life gave her a suffocating feeling inside. She wanted to order him off, but at the same time was loath to show her panic.

To distract herself, as much as to follow the lead he had set, she said, "What do men and women in this situation usually talk about?"

He lifted a brow. "Does your husband never talk to you when he is here?"

"He is never—that is, I thought Giles explained that the problem which prevents us from having a child is with him?"

"Never?" Rowan said, ignoring the rest.

She shook her head, unable to look at him as she played with the lace on her sleeves. He was silent for so long that she finally sent him a glance from under her lashes. His eyes as he stared at her had the fathomless look of mist-shrouded pools. She held his gaze for long moments, until he shuttered his own with his lashes.

"Let me see," he said, his voice low and edged with contemplation as he reverted to her original question. "If we were a man and woman bent on amorous pursuits, I might tell you that what you have on is becoming, but I would like it better if you were wearing nothing."

Katrine clenched her teeth together for an instant before she said, "Oh? And what would I say to that? Thank you?"

"You might, or you could say that I could have the pleasure of removing it if I came closer."

She gave him a severe look, though she could feel the blood singing warm in her veins. "What else might we talk about?"

"I could tell you that I love the color of your hair, that it reminds me of chestnuts and sumac and all the other russet shades of autumn. I could say I am amazed at its shining length, that I would like to wrap my hands in it and use it to bind you to me while I—"

"Please," she said in stringent entreaty, "there must be something else."

His gaze rested on the pulse throbbing in her throat before he spoke again. "I could ask if you would prefer that I shave before I come to you, or if you can endure the scrape of the beard better than the wait while I remove it. Since the night is growing cool, I could ask if you are chilled and offer to warm you. Then you might, if you were inclined, ask if my back and neck muscles were stiff from holding the lance today. You could then suggest that I take off my shirt and allow you to massage away the soreness."

The words he spoke seemed to weave a spell in her mind. She could see him doing the things he said, see herself allowing him, aiding him. She could almost feel herself kneading the muscles under the bare skin of his back with wide-spread fingers.

At the same time the images sounded an emptiness inside her. She had never quite recognized how little warm and loving contact there was in her life, how little there had been of the rich caring and appreciation that Rowan conveyed so easily.

As his voice trailed to a stop she drew a slow breath. The words soft, she said, "Is that really what men and women say to each other?"

"That and more," he answered.

She opened her lips to ask what else, then closed them again. It might be best, judging by the suggestive timbre of his voice and the ache it caused inside her, that she not know.

"Tell me about your travels," she said instead. "Did you, in truth, live with the Bedouin and ride a camel across the deserts of Arabia?"

He told her a tale of heat and sand, of monotony and thirst and bone-chilling nights. It was also one of subtle beauty, of the triumph of humanity against bitter odds, and wild battles for pride and honor. She listened, fascinated, until abruptly he reached out and took her bare foot in the warm, enclosing grasp of his hand.

"You're freezing," he said in tones of exasperation. "Why didn't you tell me? Or at least get under the cover."

"You had nothing to use to cover yourself." She tugged her foot from his hold, drawing it back under her peignoir.

"What has that to do with anything? I'm not cold."

"Nor was I until you—" She stopped as she realized how that might sound, then went on. "Anyway, I couldn't offer to share the bed covers with you."

"You would rather freeze first, is that it?" His frown was fierce as he leaned toward her.

"It just didn't seem a wise thing to do!" she snapped.

He drew back. His features were blank before they slowly relaxed. He said, "You were right, it would not have been wise. But it might have been kind."

He slid from the bed with a lithe movement. Reaching for his coat and cravat, he slung them over a shoulder and stalked into the dressing room.

It was some time later when Delphia returned. Katrine was not asleep. She lay stiff and straight in her bed, listening to every creak the house made, every whisper of the wind around the eaves. Rowan was not sleeping either; she could see the glow of a candle under the connecting door. She heard the hall door of the dressing room open, heard Rowan make some quick comment and her maid's laughing answer. Then her bedchamber door opened and closed.

"Now there's a fine-looking man," Delphia said. "He's handsome with his clothes, but without? My, my."

Katrine raised herself on one elbow. Keeping her voice low, she said, "He had no clothes on?"

"Not that I could see. Of course he was mostly under the cover."

"Oh." Katrine lay back down.

"You have been all right?" the maid asked as she made ready for bed.

"Fine," Katrine answered with a brief smile before she turned back to stare up into the rose-pink sunburst of silk lining the tester above her. The bed ropes sagged as Delphia joined her on the mattress.

Katrine and the maid spoke a few minutes about the dancing the other woman had attended. In the midst of it, the candle went out in the next room. Sometime later Katrine slept.

She was sitting in bed next morning, drinking her wake-up cup of *café au lait*, when a quick, hard knock came on the door leading to Giles's bedchamber. An instant later he stepped into the room.

Katrine was so startled that she nearly dropped her cup. Delphia turned, wide-eyed, from where she was laying out a morning costume for Katrine in moss-green velvet. She glanced at the door of the dressing room before exchanging a look with Katrine.

"Well, my dear, and how are you this morning?" Giles asked.

It was becoming annoying, this preoccupation everyone seemed to have with her well-being, as if her nearness to Rowan could have adverse consequences. She answered, however, with a bright smile.

Her husband nodded, his lips pursed. "I rather expected to find Rowan still with you."

"I'm here," Rowan said, leaning in the door of the dressing room with a coffee cup in his hand. His hair was tousled, his face shadowed with his beard, and the dressing gown he wore only half-tied. His voice was none too cordial.

"So you are," Giles returned, the words measured.

"You wanted to speak to me?" Rowan asked.

The question, Katrine thought, was an aggressive maneuver, amply conveyed by the belligerent tone. It was designed to discourage impertinent questions or other impromptu visits, she had no doubt. Whether it would serve the purpose was another question.

Giles frowned as he answered. "I thought I would see if there was anything you require for the race this morning. I understand your horse is in fine fettle, that your man Omar spent the night with him last night."

Rowan signified that he needed nothing. As he spoke he moved to the bed, casually mounting the steps to seat himself on the edge. He reclined beside Katrine with the smooth grace of a panther making himself comfortable. The smile he gave her was suffused with raffish charm and sultry appreciation in equal measure.

His black brocade dressing gown gaped open, showing a wide expanse of muscle-clad chest shadowed with dark, springing hair that trailed downward toward a flat and hard abdomen. He stretched out a hand to take up her peignoir that was flung across the end of the bed. As he handed it to her his gaze held such melting intimacy and attention to the low neck of her nightgown that Katrine could feel a flush blooming across her cheekbones.

"Good, good," Giles said. "Then I'll see you at breakfast?"

"I think," Rowan said with another smile for Katrine, "that I'll have it in bed. Omar has been so involved with the race that he's only just now begun to set up my bath in the dressing room."

"Ah, I see," Giles said, glancing toward the other room, where there were, indeed, sounds of splashing water to be heard. "Well. Until later then."

Delphia had moved to hold the door for Katrine's husband. She closed it behind him with a hissing sigh. Her expression was droll as she turned to look at Katrine. "I don't think," she said, "that this arrangement you have is going to work."

"You may be right," Katrine agreed in hollow tones. She looked at Rowan, then away again. "I suppose we could lock Giles's door."

"You've never done that before?" he asked.

"There's never been a need," she answered.

Rowan shook his head with a frown. "It would only arouse his suspicions, then."

Katrine compressed her lips. She made no reply.

"So what are you going to do?" The maid put her hands on her hips, waiting for an answer.

"I suppose," Katrine said slowly, "that there's only one thing possible."

"The gentleman and I change places, yes?" Delphia cut her eyes in Rowan's direction, but did not quite smile at him.

Katrine gave her maid a cool stare. Delphia, she knew, had thought for some time that the way her mistress lived was too limited. She said, "Don't put words in my mouth."

"She's right, you know," Rowan said, the words quiet and reflective.

"Yes," Katrine said on an exasperated sigh, "I know."

CHAPTER SEVEN

There was coolness in Giles's manner when Katrine joined him later at the tournament field where the race would be held. His mouth was tight in the pasty paleness of his face, and his grip under her elbow as he guided her toward the grandstand firm enough that she feared it would leave a bruise. She would have thought he was jealous if it had not been so unreasonable.

The arena had been turned into a racetrack by the simple expedient of laying out the course using broad, thick lines of powdered lime. In keeping with British tradition, the races would be run over turf rather than dirt, using a track in a rough U-shape including downhill and uphill gradients. The uphill grade would be near the finish to increase difficulty. Only the starting post and the finish line itself would be on the level ground of the arena, both occurring in front of the grandstand.

The races for the day would include a number of events, from a quarter-mile dash and a full-course mile-and-a-half race to a heat of three miles that would go twice around the course. The meet would pit horses from neighboring stables as well as those from all over Louisiana and Mississippi against each other. There was a great rivalry between Giles and the men of the Barrow clan in particular, though several other planters along the river enjoyed setting him a challenge. There had been much discussion in the past few days over the various horses entered, with exhaustive investigation of their home stables, handlers, and jockeys, as well as their bloodlines and past performances.

Horse racing had become a passion in Louisiana within the last decade with dozens of tracks dotted over the state. There were the Metairie and Eclipse tracks at New Orleans, the Magnolia Course at Baton Rouge, and the Fashion Course at Clinton. St. Francisville itself had a public course of some note, one that was said to be as well adapted for quick time as the Union Course on Long Island, New York. Giles, with the bias typical of most planters with large holdings, preferred the Arcadia track that was laid out to suit his own preference.

The event expected to draw the greatest interest for the day was the tournament race. This was to feature personal mounts ridden by their owners, rather than trained thoroughbreds with jockeys in the saddle. As the premier attraction, it would be run last. This was the race that Rowan would be entering with Saladin.

Katrine could muster little interest in the first races. She felt disoriented, unable to concentrate. It was difficult to smile and talk and move among her guests while knowing that a virtual stranger had spent the night in her rooms and would share her bed when evening fell once more.

She also felt a little wicked. She was aware of her body, of its shape, its responses and the way she moved, in a way she had never known before. Somewhere inside her, beneath the confusion and anger, there simmered a latent exhilaration. She liked the feeling, though she knew she should not.

Giles was collared by a neighbor who demanded that he come and look at a prize gray supposedly descended from the English racing great Eclipse. He had been gone only a few moments when Rowan appeared.

He sauntered across the field to the steps just below where Katrine sat. Mounting upward with easy grace, he stopped with one foot on the top tread and leaned toward her with his hand braced on his knee. There was warmth in his eyes as they rested on her. She wore an ensemble of moss-green velvet with a matching ribbon band and streamers on the wide hat of golden leghorn straw tied over her curls. He swept off his flat-crowned beaver with a greeting that completely ignored the short length of time since they had parted.

"Is everything all right with your mount?" she asked after a brief return of his salutations.

"Fine," he said, his manner distracted. He went on in low tones, "There was something I wanted to ask, since I saw you alone. Did you, by chance, send your maid to Giles's room early this morning, just after you woke?"

"This morning? Why should I?"

"She was there; Omar saw her leaving. She was using the hall door."

"She said nothing about it to me."

"Your husband isn't in the habit of sending for her?" he asked, his gaze meeting hers with meaningful intentness.

"You mean—no. No, there is nothing like that." She hardly knew whether to be irritated or amused that he could suggest Giles could possibly require such personal service from Delphia. Her maid had a lover, Katrine knew, a gentleman of some wealth and considerable powers of persuasion. There had been unexplained absences, also sudden appearances of perfume and clothing and bits of jewelry for which no account was given. Katrine had not required that the maid reveal the man's name, thinking it would be easier for everyone if she remained ignorant. Still, the man was not Giles.

"In that case," Rowan said, "your husband may have been questioning her about your compliance with his arrangements."

Katrine's gaze widened, then she gave a quick shake of her head. "I don't think he would stoop so low. Even if he did, it's hard to believe Delphia would tell him anything."

"He visited you after he spoke to her, didn't he?" Rowan's tones were patient.

"He may have been concerned, as you said before." She bit the inside of her lip as she considered it.

"Either way, we will have to be careful. I think Omar should develop a sudden passion for Delphia. He can try to discover exactly what she's up to and, at the same time, have an excuse for darting in and out of your dressing room."

The idea of the majestic Arab darting anywhere was so unlikely that she couldn't resist a smile. It faded quickly. She said, "I won't have Delphia upset."

"You think Omar will upset her? Don't worry; he's quite a favorite with the ladies. He'll know exactly how to handle it."

He glanced at the top of her head, then went on with hardly a pause. "Do you know you have a bee on your hat? Hold still, and I'll take care of it."

Katrine had seen no bee; but she sat perfectly still as he moved to stand over her. There was something about this man that affected her with an odd paralysis of will. She had the distinct feeling that she herself might have been "handled."

She was engulfed by the aura of quiet virility and magnetic attraction that he carried with him. The impact was so great that a species of panic moved over her. As she felt a slight tug at the crown of her hat, she hurried into speech with the first thought to rise in her mind.

"How can Omar have told you about Delphia? I thought he could not speak."

Rowan stepped away from her. "You're all right now," he said. He thrust his hands into his pockets, returning to the top of the steps before he went on. "As for Omar, he was once a messenger to the Dey of Algiers. His tongue was cut out to be certain he never betrayed what was entrusted to him. Still, he manages a few sounds, and he has sign language learned from a Cherokee Indian trader."

Katrine expressed her thanks for his service, then frowned. "You're certain you understood what he was saying?"

"I am. It would be a mistake to think he's unreliable or unintelligent because he is mute. He is neither."

"I didn't mean to suggest that," she protested.

"No," he answered, his gaze sober, "but I wanted you to know, in case of need."

What need there might be she could not see; still, she did not intend to argue the point. She said, "About the other, I'll speak to Delphia."

He hesitated before he answered. "It might be better if you said nothing."

"What do you mean? We can't change the situation between us, and you must know how unlikely it is that Delphia can be kept in ignorance of its true nature."

"You could be sending a warning that you know you are being watched."

"Perhaps it will stop then."

"Maybe," he said. Then he lifted a shoulder. "It's your choice."

He left her a few minutes later. Katrine watched him go, watched him walk away in the direction of the stables, settling his hat back on his head as he went. The swing of his long legs, the lean lines of his thighs, the confident set of his wide shoulders held her gaze long after she knew she should have looked away.

Her awareness of him was exasperating. There were reasons for it; he was a man of considerable attraction. More than that, she would not be human if she didn't consider carefully the man who had been thrust into her bed. She must understand what kind of person he was, how far he could be trusted. She needed to be able to judge what he intended. She wasn't sure of any of it, even now.

His consideration, his acceptance of the ground rules she

had requested, was extraordinary. He had his reasons, of course. She only hoped they remained strong enough to prevent him from taking advantage of the peculiar circumstances that bound them. She was well aware there was no guarantee.

Rowan returned to the grandstand just before the first race was to begin. He walked at a decorous pace with a woman in pale blue clinging to his arm. It was Musetta. Giles's younger sister smiled up into his face while she chattered and swung her wide skirts so they engulfed her escort's feet. Trailing behind them was Peregrine Blackstone. The dark looks the young man directed at Rowan's back were ferocious.

Musetta fluttered her fingers at Katrine as she and Rowan mounted to the grandstand. Her blue eyes gleamed with amusement and her smile had the tilt of a woman well pleased with the world. As she seated herself she made certain Rowan was on one side and Perry on the other.

Katrine glanced toward where Brantley Hennen stood, down near the track. Musetta's husband paused in his task of toting up figures in a small book with a stub of a pencil. There was a grim cast to his features behind his beard, and the back of his neck was red. He sent a quick glance toward his wife then looked away again, bending his head closer over his scribbling.

Brantley was not the only one unhappy with Musetta's most recent conquest. Charlotte, sitting with Georgette and Lewis, was watching the small tableau with a decided droop to her shoulders. Her gaze as it rested on Rowan had a wistful yearning that was painful to see. She was dressed in lavender in so soft a shade that it made her appear even more ethereal than usual. Her wealth of dark hair, piled in curls and loops of small braiding on top of her head, looked too heavy for the slender stem of her neck. There were dark shadows under her eyes as if she had trouble sleeping or was ill.

Katrine felt a pang of concern. She must find time to talk to the girl, she thought, before the house party was over.

Lewis was hale enough, holding forth with his usual malicious wit. He seemed to feel the warmth of the afternoon more than the others. He removed his hat now and then, fanning himself with it and running his fingers through his hair, so it stood up in metallic silver spikes.

He would not be riding in the final race of the afternoon. Lewis had not, so he said, found a mount he felt like buying since coming to St. Francisville. The horses worthy of his money all seemed to belong to his uncle, and there was no point in buying what he could use daily without cost. Candor of this kind was Lewis's most admirable trait, in Katrine's opinion. She thought, but did not say, that Giles's nephew was happy to have an excuse not to compete against Rowan again.

The excellence of the Arcadia stables proved itself during the afternoon. Giles's horses won one of the dashes and the mile-and-a-half silver-cup race. He glowed with the pleasure of it. His pride could not have been greater, Katrine thought, if he had rounded the course on his own two legs. His spirits were high during the break for the noon meal, and he drank several glasses of wine with the continuous round of toasts that accompanied the lavish repast.

Afterward Giles did not feel well. He lay down on the daybed in his office while the ladies were resting upstairs and the other gentlemen were talking cotton and politics on the back terrace. He appeared wan when he emerged again for the final heat, the amateur race.

The sun was edging down the sky, combing the lawn and surrounding trees with long, slanting fingers of light, when they gathered at the grandstand once more. The call of the bugle signaling time for the men to approach the starting post had a melancholy ring as it echoed back from the sawtooth-edged line of the woods. A flight of ducks circled the cupola of Giles's tower and dipped toward the lake in front of it, near the lower end of the sloping track. In the murmurous silence that followed the bugle's last note, the sound of crickets and peeper frogs rasped the late-afternoon stillness.

The parade to the post had a homely splendor that had been missing from the earlier races. The men on their mounts were horsemen with the natural seat of their kind; they rode with relaxed and unpretentious ease. They each had their following that cheered their appearance. As they passed there was lively discussion among the men in the grandstand on points and lineage, gear and weight handicaps. The exchange of bets was even livelier.

Rowan walked his horse into the arena among the last. His saddle was in the military style with a slightly longer stirrup than the others. His seat also had a military correctness. His accoutrements shone with polish, from his steel bit to the small brass spurs on his glossy black riding boots. He had changed into a riding outfit of perfectly cut buckskin breeches worn with a black coat of impeccable tailoring and a moss-green cravat. Fluttering at his upper arm was a moss-green ribbon.

Katrine smothered a small gasp as she saw the ribbon. She reached up to feel the back of her hat. The ribbon streamer that had decorated it was gone, leaving only the hatband. A bee indeed!

Rowan was passing in front of her. He saluted her with his crop and a tip of his dark head. She sent him a look of smoldering annoyance that he had the temerity to return with a smile that crinkled the bronzed skin around his eyes.

Giles, sitting beside Katrine, turned his head to stare at her with condemnation in his faded blue eyes. "I thought I told you . . ." he began.

"So you did," she answered, refusing to be cowed. "This is, I think, Rowan's idea of a jest. He took the ribbon from me by a trick."

Her husband studied the heat in her face a long moment before he said in soft tones, "So you call him Rowan?"

"Should I call him Mr. de Blanc after what you did to us?"

"Ah, you align yourself with him."

Embarrassment, chagrin, and a strange sadness shifted inside her. She looked away from her husband. Her voice tired, she said, "What did you expect?"

"I'm not sure," he answered almost to himself. "I'm not at all sure."

The horsemen lined up at the starting post, a field of twenty-odd, shifting, holding, jockeying for position. There were mounts of all kinds: stallions, geldings, even a mare or two, a few with respectable pedigrees, most with none. If they had one thing in common, it was that none were nags.

Finally they settled.

The starting pistol fired. They were off.

It was a wild melee of flying coattails and flashing hooves. Within moments, the leaders began to pull away from the pack. With clods of turf flying, crops flailing, they swept into the first sharp turn. By the time they reached the straightaway, they were strung out, nose to tail, over a distance of a hundred yards. Before there was time to blink, or so it seemed, the leaders were headed away down the slope, almost out of sight below the fall of the hill.

In less than no time, they were pounding back toward the grandstand. Rowan had taken a clear lead, but Alan, on a nice bay, was gaining on him. Perry was caught in the middle of a tight group of eight or so, unable to wrench his flashy white stallion clear. Satchel brought up the rear on a sluggish sorrel built to carry weight rather than for speed.

Cheers and applause and yells of encouragement rose from the grandstand. The flimsy wooden structure shuddered as hooves thundered nearer and people leaped to their feet to wave the riders on.

The racers rounded the second turn and streamed past with

shouts and cries from the hunting field. Leaning forward, with reins tight, they flung themselves into the second lap of the race.

Out on the edges of the field, the men and women from the plantation quarters whooped and hollered for their favorites. Young boys ran along the track, trying to keep the riders in sight. A cur dog or two leaped around the boys with excitement, while one hound broke free of the string holding him and raced after the pounding horses.

As the horsemen pelted out of sight again Giles dropped back into his seat. He shook his head. "De Blanc will run his gray in the ground trying to keep the lead. I should have thought he would know better. Even Satchel will overtake him."

"Maybe," Katrine said. "Then again, maybe not."

"You want him to win."

She heard accusation in her husband's voice and the rise of denial in her mind was immediate. Just as immediate was the realization that he was right. "I only care," she said, "that the deserving man win."

"And if that is de Blanc?"

She gave him a level look. "Then I will have to be glad that he took my favors."

A slow, purplish flush mounted to her husband's face. It was only then that Katrine realized the plural she had added to her final word by accident, saw the double entendre that could be read into it with that small addition. She would not retract it, however. Her murky relationship with Rowan was not by her choice.

Somewhere out of sight at the bottom of the slope, a dog yelped. It was, no doubt, the free-running hound, kicked by a flying hoof. As Katrine turned toward the sound the racing horses came into view once more.

Wild-eyed, their coats streaked white with lather, the straining mounts drove toward the finish line. Rowan was still in the lead, though Alan was moving up, plying his whip with grim-faced determination. The main body of the others was coming on, though a few straggled in the rear.

It was as they were streaking into the final turn that it happened. One moment Rowan was bending over Saladin's head, his lips moving as he spoke to him while he leaned into the curve. The next, he was plunging toward the ground.

He struck hard, then wrenched over in a powerful heaving of muscles, flinging himself from the path of the oncoming horses. His saddle bounced, then skidded directly in front of the riders. A horse broke stride, stumbled as it kicked the loose saddle, then pitched forward. Another followed in a tangle of tackle and wildly kicking legs. Riders left their saddles, rolling as they struck the ground.

Perry swerved but could not stop; he leaped from the saddle as his mount went down but was struck by a flailing hoof. He fell, tried to get up, crumpled, and was still. Alan, safely out of the melee, looked back. He wrenched back on the reins, hauling his mount to a ragged halt. Leaping from the saddle, he ran to catch the reins of Perry's rearing white stallion.

Rowan was already there. He dragged his own plunging gray free, handing him to Omar, who had come at a run, before turning back to the others.

By that time the men in the grandstand had surged down the steps to help. Amid the horrified cries of the ladies, the shouts of the stable men and field hands, and yells of the youngsters, they dragged the fallen riders to safety and calmed the plunging, limping horses. In a few minutes it was over.

Katrine was in the midst of the fray long before then. Glancing around at the Arcadia menservants nearest to hand, she sent one into St. Francisville to fetch the local physician, another running to tell Cato to remove two sets of shutters from the house windows to transport the injured, and yet another to the plantation hospital to bring bandaging, wood for splints, and her own medicine bag up to the main house.

It was just after dark when the doctor arrived. Among the five riders who had suffered spills, there were two broken arms, a broken collarbone, a dislocated shoulder, a sprained ankle, a split cheek, and a mild concussion. Nevertheless the doctor had nothing to do.

Omar, striding into the downstairs sitting room where the injured had been placed, had gently but firmly removed Katrine's medicine bag from her grasp and taken over. He would have treated Rowan first, but his master waved him toward the others, allowing him to set his dislocated shoulder only when everyone else was comfortable.

Dr. Grafton, a short and strutting bantam rooster of a man, was annoyed at having driven so far so fast only to find his patients having an early dinner. He examined them anyway, but could find nothing to fault. After being taken away by Giles for a drink and a discussion of his fee, however, he seemed inclined to be mollified. By the time he sat at the table to partake of turtle soup, asparagus vinaigrette, and roast capon in wine sauce, he was almost jovial.

Regardless, it was a restrained meal. The margin by which the riders had escaped what they considered serious injury was so narrow that it left them all thoughtful. The toll the spill had taken on the horses was not light; one had been shot, one bandaged and poulticed, and a third would never be fit for anything other than a child's mount.

There was also a rumor, as yet unsubstantiated, that the girth of Rowan's saddle had been cut halfway through. They glanced at one another now and again, obviously wondering who could have wanted victory badly enough to risk killing the man favored to win and endangering them all.

It was as the dessert was being served that Alan leaned back in his chair, surveying the table while he swirled the last of the wine in his glass. His gaze moved from Giles at the head of the table to Katrine at the foot with Rowan on her right. He looked at Perry with his head wrapped with white bandaging like a small turban, at the other injured men, and at Satchel, lounging back, sucking his teeth and eyeing the portion of caramel custard being placed in front of him. A faint smile played around Alan's mouth, but he waited until the dining-room attendant had moved back into the butler's pantry before he spoke.

"This table," he said, "should be round, you know."

Musetta smiled at him, as if ready to be amused. "You mean like that of King Arthur?"

The quiet, dark-haired young man smiled at her. "Arcadia is our Camelot, of course. Giles is our Arthur with Katrine as his Guinevere."

"How clever," Musetta said, clapping her hands. "And who should Perry be?"

"Sir Percival, of course," Alan answered.

Perry, who had been enjoying the tender attention of the blond woman that had come with his head injury, gave Alan a look of irony. "You, I suppose, are Galahad, always rescuing fair maidens, not to mention Percival?"

"I doubt I'm pure enough," Alan said. "But there can be no question that Rowan is our Lancelot. He not only has French blood, but has bested us all."

Katrine saw her husband make a jerky movement of one hand, as if he would intervene. He was staring from Alan to Rowan with a frown between his brows. As she followed Giles's taut gaze she saw Rowan watching Alan with trenchant consideration in his eyes. He looked her way for a brief moment, but there was nothing in his face to show what he was thinking.

Lewis, farther down the table, gave an abrupt laugh. "Where does that leave me, if you please? I must tell you, my dear Alan, that I don't care to be cast as Modred, plotting against my uncle."

"Certainly not," Giles said in tones harsh with censure.

"The idea is ridiculous. I would as soon think that Katrine would betray me."

"And that," Lewis murmured, "is truly unthinkable."

"Indeed." Giles sat up straighter in his chair. His gaze, as he sent a hard stare down the table, came to rest on Charlotte. "Perhaps we should speak instead of how we will entertain ourselves until our guests begin to arrive for the victory ball. Can we expect to hear another example of your lovely voice, child?"

Charlotte, thrown into confusion by being singled out, swung her wide gaze to Rowan. She blurted out, "Oh, no, sir, I would rather not, if you don't mind."

Her host inclined his head. "As you prefer." A cynical smile creased one corner of his mouth. "Then, perhaps, if we have returned to the times of chivalry, the ladies may amuse themselves with more questions concerning points of honor and romance."

He had effectively closed the subject. Katrine was not sorry. She had no wish to be forced to sit and smile while someone brought up the love affair between Guinevere and Lancelot. That would have been far too trying just now.

At the same time she was annoyed. Her husband's tone as he spoke of the questions asked and answered in their Court of Love had been slighting. She had never considered that she and Musetta were discussing matters of mind-shattering importance. The purpose had always been amusement along with the exploration of ideals and the relationship of man to woman. Still, there was no need to belittle their choice of entertainment.

Given her mood, the somewhat acerbic question posed by Musetta, moments after they were all ensconced in the double parlor, seemed eminently satisfactory.

"What is due," her sister-in-law asked with a twist to her lips, "to a husband from a wife? The church requires that we love, honor, and obey, yet we are given in marriage to men who mistake possessiveness for love, who leave us little room for honor, and who stifle rather than cherish us. At what point, then, do the vows lose their meaning?"

Katrine smoothed the black lace edging the deep flounce of her ball gown of parchment gold silk that was spread over the settee where she sat. Her voice subdued, she said, "In Eleanor of Aquitaine's Court of Love, it was considered that love between husband and wife was impossible. Marriage was a contract which conferred everything the woman owned, including her person, on the husband. A woman in that situation could not, so the theory went, love the man who held her in bondage, nor could the husband love a wife who was little more than a chattel. Matters have not changed greatly since then."

"Some marriages are based on money, but not all." The contradiction came from Rowan, who had moved to stand behind the settee.

Katrine turned her head to glance up at him before she agreed. "No, not all, but many still are."

"Yes," Musetta said, "and that being so, what meaning is left in the vows? At what point is it acceptable to look elsewhere for the human comfort which makes life bearable?"

Perry, lounging in a wing-back chair of blue brocade, cleared his throat. "It seems to me that it begins with the absence of love."

"Why do you say that?" Musetta asked, staring at him in pleased surprise.

Perry frowned in the effort of concentration. "If there is no love, then all the rest—honor, obedience, cherishing—is impossible. At least it seems so to me."

"Oh, but see here," Satchel put in, his voice gruff in protest. "If you went by that, there wouldn't be more than a dozen decent marriages left in St. Francisville."

"Sad but true," Musetta said.

Lewis snorted. "If you ask me, it's a fine excuse for scratching an amorous itch."

Musetta turned on him. "Try, please, Lewis, to be no more crude than you must."

"Of course, some people," Lewis went on with barely a pause, "need no excuse. And some have excuses thrust upon them."

The words were directed at Musetta, but his avid gaze, Katrine saw, was turned on her. The argument in favor of marriage she had been building in her head vanished. She could not prevent herself glancing up at Rowan.

"Cynicism aside," Rowan said, his voice contemplative, his eyes shuttered, "a decent marriage can hold companionship, trust, and respect. In unions based on love, this is the due of a husband, just as it is the due of a wife."

"One can see," Katrine's sister-in-law said in dry tones, "that you will make an exceptional husband. If you ever decide to marry."

Rowan gave the woman a straight look. "I will marry when I find a woman with a heart strong enough to withstand the love I give her."

"My, my." Musetta's eyes widened in sardonic amazement. She turned her head to meet Katrine's gaze, inviting her to share her wonder.

Katrine met Musetta's look, but her own face was expressionless. It was the best she could do to hide the sudden constriction of her heart inside her chest.

The race ball was without its usual glitter. Perhaps because of the accident, the candles did not seem to burn as bright, the waxen shine of the floor soon grew dull, the musicians played with less verve, and the flowers wilted earlier in the evening. There were just as many people crowding the ballroom, however, all of them laughing and talking, so that their voices made a murmur like the ocean's roar against the painted panels of the high ceiling.

Katrine danced until her feet hurt, smiled until it felt as if her face would crack. There was tightness behind her eyes that threatened to become a full-blown headache. She could not wait for the evening to end, yet dreaded it at the same time.

While circling the floor with Alan, she saw Rowan waltzing with Charlotte. The girl appeared bemused and a little faint, and incapable of raising her gaze above the level of Rowan's cravat. The smile that curved his mouth as he tried to see her face gave Katrine an odd, tight feeling in her chest.

Her own dance with Rowan was a reel. Fast moving, boisterous, it was a simple dance only if you knew the calls and steps. On this occasion it was turned into a romp by Satchel, with Georgette as his partner. Rowan seemed ready to join in the spirit of the thing, whirling Katrine around until she clung to him with a desperate grasp, diving with her under the arch made of linked hands and upheld arms, and coming up again so close together that her face was nearly buried in his coat front. She thought he did it on purpose, to discompose her, though she could not be sure.

She was standing alone, trying to catch her breath while Rowan went in search of a glass of champagne punch for her, when the next waltz began. According to her dance card, she had given it to Perry, but he was nowhere in sight. It was while she was looking around the room for her partner that she noticed Giles.

He was leading a woman out onto the dance floor, the only lady he had chosen to dance with that evening. It was Musetta.

Giles's gout had improved, for he moved with smooth expertise into the waltz. He smiled down at his half sister with a look of bemusement on his features while his gaze moved over her with wry appreciation. As Musetta returned his look with her catlike eyes touched with a peculiar vulnerability, sadness crept into his face, lingering there. For that moment it was possible to see in him the careless charm he must once have had, the consummate polish of a gentleman at ease in London society.

It was also possible to pity him, just a little. The emotion was not a comfortable one.

The evening wound at last to its end. The musicians played their final song, then packed up their instruments and departed. The guests who were not staying in the house were handed their cloaks and hats and canes as they made their adieus and straggled by twos and threes toward the door. Their carriages pulled up, one after the other, with their wheels grating in the thick layer of oyster shells that coated the drive and front court before the house. Cato, finally, closed the front door after the last of them.

The ball was over. The tournament was over.

Rowan left the ballroom by the French doors that gave onto the flagstoned loggia with its Gothic arches at the rear of the house. The loggia, in turn, led out onto the terrace across the back of the building, then descended in wide levels to the stretch of grass that sloped down to the lake.

He wished he had a cheroot. He had given up the habit of smoking since coming to Louisiana. His mother considered it unhealthy, not to mention unspeakably filthy. No doubt she was right, but it made a good excuse for escaping from confined spaces and uncongenial company.

His thoughts went back to the Court of Love earlier. He was past the age of parlor games, had no facility for such idle investigations of thought and beliefs; still, there had been a certain precarious attraction to trading opinions with Katrine, precarious because of the sympathy she had made him feel. Not that he thought she appreciated his interference.

His views were too broad for most, he had discovered; it was too easy for him to argue any given side of a question, something few people appreciated. He had his convictions, but they bore little resemblance to the rigid beliefs that were the norm. It was always easier to retreat than to explain the range of experiences that had knocked that kind of cocksure certainty out of him.

It was a pleasant night; the air was several degrees cooler than it had been when the ball began. The sky was overcast, though the round silver disk of the moon glowed behind a swath of clouds. A soft, undulating mist rose from the lake. The moisture from it and also the falling dew had plated the spiderwebs scattered over the grass with silver.

Rowan leaned against an ornate stone pillar, breathing deep of the moist night coolness and thinking of going to bed. The immediate quickening in his loins was inevitable. He had grown so used to being in a state of irritable desire since coming to Arcadia that he hardly noticed it. He could control it; he always had before.

Of course, he had seldom slept with a woman without touching her. If it came to that, he had never slept with a woman like Katrine Castlereagh.

Lascivious maids, London mistresses, Arabian women, New Orleans opera singers; they paraded across his mind. It was not a large company, but there had been more than one or two. Each had taught him something about women and their needs, each had given him some knowledge of himself and his limits. He was grateful to them all. But there was little in his association with them to guide him with Katrine. She was different.

He didn't know why he was concerned; it was not a large problem. All she wanted of him was a pretense of loving. It should not be hard.

That was the trouble. It would be too easy, far too easy.

The latch of the door behind him clicked and he heard the whisper of a woman's skirt. The scent of lilies of the valley drifted to him, surrounded him. Even before he turned his head, he knew the woman was not Katrine.

"I'm sorry if I disturbed you," Charlotte said, her voice as soft as a passing breeze and as indefinite. "I thought perhaps—

that is, I was going to walk a little. I often—I enjoy late at night, the darkness."

"To be disturbed by you must always be a pleasure," Rowan replied in the kind, automatic politeness used as a substitute for candor.

The girl was afraid he would think she had sought him out, he thought, or else that he might prefer his own company. For the first, he was not so vain. For the second, she was right, though he could not bring himself to rebuff her for it.

She drifted in his direction, pausing beside him. She glanced up at him and away again. "I hope your shoulder isn't paining you after the dancing. I mean—"

He came to her rescue as she stopped. "It's kind of you to ask, but no. At least no more than I deserve for not checking my own girth before mounting."

"It's so distressing—I've been trying all evening to think how it can have happened. Perhaps the leather was cracked or—or else it was accidentally damaged."

"Omar would never allow either one."

She frowned a little. "But to suppose that someone would be so vindictive—it's difficult to believe, here where everyone knows everyone else."

"Possibly someone resented a stranger taking the tournament prizes." The suggestion was not entirely idle; he wanted to know what she thought.

"There was some resentment, but no one in their right mind would attempt murder because of it. Would they?"

The door behind them opened once more. Charlotte whirled with her skirts twirling around her feet and her hand going to her mouth. She could not have looked more guilty if she had been caught making love on the flagstones.

"Dear me," Musetta said. "What in the world is so fascinating out here that it takes two of you to look at it?"

"Nothing!" Charlotte gasped. "I just—we were only—"

"Privacy," Rowan said, "and quiet."

Musetta gave a tinkling laugh as she looked up at him. "Ever the gentleman, are you not? I'm properly chastened." She turned to the other girl. "Dear Charlotte, I didn't mean to embarrass you, really I didn't. I only came to tell you Georgette thinks you should come inside."

"Yes, in a moment. First I would like to walk a little. Will you tell her?" There was the choked sound of tears in the pallid girl's voice, a good reason for her reluctance to return to her friend's side, Rowan thought. He watched as she turned blindly from them and scurried down the terrace in the direction of the lake.

"I could use a stroll myself," he said, and began to move after Charlotte. The girl didn't seem the kind to do anything silly, but she was more upset than was reasonable, given the circumstances.

"Let her go," Musetta said, placing a hand on his arm. "You'll only distress her more by following after her. You are her problem, you know."

He halted, a frown creasing his brow. "What are you talking about?"

Musetta tilted her head, looking up at him in the moon's soft glow. "You haven't noticed her sighing over you? Charlotte has an impressionable heart; every year she chooses some gentleman as the object of her tender affections. Last year it was Perry. This year it's you."

He said nothing while he watched the light-colored gown of the other girl fading into the dimness. His voice abrupt, he said, "I did not encourage her."

Musetta shrugged. "I'm sure you didn't; there is never a need. She will get over it, I promise, though I can see it worries you. Stay here. I'll go after her."

Rowan nodded. His host's sister flitted away in the direction of the lake and the tower standing among the trees beyond.

The darkness closed in behind her, just as it had covered Charlotte.

He expected to see the two women reappear in short order, but there was no sign of them. He was thinking of going after them in spite of Musetta's comments when Katrine stepped out onto the terrace.

He waited until she was near enough to hear a quiet request. "Walk with me for a moment, will you?"

Katrine gave him an inquiring look. "Is anything wrong?"

"Not really. I just wanted to check on something." Rowan realized he was being less than honest; still, he couldn't see himself explaining Charlotte's supposed *tendre* for him to Katrine.

She studied him a long moment, then took the arm he offered and fell into step beside him. The unquestioning acceptance of her gesture was so unexpected that he felt a tightness in his chest. He was quiet as he tried to work out why that should be. They had descended the terrace and were well out on the grass, beyond the lamps shining from the house, when he stopped.

He said, "I'm sorry, I hadn't considered. Your gown and your slippers will be wet with dew."

"It doesn't matter," she replied in low tones.

In the moon's subdued glow, her features were pale and composed, and touched by unearthly beauty. The pale gold silk of her gown made her look like a figure molded in polished metal. The womanly scent of her, composed of lavender and rosewater and rice powder combined with her own fresh sweetness, mounted to his head. It fused in his mind with the knowledge that she was his for the taking, if he chose to be a scoundrel.

Slowly he doubled his hand into a fist at his side, clenching it so hard it ached. That choice, he could see, might well be easier than he had dreamed.

"It matters to me," he said with a rough edge to his voice. "I'll take you back."

"Perhaps it's as well," she said in tones so low he had to bend his head to hear them. "The others are—going up to bed."

There came a brittle laugh from the dimness somewhere ahead of them. Katrine turned toward the sound. Rowan listened to its echoes before he said, "It came from the tower, I think. I would say it was your sister-in-law. If you will wait here a moment, there is something I would like to ask her."

"I'll come with you."

The firmness of her voice made it a waste of time to argue. He only took her arm, leading her toward the dark shape looming ahead of them.

The door opening into the tower was massive, and heavily carved with odd scrolls and symbols. It was open a crack, so that the faint gleam of some illumination inside shone around the edge. Rowan pushed it wide and they stepped inside.

Moist, warm air scented with earth and green growing things surrounded them. He stood still, staring at enormous tree ferns and parlor palms with fronds reaching ten feet before they curved in graceful arches, at floor tiles of marble in rose and green and a great stone fountain of life-sized satyrs, nymphs, and cherubs, frozen in their cavorting play.

The marble basin of the fountain was shell-shaped and deep, and large enough to house four or five lazily swimming red-gold carp. Fluttering lamps in copper holders were fastened to the carved pilasters on the inner walls that soared upward into the darkness. A linseed-oiled staircase of cypress, that wood impregnable against damp, made a sweeping curve against the wall opposite the entrance. It led to a railed gallery where doorways opened into the darkened rooms.

A man and a woman were standing half-hidden under a palm, caught in a close embrace. It was Musetta with Perry.

Giles's sister turned, her eyes wide. Seeing who had entered, she gave them a smile. "What a surprise to see you two out here. Or perhaps not, on second thought."

"Where is Charlotte?" Rowan asked, cutting across the arch sound of the woman's voice.

Musetta pouted a little, glancing from under her lashes at her escort, who gazed down on her with rapt pleasure. As Rowan stood waiting she looked back at him. "Oh, Charlotte decided to go back inside by the end door before she had taken three steps. She's a strange little thing, full of romantic fancies. Regardless, she couldn't see what a lovely night it is for a—how should I say it? For a lovers' tryst?"

CHAPTER EIGHT

"I can't sleep in a nightshirt."

The words were simple. Though spoken in low tones, they were perfectly understandable. The problem, Katrine thought, was that her brain refused to grapple with their meaning in connection with the man who stood at the foot of her bed.

"What," she said carefully, "do you wear at night?"

"My skin. It's a habit I picked up in equatorial Africa. I could try the nightshirt if you insist, but I can promise that neither of us will get any sleep for my thrashing and tossing."

Katrine was not certain how much sleep she would get with a naked man in her bed, but that seemed a moot question. She did not expect to sleep at all with Rowan beside her.

Choosing her words carefully, she said, "Isn't there some compromise that could be made?"

He gave her a wry smile. "Oh, yes, I can turn out the lights before I undress, and you can close your eyes."

"I expected that anyway," she said with asperity.

"Did you, now? What else were you expecting?"

There was a caressing note in his voice that sent panic through her. "Nothing! Nothing at all. But—if you can't stand a nightshirt, perhaps you could sleep in your clothes."

"The whole purpose," he pointed out patiently, "is to lull

suspicion, not cause it. I could strip to underdrawers, but that's worse than a nightshirt."

"Surely there is something a little less, that is, something that would still cover you?" The heat in her face was for the images in her mind, and the difficulties of finding ladylike phrases, rather than from prudishness.

He tilted his head. "Omar wears a loincloth now and then, a length of cloth wrapped about his lower body. Is that what you had in mind?"

Was it? She didn't know. She said doubtfully, "I suppose that would be better than nothing."

"Not," he answered succinctly, "from my point of view. If you want to know, he looks like an overgrown baby in it."

She sat worrying at the inside of her bottom lip with her teeth. She looked down at her hands laced together in her lap. Finally she inquired, "You really want to get into my bed wearing nothing?"

A strange look came and went across his face, lingering for an instant in his eyes before he veiled them with his thick lashes. His voice abrupt, he said, "It will make no difference to our agreement or your safety."

"I didn't think it would." She hesitated again, then spoke in a rush. "Actually it might be best if you were—totally unclothed—if Giles chances to visit again."

He stared at her, studying the pristine white of her nightgown, her hair that flowed in shining waves over her shoulders, the clear luminosity of her skin, and the set determination of her face. His tone wary, he said, "Why?"

She looked up at him, then down again. "Giles knows my feelings on this too well, which is why he is suspicious of a trick. There is a way he can be certain that I have—complied with his wishes. I tried to tell you earlier, but I'm not sure you understood."

He moved closer, resting his hands on the mahogany footboard. There was concern and alert competence in his face when he spoke, but no condemnation. "What is it?"

She drew a deep breath and let it out on a sigh. "I am still—" She stopped, then tried again. "You may find it difficult to credit after five years of marriage—but my union with Giles was never . . ."

"I understood well enough. You are still a virgin. Your husband was—is—incapable." Some emotion, rigorously suppressed, flattened his voice.

Katrine could not sustain the intensity of his clear green gaze for more than a few seconds. She looked down at her hands again before she nodded in agreement.

Suddenly he pushed away from the bed. "What do you think he will do? Check the sheets like some snooping midwife or the court doctors of a young king?"

"It seems possible," she said in colorless tones.

"It's intolerable. How a man can treat his own wife—" He took a hasty few steps, stopping with his back to her and the sound of his breathing harsh in the room.

"I'm sorry," she said as she smoothed the sheet under her hands. "I know this must be disgusting for you."

He turned slowly. "There is nothing about you that could ever disgust me; you must not think it. I find what your husband has arranged monstrous, the betrayal of everything that is good and true in marriage, but that has nothing to do with you."

Relief welled up inside her. His insight in seeing that she had dreaded his scorn when she had not realized it herself gave her an odd feeling in her chest. A part of it was gratitude, but there was also more than a trace of anxiety that he could see more, understand more about her than was comfortable.

Katrine gave him a tremulous smile. "There is still the problem of what is to be done."

"There is no problem," he said. "Come, get out of the bed."

He gave her his hand to help her down, carefully keeping

his gaze lowered as her nightgown rode above her knees. Stepping into the dressing room then, he returned with his dueling sword in its sheath. He tested the blade to find the sharpest edge, then, even as she began to guess what he intended, sliced it across his fingers. Blood welled, and he threw back the covers and rubbed the wetness over the smooth linen surface of the bottom sheet.

Tossing the sword on the bed, he moved to the washstand. He poured a small amount of water from the pitcher sitting there into the basin and dipped a cloth into it. He swabbed his fingers with the wet cloth, then stepped back to the bed to rub the wetness over the stain already there so that it spread, becoming lighter.

He glanced at her as she stood staring. His face creased in a grim smile. "If Castlereagh is callous enough to seek proof of your bedding, then he deserves to fear that you found pleasure in it."

Katrine gave a slow nod of agreement, though she was not certain she understood the precise sequence of events that might result in a splotch such as he had created. She did not intend to say so, however; she had exposed enough ignorance for one evening.

He disposed of the cloth, then moved back to the bed, where he picked up the sword and sheathed it again. He stood with it in his hands while a considering frown settled between his eyes. "In the old days," he said finally, "a knight sometimes tested his ability to resist temptation by sleeping in the bed of his lady love with a sword between them. It served as a reminder, since the cross made by hilt and blade symbolized his vows of knighthood. It was also a marker to make sure he stayed on his side of the mattress."

Katrine met his gaze, seeing the serious purpose reflected in its shadowed green depths. She moistened her lips. "I doubt that will be necessary, though I am willing if you think it will help."

Amusement tugged one corner of his mouth upward. "I won't refuse whatever aid may be available."

Despite his words, Katrine was fairly certain the addition was for her benefit. He obviously thought she was afraid to have him in her bed. Maybe she was; there was a hard knot under her breastbone that had the feel of incipient terror. Still, she had come this far and would not draw back now.

"Is your hand still bleeding?" she asked.

"It's fine." He barely glanced at it before turning from her and leaning to place the sword in the middle of the bed.

"Well, then."

She meant for the words to be calm and sedate. Instead they had the husky sound of an invitation. Clenching her teeth together to still their tendency to chatter, she swung away, moving to the lamp on the bedside table. She cupped her hands around the glass chimney and blew out the flame.

The only illumination was the faint glow of moonlight beyond the windows. Rowan was no more than a moving shadow as he stepped into the deeper darkness. Katrine turned her back on him and climbed into the bed once more. She pulled the sheet and coverlet to her chin and closed her eyes.

If she listened closely, she could hear the soft sounds of cloth brushing against cloth, of shirt studs and pantaloon buttons popping from their holes, of leather boots being levered off bit by bit. She tried not to listen, concentrating instead on the pulse beats throbbing in her ears.

By allowing a bare slit to open between her lashes, she could see shadowy movement. He undressed as he did everything else, with swift assurance and lithe grace. Catching the pale blur of a lean flank that seemed to be lighter in color than his upper body, she snapped her eyes shut again.

He moved so soundlessly that she only knew he was there when he touched the bed. Her entire body jerked in reflex. Before the movement had half begun, he lifted the covers and slid under them.

The bed ropes sagged, and the soft mattress filled with long-fibered cotton shifted with it. Katrine could feel herself sliding toward the middle of the bed, toward the sword and Rowan. She shot out her hand to grip the far side of the mattress. The movement ceased. She breathed easier.

Turning her head just a fraction, she could see him in the dimness. He lay with one arm behind his head. The sheet came to his waist only. Its whiteness made a strong contrast against the dark color of his skin.

Only slaves, day laborers, and seamen exposed themselves to the sun without a shirt to cover them, and then only if they were working well away from public view. She could not imagine what he had been doing to become so sun-bronzed.

The thought was a way of distracting herself, she knew. It made no difference, so long as it worked.

He turned his head toward her. His voice was deep and easy as he spoke. "I've been meaning to ask where Delphia is this evening?"

"I sent her to press my gown for tomorrow, one with dozens of layers of ruffles. With so many guests in the house needing clothes touched up, the laundry has been crowded until now. Besides, it seemed best to keep her occupied until—well, until we were settled."

"She does know," he said with a trace of suppressed humor in his tone, "that I've taken her place."

"Yes. Only not in that way—exactly."

"So long as she doesn't try to join us later." He hesitated a moment before he went on. "I waited until I saw her leave before I came. I sent Omar to follow her."

Katrine gave him a long look, but made no answer.

It disturbed her to suspect her maid. They had been together so long, had been through so much together. She had thought they were friends, or at least as near as their positions as maid and mistress would allow them to be. Katrine had always known there was a portion of Delphia's life she could never enter, never really understand. There were secrets her maid kept from her, details about her few leisure hours that were never mentioned between them. It had never seemed to matter until now.

It was entirely possible, Katrine thought, that Delphia was spending the evening with the man who was her lover. Omar or no Omar. Katrine had, indeed, given her tacit permission by sending her away after dark.

Katrine was concerned, but had no real objection. It wasn't like Delphia to allow her head to be turned; the association had to be important to her. Katrine only hoped she would not be hurt. If Omar could prevent that by distracting her, then that was reason enough to allow his pursuit.

Katrine noticed, suddenly, a gleam of white at Rowan's side opposite from where she lay. He was holding the arm rather stiffly across his abdomen. It seemed his dislocated shoulder from the fall on the racetrack was not so minor as he had made it out to be.

She said, "There is laudanum on the washstand, in case your shoulder is paining you."

"I saw it," he answered. "I don't think I'll need it, though it was thoughtful of you to have it near at hand."

"Delphia brought it for my headache after the carriage accident." She hesitated a moment, then went on. "I've been wanting to speak to you about that, but there has not been an opportunity. Don't you think my accident and yours have a suspicious similarity?"

"The thought had occurred to me." His words were dry.

"What can it mean?"

"Your husband seems determined that his arrangements for an heir should be kept as secret as possible. Regardless, the most obvious reason to injure either of us, so it seems to me, would be to prevent the appearance of an heir for Arcadia. The person responsible could not be expected to know the happy event has no chance of taking place."

"We might have been killed, either of us."

"That would certainly have made our liaison difficult," he said with grim amusement in his voice.

"How could anyone know anything about it?" she asked.

"Delphia knew all along, I think."

"Oh, yes, but—" She stopped. "If we must be accurate, I believe your Omar also knows."

"He does. So who else? Is there no one who might have overheard something, put two and two together, saw the direction the tournament was taking?"

"I suppose," she said in reluctant tones. "It seems to me that Lewis suspects something. But if that's how it came about, then anyone could know."

"There is that."

She heard him draw a deep breath and let it out in a frustrated sigh. She wondered if it was not in part for the strain of sharing her bed. Men, she had always been told, had stronger, more unruly physical needs than women; it was unfair to tease them, unwise to tempt them.

Her lips stiff, she said, "I'm sorry if this is difficult for you. Or dangerous."

He shifted, raising himself on one elbow in the bed. "Are you concerned for me? Don't be. Or rather, if it weighs on your conscience, you might tell me what you know about my brother. That is, if you will remember, what brought me into this."

He waited. When she made no answer, he stretched a hand toward her. She realized after a moment that he had picked up a lock of her hair that had strayed across to catch on the hilt of the sword between them. He rubbed it in his fingers, then wrapped it carefully around his palm as he stared at her still form in the darkness.

"Why won't you tell me?" he said, the timbre of puzzlement and doubt in his voice. "What is keeping you silent?"

Her throat was too tight to make a sound, even if she had wanted to speak. She didn't. She turned her head away from him on the pillow.

He settled back onto the mattress. His words were grim as he spoke once more. "You are not responsible, regardless; I am here for my brother. Whatever happens is on my own head."

His brother. She could see him in her mind's eye, a handsome, laughing young man; gentle, yet strong as the good are strong. He had been so vulnerable, so open in his ardor; it was as if he had never loved before, had no defenses against its pain.

Death. Why did it take the best? There was something wrong in a creation that removed the good and innocent and let the guilty and evil flourish. There should be some redress, some balance, even if it was brought by man, a single man.

She spoke into the darkness. "Giles killed a man in England in a duel over a woman. That was some fifteen years ago. His family kept it quiet, whisked him to the coast and onto a ship for Louisiana. He had a friend here from his Oxford days, my father. He came, invested in land and cotton, and made a fortune."

"This has something to do with Terence?" Rowan's question was tentative.

"I just thought you should know," she answered. She paused, then went on as if impelled. "Have you ever fought to the death in a duel?"

"Only to first bloodshed. My honor has never required that a man die."

"It was by choice?" Her voice was thick as she asked it. To choose to wound an opponent rather than kill him took skill and precision. It also required the courage to risk death at the other man's hands and the forbearance to settle for the satisfaction of honor rather than vengeance.

"For me, yes."

She thought of Terence, lying in dew-wet grass with the hole of a pistol ball in his forehead. Someone else had made another choice.

No. She would not think of it. That would change nothing.

She had told the truth when she said to Rowan that she was to blame. Without her, Terence would never have come to Arcadia, would never have died. She had accepted the guilt of it more than a year ago, and could not repudiate it now.

The night was not cold, yet she felt chilled. It came from inside, she thought. She shifted a little in the bed, gathering the coverlet higher around her neck.

There was a tug on her hair. Rowan had apparently forgotten it was still wrapped around his hand. She could remind him, but that would let him know she had noticed what he was doing before and had neglected to protest. She eased back into her original position.

The minutes ticked past. Outside, an owl hooted somewhere near the wood's edge, a doleful sound. A floorboard creaked in another part of the house. There came a soft rattle from the direction of Giles's room, followed by a small, oiled click.

Rowan moved on the bed like windblown smoke coiling from a dampened fire. One moment he was lying still, the next thing his long, hard length was against her from shoulder to knee.

"Just lie still and let me do it," he whispered against her hair. "Or if you want to help, you might try an artistic moan."

Her brain made sense of the words, and the need for them, just as he shifted again. His hand, dark against the white of her nightgown even in the room's moonlit dimness, clasped her breast in a hold of gentle power. His warm mouth captured her soft gasp, smothering its sound.

Giles. He was easing open the connecting door. Spying on them from his darkened room.

Anger crested in a tumbling tide in Katrine's veins. She arched toward Rowan, lifting her hand to his shoulder, sliding her hands over the bandaging there to twine her fingers in the thick curling at his neck. She felt his start of surprise. It pleased her in some manner that she could shake his self-possession, even if only for a moment.

An instant later she felt the onslaught of his kiss, and understood that until that instant she had known only the most polite of caresses from him.

Firm, possessive, enticing, his lips moved upon hers. He swept their fragile, clinging surfaces with bold strokes of his tongue, tasting, tempting. He probed the moist and tender corners, and dipped inside the honeyed depths of her mouth to urge delicate play. He tested the hesitant, fluttering edges of her tongue, gently abrading, drawing it into a sinuous duel whose winner was never in doubt. He skimmed the smooth, pearl-like edges of her teeth and sipped the nectar of her sweet and unconscious giving.

His hand at her breast tightened imperceptibly while his thumb worried the gentle bud of her nipple until it stood tight and hard under the softness of its batiste covering. He drew one long leg upward, insinuating it between her knees.

A slow, beguiling anticipation grew inside Katrine. It gathered force while her limbs grew heavy and she felt the simmering richness of desire tumbling in her veins, spreading like summer's heat through her body. An intimation of joy hovered in her mind, trembling. She pressed closer to the man who held her while a soft moan caught in her throat.

There came the quiet click of a latch.

Rowan stiffened. He lifted his head. He drew a deep breath, holding it while long seconds ticked past, holding it until Katrine thought he had forgotten how to let it go. It was soundless when he released it, though she felt the tension leaving his body, felt him easing away from her.

She let her hand trail along his arm, let it drop. For an instant she was aware of the steel-hard press against her thigh of the sword that lay between them. Then it was gone.

Not the sword. The hardness had been warm and more resilient.

She recoiled, whipping away from him, moving to the very edge of the bed. "Out," she cried in a hissing whisper. "Out of my bed."

There was no surprise in his silence, only quick cogitation. He said softly, "What if he comes back?"

"Let him. I want you out of here."

"So be it."

His voice was taut yet even as he spoke. It held no excuse, no appeal, no apology. Katrine recognized in some confusion that, shaken as she might be by what he had done, there were reserves of passion held in hard, resolute check inside him that she would never touch, a part of himself kept inviolate that she could never know.

He rose in a single, swift movement that barely made the mattress sway on the bed ropes. His body, the wide shoulders and tapering waist, the lean line of his thighs, was silhouetted against the faint light beyond the window. He swung toward the door leading to the dressing room.

He was going. She didn't want it after all, couldn't bear the dignified calm of his retreat, which told her louder than words that he would not return.

They had come this far. It would be stupid to draw back over something that mattered so little, after all.

"Wait," she said in a soft, nearly soundless entreaty.

His hearing was acute. He stopped, turned.

"Come back." The words were, perhaps, the most difficult she had ever spoken.

"Are you sure?" There was finality in his voice.

"No," she said in difficult honesty.

"Good," he answered with a whisper of humor. "Neither am I."

He retraced his footsteps, slid under the covers, but remained well toward his own side of the bed. Katrine sank back down on her side. She lay for long moments staring into the dark, trying not to think.

A shiver shook her. It was only then that she realized how chilled she had become. She turned to her back, drawing the covers up to her chin and tucking them under her shoulders.

Her hand touched the cool metal sheath of the sword. She shivered again, tensing her muscles to draw away from it. It was then that she felt the warmth.

It was radiating from Rowan de Blanc as from the sun, a powerful heat that reached out to envelop her in its steady glow. Gooseflesh moved over her, tingling, fading as a soundless sigh left her lips. She turned toward the man who lay beside her. Slowly, in minute movements, she inched her fingers across the straight metal sheath, seeking the source of the warmth. At the same time she was fearful of coming too close, of actually touching him, especially as the bed sagged in his direction. It was a delicate balance.

While she was still trying to keep it, she slept.

Rowan awoke with his usual abrupt clarity of mind. He moved not a muscle, freezing into stillness. Katrine lay against him with her back pressed to his chest, her hips nestled into his belly and her legs following the relaxed bend of his own.

She breathed easily, her chest rising and falling in soft, natural cadence. The sweet fragrance of her mounted to his head, setting off a wave of raw, aching need. She was such a lovely armful, a perfect fit. The urge to discover the clasp of her tender, virginal tightness around him was so strong his brain felt addled with it. How easy it would be to forget vows and duties and just—

No. That line of thought was forbidden.

He could feel also the sword buried beneath them. Its hilt gouged into his armpit and the point of the sheath poked the underside of his knee. A fine deterrent that had turned out to be.

Had he moved in the night, or had she? He seemed to remember, in the vague manner of a dream, the moment when she had settled into place. He must have roused then. At least he had retained the presence of mind not to gather her closer with an arm around her narrow waist.

Or had he? He seemed to recall firm, tender curves under fine batiste of the sort used in the nightgown she was wearing. Thank God she had not awoke.

He could remember little afterward. They had both slept deeply. Katrine had been so restless before, shifting her position time after time, heaving long sighs. He had heard every rustle of the bed covers, every soft breath. He had hated thinking that he was the cause of her unease. Perhaps he was not, if she could find peace in his arms.

And yet, what did that restlessness say about the life she was leading? Did it have anything to do with Terence's death? He would have to think about it later, when his mind was clearer.

As much as he hated doing it, he needed to put space between the two of them before he embarrassed them both. His bodily reactions to their position were becoming a little too noticeable for comfort. It would do neither of them any good if she woke up screaming or made a bolt for it down the hall in her nightclothes.

Removing himself to his own side of the bed without disturbing her was going to be difficult, if not impossible. Yet he had to try. It was important to him not to betray the tenuous trust she had extended to him.

Before he could move, he felt her stir, heard the whisper of her quick, indrawn breath. Too late. He lay unmoving, waiting for her to fling herself out of reach and turn on him.

He felt her muscles tense, but when she moved, it was to ease away from him. With infinite care and the smooth flexing of finely toned and turned limbs, she shifted to her own portion of the mattress. A moment later he felt the gentle tug and silken slide of a long length of hair as she pulled it from under his bent arm that cushioned his head.

She lay watching him then, he thought. The urge to open his eyes, to meet her gaze and try to decipher what she was thinking, how she felt, was so strong that it startled him. It was a luxury he could not afford. No matter how desirable she might be, no matter how fascinating, she was still his one link to his brother's killer.

Still, there was one small indulgence he could allow himself.

He mustered a soft sigh and turned to his back, away from the sword, away from Katrine. Opening his eyes, he stared up at the ceiling for a few seconds. He stretched, smothering a yawn with the back of one hand before shifting his head on his pillow to look at his bed partner.

A slow smile curved his mouth. "Good morning," he said in tones both husky and dulcet. "Did you sleep well?"

CHAPTER NINE

It was Sunday. The houseguests would have a leisurely breakfast served, for the most part, in their rooms. Afterward the carriages would be brought out so that those so inclined could go to the worship services of their choice. On their return, there would be a cold luncheon served on the terrace of sugar-cured ham, fried chicken, flaky biscuits the size of a quarter, yeast rolls, potato salad, fried yams, bread-and-butter pickles, green tomato relish, coconut custard pie, and fried apple tarts. A short respite would be allowed for those who felt the need to sleep off their luncheon. In midafternoon, then, the entire party, with baggage and servants, would be transported to the town dock to board Giles's private steamboat, the *Cotton Blossom.*

The rest of the day would be devoted to a slow cruise up the river. They would tie up for the night, then sometime the following day they would come to an island where a population of wild hogs had been allowed to establish themselves. The men would spend a day or two of hunting boar there before moving over to the Louisiana shore and a delta swamp where deer, black bear, squirrels, and raccoons were plentiful. The ladies would entertain themselves with reading and needlework aboard the steamboat or else picnics and walks on the shore. At night, there would be music, singing and dancing on board their floating home.

Giles had been planning this portion of his annual gathering for months. It was all timed to perfection, with mountains of provisions already stored on the steamboat and the galley fully equipped for cooking the bagged game. Books, playscripts, and cards had been stocked in the steamboat lounge, and an impressive list of musicians, singers, and actors transported from New Orleans and established on board to show off their skills. He was determined that nothing should be lacking that might ensure the pleasure of his guests.

There was a short time in the middle of the morning when it seemed the entire project might be abandoned. It came after the wagons returned from carrying a last load of cooking pots, plus the cook, to be settled on board the boat. One of the grooms claimed to have been told by the captain of another steamer that it would be best not to tie up at night in any out-of-the-way places.

The problem, it seemed, was river pirates. These rowdies, thieves, and cutthroats had elected themselves a new leader, a vicious thug who called himself Rooster Isom. Bent on making a name for himself on the river, the pirate leader had been on a rampage in the last few days. He and his gang had attacked flatboats, and taken over wood yards and charged exorbitant prices to the steamboats forced to stop at them; they had knifed strangers around the docks, and even surrounded a plantation house, robbing the owner and carrying off the wife and daughter. The two women had turned up the next morning more dead than alive.

After some debate, it was decided that there was little danger to a vessel the size of the *Cotton Blossom*. The men would hunt in turns, leaving a guard posted over the ladies at all times. With such sportsmen, and marksmen, as they had among them, there would be scant chance of open attack even if the river pirates dared show themselves.

Katrine was not looking forward to the outing. Compared with the spaciousness of the house, the guests would be almost on top of each other. The major occupation among the women during the long days would be gossip or discussions of babies and childbirth, none of which appealed at the moment.

A major worry was Rowan. She was not sure what Giles intended to do about her supposed intimacy with him. It seemed patently impossible to continue as they were in such cramped quarters, with so many to see Rowan's comings and goings. Yet their two nights together could hardly be deemed sufficient for the purpose for which her husband had brought them together.

She felt the heat of a blush rise in her face as she thought of her waking moments this morning. The bed and its weak ropes were to blame, that had to be it. She could not have pressed herself to Rowan de Blanc in that way for any other reason. It had been strange, waking to find herself lying so close against him. She could vaguely remember being drawn to his warmth, remember the deep and abiding comfort of settling into his embrace. She could not recall the last time she had felt so safe, or slept so deeply.

At least she had been able to move away from him before he knew. She could not even imagine what wicked amusement he might have had at her expense if he had discovered her there.

She frowned at herself in the mirror where she sat while Delphia dressed her hair. That was, perhaps, doing him an injustice. He had behaved with perfect propriety last night—other than refusing to wear a nightshirt. It wasn't his fault that his weight exceeded hers, or that she was a restless sleeper.

"Is something wrong?" Delphia asked the question around a mouthful of pins as she deftly braided a long tress and fastened it in place. "Would you rather have a more elaborate style?"

"No, no, I need something simple for today. I was just thinking."

"About last night?" the maid suggested.

"Rather this morning. You know," Katrine went on with a dry twist of her lips, "men's bodies are different."

Delphia rolled her eyes. "Just a little."

Katrine smiled self-consciously. "Well, more than a little. I was only thinking how hard they are—stop giggling! I was referring to their muscles."

"Yes, ma'am. Of course you were."

"Not all are quite so powerful in the chest and arms and legs as Rowan, I suppose. It's no wonder he had little fear of not being able to win the tournament." It was odd what pleasure it gave her to speak of him. She would not have expected it.

Delphia paused in her work to meet Katrine's gaze in the mirror. "He didn't hurt you?"

"Certainly not."

"You're not too sore? If so, I have a special salve that will have you right again well before nighttime gets here."

Katrine shook her head. "I don't need it, really."

"You don't have to be brave about it, not with me. Men don't always realize what they're doing; they go too fast, start in before you're ready. The salve will make it easier."

"There's absolutely no need, I promise." Katrine's voice was firm, though she looked away from the mirror and her maid's probing gaze.

Finally Delphia said, "You didn't do it, did you?"

"What do you mean?" Even as she spoke Katrine remembered Rowan's warning.

"You can't fool me, Madam Katrine; I know you too well. I thought you didn't have the right look, the pleased pride, about you. What did you do? Whose blood is that on the sheets, yours or that man's?"

"I don't know what you mean."

"That proves it; you should know. You're only bamboo-zling Mr. Giles."

Pain and apprehension blossomed in Katrine's chest. It became more acute as she thought of the maid reporting to Giles. Her voice quiet, she said, "You may not know me as well as you think."

Delphia put a hand on her hip and lifted a brow. "Tell me exactly what Master Rowan did then."

"Some things are private." It was not that she was unaware of the process of procreation; she had spent too much time tending the women in the quarters, their female problems and pregnancies, for that. Even if the night before had been different, however, she did not think she could have brought herself to tell her maid about it. Or anyone else, for that matter.

"I can't believe it," Delphia said, shaking her head. "You should be ashamed—and just think of what you're missing."

Katrine noticed the maid looking in the direction of the nightgown she herself had worn the night before that lay with the Turkish toweling left from her bath and the sheets that had been stripped from the bed. What additional evidence there might be in these to disprove what she said, Katrine did not like to think. It seemed best to let the matter pass and hope for the best. She began to give instructions on her clothing and also several pieces of Berlin needlework she especially wanted to take for the outing aboard the steamboat.

The day moved along much as had been planned. Luncheon came and went. The weather was unsettled; the sun sailed in and out of passing gray banks of clouds, and it grew unnaturally warm and humid. It felt as if there might be a storm in the air, one pushed along by a cool spell behind it. The prospect of a break in the Indian summer made Giles's male guests happy, since it would mean better hunting.

Those who felt the need of a restoring nap retired upstairs. During the hiatus, Giles took the gentlemen who weren't sleepy to show off his collection of firearms, including the double-action Adams revolver that had recently arrived from England. A special piece with a chased silver barrel, it triggered a heated debate over its merits compared to Colt's single-action revolver. A shooting contest was required to settle the issue of speed and accuracy, one that effectively ended the time of resting.

As the time drew nearer for the transfer to the steamboat, the upper floors of the house rang with hurried footsteps and the sound of slamming trunk lids. The chaos in the laundry rose to pandemonium as maids and valets snapped and quarreled over last-minute use of the sad irons and pleating irons. Wagons to transport baggage were lined up on the drive. Carriages, and also saddle horses for those who preferred to ride, were beginning to be brought around.

Katrine had been to the outdoor kitchen wing to check on the packing of the scones, cookies, apple tarts, and fruitcakes that would be served with tea as soon as everyone was on the steamboat. Seeing the comestibles on their way, she turned in the direction of her bedchamber to change into her traveling costume.

Giles was coming from the house out onto the terrace as she climbed to the last level. "There you are, my dear. I wonder if I could have a word with you before we become too involved in the rush to get off?"

"I still need to dress," she said doubtfully.

"I won't keep you more than a moment." He smiled as he held out his arm. The firmness in his tone showed plainly that he would not brook a refusal.

He turned in the direction of the tower. At her quick look of inquiry, he said, "It will be quieter out here, with less chance of interruption."

"Has there been a snag in the arrangements?" she asked.

"Nothing major. De Blanc's manservant has come up missing, but that's all."

"Omar? Where can he be?" The big, mute, dark-skinned

man did not seem the kind to run away or to go off on his own to drink and carouse.

"I'm sure it's a misunderstanding of some kind. De Blanc is searching for him." Her husband's voice held easy confidence.

"What will happen if he doesn't find him?"

"We'll go without him, of course. He can always join us later."

It made sense, and yet Katrine was disturbed. She had not seen either Rowan or Omar since early morning. The big man-servant had attended Rowan as he bathed and dressed in her dressing room, then Rowan had left through Giles's bedchamber. Omar had slipped away later.

The great door of the tower was locked. Katrine was a little surprised; it was usually left open as long as there were guests who might want to wander inside. Cato had charge of the key, since it was he who let the gardeners who tended the plants in and out.

She turned to go. Giles released her arm, but stayed where he stood. Reaching into his coat pocket, he pulled out the big iron door key. He opened the door and held it for her to enter.

A faint uneasiness brushed Katrine's mind. There seemed no reason for it that she could see. She moved through the door-way before her husband, walking to within a few steps of the bubbling, splattering fountain before she turned.

"Upstairs, if you please." Giles did not wait to see if she would comply, but ambled in the direction of the staircase and began to mount toward the gallery.

Katrine lifted her skirts and trailed after him. There was re-luctance in every step she took. She could feel her heart begin to thud in her chest. There was something in her husband's manner that she didn't like. She did not like it at all.

Giles reached the gallery and moved along it to a chamber door, one used as a study. He glanced inside, then pulled the door shut again. Walking along to the next room, he looked inside it also.

"Good," he said to Katrine over his shoulder. "We can be private here."

She joined him in the room he often used as his bedchamber in the winter months. He was troubled by rheumatism during cold weather, and it pained him less in the tower. The winds could not penetrate the stones and the windows were little more than arrow slits with tiny glass panes set so firmly in place that cold air did not seep around them. More than that, he had installed, at great expense, a unique system of heat much like that used by the ancient Romans. There was a boiler room in the raised basement where a fire was kept burning under a huge steam kettle during the winter months. The rising steam was fed throughout the tower by a system of stone ducts and air outlets in the thick walls. Sometimes it grew so moist and warm that water ran in rivulets down the stone and the wainscot paneling of the interior.

The bedchamber was furnished with a certain masculine grandeur. There was a large walnut bed with a pedimented tester draped in royal-blue worsted, and a great four-square walnut armoire that looked far more suitable for its original purpose of battle armor than for clothing. A pair of comfortable armchairs in worn steel-blue velvet sat before the smoke-blackened stone fireplace. The crude wrought-iron firedogs and poker matched the iron floor candelabra with branching arms that sat nearby. Rugs in faded blue and red Turkish designs softened the polished wood floor.

"Ah," Giles said, moving toward a tray sitting on a side table, "there is wine. I wasn't sure Cato had time to bring it this morning."

Katrine watched her husband pour out a glass of dark ruby liquid, then begin to pour another. She said quickly, "None for me, thank you."

"Nonsense," he said, filling the second glass to the rim. "I saw the way you ran from one task to another today, catering to my friends. You surely need something to sustain you until the evening."

He picked up the glass and held it out to her. She took it to be polite before she said, "We really should be getting ready to go. We don't want everyone to have to wait on us."

"Yes, in a moment. There is something that is troubling me."

The first thing that came to mind was the certainty that he had discovered her deception. She sipped at the wine she held as she waited for him to continue. It seemed acid and a little bitter. Perhaps Cato had been more involved with the list of wine he had been sending to the steamboat earlier in the day than with what went on the tray.

Her husband turned a stern gaze upon her. "I wanted to ask you," he said, "if de Blanc is pleasing to you?"

She choked a little and swallowed in haste. As he continued to stare at her, waiting for her to speak, she said, "I—have nothing to complain of in his treatment of me."

"There is nothing about him or his actions to offend a female of refined sensibilities?"

"No, nothing." She looked at the wine in her glass, refusing to meet her husband's hot, narrow gaze.

"Then why have you flouted my wishes? No, my express commands?"

"I didn't—" she began with anger rising inside her.

"I know you 'didn't,'" he countered, his lips twisting with the crude emphasis he placed on the words. "That is my complaint."

Outrage flowed from the center of her being to suffuse her brain and every particle of her body. "This is intolerable!" she cried. "What you ask of me is madness. Nothing in the vows we exchanged allows you to use me in this way; nothing requires that I debase myself for your benefit."

"You agreed."

"Never in words. You took my agreement for granted. I thought the idea a foolish fancy, something you would forget in time. I thought all I needed to do was refuse and keep on refusing."

Pain and sadness settled over his lined features. He gave a slow wag of his head. "If only you had not been so obstinate. If you had just agreed to a discreet liaison."

For a flickering instant Katrine wondered if Giles was right, if she really was being unreasonable and inconsiderate in refusing him his one wish. That was until she realized that was the way he wanted her to feel. She lifted her chin. "You think I could bring an innocent child into your house, one you might one day decide was unworthy of your name? I could not. Nor could I choose a man in cold blood."

"That is your problem; there is no heat in your blood. If there had been, then I might not require an heir of another man's loins."

Blood roared in her head at the insult, the first hint her husband had given that he found her inadequate. "You would blame me? There is nothing whatever wrong with my childbearing organs or my blood."

"Prove me wrong," he said, a crafty light in his eyes. "Prove to me that you know what passion is, what joy it can bring."

"I will prove nothing, nor will I go another step further in this insane scheme of yours. I've come this far only out of concern that a direct refusal from me might endanger your health."

She flung out her arm as she spoke. The wine sloshed in her glass. She would have set it down, except that Giles was between her and the table. She drank a large swallow of it to lower the level in the glass.

"I don't need your pity, Katrine. I need a heir. I warned you once."

"I am aware. I also know what you said to Rowan, and it makes me feel ill. How could you be so low? How could you spy on me? How could you think to threaten me, consider allowing someone to overpower me? How could you?"

He was silent for long moments. "If de Blanc told you what I said, he is not as disinterested as he pretends. Nor is he as trustworthy for my purpose. I will not abide having him gossip of this affair to others."

Her lips curled. "He spoke only to me. I had a slight interest, you will admit."

"Regardless, something may have to be done."

Katrine stared at him with fear shifting inside her chest. In low tones, she demanded, "What are you saying?"

"Just this," he answered, his gray features congealed into implacable lines. "I will have what I want, no matter what it takes."

"Giles—" she began. She stopped as the sick anger inside her flowed away, leaving her oddly disoriented. She swayed a little before she went on again, speaking from resolution gained in long midnight hours of worry and fear. "Go too far, Giles, and you may force me to leave you."

He was silent for long moments. "You won't do that," he said at last, "not when you have nowhere else to go, not after you know you are carrying the child who will inherit all this." He waved his hand in an encompassing gesture. "Only think; if I live no more than another year or two, you will control the estate for most of your adult life."

That kind of rhetoric was so familiar. She had alarmed herself for nothing. She shook her head in a dull gesture. "You aren't going to die."

"But I am, I feel it."

"The doctors found no disease; they told me so in New Orleans last winter."

"They are wrong."

There was no point in arguing with him. He never listened. She said, "Anyway, I never married you for your money."

"No, but there was your father's dream, and mine. The dream is still alive. Think of it, Katrine. Two estates marching side by side, one of the largest holdings in Louisiana. What good was your sacrifice if there is never a child to unite the properties?"

"What of my dreams?" she asked in sudden weariness. She really was so tired. So tired of quarreling. So tired of fighting what seemed the inevitable. So tired of only dreaming.

"A child will console you," her husband said.

She wanted to tell him consolation was not what she needed. The words wouldn't come. There was an odd, floating sensation in her head. Her hands were numb.

The high-pitched crash of shattering glass made her look down at the floor. The crystal goblet she had held now lay at her feet in a thousand pieces, each small shard coated with wine the color of blood.

She looked up at her husband. He was moving toward her without sound, looming, swelling, so that his eyes appeared enormous and glinting with dark gladness shaded with lust. He surrounded her like a chill fog, and began to tear at her clothes with his hands.

The relentless throbbing in her head woke her. She moaned, turning her head to the side. The pillow that lay under her head was hard. It was not her usual pillow. The space around her was enormous, soft, with a cold, damp feel to it. It was a bed, but not her bed. She could hear it raining somewhere, a steady, thrumming downpour.

She eased her eyes open bit by bit. Blind, she was blind. Darkness pressed down on the surface of her eyeballs as if it would coat them. She made a small sound of distress that sent sharp agony exploding through her brain.

She lifted her hand, drawing it from under covers so heavy she could barely breathe against their weight. It was reassuring to touch her head and feel it was still there, still of normal size. Yet the touch set off more bursts of pain.

Cool air wafted over her arm, her shoulder, and down under the covers to her breasts. There was something strange in that, though she could not quite think what it was.

Then she had it. There was no clothing covering her body to protect her from the draft of air. She was naked in the bed.

Memory came flooding back. The tower. Giles. The spilled wine.

Drugged. There was no other explanation.

She had read of such things in the newspapers, read of young men who visited the wrong section of New Orleans and wound up drinking some vile mixture that rendered them unconscious. Sometimes they staggered out of a dark alley without their money. Sometimes they wound up in the forecastle of some ship bound for the other side of the world. Sometimes they were found in the river.

Giles. Why had he done it? What had he hoped to gain?

In her drugged state, she had been helpless. He had taken off her clothes. What else had he done? What else had he allowed to be done to her?

She flung back the heavy covers and wrenched herself upright. She stopped as if she had hit a stone wall. Sickness rushed in on her in such a violent spasm that she clamped her hand to her mouth. Carefully she eased from the bed, knelt on the cool wood floor, and felt under the high bed for the chamber pot. She barely found it in time.

When the spasm of sickness had subsided, she sat beside the bed with her head pressed to the mattress, gasping and shaking.

It was the chill of the hard, polished wood floor that roused her. The tower. She was still in the tower. She wasn't blind, it was only that there was no light. Little enough penetrated into the rooms in the daylight hours; there would be none on a rainy night.

How long had she been there? Where was everyone? Had the others gone without her?

She pulled herself to her feet bit by bit. Her hair had been loosened from its braiding and left free. It shifted around her, tickling her bare flesh as she stood slowly erect.

She felt all right within herself. Ill, yes, but there was no pain deep inside, no bruising, no soreness between her thighs. Giles had done no more than remove her clothes.

Why? Why had he felt it necessary to do that? She could only think it was to frighten and humiliate her, or else to keep her confined more easily.

Where was he? Where were the others? Had everyone gone, leaving her alone?

Perhaps she could find a few of the answers if she could see exactly where she was in the tower, and why she was still there.

There was, she thought, a candle and tinderbox on the side table next to one of the fireplace chairs. If she could reach it, she could make a light.

She inched step by slow step alongside the bed, guiding herself by smoothing her fingers over its surface. It took nerve to let go of the bed and launch herself into the darkness. She shuffled over the parquet floor, wincing from the cold and also from the memory of broken glass. She must be far enough to the right of where she had been standing to be safe; she felt nothing underfoot.

She stumbled abruptly over something thick and long and rough. A soft epithet, bitten off in the middle, escaped her. It seemed that she heard a low echo of it, almost like a groan. She plunged forward, throwing out her hands to save herself as she fell. One hand hit a chair arm. Her fingers slipped, then grasped it. Her head hit the chair back and her knee cracked against the floor, but her fall was broken.

She huddled against the chair, fighting tears and nausea and the pounding ache in her head. She strained her ears to hear, but the only sound in the room was her own harsh breathing.

Long moments later she set her teeth and dragged herself up again. Holding onto the chair with one hand, she stretched out the other, groping once more toward the candle.

It was ridiculously easy after that. The sparks she struck from the tinder, brief as they were, showed her where to direct their fall. The points of fire caught the soft, loose cotton batting after no more than the third try. She blew on it quickly to kindle the flame, reaching for the candle at the same time. As the wick caught and yellow light bloomed on top of the taper, she felt as if she had won a great battle. She held the light up in front of her face while a tremulous smile curved her mouth.

There was a soft sound near her feet. She stepped from behind the chair, her wide gaze searching for the source.

At her feet was the thing she had stumbled over, a rolled Turkish rug, one she had last seen in Giles's office. A man was lying with his head and shoulders half out of the roll, as if he had been wrapped in it and was trying to struggle free. His hands were bound in front of him, and there was a gag at his mouth. Blood matted his hair. One eye was blotched purplish blue and swollen shut.

The other eye was open. He was staring up at her as if he had never seen a woman before and had lost hope of ever seeing one.

He was naked, as naked as she was herself.

It was Rowan.

CHAPTER TEN

She blew out the candle.

It wasn't something she thought about. Rather, it was an instinctive reaction to standing exposed and vulnerable before a man who was still a stranger.

She regretted it instantly. Her clothes might be lying somewhere in the room, on the bed, across a chair. She couldn't see them without a light, and it would be too time-consuming to search by feeling around the room bit by bit. She had to hurry. There was no telling how long Rowan had been lying, trussed up and naked, on that cold floor.

"I'm sorry," she said into the darkness. "I'll only be a moment."

There was no reply. She stumbled back to the bed where she separated the woven wool coverlet and duvet from the sheet by touch. She pulled the sheet free and wrapped it around her like a toga, tugging one corner up firmly and tucking it between her breasts and throwing the excess over her shoulder.

Returning to the tinderbox, she lit the taper once more, then moved to touch light to the candles in the floor candelabrum. That done, she went to kneel beside Rowan.

She removed the gag first. As she worked at the knot on the ropes that held his hands, he lay watching her. His gaze, considering, darkly appreciative, moved over her unbound hair, the sheen of candlelight on her uncovered shoulder, the intent look on her face.

Rowan had until short moments before been soundlessly cursing the fates, the tower, his pounding head, and his own stupidity with equal bitterness. He was beginning to feel marginally better. It was possible there would be compensation for this situation. The thought of the form it could take was enough to steal his breath and leave him lying rigorously passive. His voice when he spoke was husky with dryness from the gag. "Your husband," he said, "has a strange sense of humor."

"I don't think he meant to be funny." Katrine barely looked at him. It was impossible, she had discovered, to untie him without touching him. Her fingers brushed continuously over the flat hardness of his chest and abdomen. There was a surface coolness to his skin, but beneath it was the ingrained heat that she had known the night before.

More than that, she could not prevent the guilty curiosity that made her glance at least twice toward the flat expanse of his belly. There was a sharp demarcation line between his dark brown upper body and the paleness below the waist that fascinated her. It was bisected at the navel by a fine line of hair there that trailed from the triangular mat on his chest, disappearing under the rug's rolled edge. The impulse to follow that line with her fingertips, smoothing her palm downward from brown skin to white and under the rug, was so persistent that she bit the inside of her lip to subdue it.

"What was his intention? Was he considerate enough to inform you?" Rowan's inquiry was mild, almost as if he asked from politeness only.

"He is obsessed," she said shortly.

Rowan studied her face. "Ah," he said, "you think we are back to the-stallion-and-the-mare idea, and this is our private paddock with the gate locked behind us?"

Heat flared in her face, spreading through her, settling into the lower part of her body. "I don't know if we're locked in or not."

"We are. I heard the key turn in the main entrance door when they left after carrying me into this room."

She glanced at his face. "They?"

"A pair of field hands, I think. I couldn't see them at the time."

She loosened the last knot and took away the rope, sitting back on her heels. "How long have you been like this?"

"I've been like this, as you put it, since shortly before noon, when I was invited to Giles's office. We sat and had a drink and a discussion regarding my lack of cooperation. I passed out in the middle of it. I was carried here sometime in the afternoon, I think; I woke the first time in another room."

She remembered Giles shutting the door to the room he used as a study. Rowan must have been in there, even when Giles had brought her here. "How did you manage to fall and hit your face if you were sitting down?"

"I didn't. That is—" He stopped, lowering his lashes to shield his eyes.

"What happened then?"

"My own fault. I was careless."

"While bound and gagged?" Suspicion rose inside her at his evasive answer.

"I wasn't gagged at the time."

"If you were awake, it must have taken place here in the tower. Giles. It was Giles, wasn't it."

His battered face expressed only judicious satisfaction. "I don't think he cared for my comments concerning his morals, his ancestry, and especially his behavior toward his wife. He had come from this room, you see, and had the clothes I had last seen you wearing under his arm and a handful of hairpins in his fist."

For Giles to hit a bound man—it was unbelievable, regardless of the provocation. She twisted the rope in her hands as she said, "I think he must be going mad. His illness, possibly, or—or old age."

Rowan, who was rubbing the circulation back into his wrists, reached up and touched his eye. "He still has his strength, at any rate."

"You can't say that the thing he has asked of us, what he has done to us, is normal." She paused as she pushed to her feet and walked to the bed. She picked up the wool coverlet, dragging it off and bundling it in her arms. Over her shoulder she said, "I'm afraid of what he'll do next."

Rowan lay unmoving, staring with febrile concentration at the smoothness of her back, the slender turn of her waist and swell of her hips. The sweet shape of her was shown with such fidelity by the draping of the sheet she had wrapped around her, compared with the bulky clothing she usually wore, that he could not look away. The excess material dragging on the floor behind her should have been ridiculous, but was not. She had the regal grace of some ancient queen, one unafraid of being womanly.

Never, not even when he lay gasping his last with his grandchildren around him, would he forget the moment when Katrine Castlereagh had stepped from behind the chair with the candle in her hand. Brigades of heavenly angels, unadorned and unashamed, would never compensate him for leaving a world where such glory existed. She had taken his breath away, and the loss might well be permanent.

There hovered in his mind a suggestion, one that he was not sure, in his present state, was not dictated by pure, untrammeled need. He weighed it, abandoned it, then retrieved it again.

"There is an easy way to be certain your husband regains his senses."

She turned slowly to face him. Her face mirrored appalled anger as she said, "You mean—comply with his wishes after all?"

"Would it be so terrible?" He waited with his breath suspended in his chest for her answer.

Her eyes were huge and dark with accusation in her pale face. She opened her arms and let the coverlet drop before turning sharply and walking away. The heavy cover settled in a billowing heap. It was a good six feet from where he lay.

Rowan looked from the cover to her stiff back. A smile of purest admiration came and went across his face. He said, "I take it you don't find the idea agreeable."

She turned on him. "Am I to be cowed by fear? Should I go against everything I believe in just to save myself a little discomfort?"

"This tower is a fair prison; its possibilities struck me the first time I saw it. We could be here a long time."

Rowan pushed himself up to a sitting position. He ached in every joint and muscle, as if he had been kicked. No doubt he had been, though the hard floor had not helped matters. Clenching his teeth, he began to work his legs out of the folded rug with a total disregard for his state of undress.

"You can cover yourself," Katrine said in haste, flinging out a hand to indicate the heap of blue wool.

Rowan arched a brow in the direction she indicated. The covering was, in truth, close enough that he could drag it toward him if he wanted to stretch for it. "I'm sure I could," he said in droll appeal, "if I could only reach it."

He inched further from under his rug. Katrine spun around with her back to him once more.

"My feet are still bound," he said in tones of injured dignity, flinging out an arm to snag the coverlet at the same time. "I also have a little trouble with my sore shoulder. Help would be nice."

She hugged her arms together, hunching her shoulders. With sudden decision, she whirled and started forward. She stopped as her gaze landed on his nude body stretched out at her feet.

Rowan gave her a slow grin as he drew the coverlet toward him and twitched it into place across his body.

Her sheet had loosened with her unconsidered movements. She snatched it into place, holding it with one arm as she scowled at him. She looked lovely with the rise of heated color across her cheekbones.

"You may think this is funny now," she said, "but you'll see it differently when Giles tries to have you killed."

"Is that likely?" Under the coverlet's concealment, he hauled himself clear of the stiff rug and drew up his feet, beginning to untie the rope around his ankles.

"He practically promised it, because he seemed to have the idea that you might speak of—this."

"He thought I might dine out on the tale of my amorous nocturnal visitation privileges with his wife? His good opinion of my manners is overwhelming. Not to mention his ideas about my taste in conversation."

"He thought you might make him out to be a fool with the story of how he was duped by the two of us."

"Rather than describing him as a willing cuckold? You'll forgive me if I fail to see how one is worse than the other." He heard the bite in his own tone, but refused to soften it.

She clasped her arms around herself, as if the chill in the room was making itself felt. "There need not be a reason that makes sense, or so it seems. If there can be any just cause for agreeing to what Giles expects, then it must be this one, to preserve your life. If—if there should be a child afterward, then he will feel safe, since he can be certain you will remain silent for its sake."

He flung the rope he had loosened from him. He rose slowly to his feet then, pulling the coverlet with him like an Indian chief drawing his blanket around him. Facing her with as much pride as he could muster under the circumstances, he said, "You are offering to exchange your honor for my life?"

"Is that so amazing? You were offering yours just now for no more than my comfort."

"It isn't," he said distinctly, "the same."

She did not quite meet his gaze as she asked, "Why not? It isn't as if you asked to be forced into my bed."

The image she conjured up did nothing for the ache in his loins, not to mention the blow to his self-esteem. "Not in the way you mean," he said softly, "but I would not have refused an enticement. It was at your request that I agreed to refrain from what was expected of us. There is no dishonor for me in bowing once again to the wishes of a lady."

He watched her confusion with a species of painful pleasure. Her understanding was quick, however; he had to give her that.

"If there is no dishonor, and you are not—not unwilling, then only my scruples prevent you from—"

"From making love to you this moment? Yes, and my pride."

"Pride?"

"I object, you see," he said softly, "to being responsible for such a sacrifice."

She lifted her chin. "It is Giles who would be responsible; you would only be another pawn in his game."

His voice was dry as he answered. "I object to that most of all."

"It didn't seem to trouble you when you first agreed," she said, frowning.

"Before, I was acting of my own will, for reasons of my own choosing. I refuse to be coerced with threats."

She pressed her lips together. He followed that small movement with razor-keen interest. It seemed he could still taste the sweetness of her, feel the petal softness of her mouth, sense once more the delicate, yielding ardor with which she had accepted his kiss the night before. The tender shape of her breast, its perfection in his hand, the tight bud of her nipple nudging his sensitive palm were etched into his memory. She had allowed him greater liberties than he had dared dream. Her reasons had been plain, but she need not have been quite so compliant, surely.

Reasons. God, but he was beginning to hate the word.

What he would not give simply to sweep her up and take her away. Forget his brother's death. Forget her marriage to another man. Forget the strange request that had brought them together and the pact that kept them apart.

He could take her to his mother at the plantation just above New Orleans, or even, possibly, to England. Would she go? If he asked it, would she leave everything to come away with him?

He was the one who was insane.

La belle dame sans merci. He was in danger of forgetting.

"So," Katrine said, assuming a brisk air, "we are in agreement to defy Giles still. What now?"

He eyed her for a sober moment, then a slow smile curved his mouth. "I vote to find something else to wear. There's a certain ancient elegance to your costume, but mine is drafty."

The armoire was empty, and so were the various chests and boxe in the interconnected study and dressing room. There was nothing in the tower that might serve as covering other than a few lengths of Turkish toweling. Abandoning the search, they concentrated on matters even more essential.

There was a plentiful supply of firewood in a chest beside the fireplace to be used to supplement the steam heat rising from the basement. The water pitchers in the bedchamber and dressing room were full, and could be refilled at need from the fountain. A bowl of fruit and nuts sat on a side table in the study, along with a wooden platter of bread and cheese and fried apple pies covered by a cloth that had, at one time, been dampened to keep the food fresh. They would not freeze to death or succumb to thirst or hunger.

They were, however, well and truly imprisoned. Not only

was the entrance door locked, but a massive bolt had been thrust through the iron strap handle and fastened in place; they could see through the crack. The only windows were the arrow slits that were far too small for even a child to slip through.

In the conservatory, Rowan held the candlestick up, looking up into the massive cupola. The glass that encircled it was in small squares set within larger frames that did not open. Even if they had, the cupola was some forty feet above the lower-floor level and twenty-five feet above the gallery, with sheer stone walls soaring up to support it.

They were interrupted in their explorations by the shrill ringing of a bell. The minute Katrine heard the first chiming note, she knew what it was, what it meant.

There was a dumbwaiter in the butler's pantry next to the study. Rising through a shaft from the basement by a system of ropes and pulleys, it had been used to deliver food and drink to Giles without disturbing him any more than was necessary. It was hidden behind a panel in the wall, with an opening too small to admit much more than a loaded serving tray.

The ringing of the bell attached to the pulley rope was the signal that something was going to be sent upward. This time it indicated the arrival of their dinner.

Katrine removed the tray with its silver cover. Peering down the shaft, she called out. There was a dull silence. Then a woman's voice answered, echoing oddly up the narrow way. It was Delphia.

"Thank heaven," Katrine said. "What is happening? Where are the others?"

"Everyone is gone, Madam Katrine."

"Then you can let us out. Go and find some of the hands and have them break down the door." Katrine listened with concentration for the answer.

"I can't do it. Master Giles's orders were that you must stay up there until he gets back. I'm to bring you whatever you want or like to eat, anything reasonable to use to pass the time, but that's all."

"I insist, Delphia! You have to help us."

"I can't, Madam Katrine, really I can't. Master Giles told me not even to talk to you."

Giles was cunning, Katrine thought. He knew she would try to persuade her maid to do her bidding. There was a touch at her shoulder. She turned her head to look inquiringly at Rowan.

He held the candle in his hand to one side, leaning his head into the shaft opening. "Omar, Delphia, where is he?"

"He's in the plantation jail, Master Rowan, though it took six men to put him there."

"He's not hurt?"

"Barring a few bruises. His appetite is in fine shape; he's had six meals today and two gallons of coffee. He's to stay where he is for now, so he won't be giving you a hand."

Rowan withdrew his head and turned away with an abrupt twist that nearly extinguished the candle and sent his coverlet swirling around him like some emperor's cloak. Katrine watched him a long moment before she turned back to the dumbwaiter shaft.

"Why, Delphia? Why are you following my husband's orders instead of doing what I ask?"

The other woman's voice rose an octave in protest. "It would be as much as my skin's worth to go against him, you know that."

"Surely not." The house slaves at Arcadia were never whipped; only the threat of being sent to the fields was enough to keep them in line. Regardless, there had been a few occasions in the past years when Giles had ordered punishments for field hands and watched them carried out. She could not blame Delphia for being afraid.

The maid said, "Master Giles swore to me that no harm

would come to you from this. And he made mention of freedom, if I see that you are where he left you when he returns." Her voice rose a note. "I'm sorry, Madam Katrine."

It was a betrayal, yet how could she be faulted? Katrine turned away. A thought caught her, turned her back. "Clothes, Delphia; we must have something to wear."

"Master Giles's instructions were strict about that. I dare not."

Delphia's voice sounded as if she was leaving the basement. Katrine raised her voice. "Something, anything. A nightgown. A single pair of pantaloons."

"A guitar," Rowan said behind her. "Your needlework? Books? Pen and paper?"

"You heard?" Katrine called down the shaft.

"I'll see what I can do," the maid answered. "I'm leaving now, and I'm locking the panel down here behind me."

They heard the light click of the latch followed by the thud of the outer basement door. The noise of that heavier locking mechanism being turned into place funneled up to them. Delphia's footsteps crunched away. She was gone.

Katrine stood with a frown engraved between her brows. Delphia. She had thought they were as close as sisters. There had been so many moments of shared laughter and pain, so many memories in common. When had it all changed? How had it happened without her knowing? If something so seemingly permanent could change overnight, what else might not do the same?"

"We may as well eat," Rowan said. "There is a certain attraction to starving just to be obstinate, but it might be inconvenient."

Her dark brown eyes showed her hurt and misery. "I'm not hungry."

"Nor am I. But it will pass the time."

Katrine picked up the laden tray by way of answer, and

nodded for him to light the way through the door that connected the study with the bedchamber. He hesitated, his gaze centered on the heavy tray, as if he would insist on relieving her of it. As he was using one hand for the candlestick and the other to hold his coverlet, it was difficult to see how he meant to manage it. Catching her speculative gaze, he smiled with grim humor and did as she asked.

There was a fire laid in the fireplace. Rowan touched the light from his candle to the tinder left ready. While it caught, they set out the meal on the table between the two wing-back chairs.

Katrine seated herself before the hot potato soup edged with butter and speckled with pepper, also the roast chicken and warm bread and butter, the fruits and wine. She picked up her cream soup spoon, turning it in her hands.

Her voice was cramped as she spoke. "I should beg your pardon, I suppose, for doubting you about Delphia."

"There's no need." The words were even.

"If I had listened, we might not be here."

He gave her a considering look. "I prefer you outraged and defiant, I think, instead of contrite."

"I am trying," she said with irritation flaring in her gaze, "to tell you that you were right."

"Since I know it, I don't require to hear it, especially if it's going to turn you into a drab female who plays with her soup."

It was generous of him, she thought. Or was it only condescending? She could not decide. While she was trying he spoke again.

"How long, exactly, will this hunting party last?"

"It depends on the sport. A few days, three or four, if it's bad, as long as a week if it's good."

"A week," he repeated, his gaze resting on the ornate brass grille that covered an opening for the steam vent. "Isn't it lucky that we weren't looking forward to the trip."

"Weren't you?" She dipped her spoon into her soup and began to eat as she waited for his answer.

"Cooped up on a steamboat with dozens of people I hardly know, expected to traipse up and down corridors in the midnight hours to play at paying gallant attention to my host's wife? I had been searching for excuses for two days."

"Had you? I thought such activity was common at house parties among England's upper crust?"

"That's different. There, they know each other exceptionally well." His green gaze rested on her face with a trace of deprecating humor in its subterranean depths.

Bit by bit, as he attended to the business of eating, reaching for his wineglass, handing her the bread plate, his coverlet had slipped from his shoulders. It had settled somewhere near his waist, most of it behind him, framing him.

The firelight gleamed across the strong planes of his face, leaving the bruised side in shadow. It sculpted the smooth bulk of his shoulders, shining on the bandaging that still wrapped one, and glinted with a silken sheen in the curling tangle of hair that ranged over his breastbone. The flat expanse of his abdomen and ridged muscles of his arms rippled as he moved. His hands had the swift and tensile precision of touch of an artisan who carves in marble and stone.

She was dining with a naked man. If she had a shred of maidenly delicacy, she would shrink from the ordeal. She did not. It was disconcerting to realize how quickly she had become accustomed to the thought.

His presence, boldly, carelessly nude, was another matter. It was difficult to keep from looking at him. More than that, she felt an almost irresistible urge to reach out and touch the taut molding of his chest and arms to see if he was as warm as he looked, sitting there bathed in firelight. Or as warm as she remembered.

They finished their roast chicken in silence and set their

plates aside. Rowan offered her the fruit, then took a large pear for himself. They both reached for the silver fruit knife at the same time.

Katrine felt her fingertips graze his hand, and she drew back as if she had been stung. He froze, his gaze probing, intent, as he held her wide gaze. Beside them, the fire crackled. The candle on the small table guttered on its wick.

Rowan sat back slowly in his chair and braced his hands on the table's edge. "If this is going to be at all bearable," he said, his voice deep with strain, "we are going to have to accept each other, become used to each other. We will be the ones to go mad if we try constantly to avoid every touch, every glance, every unconsidered word or gesture."

"That's all very well," she said, "but what if we can't help it?"

"We can. All that's required is to behave naturally."

"Naturally," she repeated, her tone hollow.

"As if we were friends or, if you prefer, brother and sister. This isn't a bad prison, as prisons go. We have food, drink, a measure of comfort. The time we will be here has a limit. There is no one to oversee our actions or force us to perform."

"That is what Giles is counting on, that given propinquity with an illusion of freedom, we will—behave naturally."

"Then it's up to us to disappoint him."

He said the words so simply. Yet there they sat in their near nakedness, alone in the dark tower, while the rain drummed on the glass-roofed cupola beyond the open bedchamber door and the great bed loomed behind them.

As she remained stiffly upright in her chair, he tilted his head. "You have to trust me first, of course."

"I don't distrust you," she said.

"That isn't quite the same thing, but it will do. What is it then?"

She wasn't sure. She only knew that what he was outlining

would not be easy. She had to say something, however. She opened her mouth, and what came out was, "We have no sword to put between us."

"No," he said deliberately, "but I don't think it was particularly helpful anyway."

She stared at him. Had he been awake this morning? Did he know that she had spent some unknown portion of the night before cuddled against him? How could he, and still meet her eyes with that benign and limpid gaze?

Rowan sat quite still while his fingertips pressed into the walnut of the table as if he meant to leave his prints there. She did not know what was in her face: The memories of the morning. The fear of losing control of herself in the night. The raw need to abandon what had become a burden. The aching knowledge that she had no protection from him, and was not sure she wished for any.

She could not know. If she even so much as guessed, then he was lost.

And so was she.

CHAPTER ELEVEN

When the meal was over and Katrine had stacked their dishes back on the tray, Rowan returned it to the dumbwaiter. He would send everything back down to the basement and check to see if Delphia had sent up any of the things they had requested. Katrine, taking advantage of his absence, washed her face and hands with water in the pitcher and bowl. Pouring the water that was left into the chamber pot, she took it away downstairs to the darkened conservatory where she emptied it into the floor drain that was used for washing down the marble floor, and that emptied into the lake.

She stood for a moment, staring up at the cupola where lightning flashed in a muted glow now and then, as if it was some distance away. The rain had slackened; it could barely be heard above the splashing of the fountain. The air was growing cooler, for there were small eddies of steam rising from the warm water in the fountain's basin.

Who was stoking the fire in the basement's boiler? she wondered. Was it Delphia, or were there others who were allowed access to the lower room? In ordinary times, the head gardener tended the plants, lighted the wall lamps at nightfall, kept watch on the water flowing from an underground spring into the boiler, and kept the fire going under it during cool weather. In ordinary times.

It was pleasant in the warm, moist space with its smells of earth and greenery. The darkness enfolded her like a soft presence, soothing the restless trepidation inside her. The impulse to remain there, hiding as in sanctuary, was strong inside her. That would be the cowardly way, however. Besides, the safety was only an illusion; the person she most needed to hide from was locked up with her.

Returning upstairs, she put the chamber pot in the dressing room. She was standing with her back to the fire, warming her hands held behind her, when Rowan rejoined her.

"Clothes," she exclaimed as she saw what was in his hands.

He gave her a crooked smile. "Of a sort," he said as he tossed something soft and white at her.

She saw what he meant at once. Delphia had sent her the nightgown she had mentioned, but it was the oldest Katrine owned, one she was sure she had told Delphia to dispose of long ago. It had lost its ribbon tie at the neck, was raveling at the hem, and its lightweight muslin had grown thin from many washings. It was not quite opaque, except in dim light. Thankfully the light in the tower was seldom bright.

Her attention was caught as Rowan laid a musical instrument on the seat of a wing-back chair. It was not a guitar, she saw, but rather a mandolin. Beside it, he placed a bundle she recognized as the Berlin work she had been planning to take on the steamboat. Then he shook out the garments he had been given, holding them up with one hand.

There was an old-fashioned frilled dress shirt with full sleeves and frayed holes where studs should be used to hold the front together, and a pair of ancient knee breeches that looked as if they might not even cover his knees.

Katrine reached out to touch the shirt. "These things came

out of the ragbag, I think. I recognize the shirt as one of Giles's that Cato cleared out of an old armoire last year."

"At least it's something," he said. "My baggage must have gone to the steamboat with the rest."

"Mine also, but not my entire wardrobe." Katrine's voice was as caustic as the look in her eyes.

Rowan studied the nightgown. An appreciative light rose in his face. "I expect your Delphia means well."

"I wish I might be sure," Katrine answered. "She could as well mean the opposite. For both of us."

"Then she'll be amazed when it comes to nothing." Fishing in a breeches pockets, he brought out several items. He held up each of them in turn to show her. "Two combs, one tortoiseshell, one ivory. Two cakes of soap scented with lavender, a packet of needles, an extra mandolin string. The woman is a treasure."

"If she was a treasure, she would unlock the door."

"That's asking too much, apparently." He frowned at the clothes in his hands. "I don't know about you, but I feel the need for a bath after that gritty rug. I saw a slipper tub in the dressing room, I think, and a bucket in the butler's pantry. I could bring up warm water from the fountain for a bath when you're ready."

"You don't have to do that; I can care for myself." The words carried the remainder of an edge.

His gaze was considering. "As always, there would be no obligation."

"Are you certain?" she said.

He walked away, out the door, into the study and beyond. She heard the deliberate tread of each footstep and knew that she had, finally, angered him. He returned a short time later. He was wearing the dress breeches and the shirt open to the waist, and carrying a wooden bucket of water with steam curling from its surface. He dumped it into the tin bath in the dressing room and went away again. He mounted the stairs five times more with water, working in grim silence, ignoring protests. Finally, when the water was within scant inches of the bath's rim, he set the bucket down in the dressing room and took himself back down the stairs in the direction of the conservatory.

Katrine waited to be certain he did not mean to return. Then she went into the dressing room, closed the door, and began to unwind her sheet. There was no point in letting pique deprive her of the results of his labor.

She heard the thunder as she lay in the bath. It seemed the rainstorm was gathering strength again. Now and then lightning flashed through the arrow slits, brief, truncated gleams. She soaped herself with the scented cake left beside the tub with the bucket, then rinsed the residue away. She stood up then, reaching for the toweling she had placed ready.

A few moments later she walked from the dressing room. Her nightgown clung in places to her still-damp body, but she felt fresher and a little less unsettled. She had a long skein of hair drawn over her shoulder, trying to comb it free of tangles. She blinked as a bright flash of lightning flared, the light coming through the open doorway from the cupola. Thunder rolled immediately behind it. Drawn by the storm's furor, she moved in the direction of the gallery beyond the room.

Rain was pounding down, running over the glass in spreading sheets that shone blue gray in the lightning's glare. She shrank a little as thunder crashed directly overhead, making the glass above rattle. It sounded as if the entire cupola might come crashing down into the conservatory. She glanced down at the palms and tree ferns that stood serene and ghostlike in the lower darkness, lifting their fronds toward the rain so far beyond their reach. They should, she thought, be thrashing in the wet night instead of held captive in this protective prison.

Lightning flashed once more. Her gaze was caught by a tall shape among the greenery. Her eyes widened and she stood transfixed.

Rowan stood in the water-filled basin of the fountain with

his face turned up to the arching fall of warm water that poured from a nymph's two-handled wine jar, the pipes played by a seated satyrlike Pan, the mouths of swans and lambs. His eyes were closed and his hands hung in loose-limbed grace at his side. The water running over his body glistened in the lightning's glare. It silvered the shaping of muscle and bone, the planes and hollows and shimmering, sculpted turns. Perfect in his pure, male beauty, he looked like some ancient god among the nymphs, Mercury perhaps, molded in precious metal and with his winged feet held fast in splattering quicksilver. Steam drifted around him like undulating wisps of Olympus's clouds, concealing and revealing.

Something shifted inside Katrine, some vital image of herself, some knowledge of what she could feel and become. She had never admired the male body before, never had cause to admit it as admirable. She had brushed past engravings in books of old Greek and Roman statues with only the most furtive of glances, since staring at them, considering them even in an aesthetic light, was not ladylike, not acceptable. Musetta's concentration on men's bodies, such as at the fencing match, had always made her uncomfortable. She had not wanted to see them in terms of their physical parts.

This was different. She had, she recognized with honesty, been aware of Rowan's muscular strength and the agility of his movements for days. She knew he was a man handsome beyond most, attractive in feature as well as form. She had come to appreciate the mind that guided the body, its acuteness and complexity and swift calculation.

She had just never put all of his attributes together in her mind. She had resisted that coalescence, and with good reason. To recognize it was dangerous, not only to her peace of mind, but to her innermost self. He was formidable, more daunting, in truth, than she had known all those days ago when she had labeled him perfect.

She was not perfect, far from it. If she were, she would not be standing there staring at a naked man.

Katrine retreated a step from the balcony railing, making ready to draw back inside the bedchamber. The soft footfall in the clatter of rain, or perhaps some shift in the candlelight behind her, caught Rowan's attention. He opened his eyes, his gaze focused on the exact place she stood.

Still, utterly still, he stood, though something rose in slow heat to become a conflagration behind his eyes. Lightning limned his face in blue and gold with the silver, and crackled over his wide shoulders like the reflections from the darts of hell. Thunder shook the tower and rippled the water about his calves. Yet he made no effort to cover himself or turn from her. His gaze, striking across the dusky, steam-filled distance that separated them, scorched the air.

Katrine felt scarlet suffuse her face. Heat burst inside her, racing through her veins with a painful excitement. It gathered in the lower part of her body, throbbing so that she felt languorous and heavy. The urge to walk down the stairs, to move toward him, taking off her nightgown as she went, was so strong that the effort to resist caused perspiration to dew her skin. She caught her breath with a sharp gasp. As if released by the sound, she whirled around and fled.

Inside the room, she stood listening to the panicked thumping of her heart and wondering what in the name of heaven she was going to say to him when he came back upstairs. The answer that came to her in that same moment was simple. Nothing, she would say nothing if she could help it. It might be spineless, but she could not endure sitting and exchanging polite comments with a man who had discomposed her so thoroughly. And if he were to make some impolite comment concerning what had just happened, she would be able to endure that even less.

She climbed into bed, flouncing over to the far side next to the wall. Turning her back to the room and to the candlelight, she pulled up the cover and resolutely closed her eyes.

She never heard him come to bed. The long day, the drug still floating in her veins and allied to an excess of emotion hit her like a blow. When next she lifted her lashes, she discovered sunlight streaming into the room, marking the floor with long, yellow gashes. Rowan was lying beside her with his head resting in his hand while he watched her sleep.

She felt the impact of his lucid, inquiring gaze in the center of her being. It sent her tumbling away from him, scrambling for the far side of the bed where she had begun the night.

He reached out negligently, easily, and clamped his fingers on her arm. The grasp stopped her with a suddenness that sent her hair whipping across her face and drove the blood from her lips, leaving them pale and trembling.

He released her with a sudden opening of his fingers. He stared at his hand for a wondering instant, then pushed it under the cover, out of sight. A small frown pleated his brows as he said, "My abject apologies. I didn't mean to hurt you."

Katrine believed him. That belief dissolved the fear inside her. It also permitted her brain that had ceased working to begin again. "You meant to stop me, and you did," she said. "Why?"

"Insofar as I can understand it myself," he said, contemplating the tangled mass of her hair as she dragged it out of her face and over one shoulder, "I objected to having you run away as if you had found a monster in your bed."

She was no more anxious to meet his eyes than he was to allow her that privilege. "I was—startled. With no one here to spy on us, I wasn't sure we would be sharing a bed."

"It's the only one available, and I had had enough of lying on the floor. Besides, you can hardly claim there's anything strange in having me close by. Try again."

"It takes longer than a night or two to grow used to waking beside a man, especially one who is a stranger."

"You didn't try to run from me yesterday morning."

"That was different," she said, swallowing hard.

"In what way? Because you woke first? Or was it because I had not yet frightened the wits out of you by being careless enough to display my nakedness instead of hiding it?"

There was something in his steady regard that suggested he knew that she had spent much of the night in his arms. She was still digesting this suspicion when the sense of his last words struck her. The impulse for denial was instant. She said, "I wasn't frightened."

"No? Then why didn't you join me in the fountain?"

"I had already had my bath." It was not an answer and she knew it. The scathing irritation in his voice as he answered was no surprise.

"Besides which, it might not have been either genteel or wise?"

"You left out the question of desire," she said, then closed her eyes in despair as she realized the trap she had made for herself.

"I'm glad you mentioned it," he said. "If you didn't have the desire to join me, if you were unmoved by any such thought, then why are you leaping out of bed like a terrified virgin now?"

There was a strained silence. Finally she said, "All right, I am afraid of you. It isn't what you may do that I fear, however, but what I may be led to do by my own wayward impulses while we are in such close quarters. Is that what you wanted to hear?"

"No," he said. His eyes burned with emerald clarity into hers and his voice was fretted as a worn fiddle string.

Her irritation flared at his answer. "Then you shouldn't have asked."

The briefest intimation of a smile touched a corner of his mouth. "I wouldn't have missed hearing it for all the gold in Queen Victoria's coffers, but it makes it harder."

"What?" She could no more stop herself from asking than she could stop breathing.

"Keeping my distance."

He left the bed then, throwing back the covers and swinging his long legs to the floor. When he stood, he made no attempt to conceal the fact that he had been sleeping in his usual costume, his skin. He moved with a leisurely step to where his breeches and shirt lay over a chair. He had pulled both on and begun pushing the tail of the shirt into the top of the skintight silk breeches before he glanced toward the bed.

Katrine lay studying her fingernails, smoothing a roughened cuticle. She wished she dared meet his gaze. She didn't. Her peripheral vision, however, was excellent. Not that she needed it. Her memory of how he had looked in the fiery glow of lightning was also good.

The bruising on his face seemed better; the reddish-purple color was fading and the swelling had gone. Also, he had removed the bandaging on his shoulder, perhaps because it would have been soaked with water as he bathed last night anyway. Since he had dressed without reapplying it, she had to suppose it was not necessary. There was a long, slashing scar on his leg, but the edges were closed, beginning to look like a tight seam. He apparently had remarkable healing power.

He was altogether remarkable. What other man would have left her alone in the bed after her disastrous admission just now, especially after being given carte blanche to behave toward her as he pleased? What other man would accept being locked away in this tower without railing at her for being the cause? What other man could or would endure being slashed, thrown from his horse, drugged and beaten for her sake, and say not a word to force her to recognize it?

He had his reasons that had little to do with her, she knew, and yet she thought he was paying a high price for them. She felt the guilt he would not voice.

The ringing of the dumbwaiter bell interrupted her thoughts. Rowan, who had moved to mend the fire, stood up from where he knelt before the fireplace.

"Finally," he said as he strode toward the door. "I hope the coffee is hot."

The day wore on. They sat before the fire as it continued unseasonably cold. They could hear the wind sweeping around the tower's eaves, feel an occasional draft, but they were comfortable enough. Luncheon came and went. Afterward Katrine made a few stitches in her Berlin work. Rowan read for a while, then picked up the mandolin and tuned it. He played a series of ballads and sprightly pieces before laying the instrument aside. Clasping his hands behind his head, stretching his long legs out before him, he sat staring into the flames that tongued their way up the chimney.

There was a rough, unused quality to his voice when he spoke at last. "Tell me," he said, "how you came to marry Giles Castlereagh."

"Surely you can guess?" She spoke without looking up from her sewing.

He turned his head toward her. "I would have said so a few short days ago; now I'm not so sure. Tell me."

"It isn't a very interesting story, not really," she said, letting the Berlin work fall to her lap. "My mother married her childhood sweetheart. He was a little reckless, a little wild. Six weeks after the wedding, he rode home drunk in a pouring rain. He died of pneumonia four days later. Within the year, she married my father, perhaps in an attempt to forget. She died of a fever after I was born, or so everyone was told. My old nurse always said it was of a broken heart that my father could not mend."

She waited for some comment, but he made none, only watching her with dark, intent eyes. She swallowed a little before she went on. "I always had the feeling that my father thought my mother had failed him and deserted both of us. It seemed that I needed to make it up to him somehow. I was a dutiful daughter, and as loving as I knew how to be, but it was never enough. I wasn't my mother, and I wasn't a son who could carry on his name. My father had been sent to England for his education. He met Giles at Oxford and they became close friends. They kept up a correspondence for years; my father missed England and Giles was fascinated by all he heard about Feliciana. When Giles was forced to leave England, he bought the land here at Arcadia which ran beside my father's property. The two of them spoke often of uniting the two places. Giles was considered a fine catch; he had inherited wealth, ties to an old English family, fine property. When I was of age, the wedding was arranged."

"You could have refused," Rowan suggested.

"I suppose I might have. But I had hardly spoken to another man, was allowed no other beau except Giles. The marriage was spoken of as an accomplished fact; one of the most vivid memories of my thirteenth birthday is my nurse telling me of the man I was to marry and the splendid house Giles was building for me at Arcadia. More than that, my father was not the kind of man to accept defiance. I would have had to leave his house, and where was I to go?"

"So Giles waited years for you, pinned his own hopes of a son on you, and then nothing came of it."

"It was a bitter disappointment. He insisted we go to doctors in New Orleans, in New York, even in Vienna. Nothing helped. The problem, they told him in Europe, was his, but something in his mind instead of with his body. It might, they thought, have something to do with his failed elopement in England."

"In what way?" Rowan asked with a lifted brow.

"I don't know, Giles would never talk about it. He just seemed to accept matters for some time, then he hit on the remedy that you know."

Rowan was silent while he stared into the fire. Finally he

said, "I have been wondering about Terence. Was he, by chance, tournament king last year?"

"He and Alan shared the honors between them." She could see the trend of his thoughts, but could do nothing to change them.

"Is it possible that Giles could have approached my brother with his remedy? Could it be that Terence refused and, like the idealistic young idiot that he was, said something that Giles perceived as a threat?"

"So that Giles killed him to keep him quiet?"

His voice overrode her rejoinder. "Or forced a meeting on the field of honor for that purpose."

She looked away from him. "I don't know."

"You don't know," he repeated in tones of disbelief.

She gave him a trenchant look. "Men don't, as a rule, announce these meetings to women; I don't know why you should think this was any different. All I can really tell you is that your brother was found dead of a bullet wound beside the lake. How he came to be there, who shot him and when, are questions for which I have no answers. No one does."

"If it was a duel, it must have been a private affair, without seconds or a physician present. If it had been otherwise, there would have been someone to carry him into the house, to see to his wound. It follows then, that whoever is at fault is a sneaking coward and the next thing to a murderer, since he ran away and left him there."

"If it was a duel," she said, repeating his words as he had her own.

"Yes," he agreed in hard tones.

He pushed to his feet and left her then. There was in his movement a controlled impatience that suggested he was feeling the confinement, that he felt the need to be doing something, anything. Katrine was only surprised that it had taken this long.

He did not return for some time. He was, she thought,

prowling the tower, looking for a way out. She could hear him wandering through the rooms, opening and closing doors, going up and down the stairs. There were odd thumps and bangings. Once, when she walked out onto the gallery overlooking the conservatory, she saw him halfway up the high wall below the cupola, clinging to the minute ledges in the stone with fingers and bare toes.

She didn't stop to think. Raising her voice so that it echoed in startled dismay around the walls, she called, "What are you doing? Come down before you kill yourself."

He turned his head to glance at her, then let go and leaped down, landing in a catlike crouch. Straightening, he walked toward her with predatory grace.

Something about the way he moved made her wary. She backed away out of his path as he came nearer; she couldn't help herself. His mouth and the skin about his eyes tightened as he saw it. His lips opened, as if he meant to explain, give information, something. But he closed them again and brushed past her without speaking.

By nightfall of the third day, Rowan was tired. The condition was deliberate.

He had investigated every single panel of glass panes in the cupola and found them firmly embedded in wood and stone. He had tried each arrow slit-window for size and tested the fastening of the great door a dozen times over. He had questioned Delphia about Omar and sent messages designed to ease his manservant's mind and keep him from growing restless, and had acquired some ease of mind himself from the fact that many of the comforts and dishes of food brought by Katrine's maid could only have been inspired by the big Arabian's suggestion.

He had played cards with Katrine and made up word games to amuse her. He had pretended to read books he found in the study while watching her frown in concentration while she read or plied her needle. Until sheer, gut-wringing lust sent him away from her to try the door and climb the walls again.

Nothing stopped the turning of his mind or the memories.

He did not want to think of Terence being offered the privileges he himself had been given but could not take. Brotherly considerations did not extend far enough to make that idea endurable.

He did not want to remember opening his eyes while in the fountain to see Katrine in her nightgown on the gallery above with the candlelight behind her. He did not want to, but he did.

The perfect symmetry of her form from head to foot, every delicious curve and mysterious hollow, had been outlined in a nimbus of red-gold flame from the candlelight behind her. Her hair flowing around her like a living cape had been touched with fire. The insidious seduction of her presence had been so strong that he had been unable to move, incapable of thought, unwilling to break the alluring spell of it.

He had wanted her then as he had wanted few things in his life. The virulence of the longing had stopped his breath, torn his heart, altered some basic rhythm of his being. To be forced to mount the stairs and climb into her bed, then lie there unmoving had shredded his will and left his guts in strings fit only to make a grandmother's garters.

That was why he had flown off the handle when she leaped up and tried to leave the bed next morning. It was why he had spoken with such a whiplash in his voice.

Then later he had sat trying to distract himself, doing his best to make sensible conversation while Katrine sat within arm's length with the coral-rose aureoles of her breasts making tender shadows under the muslin of the damnably thin nightgown. That garment was an incitement rather than a barrier. No doubt it was meant to be.

There was a certain charm in her lack of awareness of how little was concealed by what she was wearing. She had no mirror, of course, other than a small square hanging on the dressing-room wall, could not see herself as he saw her. There was, in any case, next to nothing that could be done about it.

He had done what he could, forcing himself to put distance between them in order to keep his hands to himself. He had stayed away from her as much as possible, tired himself as thoroughly as he was able in their confinement.

It irritated him that Katrine was so jumpy whenever he came near. At the same time he couldn't blame her; she had reason.

This wasn't going to work, their close incarceration together. Giles Castlereagh was a clever man.

There was a solution. The problem would be persuading Katrine to see the sense of it. That was, if she could be brought to listen to him in the first place. She could be forgiven, certainly, if she thought that any advantage would be his. He wasn't at all sure she wouldn't be right.

It would not be the first time that prudence and self-interest had gone hand in hand. Nor would it be the first time that a man had tried to persuade a woman to do what he wanted for reasons that had nothing to do with the well-being of either of them.

CHAPTER TWELVE

Katrine was afraid of something in his manner that evening. It was as if he had come to a decision that, once taken, instilled the hardness of purpose in his face and his heart and, perhaps, even his soul. She sat across from him at the table that held their dinner and watched him from under her lashes while she put food in her mouth and swallowed and forked up more. She thought of asking what was wrong, but refrained. It wasn't fear that held her tongue but the uncomfortable suspicion that she knew what troubled him.

It was her. She had caused him to be caught in this trap. She had cost him his freedom and embroiled him in a strange affair that had caused him injury and threatened his life. Her constant presence that curtailed his privacy and robbed him of comfort also annoyed him. He wanted to be rid of her company and away from Arcadia. That he could do neither was a slowly festering sore inside him. She didn't blame him for it, but she would not ask about it. She didn't want to hear him explain or else watch his struggles as he sought some answer for her other than the truth.

He had finished his meal. He leaned back in his chair, cracking pecans in his strong hands and eating the nut meats with generous sips of burgundy. The flames in the fireplace beside them leaped in miniature in his wine glass, giving the rich red liquid a glowing heart of fire.

He glanced at her from time to time, his gaze resting on her face and shoulders above the neckline of her nightgown. It strayed once to the rippling sheen of her hair that trailed alongside her arms and over the soft wool of her shawl. His gaze was dark and secretive, as if involved in thought processes that required his complete inward attention.

Katrine wished he would say something, anything, wished she could think of some idle comment to ease the tension that held them. Neither happened.

The sharp crack of the pecan shells as he crushed them one after the other made her wince, then stare fixedly at the growing pile of hulls before him. The silence, broken only by his near-vicious destruction of the pecans and by the flutter and pop of the fire, made her want to jump up and leave the room. She raised her eyes to his in a long, considering look that was laced around the edges with appeal.

Rowan drained his glass and set it down. He raked the pecan hulls from the table into his hand and pitched them into the fire. Dusting his fingertips with precision, he said in straitened tones, "If this goes on, we will either be gibbering idiots by the time they come back to open the doors for us, or one of us will have murdered the other."

She followed him easily enough. "I suppose it's natural that we should irk one another."

"Irk?" he said deliberately. "You intrigue me, you awe me with your self-possession. Your elusiveness, not to mention the pulverized-pearl sheen of your skin, drives me mad. But you don't irk me."

It was their captivity, then, that had him on edge. She said, "It will only be a few more days."

"Too many. For a man and a woman to be shut up together

in a state of near undress like this is a diabolical test of nerves and will."

"It was meant to be."

A grim smile touched his mouth. "Eden all over again, complete with serpent and with childbirth the planned punishment in the end. Yes. Tell me once more why we should submit politely?"

Hearing the bitterness in his voice, it was a moment before she answered. "What else is there?"

"A plot of our own, a revenge meted out with careful embraces."

It was possible he had drunk more of the wine than she noticed. She put down her fork, used her napkin and discarded it, then rested her clasped hands on the table's edge.

"What are you saying?" she asked with stiff lips.

He regarded her a long moment before he answered. "The purpose of this charade, from your husband's point of view, is an heir. For the sake of that goal, he is willing to allow you a carefully controlled episode of infidelity with a man of his choosing. No, not allow; he insists on it. Wouldn't you say he deserves to be disappointed?"

"That is my fullest intention." Katrine clenched her hands more tightly together.

"And mine," Rowan agreed. "Still, it rankles that there is no more forceful method of defiance open to us. It is a bitter pill that in order to resist your husband's plans for us, we—or at least I—must also resist the urgings of a desire that is like none I've ever known."

Katrine, meeting his open gaze, saw that his eyes had the clarity of emeralds. He was relaxed, lying back in his chair with one long leg thrust out before him. His shirt lay open, exposing a wide expanse of muscle-wrapped chest and a small amount of board-hard abdomen. His head rested against the back of his chair with his thick, dark hair in untamed disarray, while his lax hands draped over the chair arms. The picture of weary indolence was veiled, however, by the set of his mouth and the air of barely contained force that clung to him.

"Desire," she whispered.

"Surely you knew."

She did, of course, but she had thought there was little that was personal in it. According to Delphia, and even Musetta, it was not at all unusual for a man to respond to any reasonably attractive woman. There was, however, another consideration.

She moistened her lips. "You would not say so, I hope, just because of my own ill-considered words on the subject."

He turned his head a little to face her more fully. "Only to the extent that they give me the courage to speak."

"That is one thing I would have said you could never need," she said in frank judgment.

"You think so? Then let me gather the little I have left and ask this one thing: Have you any objection to retaliating for what has been done to us, if a way could be shown that would rob your husband of the end he seeks?"

"You mean—" she began, then stopped, unable to put what she suspected into words.

"I mean," he said softly, "that I know a way to turn the tables, to permit the joys of love and cuckoldry while declining to create a small hostage for your husband's tender care."

"Why should I wish to do that?" she said.

"Castlereagh was not eager to entrust you to me; it offended his sense of exclusive ownership, I think. Can you say in all truth that it would give you no satisfaction to do the thing he dreaded even as you deny him the reward he sought in yielding you up to me?"

"I have sworn—"

"You swore not to be used as a convenient brood mare. I don't think you have taken an oath to remain a virgin your life long only because your husband is incapable of changing that state. What you may choose to do for yourself, from your own needs, is another matter entirely."

"A convenient argument, don't you think?" she said, directing her gaze toward the fire.

"One you think I make for my own ends? You may be right. I would like to believe I have come to it from concern that the pleasures of the marital bed have been withheld from you, and from a need to right the wrong your husband has committed against you. I don't dare. The truth is, I am slowly going mad from my own need to touch you, and it may be that has warped my thinking. And yet, could there be a sweeter vengeance?"

In the silence that followed his words, Katrine could hear her own heartbeat like muffled thunder in her ears. There was agreement inside her along with a sudden, ferocious yearning to be free of her celibate state and, at the same time, repay Giles in kind for the degradation of the past few days. But how could she say so and remain a lady?

He was waiting for her answer. Choosing her words carefully, she said, "It makes no difference in any case; it isn't possible to decide at will that there will be no child."

He tilted his head. "If I tell you how it may be done, will you consider a change in our arrangement?"

"I—it's possible," she said in words so quiet they hardly stirred the air.

Rowan watched her for long seconds before he gave an abrupt nod. "In the lands of Arabia, and farther beyond, in Persia and India, there are men who practice a code of loving called Tantrism, or, sometimes, Ismak. Some consider it a religion, the worship of the male and female principles; in the ancient temples and tombs there are colored drawings of men and women engaged in amorous play lasting long hours. Others only call it a method of prolonging the pleasures of love. The foremost aspect of it is the self-control learned and executed by the male partner. He does not release the fluid which causes conception. Do you understand what I'm saying?"

She could not meet his eyes, nor could she control the flush that burned in her face. Nevertheless, she was familiar enough with the parlance of horse breeding and the nocturnal activities in the slave quarters to grasp his meaning. She said, "Yes. Yes—I think so."

"Among Arabic women, there is scorn for the man who lacks this training, this ability, or so I was told by the men of the Bedouin while in the Arabian desert. The man without it not only robs his woman of her pleasure, he endangers her life by forcing childbirth on her during times of tribal migration. If he wants respect, he must learn to forfeit his own swift gratification in order to safeguard the woman and prolong ecstasy for them both. More, in Islam a man may have four wives as well as other concubines. It is considered necessary for a man to conserve his life juices, which represent his strength—this in order to keep his many women satisfied. The concept intrigued; I arranged to be trained in it."

A slow, liquid heat mounted to Katrine's brain and crept with insidious intoxication along her veins. She tried to fight it; still, it invaded every muscle and bone, pore and strand of hair. Her skin felt moist and tingling with it, as though it invited a touch. It filled her as if she were a chalice, and overflowed in the lower part of her body. Unclasping her hands, she smoothed them over her forearms, grasping her upper arms as she sat back in her chair.

She stared at the man across from her. He looked the same, yet there was fascination in the shape of his nose and mouth and long fingers, in his lean length and easy presence. The change was in her mind. She knew it, but could not prevent it, was not even sure she wanted to try.

She said finally, "If you sacrifice your pleasure, what is there for you to gain?"

"The form of pleasure is changed, not lost; it becomes a different kind of paradise. As for what I gain, I will have you, plus a degree of repose and as much content as is possible in our gilded prison."

"A temporary paradise," she said in pensive tones.

His gaze was dark as he answered. "What other kind is there?"

A waiting silence descended. Rowan de Blanc had made his appeal to both reason and emotion, Katrine thought, but he would not plead. The next move was hers. She must decide what she wanted, decide what direction their incarceration would take from this moment.

Could she trust what he said? She knew little of the miracle of conception beyond the basic mechanics; still, she had heard whispers among the area women of a few crude contrivances to be used for prevention. She had no reason to doubt his word.

There was also inside her a sense of time and opportunity slipping away. This moment, this state of isolation and secrecy with a man she could respect, one who could arouse her emotions, might never come again. She did not want to wither away into old age without ever knowing the love of a man for a woman. She could not bear the thought of leaving this turmoil of desire and fear inside her unexplored.

Giles had sanctioned her union with this man, had he not? How could it be wrong?

She knew how. Yet, what was that knowledge, what was her much-vaunted honor, compared with the long and empty years of her life that lay before her?

Words. How could she find the words that would signal her assent? It seemed so base, such a betrayal of herself and everything she was. She had been a good and conscientious wife for so long, had been so near perfect a lady, that she was trapped in the role and could not set herself free. She opened her lips in her distress, but no sound issued between them. Desolation rose inside her, pooling in her eyes.

Rowan met her gaze for long, slow-breathing moments. There was a minute change in the musculature of his face. Then collecting himself with a powerful contraction of muscles, he rose and set the table aside. Kneeling before her, he took her cool hands in the warm grasp of both his own, holding them against his chest.

"Don't torture yourself, sweet Katrine; there is no need," he said in vibrant and deep understanding. "I meant to make matters easier, not more difficult. We will go on as before, if that is your wish."

It was almost impossible to move. She gave the smallest possible shake of her head, and liquid crystal tears spilled in wet tracks from her eyes. They lay on her cheeks, capturing the fire glow in splintered prism colors.

"No? Then let me show you the first moves in the game of love. If at any point you decide to stop, then you have only to tell me, and that will be the end of it. No questions, no apologies, without blame or repining."

"Without pain?" She meant mental affliction, not physical, but she was sure he knew that. It was important that she know the degree of risk; that was the only reason she found the fortitude to ask.

"Ah, well," he said softly. "Pain is the price we sometimes pay in our search for joy."

He turned her hands palm upward and bent his head to press his lips to the sensitive, protected hollows. She felt the warm flick of his tongue like the shock of an invasion and would have closed her hands into fists. He held them open while he trailed a line of warm, moist kisses to the pulse that throbbed in her wrist, the blue veins of her forearm, the fragile turn of her elbow. He turned her hands then, placing them both flat against his chest and holding them there an instant before he smoothed his own to her upper arms. Closing his fingers around the beautifully turned contours, he drew her closer.

The heat of his mouth on her collarbone and in the hollow of her throat was consuming. Katrine let her eyelids drift shut as she felt it seeping into her bloodstream, spreading with every beat of her heart. She fanned her fingers out wide over his chest so the palms were flat against the shifting muscles. That fuller contact satisfied some need deep within, as if she could read the essence of him through it.

She wanted to know him, to discover the thoughts and the feelings that lay in the innermost recesses of his mind. She needed to know if the boon he had given her in removing the need for her verbal consent to this loving was for her sake or his own. She longed to find proof that the words he spoke were the truth, proof to refute the nebulous dread that he spoke and acted for his own adroit purpose.

Then his lips, skimming the gentle curve of her neck, brushing her chin, settled with skill and tender mastery upon her mouth. Reasons ceased to matter.

His mouth was firm and tasted of burgundy and the sweetness of desire. He traced the contours of her lips, grazing their smooth surfaces with delicate movements until they tingled, adhering to his own. Relentlessly exploring, tenaciously inciting, he probed the moist corners and invaded the line of joining for deeper incursion. The grainy surface of his tongue abraded hers, seeking the fragile underside and sensitive edges, enticing her response. Carefully he applied suction, savoring the honey-flavored nectar. He swept the glazed porcelain edges of her teeth, cupping her face in his hands as he pressed deeper.

With a soft sound in her throat, Katrine slid her hands higher upon his shoulders, smoothing her fingers along the strong column of his neck to twine among the thick curls at the back of his head. He drew her nearer, so the exquisitely tender nipples of her breasts beneath their thin muslin covering brushed the furring of hair on his chest. It was not near enough. She eased closer, until her firm curves conformed to the muscle and bone of him, until she could feel the strained rise and fall of his breathing and the hard throb of his heart.

He skimmed the shaping of her back with his hands, bridging the slender indentation of her waist and settling on the gentle flare of her hips. His grasp tightened an instant before he continued in his soothing, circling caress. With one hand spread between her shoulder blades, he swept the other around and across her rib cage, then upward between their bodies. His clasp relaxed yet sure, he cupped the swelling mound of her breast. He brushed the nipple with his thumb.

The rapture that leaped along her veins was shocking in its intensity. A tremor shivered over her and her breathing deepened. She could feel the jar of her heart in her chest. She went still.

Rowan, sensing the change in her, released her mouth, lifting his head. He loosened his hold. His voice a rattling husk of sound, he said, "Shall I stop now?"

The shake of her head was ratcheting in its slowness, but definite. He expelled his breath in a harsh sound of pent will, then reached to gather her close. Holding her to him with one arm behind her back, he thrust the other under her knees and surged to his feet. A few steps, and the tester of the bed and the wool bed curtains loomed above them. Katrine felt herself swung, then settled on the mattress. Its softness received her, cushioned the impact as he flung himself down beside her.

And suddenly she wanted to scramble off the bed and run, somewhere, anywhere, before it was too late. She opened her mouth to say the word that would set her free.

Her gaze was snared by the rich green of his eyes, and the concern and courtesy and smoldering intention that swirled in their depths. Her panic stilled, died away. As he placed his hand on the middle of her abdomen with attentive precision, soothing the terror centered there, her lips trembled into a smile. She raised her hand, resting it on his shoulder to allow him unimpeded access as she turned to him.

Diligent, merciless in his tender care, he sought the wellsprings of her pleasure, and found them one by one. He pressed his face to her belly, breathing his warm breath through the thin muslin nightgown, inhaling the womanly fragrance of her. He left a wet track of material from there upward. He delved into the tiny sink of her navel, charted the valley between her breasts, then climbed the rounded, pulsating hills before teasing each nubbed crest to the taut sweetness of summer raspberries.

He placed his hand on her thigh, gently marauding while busy elsewhere. When next she noticed, he was stripping her nightgown upward, laying her body bare. He pulled it off over her head, drawing it away with care to prevent tugging on the long skein of her hair that was caught in the folds. When she was free of it, he tossed it aside, then caught up a handful of silken tresses. He spread them over her shoulders and breasts, veiling the firelit paleness of her skin in the russet glory. Drawing a deep breath, he sought the rich ripeness of raspberries among the shimmering filaments.

Heat pulsated in her veins, collecting in heavy, vibrant anticipation just above the juncture of her thighs. Her skin was dewed with fine moisture, glowing with warmth. Every nerve resonated with glad anticipation. Her breathing was quiet, shallow. Half-formed impulses skittered through her mind. Grasping one, acting upon it, she allowed her fingers to brush over his body in tentative discovery.

A moment later he had flung off his shirt, skimmed from his breeches. Taking her hand, he guided it over his chest to the flat coins of his paps, then kissing the palm, he placed the moist spot left behind directly on the heated, silken-smooth length of his manhood. Releasing her, he left her free to do as she would.

Hard, yet velvet soft, springing but turgid, vigorous though quiescent, rampant yet obedient to his will; the contradictions of his body fascinated her. There was such wonder in discovering how he was made that it was a moment before she noticed his hand upon her inner thigh, the sure positioning that spread her legs wider, his hand cupping the moist and delicate folds at the apex of her being.

She hid her face in his neck while she drew a breath so deep it hurt her chest. But she didn't move, didn't release her hold upon him, as he separated the petallike folds and pressed gently, unerringly inside.

The feeling that spiraled up from that touch routed modesty, banished fear, threatened sanity. She was on fire. She would burst from the incredible enchantment of it. Nothing, not even the slight sting as he found her maidenhead could surmount the mind-searing pleasure of the moment. Or so she thought. Until she felt the wet heat of his mouth where his hand had been.

Time was transfigured, became aeons in which glory took up residence in her muscles and sinews. Consciousness receded in firelit ecstasy. She shivered, exploding soundlessly in his hands. Her body, her being, her very soul were malleable. She gave herself to him, and did not count the cost.

Long ages later, he drew her under him, rising above her like some rigorous god of the night. Poised with his manhood throbbing against the vulnerable entrance of her body, he spoke on a ragged, gasping breath. "Shall I stop?"

Something violent and proud and carelessly victorious rose up in Katrine. She placed her hands on his lean flanks, gripping hard. "Dear God, no," she whispered, and drove him with sure strength straight into the center of her being.

There was tightness and fullness, but little pain; he had prepared the way too well for that. For long moments he was still, then he set a slow and thorough rhythm. Even, sure, the gliding strokes opened deep internal gates of pleasure. They routed out the last vestiges of reserve and melded heart and soul into a single aching mass of desire. She wanted him with every drop of blood that boiled in her veins, every panting breath and shuddering contraction of muscle. She met his every careful descent in straining effort, gently rocking, again and again. The liquid bliss of it deepened, spread.

Abruptly she gasped as her very being coalesced around him with velvet constriction, holding. In the innermost recesses of her mind there was a turning sensation, as if she were a living lock and he the key. His movements stilled and he allowed a portion of his weight to settle upon her, pressing her down, down into the joy.

It was a blossoming. Every tight-furled constraint, every fear and embarrassment, every close-held dream and hope unfolded in brilliant, uncaring display. The rapture widened, spreading in open glory, lifting toward bright beatitude. Glowing with the sensation, Katrine clung to the trembling arms of the man who held her.

They lay while Rowan's heartbeat slowed and his breathing steadied, then he released himself with care. Rising with consummate ease and tireless tenderness, he began again.

Lost, she was lost in paroxysms of purest enchantment. Delight and perilous gratitude surged in her veins. Fast and slow, gently and with striking power they tumbled over the bed, first one on top and then the other. Relentless, inventive without end, he left no single corner of body and mind unpossessed. There was no surcease from the pleasuring, no defense from it except to trade caress for caress, plunge for plunge, joy for joy. It was a bouquet of blossomings, a garden of them, each carefully tended. And, perhaps, meant to be preserved like perfect flowers pressed in a book of memories.

But they were never, not quite ever, totally shared.

Finally they lay spent, with their hearts knocking together and their bodies fused by the dewing of moisture that covered them. Katrine, cradling his head so his face was buried in her hair, splaying her hand across his heaving back, forced a whisper from her throat, one edged with exhaustion and a curious desolation.

"Enough," she said. "Please stop."

CHAPTER THIRTEEN

Rowan stood with his forearm resting on the mantel while he stared into the fire. He was not happy with himself. He had made a mistake, a colossal one.

He had thought altering the relationship between Katrine and himself would make it easier for them to endure their captivity. He knew now it had made it harder.

Before, he had not known exactly what he would be giving up when the ordeal was over. He had recognized, certainly, that renunciation would be difficult, but not that it might be next to impossible. That newfound knowledge gave a desperate edge to every moment of the time they had left. It had wakened him from a dead sleep and set him to building a fire in the hope that she would rouse to join him.

He had almost kissed her awake. The need was a hollow ache inside him. He was not sure she would appreciate it, nor was he certain it was wise.

There were a great many things he was uncertain about.

It was possible he had loved her too long, tried her too hard the night before. She had been so amazing, so lovely and responsive, that he had forgotten everything else. He had not meant to force her to ask him to stop.

He glanced toward the bed. Katrine lay on her side with

one arm stretched above her head and her hair streaming over the edge of the mattress. The sheet covered her to the neck; it should since he had put it there moments before. He remembered well, too well, the gentle curves it covered, however, and the coral-rose-tipped perfection.

She was awake, watching him with solemn eyes. He forced a smile as he said, "Are you all right this morning?"

"Fine," she answered in murmurous tones.

She would, he thought, say that regardless. He pushed away from the mantel and stepped to sit on the edge of the bed. There was a strand of hair lying across her cheek. He reached with a hand that was not quite steady to brush it away. "No pain any-where?"

She shook her head, glancing up at him then away again.

"I didn't mean to hurt you," he said.

She rolled a little to face him. "You didn't."

"But you said—you asked me not to go on."

"Oh." She lowered her lashes. "It seemed too much effort when you weren't enjoying it."

A frown snapped his brows together. "Of course I was en-joying it. What are you saying?"

"You weren't," she answered indistinctly, "not as much as I was."

The charm of that complaint took his breath. He put a fore-finger under her chin, forcing her to look at him. "My pleasure was different, that's all. I certainly wasn't suffering through it."

"You seemed to be."

"Only because my self-control isn't as invincible as I thought," he said in wry deprecation. When he saw no accep-tance in her face, he went on. "What I felt was a series of what the French call 'little deaths,' rather than a single great release. They were actually much nearer what you had than the other would have been."

"You didn't feel there was—there was something lacking?"

she asked with trouble in her face. "You wouldn't have liked—the other?"

He shook his head in smiling negation. "Not considering the cost."

"Well, then," she said slowly, "I suppose it's all right."

She was not convinced; he could see it. Words did not seem likely to do it. There was one thing that might.

He reached to draw the sheet away from her, exposing her rosy flesh to the cool morning air even as he stripped away his shirt with his free hand. He said deliberately, "That isn't the phrase I would have used, myself—last night was far more than all right. It could be that you require a reminder of exactly what it was like."

There was nothing wrong, Katrine thought, with his control. As far as she could discover, it was perfect. He knew precisely how to achieve the capitulation he wanted, and he would not stop until he had it. She could tempt him; that was easy. But she could not make him lose his head. She knew; she had tried. Decorously, of course, but a true effort nonetheless.

She had thought it would be difficult to face Rowan after what had passed between them. He had made it easy with his naturalness, his quiet humor, his ease with his own body. If only he would settle everything else with such ready competence.

The slanting sun of midafternoon was making knife-edged rays through the window slits. The day had grown warmer, so they had let the fire die out. Rowan sat at her feet with his back against her chair as he played a rambling yet haunting melody on the mandolin. She had her needlework in her lap, though she had not set a stitch in the past hour. Her thoughts, and watching his fingers so strong and nimble on the mandolin strings, were occupation enough.

He brought the musical strain he was following to an end.

The last clear note hung in the air, echoing against the stone walls. He leaned his head back, resting it on Katrine's knee.

She reached out to barely touch the crisp waves of his hair. In quiet concern, she asked, "What are we going to do?"

"Something, nothing, whatever is necessary," he answered, and sighed.

"What if—" she began, then hesitated, biting her lip.

"Yes?" He tilted his head, but did not turn to look at her.

She forced the words through the tightness in her throat. "What if Giles decides to kill you anyway, regardless. What if he decides you are a threat that he cannot risk?"

"What if he decides that he would prefer the man who made him a cuckold not live?" Rowan said in amplification. "I don't intend to go quietly to the execution."

"But you are unarmed now."

"You think he might order me slain as soon as the *Cotton Blossom* docks? You may be right, though I would think, since he's gone to such trouble, that he will at least show some curiosity about the success of his maneuver to get us together."

"I can't imagine what he could say to discover it," she said with some asperity.

"It will be simple enough, I expect, so long as you are not there."

"Oh, I see, a direct question, man to man."

Rowan straightened as he turned, and rested an arm on her knee. His gaze was clear as it rested on her face. "Does that bother you? I give you my word there will be no backslapping discussion, no details."

"No, I'm sure there won't." That was not Rowan's style, Katrine thought, any more than it was his style to make love to a woman at her husband's behest. And yet, here they were.

Rowan picked up her hand, placing it against his own, palm to palm. He pressed them together until every knuckle and line touched, measuring the length of the fingers and the width of the thumbs. "Don't distress yourself," he said, his gaze on what he was doing. "I won't hurt him unless I must."

"It wasn't Giles—" she began, then stopped as Rowan cocked an interested eye up at her. She snatched her hand away. "You may think it's funny that I'm concerned for you, but the responsibility for your death would be mine. I would rather not have to bear it."

The light faded from his face. He shifted position, turning back to stare once more into the fire. "I will do my best," he said dryly, "to see that you don't have to."

Katrine was something less than mollified. It was not a new feeling. There had been a singing disquiet inside her since the night before. In spite of Rowan's explanation, she was still disturbed by his incredible command of his emotional responses. She didn't like it that he could control hers so easily without forgetting himself. It made her feel manipulated, made her wonder if there was more than mere desire or concern for her behind his suggestion that they change their circumstance. She thought he might be trying to influence her emotions, though he could have other reasons for making her respond to his artful caresses.

There had been a time not so long ago when such a thing would not have entered her head. The events of the night had changed that. She had not only gained a great deal of knowledge about the art of making love, she had learned much about herself. She might easily, she thought, become dependent on the kind of closeness she had discovered with him. She was doing her best, however, to keep that fact to herself.

She hated being suspicious, hated the doubt and confusion in her mind. She wished with sudden virulence that she could have met Rowan before her father died, that what was between them could have developed along more normal lines. She wished they could have courted as young lovers did, with waltzes and valentines and tokens of affection, with quiet walks and discussions of likes and dislikes, wishes and dreams. How lovely it would have been to have long months to get to know each other, to touch, to kiss, and to come slowly to love.

Yet the question was, would they have loved at all? Would he have felt anything for her? Did he feel anything now beyond compassion and the attraction of the moment?

She had to know. It seemed that if she could break his control, make him forget everything except her, that would be an indication. She would have to try again, this time less decorously.

She spent some moments staring into the fire, then a slow smile curved her mouth. She straightened one knee, lifting her foot and leaning at the same time to scratch her ankle. As she bent forward, the fullness of her breast brushed Rowan's cheek.

He shifted his position, moving away to give her room. It was, perhaps, a natural thing for a man of good manners to do; still, it was annoying. She touched his shoulder as she settled back into place, and he resumed his position.

After a few moments Katrine put a fingertip to the outer edge of his ear in a pretense of idle exploration. There was nothing idle about it, however; she had discovered that he was stirred by being touched there. She followed the whorls and subtle shaping that lay close against his head with care before dipping into the small opening at the center.

A faint smile curved his mouth as he sat staring into the fire. Reaching up, he caught her hand and carried it to his lips to kiss her knuckles. Then he sat holding the hand he had captured, smoothing the palm with gentle, even strokes of his thumb.

Frustration shifted inside Katrine. It crossed her mind to wonder if he was aware of what she was doing. It was possible he knew and was trying to give her a hint that her shy advances were not welcome. The idea gave her a hollow feeling inside. There was only one way to find out, and that was to continue.

She set her needlework on the side table. Resting her weight on her elbow on the chair arm, she reached to press her fingers into the small troughs formed by the soot-black waves of his hair.

"Take care," he said in lazy tones, "or you're going to find yourself in trouble."

"Is that a threat?" she said, carefully training an errant wave to curve over his ear.

"It's a promise," he returned.

"Somehow," she said softly, "I'm not terribly frightened."

There was a sudden tug on her captive hand, and she catapulted headfirst from the chair. His hard arms caught her, dragging her down against an equally hard body. A shift of taut muscles, and she lay in his lap with her back against his chest and her arms crisscrossed before her. She was held in a vise grip made by strong arms and hard swordsman fingers.

"Good," he said against her ear. "I like bravery in women. It makes them adventurous in love."

It was a moment before Katrine could catch her breath. She tested the strength of his hold by twisting her wrists back and forth. There was no give in her hands. Her voice tight, she said, "I'm sure you should know, after all those foreign females."

"All? You give me too much credit, there were only one or two."

"The one or two who taught you how to—to conserve yourself, I suppose." Her face burned at her daring in speaking of such a subject.

Laughter sounded in his voice as he answered. "No, as a matter of fact. The knowledge came from the precise instruction of an elderly scholar of the art, an Arabian gentleman."

"You must have had practice with some woman—women," she persevered, even as she pulled at her hands held in his grasp, hoping for a moment of inattention.

"What an indelicate mind you have, my love, and how busy it has been. Does my practice, as you call it, disturb you?"

My love.

Indignation and a species of alarm struck through her. "Why should it? It's nothing to do with me."

She could feel the thudding of his heart against her shoulder blades. It gave her a yielding sensation deep inside that she was beginning to recognize. She stiffened against him on a quick intake of breath. The movement caused her breasts to press against his forearms.

"How astute of you," he said in lazy approbation, at the same time transferring her wrists to the grip of one hand. He curved his free hand to cup the gentle weight of a breast, weighing it, caging it within his wide spread fingers, caressing the nipple in slow circles with his hard palm. He went on, "No woman known before I met you means anything; they are forgotten."

Why had he said that? There had to be a reason. Doing her best to ignore the sensations spiraling through her body in time to his movements, she said, "Poor things, to give themselves to so fickle a man."

"I will be constancy itself, to the right woman."

She could feel his warm breath against the side of her neck, sense his voice resounding in his chest, vibrating down her backbone. She was affected by it, and the promise she heard in its low timbre, against her will. It seemed advisable to distract him before she became too affected. The sight of his hands, so sun-browned against the white of her gown, was her inspiration.

"Was it the Arabian sun that darkened your skin?"

"Do you dislike it?" he asked.

She arched her neck, trying to see his face, but he kept his gaze on his effort to tease the berry-hard nipple of her breast into greater firmness. There was a small catch in her voice as she answered truthfully, "No, I rather like it, only it seems a little odd."

"I know a gentleman is supposed to be lily pale to show that he need never labor, but I like the sun. It comes from being reared in England's gray skies and gales, I expect. But no, I didn't brave the desert heat; that would be foolhardy. I was once captured by Barbary pirates, and made to work as a seaman. I discovered it had its benefits, up to a point."

"Oh, I remember," she said, going still. "Terence said you were supposed to be ransomed, but made such a good pirate that they gave you back your sword. Whereupon, you cut your way to freedom."

"Something like that, though it wasn't quite so simple. What else did Terence tell you?"

"He said you were with the expedition led by some explorer trying to find the source of the Nile, though you weren't entirely successful. He said that you met the man—Burton was his name, I think—while you were both living among the Arabs and that you translated for him some of the more risqué passages of the *Arabian Nights*."

"My brother, it seems, was not always discreet."

"He was entertaining, possibly because of it. He said you once fought and killed a lion with your bare hands."

"Wrong. I only scared the beast away when he invaded my tent in search of midnight supper."

It was said with such modesty, yet such confidence, that she could not help smiling. "Was it as a pirate, or while you were in Africa, that you came upon Omar?"

"It was on the Barbary coast. We shared an oar in a pirate galley; Omar had been given to the pirates after the loss of his tongue. It was an excellent way to become friends, where a willing partner can carry the rowing while the other snatches a precious moment of rest without danger of a whiplash across the shoulders. Later, when we won free, I went with him to his hometown, where he had left a woman he loved, a woman who had married in his absence. They were discovered together. The woman was tied in a sack and drowned in a well, and Omar beaten and left to die in a ditch, and would have if I had not found him."

A small sound of distress rose in her throat. She shuddered with horror at the vision he had conjured up. "So barbaric."

"It's not quite so civilized as slicing a rival to pieces in a duel, but the result is much the same. At any rate, I forced Omar to live when he wanted only to die. It was a long time before he was grateful, but he has been with me since."

There was a pensive silence. Finally she said, "Terence also talked about the time you saved his life."

"The brat dived out of a rowboat, trying to imitate his older brother. He was seven at the time and had never swum a stroke in his life. I happened to be closest to him, but there were two other men who could have gone in after him."

He seemed determined not to be considered heroic. "You fought an undertow for him, so he said. He never forgot it."

"Nor did I. He would never have been in danger if I hadn't taken him out in the rowboat in the first place." He was smoothing his hand down her body in sweeping strokes, making the thin gown conform to her curves.

"He wanted to follow in your footsteps, only his mother forbade it," she said, her voice quiet. "He worshiped you."

"Did he tell you everything he felt about me?" Rowan's words were striated with pain. His hand grazed across the small mount that protected her pubic bone and the entrance to her innermost self. He paused, holding. "Did he talk about nothing else while the two of you lay in bed together?"

Swift anger rippled through her, though she sat perfectly still. She had almost persuaded herself she was wrong, that he was not trying to use her bodily responses against her. She should have known better.

"What if he did?" she said, the words reckless with the pain of disillusion. "What difference does it make now?"

His hold tightened, so she could hardly breathe. His hard fingers sank into her unprotected flesh. "I have to assume, since you were still a virgin, that my brother was better at playing the gentleman than I."

"He didn't have to play," she said.

She felt him flinch at the cruel thrust of the words that

damned him as a lesser man than his brother. She expected to be flung away from him, set free. It didn't happen. Instead he relaxed his hard grip as if by conscious effort, then began to caress her with slow, insistent strokes. Fear seeped into her mind, fear not of pain but of an extreme form of humiliation. He meant to punish her with pleasure for her insult.

She could retract what she had said, or she could suffer his attentions and struggle to remain indifferent to them. But could she resist his touch when it was driven by experience, whetted intelligence, and quiet wrath? It was so new to her, so powerful; she might be taken by surprise with variations she did not know existed.

She had already lowered her defenses for him. What might she not do and say if they were all stripped away? And how would she live, afterward?

"Don't do this," she said in strangled tones.

His movements slackened, but only so that he might grasp a handful of her gown and draw it upward to slide his hand underneath. His voice pensive, absorbed, he said, "Why? You only tell me what you want me to hear about Terence. What are you hiding? What reason can there be for keeping back what you know, unless it's something not to your credit? And if it is that, then why should there not be retribution?"

"Retribution, or torture? Either way, there's nothing to tell."

"I don't believe you. I want to know who invited my brother here, and if he was selected for the same reason that brought me. I want to know how he gained your company without a clear win on the tournament field. I want to know what happened afterward, how it came about that he never left Arcadia. I have been patient, thinking you would tell me in your own time. But our days together are growing short, and now you must tell me in my time."

"Are you sure," she said, her voice ragged at the edges,

"that you didn't wait until now because you think I can't resist you?"

There was a pause in his movements before he began again. "There is rare pleasure in that thought, but if I entertained it for a moment, I could not continue. For obvious reasons."

That honesty, and the care for her secret fears that it showed, deserved some small recompense. "If I told you that your brother came of his own accord, because he had heard of the tournament from Alan, if I swear once more that he never shared my bed, never touched me except in a waltz, would that satisfy you?"

"It might," he answered, his voice absorbed, "if I didn't know there must be something more that you are keeping from me."

"Suppose—" she began, then lost her voice as he pressed deep inside her and she felt the hot ripple of desire through every smallest particle of her body.

"Yes?" he said.

It would have been better, easier to fight him, if he had been more domineering and vicious in his approach. Pain she could have surmounted with teeth-gritted resistance. His diabolical control and relentless attention to her responses was soul-shattering. Tears rose inside her. She swallowed them with a difficult movement of her throat.

"You were saying," he prodded with words, and otherwise.

"Suppose—suppose I should tell you something of your brother you may not want to hear?"

"I doubt you can," he answered simply. "Terence was young and given to grand gestures and quixotic impulses, but there was no baseness in him. Unlike his brother."

She was on fire, and he knew it. There was nothing she could do about the pounding of the blood in her veins, the swollen moistness of her flesh, or the tight buds of her nipples. She wanted to be aloof, to turn off the sensations that flooded her.

She couldn't. While some corner of her mind shrank from him, simmering with rage and injured amour propre, her body contracted around him and urged him to greater liberties.

She could fight him. She could kick and scream and force him to hurt her to subdue her. What would be the point, when it must end the same way? The steel-manacle grasp of his hands that was just short of painful, the instant reflexes that countered her every attempt to break free, told her it was useless. No, there was greater dignity in remaining still, allowing him to do his worst. The best defense might well be if she could manage to enjoy his ministrations while retaining her secrets.

The true triumph would be if she could persuade him to join her in the enjoyment.

"Your brother," she said softly as she leaned her head back on his shoulder and turned to gaze at his profile, "was a dear young man, handsome, funny, and a little wild. He was a great favorite; all the ladies loved him. But he was not his older brother's equal."

Rowan's movements stilled. He turned his head to stare at her. She held his gaze, her own wide and vulnerable. He was so close that she could see the individual hairs of his brows and the faint trace of beard stubble under the skin. She knew the instant his pupils began to dilate, saw his glance flicker to her mouth and the first tentative dip of his head toward her.

His mouth touched hers, and rich elation exploded inside her. He was not exempt from seduction himself. She could tempt him, she really could.

Her lips were firm and possessive. He did not release her hands. Katrine, feeling his efforts to dominate, softened her kiss, becoming endlessly receptive. She tested the hardness of his mouth with tiny flicks of her tongue, teasing her way inside. Advancing, retreating, she incited him to follow. He plundered her sweetness, seizing the lead from her as he abraded her tongue with his and drew it deeper while he probed the smooth underside.

Sustained by her achievement, she allowed her body to conform to his, pressing against him. She could feel his breath swell in his chest, sense the tensing of the muscles of his abdomen. He wanted her; there was no mistaking the hardening of his body that she felt under her hips. Her breasts rose and fell with her sigh as she fitted herself more closely against him.

His grasp on her wrists tightened with cruel force, then was released abruptly. He tore his mouth away and heaved upward. Katrine, propelled from his lap, would have fallen if he had not caught her. He loomed over her with a scowl drawing his brows together. His gaze flickered over her, resting an instant on the quick rise and fall of her breasts, returning to the moist and tender rose of her mouth.

A soft oath left him. He swung from her, striding to the door. It slammed behind him with a thunderous crash as he left the room.

She had won. She had, somehow, broken through his absolute self-mastery, if only in a small degree. She could hardly believe it. Somehow, she did not feel victorious.

She had made him forget his design of forcing answers from her. She had roused him to desire to the point that he had to break off what he was doing and either possess her or leave her. He had chosen to leave. What did that mean? Could it be that he did not trust himself to make love to her with the same detachment he had used before? Or had he left to prevent himself from beating the answers he wanted out of her?

A shiver moved over her. She wrapped her arms around her body, edging closer to the fire. A part of the chill, she realized, was from the removal of Rowan's body heat, but a part of it also came from the desolation inside her.

Lust. That was what she had aroused in him. It was all he felt for her.

He could not be blamed for that, of course; hadn't he told

her it was one of the reasons he had agreed to this charade? He had, at least, been honest.

Nor did she have a right to expect more. She was well and truly married, bound by tradition and her own closely held principles. There was no way that she could, with honor, respond to more from him if he had offered it.

Did she want him to offer it? She hardly knew. She was so confused and overwhelmed by everything he made her feel. The tempest he stirred in her blood with his touch was not love. Or was it? The yearning he roused in the secret recesses of her soul was not love. Or was it? The inner delight she felt in watching him, touching him, was not love. Or was it?

Did these things, together, add up to something more than mere desire? Was supreme lust for a particular man, a particular male body, a form of love?

She wished she knew. She really wished she knew.

CHAPTER FOURTEEN

He was a fool, twice-damned, utterly hopeless.

Rowan stood with his wrist propped on the wall beside an arrow slit in the study, staring out at the gray afternoon light and the narrow section of trees afforded as a view. He was blue-deviled, and as jumpy as a chicken with a snake in its nest box. The worst of it was he had no one to fault except himself.

He should never have tried to force answers from Katrine. He had miscalculated; it was not a mistake he made often. Jealousy, that was the cause. He had been driven, at least in part, by jealousy of his dead brother. Could anything have been more asinine. Still, who would have guessed she would be so stout of heart?

He had expected pleading, tears, recriminations before the inevitable capitulation. Instead she had used reason and, when that failed, a deliberate assault upon his own emotional defenses.

He had not been ready. Nothing had so unnerved him in years as seeing the fortitude and accusation and stalwart resistance in her eyes. He had felt like the lowest of the low. He had wanted to lay his heart, bloody and still barely beating, at her feet as a recompense for the harm he had done.

The worst of it was knowing that he had destroyed the tenuous accord between them. He had, of his own will and by his own actions, exiled himself from her bed. There was no way he could now go back to the way they had been.

The tower had not, until today, truly felt like a prison. Now it seemed he could sense the weight of the stone on the surface of his skin, see the walls closing in on him. He thought he would detonate like an overstuffed powder house if he didn't get out. At the same time he was reluctant to end the time he must spend pent up with Katrine.

He had done his best to stay out of her way since the morning. His inclinations were too volatile to remain in the same room, even if he could have found a pretext. He had spent hours trying to decide which he wanted most, whether to have her naked and willing in his bed for the remainder of their time together, or simply to take her quickly, completely, wherever he next came upon her: in front of the fire, on the marble floor beneath the palms, on the wide stair landing.

He was beginning to understand Terence's obsession. It was possible he even shared it. He had never burned for a woman as he did for this one, never let one take over his thoughts and dreams, rout his plans and concerns. Her sweet, unique scent seemed to be impressed indelibly in his pores, to have lodged in his lungs and mind. The taste of her lingered like some delicious, magic elixir that, once savored, became an addiction.

Her beleaguered state, and the valiancy with which she fought against it, must have been irresistible to Terence. To save the lady in distress would have seemed a noble cause. To do it without hope of reward would have been nobler still.

Rowan acknowledged a virulent wish that Giles would try to eliminate him as he had his brother. Katrine's husband might find it a shade more difficult, or so he hoped. Revenge, quick and violent, if it offered itself, would be pleasant. More important, the attempt would be an excuse to take Katrine away.

That urge, astonishing in its power, had surfaced often in

the past few days. It seemed that it had always lain, half-hidden, in some strange corner of his mind.

He had no idea that she would come away at his behest. His one chance, so it seemed, would be if he appeared endangered for her sake. Only something so desperate was likely to make her forget her principles, which required that she stay with the man who had shared her wedding vows.

What would happen afterward was difficult to assess. So much depended on how and why he took her away, and what she made of it. It was doubtful she could ever feel anything for him, especially after this morning. It didn't matter. He could at least see that she never again had to accept a man she despised into her bed.

That sentiment, he thought, was a lofty one for a man who would himself invade her bed, unrepentant, at the first excuse that offered. He had told her, when he could keep the secret no longer, that he was not a gentleman. It turned out she had known it well enough.

He wondered how long it would be before she realized that she was first a woman, and then a lady. He would give a great deal to be around when she discovered it.

Dinner time had the advantage of being an unimpeachable excuse for rejoining Katrine. In strained and helpful silence, he took the heavy tray from the dumbwaiter and carried it into the bedchamber. He would have given her a hand in placing everything on the small table, but she waved him back while she attended to it. He took his place across from her, hoping all the while that he would be able to swallow without making noises like a boar hog finding a pork-chop bone in the slops.

There was wine with the meal, and brandy for afterward. He was meticulous in his offers to share both, but just as happy when she took no more than a single glass. He needed the spirits—or rather, needed the lightening of mood they could bring.

He watched her as he tried to eat. She was pale and kept her eyes downcast. She pushed the food here and there on her plate without transferring a great deal of it to her mouth. Her hair shimmered in the firelight, lying like scattered strands of russet embroidery silk over her thin nightgown. It seemed to bother her, for now and then she would catch a tress that swung forward and toss it back over her shoulder, out of her way. He enjoyed seeing that: the quick, graceful movement, watching the strand drift down to join the rest of the thick skein behind her back. He wanted to sink his hands—

He wanted too much. He had always wanted too much. It was the reason he had left home for foreign climes. It was the reason he was here.

In an effort to ease the tension, he said, "I heard a rider earlier this evening. There was activity in the direction of the carriage house a short time later, as if they were getting ready to go out in the morning. It may be that our idyll will be ended ahead of time."

"You think the *Cotton Blossom* has docked?" Her eyes were wide and dark as she put the question.

Rowan tossed aside the yeast roll he had been crumbling and picked up his wineglass again. "It seems likely."

"So soon," she said, or that was how it sounded. The words were almost too soft to hear. Even so, his heart leaped inside him with fearsome pleasure.

She put down her fork and pushed back her plate. Folding her hands in her lap like a nun, she looked up to meet his gaze. Her eyes clear and a little feverish, she said, "I would like very much to have your child."

The words struck him like a scourge, a cat-o'-nine-tails with a barb in each individual word that took away strength and power of speech. He waited for one or the other to return while he stared at her with eyes narrowed to conceal his fierce elation.

"I know," she said on an inadequate breath, "that it isn't what we agreed, but what will it really matter, in the end?"

"What indeed." His elation seeped away, leaving desolation behind it. His voice had a sword's honed slash when he spoke. "Have you decided you would rather please your Giles, after all?"

"I have decided," she said incisively, "that I prefer to please myself."

"By having a child to dandle and suckle and, eventually, to inherit Arcadia for you."

"And to love."

The censure in her gaze touched him; he deserved it, he knew. The knowledge could not obliterate his feeling of betrayal. Their mutual defiance had meant more to him than he realized. Or else he was jealous, not only of her husband and his own brother, but also of his unconceived child.

"Only think," he said with a twist of his lips, "of the bliss there might have been if you had been so accommodating when the subject first came up between us."

"There is still time. Barely. Perhaps."

His gaze had a dark red haze over it and the tops of his ears were hot. His impulse toward self-destruction was still strong. "No, there is not," he said in soft finality. "There will be no child of mine brought up in the shadow of a killer, no child left behind to suffer for his absent father. I will not leave here remembering a babe in my image, and thinking how easily it could die."

She put out her hand toward him. "I would cherish it."

"Would you, and forever? Despising its father?" His gaze, dragged from her face, landed on her outstretched arm. There were bruises there as round and purple as grapes, and just the size of his fingers. He cringed inside, but reached out to touch one livid spot. "For this I am sorry, but not for my refusal."

She drew back her arm, hiding it under the table edge. Studying him as if in search of a weakness, she said, "You were willing once."

JENNIFER BLAKE

"Once I was thinking only of bedding, not babies. I have re-considered." There was often effectiveness, he had found, in selective brutality.

"You would deny me this because I refused you knowledge of Terence. Is that it?" She leaned back in her chair, her eyes never wavering from his face.

He met her gaze for long moments before he said in laconic disbelief, "You are suggesting that we trade favors?"

She looked away then. "No. No, I can't do that."

He had had a vast aeon of time during the day in which to think. He said helpfully, "I would ask why, but cannot be certain there is a need. You are protecting someone. Not Giles, if Terence never shared your bed, but someone else whom you hold in affection. Except, like the tinker's wife who loved pots, there seems no single person who might reign so high."

"You know nothing of my capacity for love."

"There," he said with quiet bitterness, "you are in error."

The loveliness of her response to him the night before had told him everything he needed to know. Making love and loving were two separate things, but were close enough to draw comparisons. One he had experienced, but it was unlikely he would ever know the other. There would be no place in her life for him when this was over. He would have served his purpose and could be dismissed.

The fire burning beside them crackled in the silence. A shower of red sparks shot from under the mantel and drifted, dying, to the hearth. Katrine spared the pyrotechnics not even a glance. "If you refuse me," she said, "I may never have another chance for a woman's fulfillment."

"Complain to Giles. His sympathy may lead him to arrange another tournament."

"If he does, I will leave him."

The simplicity of the words robbed them of bravado. However, Rowan could not, for his own peace of mind, accept them.

He said, "If you can find the courage, and the money. And if you can find a place to go, and if it's a Wednesday in August with sleeting rain." He paused, the words torn from him against his conscious will, he said, "Come away with me now."

"I don't see," she answered with resentment chasing the pale fortitude from her face, "that you are going anywhere."

He gave her a look with all the power of his pent yearning in it, and had the pleasure of seeing her quick indrawn breath. His voice intent, he said, "And if I were, what then?"

She made no answer, nor could she sustain his gaze. He waited while the fire fluttered and the wind sighed outside. After a long moment he nodded. Getting to his feet, he picked up the brandy bottle and his glass. "I understand. Marriage is, of course, a consecrated institution. So is a graveyard."

Rowan swayed a little, the effect of verbal blows and violently suppressed impulses, all combined with four glasses of wine and a large brandy on a stomach that had barely known dinner and received no luncheon. He intended to add as much more of the brandy as he could swallow before oblivion found him. He did not indulge often, but was a tidy drunk; there was seldom any evidence of his dissipation. His footsteps were steady and his path straight as he walked to the door.

"Where are you going?" She rose from her chair and took a step after him.

"To Eden, my own damp and warm paradise. Away. Below." He turned, leaning his broad back against the doorjamb. "Will you miss me?"

"Stay," she said, moving toward him with slender grace and earnest provocation. "I would rather not be alone."

She walked to within inches of him, putting her hand on his chest where his shirt fell open. He could feel each separate fingertip searing into his skin in a brand that might never be erased. A thunderstorm swept into his head, rattling his brain with its flash and sound. It pounded in every fiber, every body member.

The distraction was great. To counter it, Rowan spoke in hoarse inquiry. "Turning temptress?"

"Do you mind?" she said, stepping closer still.

He paid mental homage to the effort it must have taken to bring her to him. He did not make the mistake, however, of taking credit personally. "God, no," he answered, "so long as the consequence doesn't share my bloodlines."

"That is your choice, I think, or so you gave me to understand." She raised on tiptoe and pressed her soft lips to his.

He enclosed her in his arms with the brandy bottle resting on her hip; there was nothing else to do. Her mouth was nectar rich with promise and intimations of defeat. Her arms were cool and rounded and binding. He could feel the points of her breasts driving into his chest, driving him to madness. The urge to give up, give in, give way was so strong that it seemed to carry him along like a piece of flotsam. Until he remembered that it was not him she wanted, but the slim possibility of a child of his making.

He let his arms fall to his sides. He allowed his lips to slacken. As she released her arms from his neck in slow, unbelieving reluctance, he said, "I mind, after all."

She searched his eyes, her own liquid with unshed tears. Her breath gentle, sweet in his face, she said, "Why?"

"Family pride, ego, stubbornness. You might try again, when you want me alone. Not absolution, not relief from loneliness, not some vague maternal dream, but me. Then I will give you whatever you want. And the only thing that will be able to stop me is for you to cry enough."

Her hands clenched for an instant on his shirt before she let him go. Still, she made not a sound as she watched him bow and turn from her. She was standing where he had left her, staring at nothing with her arms wrapped around her, when he looked back.

He had done the right thing, the only thing possible. Why, then, did he still feel like a fool?

Never, Rowan thought a few hours later, had there been such a moon. It was rounded as a pregnant queen, bright as a dawning of heaven. It gilded the trees and glittered on the grass and struck through the arrow slits of the tower like chased-silver Saracen blades. Streaming down through the glass cupola, it turned shadows to jet darkness and outlined the shapes of palm leaves and fern fronds in black dragon's teeth on the marble floor.

Rowan was drunk and fanciful with it. He wandered from one slitted window of the study to another and up and down the stairs. He circumnavigated the conservatory, ducking under palms and touching the warm, wet breasts of the fountain nymphs with delicately questing fingertips.

They were no match for Katrine. Sighing, he turned away and found a seat in the largest palm's serrated shadow, with his back to its giant Chinese ceramic pot. He drank the last of the brandy with a cool strip of moonlight in his eyes.

He was still sitting there, holding the empty glass, when Katrine came down the stairs. He put the piece of crystal down, carefully, noiselessly, before he dropped it. Then he sat in perfect stillness in his dark ambush.

The glowing light from above turned her hair to spun copper gold and her thin nightgown to silver gossamer. Like some goddess descending from Olympus, she floated down the curving treads with consummate grace and without sound. Her cheekbones, the proud globes of her breasts, the tender turns of her arms and lengths of her moving thighs, caught the play of moonbeams, reflecting them in a soft luminescence that hurt his eyes. There was a length of toweling over her arm.

He should rise and make his presence known, should give her privacy for her ablutions, if that was what she intended. The inclination, much less the effort, was beyond him. All the devil's horsemen could not have dragged him from his place.

She glided down the last step and across the marble floor, passing him without a glance. Reaching the fountain, she held out her hand toward the silver streams of water pouring from the urns held by the nymphs and the mouths of a pair of swans. The delight in her face as the droplets splattered over her fingers, beading her face and shoulders like warm diamonds, caused Rowan's breath to lodge in his throat.

She rubbed the drops into her skin, smoothing her hands over her face and shaking back her hair, so it shimmered like a living flame. Putting her hands to the bodice of her nightgown, she began to loose the buttons that held it.

One shoulder at the time was freed and the small, cap sleeve drawn down her arm. Slowly, with great care for the fragile fabric, she peeled away the batiste from her breasts, pressed it down to her narrow waist, and slid it along the gentle curves of her hips. It clung for a tantalizing instant, concealing her lower body like the drapery on some classical statue. Then it slipped to the floor, settling in soft folds around her feet.

Rowan ceased to breathe. He had known she was lovely; his hands, his mouth, every inch of his own body had told him so. Regardless, these means of judging were poor substitutes for the pleasure of seeing her naked in the glare of the moon.

The image, he thought, was engraved on his pupils, burned into them with the acid of his own feverish enchantment. When he was old and the time came to close his eyes in death, whoever was entrusted with that task would see her likeness imprinted there still. And they would marvel.

Now Katrine stepped from the discarded nightgown. With fluid movements, she climbed over the wide ledge of the fountain. She straightened, a nymph of living flesh and blood. Moving through the knee-deep water, she made toward the place where the flowing streams met and mingled.

The water struck her, shattering into dazzling spray. As she found its center it sleeked her curves and hollows with glistening cascades that chuckled and gurgled as they streamed down to splash around her feet. She closed her eyes on a long indrawn breath, revolving slowly under the steady shower with arms out and palms turned upward to catch errant currents of the warm flow.

Finally she faced forward. Stepping back to the wide ledge where she had placed her towel, she picked up the cake of soap Rowan had left lying there. Bemusement on her features, she smoothed it over her body in slow strokes, along her arms and down her sides, across her breasts and abdomen, along the insides of her legs from knee to knee. The lather left in the soap's wake gleamed like an adornment of silver lace. Spreading, sliding downward, it covered her with the intimacy of an embrace, riding crests, disappearing into crevices on silent, secret meanderings.

She glanced behind her, then eased back to sit on the knee of the satyr while she lifted her feet, one after the other, to soap them. Raising her arms, she rubbed lather into her hair until it was a lank mane frosted with white, until lather coated the surface of the water in the fountain and flecked her audience of statues. When she had finished, she stepped back beneath the water, letting it chase away the foam while she turned slowly in the converging streams.

She appeared to notice the grinning, lather-bedecked satyr after a moment. Leaning toward him, she splashed the bubbles from his chest with water, chasing them with spread fingers down the sculpted musculature, skimming over the too-hard belly, pausing a fleeting instant with her hand on the wet, foam-flecked male member.

Rowan swallowed, and drew air with a hoarse, whistling sound into his lungs. At the same time a pair of memories edged upward from the swollen, drink-fogged bottom of his mind. Katrine had once stood and watched him in the fountain. And he had told her he was going to be down here, in the conservatory.

She knew he watched. She knew, and wanted him to see.

He saw very well, too well, but it made no difference. She had won this skirmish.

The greater battle, however, was still to come.

He got to his feet with slow care, and moved from the shadows into the light. She jerked around, her entire body shuddering. She was an inexperienced temptress, as he recalled. It was, perhaps, a good thing.

She made no effort to cover herself, but straightened, standing tall. He applauded that, not only as a show of courage, but because it permitted him a total view. He took advantage of it as he closed his hands on the edges of his shirt, ripping it from his breeches.

"What are you doing?" she asked, her voice not quite steady.

There was raffish intent in his smile. He said as he loosened his first breeches button, "Abandoning an untenable position for a better one. It may be a bit damp, but I expect compensations."

"If you mean—"

"I do mean," he interrupted. "Are you going to tell me I'm not welcome?"

It was long moments before she answered. Her gaze, dark with some emotion he could not read, followed his movements as he stripped his breeches down the ridged muscles of his thighs and over his feet, then kicked them from him. Dropping his shirt behind him, he moved forward in rampant readiness.

Her eyes widened. She took a step backward. The jets of water struck her in a splattering flood.

"Stay where you are," he said, vaulting over the fountain's edge. He reached her in a single, plunging stride.

Alive, he felt so alive. The befuddlement of liquor was gone, banished from his bloodstream by lust and fascination. His every sense tingled with an alertness that bordered on pain. The spice scent of the ferns, the musty richness of earth, the lavender perfume of the soap foam all swirled around him, rising to his head in overpowering intensity.

He could hear the cry of a night bird and the sweep of the wind beyond the tower's wall. It was easy to see the throb of the pulse in Katrine's throat, the quickening rise and fall of her breathing, the glint of incipient panic in her eyes.

There was power in his sinews and pounding ardor in his blood. He wanted this woman, needed her with some deep internal ache that he had never felt before, and nothing, nothing was going to prevent him from taking her.

She put out her hand as if to ward him off. He stopped stock-still. For a long moment he stood with his hands on his hips and water splashing from her body into his face. Then he reached to take her hand, cradling it, carrying it to his lips before he placed it on his shoulder. Circling her waist with one arm, he flexed his body to catch her under the knees. With a single, careful heave, he placed her back where she had been moments before, in the lap of the satyr.

Before she could move, before she could protest, he stepped between her knees and knelt. Holding her hips immobile, he bent his head to the tenderly folded, lavender-flavored juncture of her thighs.

The blood was so close to the surface there, ran so swift. He thought he could taste it through the fragile skin, taste also the tart-sweet essential essence of her. His heart swelled in his chest, aching. Artistry came easy then, along with the relentless intent to render pleasure.

He adored the soft sounds she tried so hard to stifle, the quick convulsions of rapture that trembled through her under his hands, the way she flattened her palms and spread her fingers against him as if to welcome all the joy. He worshiped the perfect shape of her that fit his grasp as if made for him alone, the thick, wet coil of her hair, the pert tilt of her breasts and the way their nipples ripened like sweet berries in his mouth. He loved the delicacy of her movements in answer to his, the rapture in her face.

He loved her. It was the reason he was there.

In the tower, in the fountain, in her arms.

And when he took her, pressing his body into the soft core of her again and again, feeling the warm, velvet-lined iron band of her closing around him, the words echoed in strong, endless rhythm in his head. He shouted them in the straining silence of his mind, felt them running in unshed tears down the back of his throat.

But he never made a sound.

His control was superb, and damnably complete.

CHAPTER FIFTEEN

Katrine clung to Rowan as he lifted her from the fountain and, leaving wet footprints behind him, carried her up the stairs. His hard strength was a secret pleasure; the way he held her cradled to him made her heart ache.

She would never forget how he had come to her, naked and unashamed in the warm and splashing water. Nor would she forget what had happened afterward. She would never be the same, did not want to be the same.

Her change of heart concerning a child had not met with Rowan's approval. He didn't understand. She could hardly blame him, considering how opposed she had been to intimacy between them in the beginning.

She was not being irrational, not really. It was his own tender instruction in the ways of love that had caused her about-face. It had been impressed upon her in the last few hours just how bereft she was going to be when he was gone, how much she was going to long for a reminder of him and of their loving.

She had never objected to having a baby, only to having its father and the timing of its birth chosen for her according to Giles's will. She could think of nothing more lovely than to have a small, living being to hold against her, to fill the emptiness of her heart.

The fact that by conceiving she would also please Giles could not be helped; certainly, it had nothing to do with her decision. Giles would undoubtedly be generous in his victory and a doting parent afterward; she had no real fears on that score. Still, it was the child that was important, not her husband's feelings.

Her heart misgave her when she thought of what might become of Rowan, of what might yet be attempted against him. The fear only added strength to her desire, since the danger seemed the same whether he gave her a child or not.

If he should be killed—no, she would not think of that.

Time was growing so short. If Rowan was right, a message had been received from the steamboat landing requesting the carriages to be dispatched to pick up Giles and the others. Supposing her husband kept to the usual program, he would wait for morning to disembark and begin the journey to Arcadia. Everyone would be at the house once more by midafternoon.

They would be asking after her, wanting to know when she would be returning from her supposed journey. Giles would have to produce her in short order. Surely someone would come to release Rowan and herself soon.

There might be only tonight, then.

She had no great experience in these matters, yet she was almost certain Rowan had withheld his seed from her again, there below. There must be a way to breach his defenses in the time left to her.

Rowan shouldered into the bedchamber and placed her in the big wing-back chair before the hearth. He draped the toweling he had flung over his shoulder with his breeches around her, then knelt to build up the fire. She sat where he had left her, too lost in languorous well-being and her own thoughts to move. She followed him with her gaze, however, as he stepped into his breeches and buttoned them with swift movements, then picked up her hairbrush and comb from the dressing table and came toward her with lounging strides.

He really was magnificent. Giles had, in his peculiar fashion, chosen well.

Rowan paused, his gaze on the involuntary smile curving her lips. The look on his face was unreadable, but far from trusting. She wished she knew what he was thinking. Since she could not, she must proceed without it.

He reached for her hand and she gave it to him, allowing him to draw her from the chair. He seated himself, then pulled her back down between his spread legs. She leaned gratefully into his warmth, becoming aware as she felt it that she had been chilled. Taking up the towel, she began to dry the water droplets from her arms.

He set aside the brush and comb and took the toweling from her, using it to blot her arms and shoulders dry before moving on to her breasts. His touch was gentle yet deliberately chafing as he buffed the tender globes to a soft shine. Her nipples tightened, tilting upward.

Katrine felt the movement of the facial muscles in his lean cheek against her temple as he smiled. That evidence of his enjoyment caused the slow spread of warmth downward through her body. She arched her back a little, giving him freer access.

His movements stopped. His diaphragm swelled as he took a deep breath. With a quick shift of his shoulder, he raised her to an upright position and began to dry her hair. Dropping the towel in her lap, he picked up the hairbrush and drew it through her damp tresses.

His touch on her hair was soothing. She sat for some time, staring into the fire, enjoying its increasing heat and his careful ministrations. She turned her head to watch him curl the ends of a long strand around his palm to brush it free of tangles, then let it drift to join the heavy mass spilling around her. There was such concentration and purpose in his face. She longed to know what he was thinking, what he was feeling, but did not dare ask.

She could not sit there forever, as pleasant as that might be. She had to act. She had had some success at it in the fountain. She needed the encouragement of remembering that.

It had felt good, taking the few small steps to gain what she wanted. She wondered that she had been so long in coming to it. She had not been reared to independent thought, of course, much less independent action. Every facet of her life to this point had been planned and contrived for her. Her resistance to Giles's wishes, passive though it had been, was the beginning of the great change in her. It would not be the end.

Now. It must be now.

Katrine's foot was resting on Rowan's instep. She bent her knee a little, pressing, caressing the arch of his foot with the underside of her own. Her voice soft, almost dreamy, she said, "I'm glad someone taught you to make love, whoever it may have been."

"Are you?" His voice feathered in a warm gust over her shoulder. "Now, why?"

"Because I have reaped the benefit, and nothing can take that from me. Because there was no time for us to learn how to accommodate each other in the way of most couples, by trial and error over long years."

"More time might have had its advantages."

"Yes," she agreed quietly, thinking of how it could have been if the two of them had come together as young newlyweds. At the same time it was pleasing to her to know that he would also have wanted their time together to be longer. "Yes," she said again before she added, "I am indebted to you for showing me the—the pleasures of the body. I would have hated to have missed knowing them."

His movements stilled. His voice was compressed as he said, "If it had not been me, it would have been someone else, some other time."

"You mean in years to come, if I were widowed? Perhaps I would be too old then, too set in my chaste way of life to allow it."

"I doubt," he said in dry and grating tones, "that it would have been so long."

"You mean I would have succumbed to another man eventually, by Giles's will if not my own? No. That could never have happened. Only someone—someone like you could have prevailed."

He lifted his hand to her face, forcing her to turn to him, meet his gaze. "What are you saying?"

She could sustain the dark inquiry in his eyes for only a moment. Hiding behind the shields of her lashes, she said, "You are the champion, are you not? The qualities which make you an excellent sportsman also make you a good prospective father and superior lover."

"How do you know what manner of lover I am," he said, "never having had any other?"

Warm color suffused her face, though she considered only a moment before she answered. "Instinct, I think. Am I wrong? Is it possible that any other man could make me feel the same or respond to him with more abandon?"

A wry smile tugged at his mouth. "I hope not."

"Well, then."

"Modesty forbids that I agree, just as prudence forbids that I overlook the reason for the flattery."

"Meaning that you suspect me of saying it only to tempt you past endurance for the sake of a child?" she asked, sweeping her lashes wide open. "But I thought you were invincible, that nothing could make you lose control of your desires?"

"I never said that."

"Then your resolve might be tested if I did this?" she said, pressing her lips to the taut corner of his mouth. "Or this?" she added on a softer note as she reached to press her hand to his bare chest, searching out a tight pap in the curling, still-damp mat of hair that cushioned his breastbone.

He captured her hand, holding it in a grasp so tight that his fingernails whitened. His voice was rough as he demanded, "What other reason is there?"

"Perhaps," she said on a soft, indrawn breath, "I would like to give you pleasure for pleasure. Since there will never be your equal to share my bed, perhaps I would like to discover all the ways of loving that you know so well. Will you teach me?"

"God, Katrine . . ." he breathed.

Elation ran with daring in her blood as she saw his confusion. She said, softly, "Is there something I could do, some way of touching you I could learn, some technique that would return to you the same pleasure you have given me?"

"You—you must not say such things," he said, his voice hoarse.

"No? But how else am I to know what you would like?"

His face was grim as he said, "You require no technique. All you need do is look at me as you're doing now."

"There must surely be more," she said with a slight tilt of her head. "Women are so dependent on men that there has to be a means of pleasing that will aid in holding them."

His eyes narrowed. "There might be, if you are thinking of the need to revive a lagging ardor. That of your husband, for instance?"

She blinked, drawing back a space. "It never occurred to me."

"Then you really must explain this sudden desire—unless you are being less than truthful?"

There was a pause long enough for Katrine to take several shallow breaths. Her eyes, dark with the current of swift emotions, were fastened upon his intent gaze. He was more right than he knew, she thought. She wanted many things, beginning with complete knowledge of his methods as a lover and ending with a child. Most of all, however, she wanted him to wipe all thought or need for self-control from his mind. She wanted him to desire her so intensely that nothing else mattered. She wanted him to love her enough to give of himself without reservations.

Her hand clenched slowly upon his flesh as she saw what she should have known days before. She needed to know that he loved her for one reason only. She needed to know because she loved him.

Her voice was a strangled whisper as she spoke at last. "You will soon be gone; you must be. You will know other women, other loves. For me, it will be different. Is it so wrong, then, to seek to take and hold a lifetime of loving in a few short hours?"

"Am I supposed to feel guilt now?" he queried in quiet watchfulness.

Her heart contracted inside her; still, she answered with the truth since that was all that was left. "Yes," she said, "if it will sway you."

"And what then?"

"Make love to me only once without your special methods, and I promise you that you will never know the results. You can leave here and not look back. I will never contact you if there is a baby, never place any claim upon you in its name. You need have no fear for a child that is never known to you."

"Suppose," he said softly, "that I should send to know?"

She swallowed, and had to make the second attempt before she could produce sound. "That—would be your right, of course."

"My right?" he repeated, his voice taut. "What of my hope, my fear, my maimed and mishandled desire? Is that what you think of me, that I want no ties, no responsibilities? Don't you know that my days would be forever haunted by that one unendurable possibility, that you should bear a child in my image and I never be allowed to know it?"

She searched his face. "I wasn't sure."

"Knowing it now, would you tell me the truth? Would you dare, if you understood that should there be a babe born of our loving, I would come back to you through fire and storm, that I would seize you by force, if need be, and take you so far away that your husband would never find us?"

Fierce gladness mingled with distress swept in upon her. It was admirable that he should be so determined to hold and keep his own, yet she could not prevent the pain brought by the knowledge that his threatened protectiveness extended only so far and no further, that he would not come back, apparently, for her alone. It made her reckless.

She said, "Even at that risk, why should I be denied the comfort of a child? What right do you have to withhold it from me?"

"What right do you have to withhold knowledge of my brother's death from me? My scruples or yours; which holds the most potential for grief? Which is stronger?"

"Scruples," she said quietly, "can be terrible things."

There was agreement and regret in his voice. "I would give you anything you ask, do anything you ask, if there was no one to consider except the two of us."

"Would you?" Her tone was uneven, her smile strained.

"Can you doubt it?"

"I'm not sure," she said, and leaned slowly toward him until her breasts touched his bare chest and her lips were only inches from his.

He knew what she was doing; she could see it in his eyes. He did not draw back, but set the brush aside and smoothed his hands up her back, turning her more fully toward him, bringing her closer. "I am sure," he said, "that no matter the cost, it would be a crime to waste the time left to us."

His mouth was warm and sweet and generous; the blending of care and authority in his kiss was uniquely his own. She gave herself to it with a soft sound in her throat, pressing herself hard against him and twining her arms close about his neck and shoulders. The feel of his body molding to hers inflamed her.

Her need for him went beyond mere desire. It was wide and deep and edged with intimations of loss. There was desperation in it and rage, and a wild hunger fueled by terrible, aching fear. It hurt, that need, and only he could give her the antidote for the pain.

Permanence. Someone to cherish. A child to replace him, at least in part.

She would take that much from him, by guile and with love, if she could.

She brushed her hand over his ear and along the square shape of his jaw, then cupped the jut of his cheekbone with its faint trace of bruising and the taut plane of his cheek. She laid her lips upon his, slanting across the smooth, warm surface. Delicately invading, she engaged his tongue with her own, advancing, retreating, inviting him to join her in the amorous prologue to love. He accepted, enlarging on the theme with wit and courtesy and sudden, thrusting power.

The clasp of his arms tightened. Katrine felt a shifting sensation, then he was easing from the chair with her held firm against him, sinking toward the floor. A moment later she lay on the hearth rug while he braced on one elbow above her with orange-red firelight and determination leaping in his eyes.

Trepidation shivered over her, lodging in the pit of her stomach. For a single instant she was reminded of how little she knew this man, and how vulnerable she was to him. Then her gaze touched his mouth with its faint, quizzical smile at the corners. She reached up to him.

He bent his head, brushing her lips to exquisite sensitivity, feathering the line of their molding with the warm tip of his tongue. "Tell me," he said in husky tones, "if Terence did not win your embraces, why did he stay on at Arcadia?"

The shock of it held her perfectly still while with wide eyes she searched his face so close to her own. Something he had said—was it earlier in the day or the night before?—hovered at the edge of her mind. It seemed an explanation, if she could only remember. Then she had it.

You are suggesting that we should trade favors?

Those were the words he had spoken. He had pretended to think she meant to exchange her knowledge of his brother's death for the prospect of a child. Now it was what he intended; she knew it.

She drew a gasping breath, said, "You—you tried this once and could not see it through."

"So I did," he said in low agreement, "but there is a difference. I set out before to test your desires while restraining my own, to take from you without offering anything in return. That was unfair. This arrangement at least has equal compensation."

There was an uncontrollable quiver in her voice. "If you think this fair, you have a strange idea of justice."

He lowered his head, pressing the moist heat of his tongue to her breast, tasting it before drawing the nipple into his mouth. He held it a long, tingling instant before he answered. "You have something I need, I have something you want. An exchange doesn't seem unreasonable."

"Your methods—" she began.

"—are double-edged," he finished for her. "I cannot tempt you without tempting myself. As you well know. And you are free to serve me the same, if you dare."

It was not the greatest act of chivalry, his laying bare the exact nature of the contest between them, but it was honest. It was, in truth, much more just than what she had attempted to do moments before.

A great stillness gathered inside her. It began in the warm and beating center of her heart and spread outward in slow-moving waves. Her very being expanded, turning warm and liquid and calm; it was fearless, accepting, welcoming. She wanted him, and she would not be denied. She wanted him, and nothing else mattered.

She lifted her hand to his chest, trailing her fingers over the firm padding of muscle, combing her nails through the dark and silkily curling hair. Spreading her fingers, she pressed her palm to the chiseled definition of his shoulder and the bulge of his upper arm. The pleasure, and the importance of what she was doing, were both so great that her throat swelled with them; still, she forced words to her lips.

"Your brother," she said, "was not in love with me, never looked at me, never touched me except with respect. I was his hostess, nothing more."

"He admired from a distance, did he? He was always a well-mannered cub," Rowan said, fitting his hand carefully around her breast, pressing upward so that the damp and rosy nipple was lifted toward his lips. "But you haven't said why he stayed."

"He enjoyed the music, the dancing, the food and wine, and there were other distractions, other ladies."

The toweling had been caught between their bodies. She glanced at it from beneath her lowered lashes, then skimmed her fingers downward through the triangle of his soft chest hair, following the kite-string of it that disappeared under the waistband of his breeches as she had once longed to do. Just before she touched the bulge of his male member under the cloth, she caught the toweling and tugged.

He shifted, reaching to aid her in dragging the toweling from between them. His hand lingered at the level of her abdomen as he rubbed his knuckles across that flat surface and, in imitation of her own action, let them drift lower, into her smaller triangle of soft and damp russet down. "When last I heard of Terence, he had learned gallantry as well as manners. If not you, then which lady did he choose to honor with his bows and graces?"

"None," Katrine said, and drew in her breath sharply as he

touched, and centered his attention on, the most exquisitely sensitive place on her body.

"Are you sure?" he asked, the words whisper soft against her ear, the movement of thumb and forefinger upon her deliciously coordinated to the rhythm of his words. "Who could it have been? Not Georgette, I think. She would have been rough for his tastes, much more suited to the Satchels of this world. Sweet Charlotte might have aroused his protective instincts, but not his ardor. Musetta is too much the flirt to have held his interest for long. There seems to be no one. Yet he spoke of love in his letters. And of you."

Doubt and confusion made her voice tight. "He could not have meant me."

"No? Why not, if he loved you in secret, from a distance? You might never have noticed, though Giles could have, and possibly did."

"No," she murmured in near incoherence. Her blood was simmering in her veins; she could hardly breathe. In self-defense, she reached to place her palm on the hard length of him through his breeches, matching, mocking his rhythm.

He caught his breath, stiffened. He lifted his head. "What was that?"

She paused, listening. There was nothing to be heard except the thunder of her thrashing heart. It had, she thought, been a trick, one designed to give him time to steel his responses. She released him, thrust her hand under the waistband of his breeches, and curled her fingers around his maleness, holding tight.

He shifted his grasp to her hip. Kneading the smooth and rounded shape of it, smoothing the soft skin, he drew her closer. He reached lower to the bend of her knee and lifted it to lie across his thigh. The movement gave him unimpeded access to her softness, and he took instant, total advantage of it.

The penetration was sure yet careful, deep and knowledgeable, hard and strong, but without pain. Katrine shuddered with the sudden onslaught of sensation. A low sound, half cry, half supplication, caught with the pent breath in her throat. Her interior being contracted around him, drawing, holding. Slowly, blindly, she pressed against him.

His muscles quivered in a long, shivering spasm. Moisture broke out across his forehead and upper lip, and made a damp sheen along his arm. His chest swelled with the depth of his inhalation.

For long moments they lay unmoving, with eyes tightly closed. Then he lay his chin against her forehead. His voice as ragged as a banana leaf caught in a windstorm, he said, "There must be some reason you won't speak. Tell me that much at least, I beg you, before I lose mind and soul and take you like the most dumb and rutting beast."

"Gladly," she whispered, since she could do no more. "I keep my counsel because I gave my word, and because there has been enough pain, enough death."

"Honor," he said in rasping stringency, "can also be a terrible thing."

"Yes." She sighed, and opened her hands, releasing him even as she curled against him. "Please—please love me now, as you will, in any way you choose. I don't want, can't bear this anymore. I want—"

"Shh," he said against her hair. "I know. God, but how I know."

He covered her with his body; she opened her thighs to him with simple grace. He held her gaze there in the flickering firelight as he sank deep into the liquid heat of her. She took him inside, wanting to be filled, aching with the need. So intense was the satisfaction of that longing that gooseflesh prickled over her skin. Like a contagion, his skin surface caught and carried the same prickling, until the dark hair on his arms and chest stood in stiff ardor.

Rowan began to move. Then he whispered in hoarse, desperate demand. "Who was it? Who did my brother love?"

And Katrine, inhaling in sudden, hurtful shock, breathed the first nose-burning whiff of disaster.

Scorched wood. Burning cloth.

Smoke.

CHAPTER SIXTEEN

A haze of smoke hung in the upper air of the conservatory. Tendrils of it drifted toward the open bedchamber door, drawn by the draft of the fireplace where Katrine and Rowan lay. An ominous crackling noise could be heard somewhere below in the midnight quiet.

The tower was on fire.

Trapped. Trapped in a burning building with no way out. It was a horror in the mind, one that had always haunted Katrine.

Rowan rolled from her. He flung the nearest cover to hand, the length of toweling, in her direction, then scrambled for his breeches.

Katrine pushed to her knees. Her voice uncertain, she said, "Whoever was tending the boilers down below must have let the fire get out."

"Maybe," he answered in grim tones. A moment later he was gone, pounding down the stairs.

Katrine was not far behind him. Her nightgown lay where she had left it on the floor beside the fountain. She struggled into it in haste, fighting the folds that seemed bent on keeping her from pushing her arms into the short cap sleeves. She could hear Rowan moving at speed from one steam grating to another, saw him stop once and feel of the marble floor, seeking the source of the fire. He paused a moment at the entrance door, fruitlessly checking the lock and bolt.

By the time Katrine could push her head through the neck of her nightgown and drag its fullness down around her, Rowan was leaping up the stairs once more. She followed him at a run as he disappeared into the butler's pantry. By the time she reached him, he was coughing in the midst of the thick cloud of smoke shot with flames that boiled up through the dumbwaiter shaft. He slammed the door of that opening shut as she reached him.

"The fire is below, around the boiler, all right," he said. "We can't get out this way."

"Get out?" Katrine echoed, searching his face with wide eyes.

He gave a decisive nod. "The lock on the door at the bottom of the shaft could be forced; it was made to hold from the outside, not the inside. We could have climbed down that way if the fire had started somewhere else."

"Climbed down?" she said slowly. "You mean we could have escaped."

"There was a man on guard duty," he answered with wariness in his face. "The gardener who tends the fire, I think."

"He would have been no match for someone like you."

"There might have been others."

"Oh, yes," she said in swift and totally spurious agreement. "But you didn't bother to find out, did you?"

He lifted a brow while a grim smile tilted one corner of his mouth. "No," he said, "I didn't. I didn't want to see, didn't want to escape. Is that what you wanted to know?"

It was, of course, yet his frank admission still took her breath. She had known that he wanted her. She had not known how much.

"Why?" she said in bald query.

Cogent thought flickered in his eyes, then was gone. He

reached to touch her face. "The question is, where are those guards now? Or the gardener for that matter. I would love to discuss this with you here and now, with special attention to reasons and rewards, but we might get a little warm doing it."

It could not be denied. She made no protest as he caught her hand, swinging toward the door.

In the short time since they had left the conservatory, the air had filled with dense gray-black smoke. It rose through cracks in the walls to boil against the glass overhead. Snake's tongues of flame licked at the bases of the cypress pilasters here and there. The hiss and crackle of eating flames was louder.

"It's in the walls," Rowan said. "Whoever set this place to blazing knew what they were doing."

"How do you know it was set?" she protested.

"It makes sense, doesn't it? After the other things that have happened?"

The sawn wheel, the cut saddle girth. Yes, it made sense, of a terrible kind. She closed her lips tightly together. She preferred not to think of who might be responsible.

When she looked back at Rowan, he was measuring the grooved stone of the wall underneath the glass cupola with his eyes. His gaze stopped at several fixed points, as if marking hand- and foot-holds.

Katrine watched him an instant, then tugged at his hand. "No," she said, "not that way; the smoke is too thick. Let me show you."

She hurried, half running, back toward the bedchamber. It might have been imagination, but it seemed that the floor was growing warm under her feet. There was an acrid layer in the smoke that caught in the lungs and made her eyes stream. She breathed too deep, and a spasm of coughing doubled her over, though she never stopped moving.

She led the way to the bedchamber. Running toward the great armoire wedged into a corner, she flung open the door. She reached inside, lifting a hidden latch. The small door panel fitted into the end against the corner wall swung wide.

Revealed in the opening was a narrow stair lined with stone, winding down into the darkness. Spiderwebs and dust floated in the heated air wafting up from below, but there were only a few wisps of smoke.

Rowan gave a grunt of surprise. As Katrine stepped into the armoire he shot out his arm, barring her way. His voice taut, he said, "It's your turn to explain."

"It's a servants' stair," she answered in careful tones, "one built into the stone wall so Cato could come and go without advertising his presence. Or a woman, before Giles's marriage. It leads to a hidden door on the side facing the woods. Delphia told me about it when I came here as a bride."

"That isn't what I meant, and you know it," Rowan said evenly.

She didn't like the tone of his voice. "As you said yourself, there's no time," she told him. "We have to be quick, before the smoke finds its way through the cracks in the stone."

She bent her head to duck under his arm, but he stopped her again. "You could have left the tower, too. Admit it."

She turned her head to meet his gaze and arched a brow. "There might," she said stringently, "have been a guard. Or a lock."

"But you didn't look to see."

"What was the point?" she said, avoiding his eyes.

He snorted. His tone laden with grim promise, he said, "We'll discuss it later. Wait here. I'll be back."

He didn't linger for her agreement, but sprinted away back into the bedchamber. He returned seconds later carrying one of the wrought-iron floor candelabra. The candles had been removed. Without them, the tridentlike head made a formidable weapon.

Rowan drew Katrine aside. Bending his head for the low

portal, he went before her through the end of the armoire and down the winding stair. She followed after him with hasty steps.

The two men appeared halfway to the bottom, shadows of brute size with pale skin and cloths tied over their faces, rising out of the dark. The one in the lead cursed as he saw them. He made a fast movement, and a blade caught a gleam of light. The two moved in to the attack.

Rowan spared Katrine a quick backward look. Certain of her position two steps behind him, he braced his back on the curved wall, brought his weapon up, and swung.

The leading attacker took the blow in the stomach and shot backward into the other man. The two tumbled, sprawling down the stairs. The clatter of metal on stone could be heard. Rowan bounded down after them.

Katrine smothered a cry of alarm. Eyes wide and staring, she searched the well of darkness. She surged downward a few steps, then stopped. She had no weapon, could not help Rowan. So long as she was out of his way, every person in the dark was a foe; he need not take care who he injured. She was better out of it.

At the same time her mind raced. She could smell fresh air and the fishy smell of the lake; the door below must have been left standing open. The two men were not servants or field hands from Arcadia, not ordinary guards. Their skin had been white and they had been moving upward. They had not, she thought, been intent on rescue.

Below her, there was the sound of blows and grunted oaths. Something soft slid over stone. There came a deep-throated shriek, suddenly cut off.

Quiet fell. In it, a man could be heard, panting for breath.

"Rowan?" Katrine's voice echoed with a desperate timbre in the enclosed space.

"Come," he said on a ragged gasp. "Hurry."

The stone steps hurt her feet as she sped down them. One

moment there was darkness, the next a hard arm reached out to whip around her waist, arresting her progress.

"Not that fast," he said on a husky laugh. "You'll break both our necks."

Her heart was beating so hard she felt sick. She wanted to kiss him or slap him, and wasn't sure which to do first. Instead she stiffened and drew away.

He reached out and caught her wrist, snatching her back. Moving with care and without sound, he pulled her after him down the last few steps. There, they flattened themselves against the wall.

For long moments they searched the night beyond the open door with their eyes. Nothing moved. An orange light was growing, radiating through the glass of the cupola above them. In its light, the woodland that crowded up to the tower on that side stood dark and silent. Nothing moved in the tree shadows.

"Let's go," Rowan said, and stepped out into the darkness.

He kept close to the tower, following its curvature, watching the night around them. He had taken no more than a half-dozen steps when he stumbled. He dropped to one knee beside a long, still shape in the dry grass. A soft imprecation left him.

Katrine, sinking down beside Rowan, leaned past his shoulder to see the face of the man who lay there. His features were gray and splotched with blood from an ugly cut in his scalp. If he was breathing, it was not possible to see it. It was Giles.

The eyelids quivered in the waxen mask of a face, opening with jerky slowness. The older man's gaze wandered, then fastened on Katrine. His eyes widened in wild dismay. He lifted a trembling hand. His mouth opened and closed. The sound he produced at last was dry and weak. "Run," he said. "They're coming for you—to kill you. Run . . ."

"Who?" Rowan said, leaning over the other man in urgent appeal.

Giles opened his mouth, but nothing came out. His face

twisted and he dropped his lifted hand to his chest, plucking at the front of the dressing gown he wore.

There were footfalls coming toward the tower. Heavy, fast moving, without extra sound, they could only belong to the killers Giles had tried to warn them about. Rowan sprang to his feet, then moved to Giles's head and bent to grasp him under the shoulders.

"What are you doing?" Katrine asked, even as she ran to her husband's feet and lifted his ankles so he would be easier to move.

"Getting him away from the wall, in case it goes—and away from the door."

He meant out of the sight of whoever was coming, Katrine thought. It would be a miracle if they made it.

She reckoned without Rowan's strength. Short moments later they laid Giles down with his back to a tree at the edge of the woods. Rowan hesitated, as if loath to leave him there, but there was no choice. The men pouring around the side of the tower were not from Arcadia. In the orange-red light from above, they were white men dressed in ragged blanket coats and shapeless twill pantaloons held up with homemade suspenders. With their ragged hair and hard faces, they had the look of the worst kind of riverfront scum.

"Rowan," she whispered.

"Not now," he answered just as quietly, and motioned her back into the woods.

She looked back just once. The river pirates thought she and Rowan were still in the tower; they were pushing and shoving, snarling and cursing each other as they tried to get inside. They carried cocked pistols in their hands and thick-bladed knives without guards, and there was bloodlust in their eyes.

Katrine swung sharply away from the sight. It was then it came to them, the clanging of the plantation bell. Close upon it could be heard the noise of people yelling. The fire had been discovered in the slave quarters. Soon the grounds would be swarming with the people of Arcadia. It was possible the alarm, and the prospect of discovery, would drive off the river men.

Rowan did not seem ready to depend on the chance. He caught her arm to pull her deeper into the covering underbrush. Putting her head down, Katrine concentrated on following where he led, and keeping her feet in the darkness closing in around them.

Tree limbs reached down to drag at her hair and brush slapped her in the face. Briers pierced her feet and scratched her ankles. Vines wound around her legs, threatening to trip her. They scrambled down into dry washes and out again, and crossed the winding branches of the shallow creek that fed the tower fountain so many times that the rag that was left of Katrine's nightgown was wet to the waist.

The underbrush around them rustled to the retreat of wild things scurrying out of their path. The smell of leaf mold and crushed leaves and disturbed earth rose around them, covering the scent of smoke. The cool wetness of dew shaken from spiderwebs and dangling evergreen leaves cooled their heated faces.

The roar and snap of the fire and the frenzied ringing of the plantation bell receded behind them. They could not seem to lose it, however. It even seemed to grow louder now and then, as if by a trick of a vagrant wind. It was one of those times when Katrine, fighting for air with laboring lungs, grasped Rowan's arm and dragged him to a halt.

"Stop," she pleaded. "Rest. Just a—minute."

"We're almost there," Rowan said.

His own breathing was deep, but without apparent effort. It would have been annoying, if she had allowed it to be. She peered closely at his face. "Where? Where are we going?"

His mouth seemed to move in a tight smile. "The one place we'll be safe."

"And that is?"

"There," he answered, and stepped aside, gesturing ahead of them through the trees.

A darkened house loomed before them, a great house of two stories embellished with Gothic arches at the gable ends, with balconies, and a carpenter's nightmare of arabesque carving and sawn woodwork. A front court white with crushed oyster shells and a long drive of the same material lay before it. The rooftop was outlined in an orange nimbus of glowing light.

"Arcadia," she said in blank wonder.

"Where else?" he said, and began to move toward the house.

"No, wait." She wrenched him to a halt once more.

He turned, stepping so close that his thighs brushed hers. His voice quiet and deep, he said, "Is there somewhere else, sweet Katrine, that you want to go?"

There was something in his words that brought the ache of tears behind her eyes. She couldn't prevent them from sounding in her voice as she answered, "Yes. Anywhere."

"I had thought," he said, almost as if speaking at random, "that it might be possible to get into the main house during the excitement. We could find something to wear, then show up as if just wakened. In separate beds, of course."

"The others may have returned with Giles. We could run into them in the halls."

"There would be some sign by now, more lights and noise in the house."

She bit her lip before nodding in reluctant agreement. "But—suppose we are seen by the men sent after us?"

"I would try my best," he said dryly, "to avoid it."

She shook her head. "I don't know."

He watched her in silence for long moments. When he spoke, his voice was even, without inflection. "If you have no objection to being seen together in our current state of dishabille, then I have none."

She saw his point at once. "It's kind of you to consider my good name, but it's hardly worth the risk of our lives."

"And more than that," he said, tilting his head to one side, "you discovered a certain freedom in our enforced idyll, and are not sure you want to return to your other prison."

"Freedom?" she repeated.

"To say what you wish, to do as you wish without censure; to go naked if it pleases you, to tempt a man if you dare. To know that someone will not only understand and accept what you do and what you are, but will encourage you—if that's what you need."

Her throat ached with the press of tears as she listened. Against its tightness, she whispered, "Yes."

He was silent while beyond them the flames leaped and the bell tolled. Finally he said, "And so?"

She swallowed, and had to try the second time before she could speak. Even then, her voice was no more than a thread of sound. "So it's impossible, isn't it? Someone must see to Giles, get him into the house, and send for a doctor. And the tower; we can't just let it burn." She hesitated, went on with difficulty. "It's our duty to do what we can."

"Yes," he answered on a soft sigh, almost to himself. "It was always—impossible."

They kept to the deepest shadows and used every scrap of cover on the way in to the house. No one challenged them, no one tried to stop them. The side door was wide open, the great rooms inside empty. The house servants had run out to the back to see the fire, and there was no sign of Musetta and the others.

Katrine and Rowan parted at the door to her bedchamber. The fear that someone might appear and see them at any moment made their leave-taking brief.

"I'll go out and pretend to discover Giles as soon as I've thrown on my own clothes," Rowan said.

She nodded. "Look around for Cato. He'll know how to make his master more comfortable, also who best to send for the doctor."

Rowan agreed. "If I see Delphia, I'll send her to you. After that, I may be busy for a while."

With Giles down, and Brantley and the other men still at the steamboat, someone would need to organize the effort to control the fire and see to it that the flames did not spread to the main house. There were also the river pirates out there some-where. It was unlikely they would attack Rowan with the people of Arcadia behind him, but there was no way to guarantee that.

"If you'll wait, I'll come with you," Katrine said abruptly.

He shook his head. "It will take too long; you'll have to dress. I love the way you look, but the others might not under-stand. And time may be running out for Giles."

"Yes," she said, her gaze dark as she stared at him. She moistened her lips. "Take care."

He caught her hand, pressing a kiss into the palm. There was rare sweetness in his smile as he said, "I will do that."

He inclined his head while holding her gaze, then he whirled away and was gone. Katrine stepped into her bedcham-ber and closed the door slowly behind her.

A shadowy movement caught the corner of her eye. It was her own reflection in her dressing-table mirror. There was enough fire glow from beyond the windows to light up the room. In that peculiar orange-pink illumination, she moved slowly toward the mirror.

I love the way you look—

It was a compliment to be treasured, to be put away in layers of rose leaves and brought out for remembrance when she was gray and near senile. What had Rowan seen, really? She needed to know.

The woman in the mirror was different; she saw that at once. It was not just her hair flowing in wild abandon down her back. It was not the near-transparent rag of a nightgown she wore with a rent from waist to jagged hem that showed a scandalous length of bare limb. It was not the flush of color in her face and lips, nor the easy way she moved. No, it was something in the eyes. They held a softness and warmth and rich self-awareness that had not been there before. There was vulnerability, also, combined with the beginnings of desolation. It was the look of love, she thought, and of renunciation.

She closed her eyes and lifted her hands to cover her face, pressing tight. She would not remember, she wouldn't. This was not the time for vain regret, for mourning the loss of closeness of mind and heart, of bitter words and challenging will and sweet surrender, of loving, of the prospect of a child.

She was the chatelaine of Arcadia. No matter where she had been for the past few days or what she had been doing, she must step back into her old position. There were tasks to be done, duties to be performed.

Pride and duty, these were the underpinnings of her life; they always had been, always would be. She had nothing else, would never have more.

She lowered her hands. Taking a deep breath, she squared her shoulders and shook back her hair. It would be all right. One day, when she was near death, perhaps, she would begin to forget, and it would be all right.

She stepped to the washstand and poured water from the pitcher into the bowl. The scratches on her arms and neck stung as she bathed them. Her feet were cut also, and there was more than one thorn buried in the flesh of her heels. A quick wash would have to do for now, however.

She dropped the cloth and moved to the armoire, searching through it for something that she could get into with a minimum of effort, but that would cover her arms and shoulders. A rose poplin with a high neck edged with lace and closed by pearl buttons up the front came to hand. She turned with it to place it on the bed.

There came the scrape of a footstep from the direction of the door into the hall. Katrine looked up, expecting to see Delphia.

"Well now," the man in the doorway drawled, "just look what we have here. I says to myself, Isom, old coon, the bitch you want will circle back to 'er den, sure's you be born. And just see here how right I was."

The shapeless hat with a hole in the crown as if someone had taken a bite out of it, the raccoon vest worn over faded wool underwear, the greasy breeches tucked into ancient, water-stained boots, the oily beard and dirty skin; everything marked him as being from the river. She dropped the gown she held and backed slowly away from him.

"What are you doing here? Who sent you?"

"Oh, now, just listen," he said with a smile that showed blackened stumps of teeth. "She knows a thing or two, she does." He moved after her, his eyes roving over her, coming to rest on the small triangular shadow beneath her ragged nightgown. "Seems sinful, damned me if it don't, cutting the life out of such a fancy piece of goods. But money's money."

"Whatever you were offered, my husband will give you more." Behind her on the washstand, where Rowan had left it after taking it from the bed so many nights ago, lay his sword in its sheath. Could she use it? She didn't know, but at least it was a chance.

"Aw, now, they all say something like that. But where would this old coon be, iffen I listened? 'Sides, nothing was told me 'bout what to do, or not, to you, fancy piece, and I got me a powerful urge to—"

Katrine closed her mind to the rest of it, did her best to ignore the rank smell of old wood smoke, old animal hides, and old sweat that rose from him. It was easy to see from the swagger in his walk that he did not expect resistance from her. She would have surprise on her side, then. She also needed some way to distract him, if only for a moment.

"Suppose," she said through the tightness in her throat, "suppose I let you. What then?"

Ribald delight spread over the man's face. "Say, you something, ain't you, fancy? Let me. Gawd. Let me? Why, ain't nothing you can do to stop me."

She wanted to kill him, in that moment, with a passion shocking in its virulence. She hated his crudeness, his overweening confidence in his superior strength, his enjoyment of her fear. She was disgusted by his drooling pleasure in what he meant to do.

None of it mattered. She could not let it cloud her thinking. There was something nagging at the back of her mind. She could not quite capture the whole, but a portion had to do with what the man was saying.

She took another step backward. "You may find it harder," she said in scathing tones, "to kill Rowan de Blanc."

"The man left with you out there?" He gestured in the direction of the burning tower. "I'll make fish bait out of him, he gets in my way."

It was her the man was after; Rowan, it seemed, was important only as a possible impediment. There could be only one reason. She had known it must be so, yet how difficult it was to believe it, even now.

She thought of Giles lying in the grass with blood matting his hair and shining in the grooves of age in his face. She thought of Terence, gentle and kind and so young. She thought of Rowan, serious, dedicated, as he raised himself above her in the firelight. They made a kaleidoscope in her mind, those images, and because of them she knew she had made a wrong choice days ago, desperately wrong.

"Ho, now I see what you're after, fancy," the man who

called himself Isom said with a salacious grin. "You want to poke me with that there long hog-sticker behind you. Now, that ain't no thing for a lady to do, you know it ain't. But you can try, be you of a mind."

He pulled a knife with a crude hilt, a tapered blade, and wickedly sharp point from his waistband. Flourishing it in wide swipes, he dropped into a rough-and-tumble fighter's crouch.

It was at that moment that Delphia appeared in the doorway. Her eyes snapped open as she saw the man. Her mouth flew open and a scream of throat-tearing horror blasted the air.

The man's head snapped around toward the sound. In that second of inattention, Katrine whipped backward and snatched the hilt of the sword. The pitcher on the washstand went flying, crashing to the floor, as she ripped the blade from the scabbard. The sword was heavier and longer than she remembered. As she brought it around, the tip plunged downward, striking the floor. She grasped it with both hands, bringing it up.

The man snarled as he swung to face her. He lunged. Katrine whirled the sword, bringing it up from below to parry his slashing cut. The blow vibrated along the blade to numb her wrists; her backhanded slice at his midsection lacked the power to cut through his heavy coat. It gave her attacker pause, however. He stumbled backward a step. Then his eyes narrowed in vicious intent. He leaped toward her.

He meant to overpower her with sheer brawn. Katrine set her feet, clenched her teeth, and steeled her grasp on her sword.

There was a soft, whisper of sound behind her, a shadow of movement. Another one was behind her; he must have come through the open dressing-room door beside the washstand. There was no time to turn, no time to react. His arms, long and hard with muscle, settled around her, gripped her hands that held the sword.

The man called Isom drew his lips back in a grimace. He drove at her heart with his knife.

Katrine lifted the sword that had suddenly become a feather's weight. She circled the knife blade and brushed it aside. With Rowan's arms around her and his weight behind her, she bent one knee in a graceful lunge, and thrust the steel in her hands deep into the river pirate's heart.

"God," Rowan breathed. He jerked the sword free, letting the man fall. Wrenching the blade from her convulsive grasp, he flung it, clattering, against the wall. He turned Katrine to him then, dragging her tight to him with her face pressed into his shoulder. His voice was low, jerking as he went on. "I saw that scum—I was with Giles when I saw him sneaking into the house. I was so far away. I thought—I was afraid I wouldn't be in time."

Delphia moved into the room. Her face was gray and her hands clenched tight upon the starched and frilled cloth of her apron. There was a curious expression, half scorn, half jealousy, on her face as she said, "You nearly were not."

Katrine stirred in Rowan's hold. She pushed at him a little with her hands and arms that were folded between them. As he released her she said, "It doesn't matter. He came."

"Yes," Delphia said, "and now he must go. I was about to tell you, madam, that the wagons are coming up the drive. Master Brantley is riding alongside them, and Master Lewis."

Katrine turned to look at her maid. "If that's so, the carriages cannot be far behind. I wonder what brought them so quickly."

"I would guess it was Master Giles," Delphia said, her tone expressionless. "No doubt he was anxious."

"I suppose that could be it," Katrine agreed in low tones.

"Whatever the reason, we must be glad, under the circumstances," the maid said with a slight tightening at the corners of her mouth.

"Yes," Katrine echoed, lifting her eyes to meet Rowan's dark green gaze. "I suppose we must."

CHAPTER SEVENTEEN

"My dear Katrine, what have you been doing with yourself since we have been gone? Your poor hands have such scratches that I cringe at the thought of the pain."

Musetta made her observations halfway through dinner. It was a late meal after a sketchy luncheon and nonexistent breakfast due to the uproar and unsettled nerves of the household.

The table was laden with candles and flowers, along with an extensive menu of food and wine. Everything possible had been done to try to make this first time everyone had come together since the return from the hunting expedition seem normal; but, the gathering had, until now, been subdued. They were too tired, too anxious, too aware of the empty place at the head of the table for anything approaching easy conversation.

Katrine barely glanced at the marks marring the backs of her hands before giving the first answer that came to mind. "I gathered a bouquet of roses for my aunt's sickroom during my visit with her. Unfortunately her garden has been allowed to run wild these past months since her illness."

"Without gloves? Insane." Musetta shivered.

"It was an impulse, after I saw the roses from a window."

"Was Rowan there? He seems injured also."

Katrine met Rowan's steady gaze as he sat on her right.

Holding it, she said, "He was kind enough to lend his aid and comfort when I found myself in difficulties."

"There was no question of kindness," he said, inclining his head. "I was honored to have been of service."

Katrine could not prevent the rise of heat to her cheekbones. She should have known it would be dangerous to attempt any sort of veiled communication with Rowan; he was far too daring, and adept at the double entendre, for her comfort.

The only one who appeared to notice her discomfiture was the stranger at the table, a gentleman who peered intently at the scratches on her hands and the color in her face. He was the doctor brought to attend Giles. Arriving early that morning, he had scarcely left his patient since. A heart attack brought on by the shock of the fire and the head injury had been his diagnosis.

It was toward this gentleman that Musetta turned her attention now. "You say, Dr. Mercier, that my brother is holding his own, yet you won't allow anyone other than his wife to see him. You must realize that as his sister I have a natural anxiety. When, pray, will we all be allowed to visit with him?"

The doctor put down his fork and wiped his mouth with the square of damask napkin that he had tucked into the top of his waistcoat. He folded the napkin and placed it beside his plate. Thin and tall, with precise movements, a pince-nez perched on his nose, and a pronounced French accent, he was a man well aware of his own importance.

"Your brother, madam," he said when he was quite ready, "is gravely ill. Stronger men than he have perished under the triple blow of concussion, heart attack, and prolonged delay before treatment was begun. *Le Bon Dieu* alone knows why your brother still lives, especially given the chronic weakness of his system."

"Chronic weakness—you mean Giles has actually been ill all this time?" The blank surprise in Musetta's face would, at another time, have been comical.

"Undoubtedly. There are matters concerning his case which puzzle me greatly, coming new to it as I do, matters I would like to discuss with his previous physician. But above and beyond this problem, we must consider his precarious condition at present—not to mention his expressed wishes."

Lewis, listening to the exchange with a keen look in his eyes, spoke in sharp tones. "His what?"

"My patient has no desire to see anyone at present. The exception is his wife. To this I can only add that I feel his decision to be a wise one. It has been my experience in these matters that visitations from relatives are often fraught with tension. This is especially true when there may be expectations of a monetary nature depending on the outcome of the illness of a loved one."

"Well, of all the nerve!" Lewis exclaimed with outrage in his narrow eyes.

The doctor pushed to his feet. "I apologize," he said, unperturbed, "if I have given anyone affront. It was, I hope I need not say, unintentional. My concern is for my patient. If you will excuse me now, I must return to him."

The table was quiet while the doctor's footsteps faded from the room. When he was gone, Lewis flung down his napkin, declaring, "Unintentional my ah—eye."

Musetta looked from Lewis to her husband, her gaze barely resting on Katrine in the process. "Can Giles really have barred us from his rooms?"

Brantley pursed his lips. With a shake of his head, he said, "I see no reason for the man to lie."

"Oh, but why? He should know none of us cares for—for our expectations. It's ridiculous."

"This man is officious beyond permission," Lewis said waspishly. "I don't care how good he's supposed to be, I prefer old Grafton. What did you say happened to him?"

It was Rowan who answered. "Dr. Grafton broke his leg while taking a fence during a fox hunt up near Natchez. Dr.

Mercier, it seems, is an acquaintance of the Barrows family, a New Orleans physician visiting with them for the expected confinement of a Barrows daughter-in-law." He added, "Cato knew where to send for him."

Alan, seated farther down the table between Georgette and Charlotte, leaned back in his chair. "It looks to me as if it was lucky Mercier was close by. I'm not sure Grafton could have handled the problem."

"It was also lucky, I think," Charlotte said in her whispery voice, "that Rowan was here. I can't bear to think what those horrible men would have done to Mr. Giles if he hadn't stopped them."

"You give me too much credit," Rowan said with a steady look in the girl's direction. "The river pirates took off soon enough when they discovered there was someone on the place other than the people from the quarters."

"But why did they ransack Giles's tower?" Musetta asked, spreading her hands. "It isn't as if they expected to find the family silver there. I don't understand it."

"No, but I'm still glad they're gone," Charlotte said with a shiver.

"I wish they would come back," Georgette said, entering the discussion with a gleam in her eyes. "I'd like to take my pistol to them, or a whip. And I'd love to see Rowan run one through with his sword."

There was a small silence. Katrine glanced at Rowan, but he was studying the rim of his wineglass. He did not, she thought, find the role of hero agreeable. No one other than the two of them and Delphia knew that the man killed by a sword thrust had died inside the house. No one else was aware that Katrine had had a hand in it, or that she had been his chosen prey. It had seemed best that way, though it placed Rowan in a false position.

It was difficult to see why he should mind, since he had certainly defeated the two men on the tower's secret stair. It was not his fault they had recovered in time to make their escape with the others when the alarm began to ring out.

The awkward lull in the conversation seemed a good time to give the signal for the ladies to leave the gentlemen to their port and pecans. Katrine was about to suggest it when Rowan spoke again, this time to the table at large.

"Does anyone know," he said in neutral tones, "why Giles returned to Arcadia in advance of the rest of you?"

They looked at each other. It was Brantley who finally spoke. "I'm not sure he gave a reason. I assumed it had something to do with the comfort of his guests."

"Or else he felt the need for activity after being on the steamboat, and decided to ride on ahead," Alan added.

Rowan watched them all, his gaze measuring. "So far as any of you knows, he had no reason to suspect that something might be wrong here?"

"Surely he would have gathered us together and requested our help if that were so," Perry suggested.

Brantley, his prominent forehead creasing in a frown, said, "Just what are you getting at, sir?"

"Nothing of importance," Rowan answered with a shift of his shoulder. "It seemed an unlucky coincidence that he arrived just in time to be struck down."

Katrine, watching the fleeting expression of Rowan's face, thought she saw where his thoughts had led him. Giles had doubtless ridden for Arcadia in advance of his guests for the sole purpose of releasing Rowan and herself from the tower. He had, perhaps, thought to allow them time to return to the house and make themselves presentable before the others arrived. That he had appeared at the same time as the river pirates was either a colossal piece of bad timing, or else someone had known he would be there, had known his errand.

That last possibility required a readjustment of her thinking. If someone had known he would be at Arcadia, then her husband's injury was no accident; he had not been beaten and left for dead because he happened to interrupt the attack on the tower. No. He had been meant to die with Rowan and herself.

Someone had tried to use the scum from the river to be rid of the three of them. The question was, who hated them that much?

"While we are on this subject," Rowan was saying with a trace of steel in his voice, "has it occurred to anyone that this is the second year the Arcadia tournament has ended in calamity? Have none of you thought to wonder why?"

Lewis, leaning back in his chair and making a plaited bridge of his fingers, said, "We were all sorry for the death of your stepbrother, de Blanc, but if you are suggesting that there is some connection between that tragedy and this attack by river scum, I, for one, fail to see it. The river pirates are a recent evil."

"My brother," Rowan said deliberately, "was found dead on the grounds of Arcadia. Our host was also found lying injured outside the house. Will you say there is no similarity there?"

"We know who felled Giles," Lewis said reasonably.

"Do we? Or do we know who we are supposed to think felled him? Was there no one else who left the rest of you to ride ahead? Is there no one who was missing from among you on the night my brother died?"

Lewis looked slowly around the table, his gaze resting on the other men and women one by one. His smile was pitying as he returned to Rowan. "No one."

Charlotte, her eyes wide in her thin face, whispered, "But I thought Terence—that is, I understood he—did away with himself."

"De Blanc thinks otherwise, or so it appears," Lewis told her.

"So do I," Georgette said, "always did. He wasn't the kind, liked living too much for it, not to mention liking himself."

Rowan, his gaze steady on her broad, high-colored face, said, "What do you think happened?"

"Some silly quarrel that got out of hand, most likely over cards or women or horses. Kind of thing that happens too often, in my opinion." Georgette's tone was morose.

"Yes, and in mine also," Katrine said into the quiet that followed. She rose to her feet with a significant glance around the table at the other women. "Ladies, shall we?"

Her hands were trembling, she discovered as she led the way toward the parlor. It was nervous reaction, she thought, along with exhaustion and the necessity of appearing the composed and capable hostess while her mind was in turmoil. How she wished she could go somewhere this moment and lie down and close her eyes; she had not closed them in days, it seemed, not since she had slept in Rowan's arms in the tower.

It was impossible. She could, however, be alone for a few moments. She needed desperately to be able to stop smiling and pretending for that long.

When the other women were settled in the parlor with their needlework, cards, and gossip, Katrine excused herself to check on Giles. He was lying quiet and still, his breath barely moving the covers over his chest. Against the starched linen of his pillowcase and the bandaging around his head, his face was pallid, with a waxen look about the nose and mouth.

Dr. Mercier looked up from where he sat with a book in his hands to nod as she entered. He did not speak, nor did Katrine. There seemed no reason to inquire as to the progress of his patient; it was easy to see there had been no change. Her husband was as he had been since they had put him in his bed, hovering in a state somewhere between sleep and waking. Once or twice he had roused to cry out and mumble half-coherent phrases, but lapsed each time into his light coma once more.

Katrine spoke his name in a low tone. His hand twitched,

briefly, at the sound, but he did not waken. She touched his fingers lying on the coverlet, then turned and went away again.

She did not return to the parlor immediately, but swung toward a doorway at the end of the long hallway. It led to one of the balconies that decorated the side of the house facing the tournament field. She stepped out onto the small parapet with its drapery of ornate wood carving.

The air was fresh, the darkness welcome. These things, with the open height, reminded her of the tower. Most things did that now. She took a deep breath and let it out slowly. She had thought to find a few moments of peace, but it seemed none was to be had anywhere.

The door latch clicked behind her. She turned to see the tall, dark figure of a man step out on the balcony.

"Don't say it," Rowan cautioned her before she could speak. "I know I shouldn't have followed you, but I saw you step out here, and thought there might be a chance for a few words without interruption."

"There may be," she said with wry weariness, "if we are quick."

His nod of understanding was only a vague movement in the dimness. Still he stood without speaking.

To fill what was becoming an uncomfortable silence, she said, "There's been no opportunity to ask about Omar. You found him none the worse for his stint in the plantation jail?"

"Actually I think he enjoyed it. He seems to have kept Delphia running back and forth at a pretty steady pace. She may be more glad he's free again than Omar is himself."

"She hasn't had much to say about it."

"He told me she came of her own will to let him out when the tower started burning. It was as well, since he was about to tear the jail down, though he appreciated it all the same."

"Delphia did say Omar was magnificent in the fight to keep

the fire from spreading. I believe he has impressed her, which isn't easy."

Rowan made no reply. He moved to stand near Katrine at the railing. After a moment he said, "I've been thinking that it's time for me to go."

Katrine took a deep breath and let it out carefully. "I have been wondering when it would be."

"It wasn't possible before, not when it seemed that gang of river cutthroats might return. Every hour that passes makes that less likely. With that consideration fading, there is another that has to be weighed. If by chance it was my presence that was the trigger for the attacks on you and Giles, then it's better that I don't linger."

There was cold distress inside Katrine that had not been there before. She moistened her lips. "Suppose your being here had nothing to do with it?"

"Then I should still leave, if only to prevent talk."

"Yes," she said unsteadily. "Anyway, I expect you have duties and obligations elsewhere."

"None that would interfere with staying," he answered, turning to lean with his back against the balustrade beside her. "But I would not injure you more than I have already."

"And if I said there was no injury?"

"I would be glad," he said quietly, "if I believed it."

She could not hold him, and had no right to try. The kindest thing she could do, then, might be to set him free.

With a lift of her chin, she said, "I'm sure whatever damage has been done will be mended soon enough. Perhaps it will be better if you don't remain, after all. If Giles wakes and finds you here still, he may be overwrought."

"We would not want that," Rowan said, the words short, without expression.

"No," she agreed, but could say no more for the hard knot in her chest.

"As your husband, he has your fears and prayers and, of course, your love. Just as he deserves."

"Of—of course." She turned her shoulder to him, though she knew he could not possibly see her face.

A stray night wind with dampness in its chill found them on the balcony, stirring Rowan's hair and lifting the heavy hem of Katrine's skirt. After a time Rowan pushed away from the balustrade. In pensive tones, he said, "*La belle dame sans merci.* I see what Terence was saying."

He left her then, reentering the house with swift and silent treads. Katrine made no move to stop him. She stood with her hands clenched on the railing, staring wide-eyed into the dark. The pain inside her was grinding, like a stone weight slowly crushing her heart. It took every ounce of her will, every minute particle of her strength, to prevent her knees from buckling under her. She breathed in tiny, aching gasps, because that was all she could do. She didn't cry. That was a relief, and a solace, denied her. There were some things beyond tears.

The gentlemen had deserted the dining room for the parlor by the time Katrine reached it. It appeared Rowan must have said something to the others about going, for there was a general discussion concerning leave-taking in progress. She paused for a moment with her hand on the doorknob, shamelessly listening.

"I was thinking it was time and more I pushed off toward home," Satchel was saying in his booming voice. "Be happy to stay if I could be of use, but don't want to be in the way."

"Exactly so," Georgette seconded him. "Besides, I'm promised for the hunting at the Cavendishes' place. I wouldn't mind missing it to help Katrine, but don't know that I can."

"But I don't want it all to end," Charlotte said in a soft wail.

"None of us do," Alan told her, his voice severe, "but there's no point in giving Katrine and the Arcadia servants more work."

"I would not wish to do that, of course," the young girl answered. "Still, this has been such a fine tournament, in spite of everything."

It was Lewis's poisonous drawl that broke in on the exchange. "Dear me. Such sentiments from someone who just a few days ago, aboard the steamboat, could not stop lamenting about the boredom. It isn't the tournament that has you in thrall."

"I don't know what you mean." The girl's voice was even smaller than usual.

"Ah, but I'm sure you do," Lewis said in insinuating tones.

"Stop teasing poor Charlotte," Musetta ordered. "Have you never been in love?"

"Not recently," Lewis said in contempt.

"No," Perry was heard to say in his measured baritone, "you are too fond of yourself."

There was a short, pithy silence. Into it, Charlotte said in faltering tones, "I'm—not in love."

"Oh, no. That's why you looked at our brave and noble champion before you spoke." Lewis's laugh was edged with spite.

"That's enough." The words, spoken by Rowan, had a hard finality about them.

"More than enough," Alan seconded in disgust.

"My, my. Maybe I should beg your pardon, Miss Charlotte. Otherwise I may be called to account for my poor little jest. Such a paltry thing, to be forced to die for it."

The girl's cry was soft but filled with pain. Katrine, hearing the quick patter of running feet, opened the door. Charlotte was hurrying toward her with a hand over her mouth.

"Wait, Charlotte, stay, please," Katrine said, trying to catch her arm.

The girl drew back, sidling around her. "I can't," she sobbed, "Oh, I can't." Whirling, she ran away down the hall in the direction of the stairs.

Katrine turned slowly back into the room. As she moved

inside, her gaze was directed with scorn at Lewis. He fidgeted under it for several seconds before he burst into speech. "Can I help it if the girl has no sense of humor?"

"It isn't humor she lacks," Alan said, "but self-protection. And yes, you could help the situation greatly by not attacking an unworthy subject."

"How fascinating," Lewis said. "I believe you are in love with shy Charlotte."

"There are other reasons for protecting a lady besides personal interest," Alan said shortly.

"You must forgive Lewis," Musetta said. "To acquire an understanding of loving, one must first love."

Lewis turned on the woman who was his young aunt with fire kindling in his eyes. In the chair beside her, Perry sat up straighter while a frown drew his brows together.

It was then that Brantley, silent and morose on his wife's far side on the settee, turned his head to give his nephew by marriage a hard stare. Lewis turned dark red and his mouth tightened into a straight line. His hands clenched into fists. After a moment he flung himself back into his chair and turned his gaze to the ceiling.

In the taut silence that fell, Rowan's voice came quiet and reflective. "A question for the Court of Love before it is dismissed for another year. Does anyone mind?"

Musetta turned toward him in surprise. "Not at all. How intriguing."

"It is this, then: What does a man owe to a woman whom he has injured. What deed or vow is sufficient to remove the stain of the insult?"

"Nothing," Georgette said in gruff tones. "Nothing can remove it." She flushed a bright and unbecoming red as they all turned to stare at her in surprise.

"It depends, I would think," Alan said, "on the nature of the injury."

"The worst possible." Rowan's words were clipped short.

"His hand, his worldly goods, his life," Musetta said in whimsical tones that showed clearly the trend of her thoughts. "Marriage is a fairly potent salve for wounds."

"Only for some," Perry said tiredly, avoiding Brantley's gaze. "For others, it's useless."

"Love," Katrine said in low, distracted tones. "It is, or should be, the sovereign antidote for most ills, the remedy for most wounds." She fixed her gaze on a picture on the far wall, a still life of fruit and flowers. She refused to look at Rowan for fear of what she might not see, rather than what she would.

"And if that isn't enough?" Rowan said, his voice pensive.

"That's when you give your life," Lewis snarled as he came erect. He surveyed them all with outrage in his face. "Do any of you seriously expect me to offer love and marriage to Charlotte because of a few words spoken in fun? It's ludicrous!"

Musetta lifted a brow before she spoke in pitying tones. "No, Lewis. We know better than to expect anything whatever of you."

"Yes, and it's a good thing, too." He came to his feet with a jerky movement. Casting a look of revulsion at them, he stalked away out of the room.

Brantley put his hands on his knees and pushed his bulk upward until he was on his feet. "I think I'll take a turn about the place, just to check, then have an early night."

"Maybe I'll join you," Satchel said in his rumbling voice.

"Don't leave good company on my account, please," Brantley protested.

"No, and I wouldn't, except I just had the thought that I better tell my man to get on to the packing. That's if I'm to make an early start for home in the morning."

"Is everyone leaving so soon?" Katrine asked. Only a short time earlier she had been wishing for solitude, but the prospect of it now made her less than happy.

Georgette shrugged so joltingly that her high-piled red curls slipped farther down the back of her neck. "I will have to talk to Charlotte, but I expect we'll leave with the others."

It was a kind gesture on the gruff woman's part, Katrine thought, to speed the departure for her friend's sake. Still, she had not heard the answer for which she waited. Then it came.

"It seems best to relieve the household of my presence also, and that of my servant, as soon as possible," Rowan said quietly.

"I can do no less." Alan smiled at Katrine and gave a small shrug.

Perry, his gaze on Musetta, did not speak.

They did not linger in the parlor; the time for idle amusements and word games was over. They spoke their farewells with politeness and constraint. Even the bow Rowan made over Katrine's hand was dutiful, impersonal. Her voice as she accepted it was composed.

Nothing was said by anyone about next year's tournament. The reason had less to do with the fact that there might not be one, Katrine thought, than the probability that no one felt any anticipation for it. Everyone seemed relieved when they could, finally, go to their separate rooms.

She stopped at Giles's bedchamber before she went on to her own. This time Cato was sitting with him. She tried to persuade the elderly butler to let her take his place for the first portion of the night, at least. Cato would not hear of it. Yes, ma'am, he had stayed up the night before, but the French doctor had spelled him most of the day while he caught up on his sleep. He was fine now. Anyhow, there was nothing to do except wait. The master's heart would either heal itself, or it wouldn't. It was in the Father's hands, not old Cato's. She should just go along to her own bed. And she wasn't to worry; he would call her if there was any change.

Katrine didn't want her own bed. It was empty and cold and far too big. She had not been able to sleep there at all. There was nothing to be done, however, except to try to get used to it again.

Moving to the connecting door between her husband's bed-chamber and her own, she turned the silver-plated knob. The door was locked. There was no key. She turned toward Cato with lifted brows.

"I don't know, Madam Katrine, really I don't. Maybe Delphia did it. Or the French doctor."

"I suppose they must have," Katrine said. "Don't fret; I'll just go around."

Shut out of Giles's room. What did it mean? Surely Dr. Mercier did not suspect her of wishing to harm her husband. And yet, she could not quite blame him. The difference in their ages had never seemed greater than in these past hours. The lure of freedom from her vows had never seemed so sweet. Somewhere inside her, to her shame, she had heard a small, quiet voice whisper: *If Giles should die, what then?*

She wouldn't think of that, she wouldn't. She shook her head to dislodge the thought as she pushed into her bedchamber.

"I would have opened the door for you just now, but I didn't think Cato would approve."

Rowan.

Relaxed, looking perfectly at home with his hands behind his head, propped on piled pillows, he was lying in the middle of her bed. She stared at him there, outlined in the wavering gold light from the single bed candle, and her hard-won composure flew to the four winds. She had thought she might not see him again before he left, had thought she was prepared for it. Now she knew it was not so.

Katrine glanced into the hall behind her, then quickly closed the door. Her voice taut, she said, "You locked the connecting door?"

"It seemed best."

"Is something wrong?" She advanced into the room. His

feet were bare, she saw, his boots placed neatly beneath the edge of the bed.

He raised himself upright with a lean contraction of muscles and slid off the high mattress. Moving around her, he stepped to the door she had just shut, and locked it. Turning, moving toward her, he said, "There is some unfinished business between us."

He reached for her, pulling her against the hard length of his body. His eyes burned into hers with green fire in their depths before he lowered his head and placed his lips upon hers.

She should be angry at his audacity; she should resent his assumption of right and certainty about her surrender. She felt none of those things.

This was what she wanted, what she needed; this was proof that he was not as indifferent as he seemed with his talk of leaving and his coolly correct good-bye. Her heart turned a slow somersault inside her and she melted against him with a low sound of joyous reprieve.

His chest swelled and he caught her closer, holding her so tight she could not breathe. It did not matter; she had no need for air, not when there was so much love inside her.

There was mastery in his touch, and heated desire in the encompassing power of his arms. His clean scent of starched linen, leather, bay rum, and warm male invaded her senses. His mouth tasted of port wine and limitless resolve.

Her lips burned under his so she gave way with grace and sweetness, inviting his entry. He took instant advantage, tracing the porcelain edges of her teeth, grazing her tongue with his in sinuous play, demolishing defenses and stratagems and will with skill and abiding desire.

Katrine welcomed him, endlessly giving, holding nothing back in the strength of her need. She wanted him, and would deny it no longer, either to herself or to him. No matter what came, she would have this much to remember.

He drew back by degrees. Smiling down at her with pain and whimsy in his eyes, he said, "So, *la belle dame*, you can sometimes be merciful."

"Often," she answered, her eyes grave, "for the proper man."

"I should be honored, except I should warn you that all my inclination at this moment is to be totally improper."

"Call me depraved," she said with a quivering attempt at a smile, "but I have a definite predilection for improper men, too."

"Depraved?" His tone was intrigued as he tested the word, and tested also the swell of her breast that he clasped with one firm hand. "Let us see how far you have advanced toward this depravity, and how much further the proper, or improper, man can take you—"

He undressed her where she stood, slipping buttons from holes with swift ease, peeling away layers of heavy silk and embroidered cotton. He pressed his lips to the soft curves of her breasts above her camisole before lifting her free of the standing stiffness of hooped petticoats. Then, as he stripped away the camisole in turn, he saluted the rose-coral-tipped perfection he uncovered.

Katrine kicked from her slippers, then in only stockings, corset, and underdrawers, she slid her hands inside his coat, pushing it from his shoulders. Wanton delight spread through her as she unbuttoned his waistcoat and slipped his shirt studs from their holes. She had never removed a man's clothes before, never fended off his attempts to snatch kisses while she helped him shed pantaloons and underdrawers.

She would have unhooked her own corset, but he brushed her hands away from the ribbon closure at the top. Bending, he thrust a strong arm under her knees and heaved her up onto the mattress. Before the bed ropes had stopped jouncing, he had joined her there.

He knelt over her as he unfastened her garters and unrolled her silk stockings. Drawing them down her legs, he tossed them away over his shoulder one at the time.

"In Arabia," he said as he worked, "an odalisque sent to entertain the potentate, enters his bed from the foot. Keeping her head always lower than his, she advances up toward the pillows in a series of carefully calculated steps. The technique is interesting. Shall I demonstrate?"

There was such wicked promise in the dark green of his eyes there in the candlelighted dimness. She could not resist testing it. She murmured, "For my edification?"

He smiled. "For your pleasure."

"Please me, then," she whispered, and felt the shiver of a perilous thrill at the light that leaped into his face.

Nothing in her constricted, encapsulated life had prepared her for the effect of the wet heat of his tongue on the inside arch of her foot, brushing across her toes, encircling her ankles, then wending upward. She had not known her knees were so ticklish or so sensitive, or that she could be driven to madness by a warm breath on the insides of her thighs.

Turbulent bliss poured through her veins. Her heartbeat jarred her chest. The surface of her skin glowed with the inner fire that threatened to flame out of control. Desire, stirring deep within, became longing, longing gained force, became yearning. She wanted him, needed him, could not bear it if she did not have him.

Tireless, inventive, he sampled and suckled his way. There was no soft hollow, no tender curve that went unnoticed, untasted. Gently marauding with hands and mouth, he tended the rise of her passion, building it, shaping it, controlling it.

Desperation brushed her mind, lodged there. His mouth on her breast sent convulsive shudders through her. Her stomach muscles were so taut they fluttered involuntarily. The deep press of his fingers, carefully moving, turned her body into a caldron where molten liquid boiled, overflowing. She gasped, writhing against him with her breath caught in her chest.

He shifted yet higher, high enough to brush his lips across her eyelids, her cheekbones, the point of her chin. Then he took her mouth, probing sweetly, retreating. And again.

She gave a low cry as the world inside her expanded to its outermost limit, then collapsed in tumbling rapture upon itself.

With a powerful flexing of muscle and sinew, Rowan heaved himself above her, entering her in a searing, liquid glide. She took him, encompassing him while the joyous, radiating fulfillment of it sent gooseflesh prickling over her. He plunged deep, sounding the heated center of her being, driving for her soul. She raised her hips to meet him, and absorbed each wrenching shock with a soft sound of release.

Heart to heart, thighs entwined, they strove. Until he shifted, revolving with her over on the mattress in a change of position that brought a different, more intense pressure. Then the waves of ecstasy that had been fading inside her contracted on themselves, turned, and took her spiraling higher once more.

She was transfigured, knowing herself mortal yet sensing immortality, soaring with gasping breaths and wildly throbbing heart. She wanted the wonder never to end, and it seemed that with his infinite strength, his skill and his will, Rowan could make it last into their private eternity.

He turned with her once more, shifting again to rise above her. She took his weight that pressed her into the bed, wanting it, needing it. She held him tightly, cradling him with encircling arms and thighs while internal tides of sensation crested, compressing upon the heated rigidity of him in rhythmic spasms of bliss.

He kissed her forehead, her temples, delved into her mouth with slow, heart-stopping thoroughness. Cupping her breasts, he took the pointed nipples into his mouth, while with one hand he reached between them to smooth his hand down the taut surface of her abdomen. Testing, easing their joining, he also soothed the cortex of her pleasure with small, sure strokes.

She drew an abrupt breath of rapture and disbelief as she was caught once more in the maelstrom. He rose above her then, supporting his weight on his elbows. His voice husky, shaded with anguish, he said, "Now."

Katrine opened her eyes. Rowan's face was flushed, his hair damp with perspiration, and his arms trembled with the effort of control. The pleasure he had given her was not, she saw, without cost. She saw also that he did not count it, or expect it of her. His eyes were slumberous, exalted, and darkly green with some emotion she dared not name. There was promise in his face, and purpose.

Holding her gaze with his, he abandoned restraint with conscious will, and drove into her with leashed power. In rising, falling tumult, he swept her with him into glory. She spread her palms wide over his chest, sliding them with trailing nails to the lean, muscle-padded expanse of his waist, where she clenched her hands. With that support, she rode with him, reveling in his thrusts, feeling the mounting joy of them vibrating through him, acknowledging her own sensual elation at his desire for her. She gave herself to the last final recess and unbreached fastness. With heart and soul naked in her eyes, she took him deep, dissolving, liquid with the passionate longing to have and retain something of him always within her.

A low sound resonated in his chest. Heated, liquid, he gave himself to her in vigorous, vibrant surging. She felt the pulsing flow, and her being closed tightly around him, pounding into rapture so intense that the only earthly bonds that could hold her were his arms.

Together they soared, buoyant, vital, locked together in perfect, vital communion. The rapture was so intense that it hovered on a razor's edge of perception between pain and pleasure.

Dense, vital, immense, it surrounded them, held them, carried them beyond themselves into a realm of ancient, intimate glory. There they were alone, secret, safe. They were one.

Stillness settled over them by degrees. They subsided to lie close, breathing hard, in stunned quiescence. He cupped her shoulder in his hand, smoothing it with his thumb in an endless, compulsive caress. Her fingers were curled in the thick silk of his hair at the nape of his neck.

Long moments passed. At last Katrine sighed. She unwound her fingers from his hair, slid them along his neck and downward to his chest, where she exerted minute pressure, enough that he released a fraction of his hold. She raised herself upright, then brushed her hand along his lean flank to the purplish scar of the sword cut that striped his skin.

Leaning forward, so her hair fell in a tangled mass around her face, she soothed that long hurt with lips and tongue.

"I think," she said between soft kisses, "that I understand the way of the Arab women with their potentates now."

There was aching enchantment in his voice as he said, "What about an exhausted potentate?"

She pretended to consider. "Given past performance, I expect he can be revived."

"What if," he said, taking a strand of her hair and brushing it over his lips, "his revival is more than you bargained for?"

"That is a chance I'll have to take," she said, slanting a quivering smile at him through a curtain of russet-gold filaments.

He released her hair and shifted, stretching hugely with his arms above his head. His tone nonchalant, yet not quite even, he said, "Shall we see?"

It was sometime later, when they lay, considerably more weary, watching gray light sift through the window curtains, that Rowan stirred and drew a deep breath. The words he spoke fell soft and desolate into the dawn quiet.

"Before," he said, "the thought of leaving you behind to face the dangers here, known and unknown, was a barbed sword pushed into my flesh. It seemed the best way to deal with the pain of it was to jerk it out with one swift pull. Now it's more like a blade to the heart. To draw it out can only mean death. How can I go, then? How can I ever go?"

CHAPTER EIGHTEEN

Rowan eased from the bed. He should have gone long before, he knew. It had been impossible with Katrine so delectable and yielding in his arms. Even now, it was all he could do not to kiss her awake once more. If he didn't look at her lying in the center of the warm mattress, if he didn't think about the taste and feel of her, then he might be able to do the right thing.

She needed whatever rest she could snatch before the household awoke. He had not been easy on her. Driven by a species of despairing anger, he had taken everything she had to give, given everything he had inside him. His remorse this morning was strong, yet he had not regretted it at the time, and suspected he would not in the empty years to come.

He searched out his clothes in the early-morning dimness. They were somewhat the worst for being left in a crumpled pile on the floor, but Omar could fix that, given time. Skimming into pantaloons and shirt, he looked around for his boots.

There was a muffled thump and the sound of voices from the connecting room. He paused in the act of pulling on his footwear. It was just the doctor, he thought, or perhaps Brantley. Hopefully they would not try to disturb Katrine at this hour. The last thing he wanted was to make a dive for hiding.

God, how he hated this sneaking in and out, hated the underhanded wooing, the feeling of sullying another man's marriage vows. That he had been pushed into it changed nothing. If he was half the gentleman he had always thought himself, he would have refused the moment he understood what was expected of him, and held fast to that refusal no matter the provocation.

He had been right when he told Katrine that he was no gentleman. More right than he knew.

He stood and picked up his coat, shrugging into it. With his cravat dangling from one hand, he ran the fingers of the other through his hair. What he looked like made a difference only in case he met someone of the household in the hall. He didn't care to appear as debauched as he felt.

"Aren't you going to say good-bye?"

The soft timbre of Katrine's voice fell like a chime on the morning air. He swung toward the bed, moving closer so as to be heard while speaking just above a whisper, going to one knee on the bed steps. "I thought we had said our good-byes last night."

A smile flickered across her mouth. "I suppose you could say that." She sobered. "There is something I wanted to say to you while we have the chance. I—would have told you before, only it seemed a betrayal. I know now that there are some things more important."

He watched her face, the earnest, yet doubtful light in her eyes. When she paused, he said, "About Terence?"

She nodded. "Your brother was not in love with me, but there was a woman for whom he had a special attachment. She shared it, I think, in spite of everything—"

A scream shattered the morning quiet. Full-throated, a collision of outrage and horror, it seemed to echo through the house.

Rowan leaped to his feet. He strode to the door into the hall, only to check as he heard running footsteps outside; he had almost forgotten that he could not be seen emerging from this room. He waited until the sound had died away before he opened the door a cautious crack.

There was no one in sight. He sent Katrine a quick backward glance. She was already out of bed and searching for nightgown and wrapper. He checked, torn by the need to remember the loveliness of her naked form in the morning light and by half-formed impulses that were better repressed. She flashed him a quick smile edged with mystery and trepidation. He took it with him as he slid through the door and closed it behind him.

It was Georgette who had roused the house. She was standing at the edge of the lake, moaning and wringing her hands. As Rowan came nearer she indicated with a frantic wave of her hand that she was all right, before pointing toward something floating in the water.

The body of a woman, dressed in a long white nightgown and dressing gown, with her hair drifting around her like dark water weeds, was floating in the lake.

Charlotte.

Alan joined them, coming at a pounding run from the direction of the side door of the house. Together, he and Rowan waded out to the still form of the girl. Rowan had no hope from the moment he touched her; she was too cold, her limbs too stiff. He picked her up and carried her toward the bank.

Dr. Mercier was waiting with most of the others gathered behind him by the time they reached dry ground. As they placed Charlotte on the ground the doctor knelt beside her.

"Gone, I fear, poor child," he declared after a cursory examination. "Death occurred some hours ago."

There were small cries and sighs from those assembled. Georgette burst into noisy tears. Hiccuping and sobbing, she tried to answer the barrage of questions hurled at her.

She had gone to Charlotte's room because the other young woman had asked to be wakened early so they could get on the road. Charlotte's bed showed no sign of having been slept in, and her maid had not seen her since her mistress had dismissed her the night before. Alarmed, Georgette had begun to search. The thought that Charlotte might have gone for a walk finally took her outside. There she was.

"Why?" Musetta said with horror in her voice. "Why would she do it? I think this house must be cursed, that such terrible things happen here."

"If you are assuming, as I must suppose," Dr. Mercier said in his precise, dry tones, "that the lady did away with herself, then you are mistaken."

"What do you mean?" It was Alan who asked it, his voice sharp.

"If you will notice the abrasion at the neck area, you will understand at once. This unfortunate young woman was strangled."

In the shocked silence that followed, Rowan sent a keen glance around at those gathered at the lake's edge. He had noticed the marks on Charlotte's neck when he picked her up. That, with the fact that she was floating so easily, as though her lungs had not filled with water, made him suspicious. However, if any of their number knew more of what had happened to Charlotte, they were good at covering it.

Georgette, standing only a few feet away, turned slowly to stare at him. "You," she said with loathing in her pale, freckled face. "It was you who killed her."

"Oh, here, I say, no," Satchel objected in gruff tones. The rest, after a few gasps and murmurs, were quiet.

Rowan felt a chill on the back of his neck. He resisted the need to look behind him, to see if there was someone else she could mean. His voice even, he said, "I will make allowances for your distraught condition."

"Don't bother," the tall young woman recommended. "I'm not too upset to know what's what. Charlotte showed me the note she meant to send to you last night. She was so unhappy, but excited, and quite determined to declare herself to you. I told her to be careful, that you were a dangerous man to know, and anyway, your attention was turned elsewhere. She wouldn't listen to me."

"I received no note," Rowan said. The suggestion in Georgette's words that everyone knew of his feelings for Katrine he let pass as unworthy of comment.

"You must have. She said there was something she could tell you that you would want very much to hear, something about your brother."

A cold, hard dread settled inside Rowan. "I wonder," he said softly, "what that might have been?"

"I have no idea," Georgette said in red-faced scorn. "All I know is that Charlotte came down here to the lake to keep some nonsensical romantic rendezvous with you, and now she's dead. If you didn't kill her, who did?"

Rowan sent a frown around the gathered group. His gaze rested last on Katrine, standing near the back. She looked beautiful, with concern in her eyes and her hair spilling over the shining rose brocade of her dressing gown. There was also a shading of anger in her face that made him uneasy.

He said, "If there was information Charlotte could have given me about Terence, I would have been delighted to hear it. But I had no reason to harm her."

"Maybe you didn't like what she told you. Maybe you thought she meant to offer you something besides information, and you became angry when she refused your advances."

"That's ridiculous," he snapped.

"Is it?" Georgette said, her face twisting with resentment. "She was just an innocent girl, while you—everyone knows you are a man of the world who may have brought heaven knows what kind of foreign vices here among us."

It was an attitude Rowan had noticed before, an insular certainty that this backward community represented everything that was decent, while any foreigner must naturally embody what was indecent. It was as though this prejudice was necessary to balance the feelings of inferiority aroused by someone of European extraction and habits.

"I assure you," Rowan said with the ring of cold steel in his voice, "that I never touched your friend."

It was then that he heard the sound he feared to hear, Katrine speaking in clear, carrying tones. "He could not have done so, could not have received Charlotte's note or met her last night."

He whirled. "Katrine, no!"

Her gaze was steady as she moved to stand beside him. "Do you think," she said, "that I would let you be falsely accused?"

From somewhere behind them, Lewis could be heard saying in mock astonishment, "Dear me. How interesting."

Brantley, rocking back and forth with his hands behind him, frowned at them. He said, "I don't think I understand, Katrine. What do you know of de Blanc's activities."

"A great deal," she answered quietly. "He was with me most of the evening, and all of the night."

Alan looked away across the lake with an expression of acute embarrassment. Perry scowled. Musetta appeared both intrigued and cynically amused. The doctor ignored them as he gave the marks on the body closer attention.

Georgette turned on Katrine. "Yes, and you're another reason Charlotte is dead. She would never have gotten such notions as midnight meetings into her head if it wasn't for you and your ridiculous Court of Love. She believed all that stuff about knights and fair ladies, sacrifices and dying for love; it wasn't just a game for her. So maybe she came down here hoping to meet Rowan, but ran into one of those river pirates instead. It's still your fault, yours and your fine champion's."

The accusations took Rowan's breath, not because they were so sweeping but because some part of them might, just possibly, be true. Gazing at Katrine's face, he saw that she knew it, too. Fear more blighting than any he had ever known rose inside him then, not for himself, but for the woman beside him.

In the sudden silence, Brantley spoke again. "I think," he said with ponderous consideration, "that this is a matter for the sheriff."

"Of a certainty," Dr. Mercier agreed, getting to his feet and wiping his hands on his handkerchief. "There appears to be a number of possibilities which should be brought to the attention of the authorities."

The doctor's words, along with his unmovable request to be left alone to see to the body, raised the specter of further examinations and, possibly, further charges of a criminal nature that might be lodged with the sheriff. It left them all thoughtful as they straggled back toward the house.

It was toward noon before the sheriff arrived. By that time most of the house party had made themselves presentable and partaken, in a desultory manner, of the late-morning repast laid out for them. The exception was Georgette, who had shut herself up in her room while she struggled with the letter that must be sent by a groom to inform Charlotte's mother of the tragedy.

There was a sense of strain in the house. It was not to be wondered at, of course; still, it wore on the nerves. It was impossible to ignore the feeling that everyone was watching everyone else, that there were whispered conversations in corners, that there were places and persons that most felt it wisest to avoid.

Rowan was one of the last, as was Katrine. For himself, it was easily endurable; for Katrine's sake, he despised it.

The sheriff was rotund, dyspeptic, and profane. No one in his life had ever given him cause to doubt his intelligence, or the privileges of his office, and he had a high opinion of both. Other than an occasional knifing among the river rats, petty thieves, and cardsharps at the dock, there wasn't much in the way of murder around St. Francisville. Murder among the gentry wasn't exactly in his line, but he knew how to handle it. All he had to do was use the power of his office. It was a mistake that went unrecognized by him, though not by the household and guests of Arcadia, for the better part of an hour. By then, it was too late.

"Did you kill the woman?" the sheriff demanded of Rowan.

Rowan's glance was heavy with weariness and contempt. The sheriff had, apparently, left him until last since he was the best suspect. "Was I overcome with wild lust that caused me to ravish the poor child, then wring her neck and toss her like a drained orange rind into the lake? Yes, certainly. I would have confessed it sooner if I had known the delay would cause a lady to perjure herself for me."

"Rowan, what are you saying?" Alan exclaimed. "The damage has already been done."

"What damage?" he demanded in tones of steel. "The lady and I sat beside her husband a few hours, that's all there is to it; I'm amazed anyone who knows her could think otherwise. Still, it's plain to see some of you did. I can only try, then, to retrieve the lady's good name."

"By hanging?" Alan said with admirable brevity.

"See here," the sheriff said, as red in the face as a turkey cock, "I'll ask the questions. Or maybe we should have the lady downstairs to find out exactly what went on."

"Do you doubt my word?" Rowan asked, leaning against the wall with quiet inquiry in his face and his hands pressed against the paneling behind him.

Lewis, glancing at Rowan, and at the white-tipped nails of the half-concealed hands that spoke of rage, edged away from between the other two men.

The sheriff was not as great a fool as he appeared. He drew a whistling breath as he frowned at Rowan. "I'm trying to get to the bottom of as ugly a deed as I've ever seen. Now I want a straight answer. Did you meet this girl last night?"

"Must I declare it from the rooftop?" Rowan said, his gaze opaque. "I have said that I did."

"Why? And don't give me any of that lust business. She wasn't molested that way."

"She wanted to be married. I didn't."

The sheriff narrowed his eyes. "A lot of women want to be married, but where would we be if men went around killing them for it?"

"A good question; the institution could fall into disfavor."

Perry rose from the settee where he had been sitting with an abrupt movement. "He didn't meet Charlotte."

"Are you saying you did?" Rowan asked with something less than gratitude in his face.

"Of course not!" Perry said with heat. "I had another appointment."

"Assignation, I think he means," Lewis murmured.

"I was in the hall," Perry went on doggedly, "when I saw de Blanc going into the bedchamber of another lady."

"Hell's bells," the sheriff said. "Didn't anybody sleep in his own bed last night?"

Brantley sat staring from Perry to Musetta with the frowning malevolence of a chained bulldog who is being teased, but he said nothing. Musetta, with defiant color in her cheeks, kept her gaze on the sheriff.

"It seems," Rowan said quietly, "to be an exchange of alibis."

Perry swung on him. "Meaning that I make excuses for myself by coming to your rescue? You are a hard man to help."

"No aid was required." Rowan's words were trenchant.

"Does it trouble you to take it from one who acted the knave by cutting you with a sword?" the younger man said, clenching his fists. "Well, I'm sorry, but you have no choice. Sportsmanship aside, it goes against my conscience to let a man be arrested for a murder he didn't commit for the lack of a few words."

The other man was trying, against his own better good, to do the right thing. It might be possible to make use of that saving grace. Rowan said with deadly softness, "Recompense for past injuries? Then I can only accept, but did you have to damn the lady?"

Perry flinched at the whiplash of the last words. "I didn't mean—"

Musetta entered the fray then. "I see no reason my sister-in-law's honor should be impugned. There is a connecting door between her bedchamber and that of her husband, my half brother. No doubt M'sieur de Blanc took that route because Dr. Mercier had caused the hall door of the sickroom to be kept locked. I know it must have been necessary to enter that way since I tried to get in through the hall door myself."

"For what reason?" Rowan asked, his tone no whit more accommodating.

"Sisterly concern, of course," Musetta said, and dared him with her eyes to accuse her of more.

"I want to know one thing," Georgette, who had come downstairs for the sheriff's inquiry, said, frowning at Rowan, "if you didn't intend to meet Charlotte, why didn't you at least send a note to tell her so. Then she would not have been out there where this could happen."

"I had no note," Rowan said in bald answer. It was a point that had already given him a few bad moments.

"But I saw her writing it," the red-haired girl insisted.

"And who delivered it afterward?"

A considering frown rested between Georgette's eyes. "I suppose she must have handed it to her maid to give to your Omar."

"Omar says not," Rowan said shortly.

"From what I could get out of the girl's maid," the sheriff said, "she put it under the door of your room."

Alan cleared his throat. "Anyone walking down the hall might have taken it, if it was not quite hidden."

"Looks to me like a mighty big if," the sheriff said.

Rowan could only agree. There was another possibility, however, one in need of exploration.

He said, with what charm he could muster, "Shall we blame it on the river pirates then, at least until a better candidate presents himself with a signed confession?"

"Don't put words in my mouth," the sheriff said. "I see what it is. You folks think you can protect your own, and to the devil with justice. Well, just you remember, I'm the law. Whatever happens, you'll still answer to me. This thing ain't over, not by a long shot!"

The sheriff left soon after. Rolling his buggy away down the drive, he took with him no one except his deputies for company.

In due time, Charlotte's mother sent a message by the returning groom to say that she was too ill to come personally to escort her daughter's body homeward, but wished the arrangements for the journey to be completed as soon as possible. The black wagon carrying Charlotte in a plain coffin of the kind kept ready against need on most plantations trundled away toward St. Francisville and the river road. Georgette and Satchel went with it, riding honor guard. The dust of its passage down the drive faded away into the trees.

The others, turning from seeing the somber procession on its way, straggled back into the house.

Cato, after carefully counting the reduced number of heads, waited a respectable time, then brought the tea tray with the correct number of cups into the parlor, where they had gathered once more. When he was certain he had their attention, he made his announcement.

"I have been instructed to tell everyone, ladies, sirs, that Master Giles has come back to his senses, the Lord bless him. He just might be up to visitors by tomorrow noon."

Katrine sat sewing, embroidering a blue Delft design on white linen for a tablecloth that Arcadia's dining room didn't need, when the connecting door from bedchamber to sickroom opened. It was Rowan who stood in the opening. She met his dark gaze with a quickening in her heart, then she noticed the flintlike hardness in his face.

She glanced at Giles. His eyes were closed, though whether he slept or was only resting she couldn't tell. Motioning to Rowan to remain where he was, she got to her feet and placed her sewing in her chair. She went silently to him, slipping past into the other room.

She turned to watch him close the door behind them before she spoke in strained tones. "When do you go?"

"Never," he said, and turned to face her with his back to the panel.

"But—you must," she whispered.

"And leave you to the gentle care of a midnight strangler? No, I thank you. I will go, if there is no other way, to keep you safe. I will not go leaving you to certain harm."

She searched his face while a slow, sweet singing ran through her veins. Then, as she saw the darkness in his face, the jubilance died away. "You know who killed Charlotte?"

"And who tried to have you killed. At least in theory. Tell me quickly, while there's time, about this woman Terence loved. How do you know he was enamored of her?"

She gathered her scattered thoughts, then said, "Well, they went riding together often, and once or twice managed to lose their way. Another time they were discovered coming from the stable with straw in their hair. They were both a little careless, but their passion made a fine excuse."

"Musetta," he said, moving away from the door, coming to stand before her.

"You guessed?"

He took her hand. "If it was not you, then it had to be the only other woman who would need to be discreet. The others Terence could have courted openly. But I wanted to be sure."

"I think he wanted her to go away with him; he seemed to neither notice nor care that she was a few years his elder. Whether Musetta actually agreed, I don't know; she is a woman who prefers security. At any rate, he died a few days after he declared himself."

"You feel his death had something to do with this love affair?"

"I—don't know," she said, looking past him. "I've often wondered. I mean, it's possible he may have killed himself if Musetta refused to give up her life for him."

"No, I don't think so," Rowan said. "I can feature Terence angry and dejected, but not to that extent. What of Perry? Was he a conquest for your sister-in-law last year?"

"He was smitten," Katrine admitted, "but though Musetta flirted with him a little, it was Terence she preferred. Do you think he and Terence quarreled, and it ended with them facing each other with pistols?"

"No," he said, and lifted her hand to his lips, though his eyes looked past her, unseeing.

She watched him, her mind moving in swift, not quite coherent thought. The blankness of his expression was a screen to conceal things he didn't want her to know. The idea did not trouble her since it was her he was shielding, rather than himself. Whoever had killed his brother had also tried to harm them both. Poor Charlotte had died, perhaps, because she had written a note indicating that she had knowledge of the events of the year before. Rowan had somehow discovered the thread that tied these things together. If he knew it, then she must be able to discern it also, if she tried hard enough.

She released her hand and, turning from him, walked to the window. The early evening of autumn was drawing in, turning the world outside to purple and lilac velvet. The dimness made the glass reflective with the lamp left burning on her dressing table. She could see Rowan behind her, see the lamp and her own face. He was watching her with doubt in his face that tore at her heart.

She said into the stillness, "You did not get the note from Charlotte because you were with me. Where is it now?"

"Gone," he said without encouragement.

"If Omar had received it in the usual way, you would have it. And so—"

He stood without moving, watching her back. "So?"

She knew what he was protecting her from, and why.

The pain started in the center of her being and flowed upward, burgeoning into a hard anguish that must, somehow, be contained. She searched her mind for fault, and found it in her unwavering, thoughtless trust. The indictment was blighting. Terence she might not have been able to save, but there should have been no danger to Rowan, ever. And Charlotte should still be sighing after love, instead of dying for the misguided passions of someone else.

Rowan's voice, as he spoke again, was like a bludgeon. She knew, then, that there was another casualty, and it was love.

"Who," he said, "is Delphia's lover?"

CHAPTER NINETEEN

Into the hard and ringing certainty of that question, there came shouts of weak rage edged with dread. They issued, quavering and cracked, from the next room. It was Giles.

Katrine swung toward the sound. Rowan was before her, striding to the connecting door and flinging it open, pushing into the brighter light of the sickroom.

He halted so abruptly Katrine nearly ran into him. Whirling, he caught her arm, giving her a strong shove so she stumbled back into the bedchamber. He snatched at the door to slam it shut on her.

"Stop!"

The command, with its vicious promise of violence, had a strange ring. That was because it came from Brantley.

Katrine, looking around Rowan's broad shoulders that were blocking her view, saw Musetta's husband standing on the far side of the bed where Giles lay. The bovine placidness of his broad face had been replaced by glittering cruelty. In his hand there shone the chased silver of Giles's Adams revolver.

"Very good," her brother-in-law went on with a twist of his thick lips. "I require that Katrine join us, otherwise there is no purpose in this charade."

Giles cursed, gasping. His face was purple with a white line around his blue lips.

"What are you doing?" Katrine asked as she stepped from behind Rowan. "Where is Dr. Mercier?"

"The good doctor was called back to the Barrows house—for the daughter's confinement, you understand. He felt his patient here was sufficiently recovered that he could be left to Cato. Dr. Mercier will be saddened to discover Giles has had a—severe setback—in his absence."

"You are a fool," Giles said with croaking difficulty. "Mercier knows someone's been feeding me arsenic for months—even years. Told him so myself, just today."

Brantley smiled. "Then I shall have to discover that it was Katrine, won't I? That should be easy enough, since everyone knows now that she's been carrying on an affair under your very nose. No one will be surprised that she wanted to be rid of her elderly husband."

"Affair was—my choosing," Giles panted.

"Oh, I know that, but who else would believe it? Especially if none of you are alive to explain."

Rowan spoke then, his tone flat. "A double murder followed by a convenient suicide. Do you think you can get away with it?"

"I think so. People underestimate me, you see. They think I'm a plodding idiot who is easily hoodwinked. Even my wife. She thinks I don't see her little games. She doesn't know I let her go her own way because I have more exotic tastes."

"Delphia," Katrine said in a strained whisper.

"Precisely. A useful tool, once she was flattered into thinking I loved her. Not to mention being far more interesting than dear Musetta when naked between the sheets."

"She brought you the note that told you where Charlotte would be."

"A pity, that. The silly girl was always mooning around. She saw me with Terence that night, but thought it was an affair of honor over Musetta, something that should be kept decently quiet. She considered it a matter of loyalty, until something changed her mind, made her decide to tell de Blanc. I couldn't have that."

His weakness, Katrine saw, was his egotism, his certainty that they were all his inferiors, whom he could control. It might be used to delay matters long enough for something to happen.

She said softly, "Funny, but I had the same idea, to shield Musetta. That didn't matter, though, did it? You weren't jealous, didn't care about the affair so long as it remained a brief attachment. That changed when you thought Musetta might run away with Terence. That wouldn't have done at all."

"I had not slaved here at Arcadia for years just to have her do me out of my rightful place as master because she couldn't keep her legs together." Spittle gathered at the corners of Brantley's mouth as he spoke, and there was cold enmity in his eyes.

Rowan, shifting a little so that his body intervened once more between Katrine and her brother-in-law, said, "That was the problem with Katrine, too, wasn't it? If she became pregnant by me, as Giles wanted, then the child, once acknowledged as Giles's legal heir, would block you from owning Arcadia through Musetta."

"Giles went to great lengths to break through the scruples that were keeping you apart. Delphia told me she thought he had succeeded, finally."

"Did I, by God," Giles exclaimed. "That's something, anyway."

"Crow, and be damned to you," Brantley said. "It won't do much good when they're both dead."

Giles made a hoarse sound that might have been a laugh. "No, but I almost won. I almost did you out of it all. I've known for years you wanted to step into my shoes. Why else do you think it was so important to get an heir on Katrine, no matter who the father might be?"

"You might have chosen me for the father," Brantley said bitterly.

"Never," Katrine exclaimed.

"Never," Giles said on a choking growl. "I remember too well who told me after the duel that I'd killed my man—who hustled me out of England before I could say good-bye to the woman I loved with all the passion I had in me. The woman whose fiancé I had killed. The woman you decided, in cold blood, to marry."

Brantley said with a chill smile, "But you arranged it."

Giles raised himself in the bed. He was trembling so hard that the bed frame shook with it. He said, "It was blackmail. What else could I do? People don't understand love for a sister—half sister. But I never forgave you for it, never forgave you for escorting her here, where it could be done. Never."

Katrine drew a quick, piercing breath. The air was heavy in her chest, flavored with burning oil from the bedside lamp, sickroom sourness, ingratitude, and old sorrows. In it also was a heated tension that coiled, tightening, around her nerves. The bed curtains swayed in a draft, turning from red to black in their folds. On the wall behind the bed, the dogs in a hunting print pointed at unseen prey. Beside her, Rowan was still.

Brantley ignored them, concentrating on the man in the bed. He said, "You took a bride yourself to spite me, so it's your fault we've come to this."

"You would have preferred—that I died of my—so-called stomach problems," Giles said on a gasping, shuddering cough. "But Cato saved me. He guessed about the poison a year or so after I was wed. Too late to save my digestion. Tested Katrine, but wasn't her. Couldn't be Musetta. Lewis, for all his bile, is a coward. Had to be you. Not too late to put a spoke in your wheel."

"This seems," Rowan said, his thoughtful gaze on the wavering barrel of the pistol in Brantley's hand, "to be where the tournament came into it, and Terence, and I."

"You were ideal," Brantley said with sneering disgust. "Strong enough and with the skills to win the prize, handsome enough in form and face to suit Giles's ideas of a suitable breeding mate, different enough from all the others to catch Katrine's attention. It was obvious from the beginning that one or both of you would have to be eliminated."

"So the crudely engineered accidents," Rowan mused, his gaze lifting to Brantley's face.

The gun in Brantley's hand turned, centered on Rowan's chest. His features mottled with color, he said, "They should have been sufficient, with so many people, so many competitors, around. They would have been, if you had been less lucky."

"Or more trusting?" Rowan suggested. "Or if I had slept more soundly—or just slept more—while imprisoned. Or if I was less careful of those I protect. I'm sorry if I caused you hardship. I only wanted life for Katrine and myself. For obvious reasons."

"Yes, too obvious," Brantley said in acid tones. "I doubt Giles planned on so strong an attraction."

"I did not," Giles said, gasping, "though perhaps I should have. I will admit, it—pained me more than expected. It made me more brutal than . . . Anyway. I apologize, my dear wife. But I'm not sorry, really. Not sorry, seeing—how it's turned out."

"In that case," Rowan said with a slight inclination of his head toward both men, "neither of you will mind if I say farewell, or if it is somewhat prolonged?" He turned to Katrine and took her hands, carrying them to his mouth before holding them against his heart.

It was as if, by the shift of his body, he enclosed the two of them in a space where there was nothing except honeyed light and dazzling memories. She said, her gaze open and dark as she searched his face, "I never meant to lead you to this."

A smile of wry sweetness curved his mouth. "I was behind you, pushing with both hands while laying down a pathway greased with half-stifled impulses, platitudes, and impure inclinations. I am grateful," he said more softly, "for prizes won, and also those given with grace."

"And with love," she said, her throat aching.

"Enough to enamel a few stolen hours in colors to stun spirit and mind. You are my wonder and my lifelong dream, my valiant minion and my sovereign, my moonlight-crowned nymph naked and kissed with warm dew. You I worship with body and every other weak, shivering, but well-intentioned faculty, and will hold like a sweet apple in the pocket of my hungry soul, Cupid's arrow in my heart."

She pressed her cheek to his hands that held hers. "I honor you for what you meant to be," she said, "but most of all for what you are, what you gave me of yourself, and what you made of me."

"Then will you hear my vow?" he answered, touching her face with warm fingers and tilting her head to meet the intense green of his eyes. "I swear that not even death can or will send me from you."

Breaking through newly discovered realms of despair and pure, unsieved anguish, she heard in that instant the message couched in his phrases of love. Heard, and steeled herself, waiting, even as his lips touched hers with perfect, transcending accord.

Push. Behind her. His death.

A protest rose, screaming in her mind. There was no time. He caught her against him with hard, suffocating closeness. His fingers bit into her hands. He drew back sharply and, in the same, abrupt movement, sent her hurling from him like an arrow released from a straining bow. She flew, skirts billowing, toward the curtained head of the bed, the only place in the wide room not covered by the pistol in Brantley's hands.

Brantley swung, instinctively, to cover her swooping flight.

And Rowan, as silent as a serpent's shadow, and as swift, launched himself straight at the deadly revolver, which needed only a strong pull of the trigger to fire and fire again.

They had discounted Giles, if not forgotten him.

Katrine's husband growled in hoarse savagery and leaned to grab Brantley's right arm. He dragged him, off balance, across the edge of the high mattress.

The percussion of a shot thundered through the room. Blue-black smoke erupted in an acrid, throat-searing cloud. There came a choked cry. Someone cursed.

Katrine, clinging to the bed curtains that she had caught to halt her flight, saw through drifting smoke a melee of struggling bodies on the bed. She did not hesitate. Using the curtain for purchase, she launched herself into the fray.

Blood poured from a cut on Rowan's brow. He was half-blinded by the flow. There was blood staining the coverlet, blood splattering the three men. It was impossible to tell where it was coming from.

Giles, gasping, was flung this way and that as he held to Brantley's arm. The bigger man, bull stout and enraged, ignored his brother-in-law's weak efforts while he weaved back and forth in Rowan's grasp. As he saw Katrine bounce onto the bed he strained to bring the revolver around to bear on her.

Rowan flung out a hand to snare the wrist of Brantley's gun hand. With bared teeth, he applied pressure. The grinding of the bones in Brantley's wrist could be heard. The other man muttered a curse and reached for Rowan's eyes.

Rowan heaved away from the rake and gouge of yellow nails. The movement took Brantley with him. The heavier man used his weight to overbalance them both, pushing Rowan down into the softness of the mattress. Slowly, with teeth bared in an exultant snarl, he began to bring the end of the revolver barrel around toward Rowan's side.

Katrine couldn't breathe, couldn't think. Her chest ached.

Her heart battered her lungs and ribs with sickening thuds. Her eyes stung with the unblinking need to see. She wanted to help, but was terrified of hindering.

Fear for Rowan was acid in her blood. So recently, he had been slashed, injured in the fall from his horse, and beaten. With such injuries, how long could he match strength for strength with the bull-like heft of Musetta's husband.

Somewhere in the distance she heard shouts and running footsteps. That would be the others, alerted by the gunshot. Brantley heard them, too. He redoubled his effort, wrenching the revolver around with the full force of his body.

Rowan struck out with a knotted fist. It caught Brantley on the point of his chin. He pitched over on his side. Rowan hurled after him. Grunting, the two thudded to the mattress. Brantley's head snapped backward, hanging over the edge. His gun hand was flung outward.

The revolver struck Katrine's knee. She pounced with fingers like claws. With darkness in her mind and rage in her soul, she tore it from Brantley's hand.

Giles clamped shaking, bloodstained fingers on her arm. His eyes burned into hers, clouded yet deadly. "Mine," he said in a rattling whisper. "It's mine." He caught the pistol in a palsied grasp.

Rowan, freed of the need to control the revolver, gathered power and honed will. He struck again with a powerful fist.

Brantley reeled under the impact. He saw the revolver in Giles's hand. He heaved himself over, grasping for it.

Giles was shaking so violently that his teeth rattled in his head. Blood, wine red and wet, matted the bedclothes around him. His eyes were red-rimmed, opaque, already glazing. He shoved the revolver toward Brantley, pressing it into his breastbone. He panted, closing his eyes. His face twisted and he gave a gurgling cry. His head fell forward.

Brantley's hand closed on the gun barrel. A cruel smile

twisted his lips. He wrenched at the gun to pull it from Giles's failing grasp.

The revolver exploded. Brantley, half-hidden in the billow of gun smoke, snapped his eyes open in terrible understanding and disbelief. He did not close them.

They left them there, Giles and Brantley, lying on the bed with the gun between them. The purpose was so the sheriff, an avowedly suspicious man, could see them. It was hard to do.

There was so much blood, and the smell of fear and dread and unreasoning violence in the air. It would have been far easier to rid them both of it all, to clean them and compose their sprawled limbs and place them side by side in coffins in the parlor. Everyone could then have forgotten the terrible things that were done, the terrible things that were said.

As it was, they only pretended to forget a portion.

Closing ranks, the gathered guests decided that a few details of the terrible confrontation should be omitted from the public record. Nothing was said to the sheriff, then, of a brother's unnatural love for a half sister. The hatred and plotting and failures of honor were distilled into a tale of misdirected greed and jealousy. The fight on the bed was presented as a tragedy caused by an act of madness.

There was no one who would admit to seeing a connection between the two dead men and the attack of the river pirates. None of them acknowledged any possibility that the men might have been hired to fire the tower or make the previous attacks along the river, which made the one on Arcadia less unusual. And if there were glances exchanged between Alan and Rowan, Perry and even Lewis, that suggested the marauding days of the river men might soon be forcibly ended, none felt the need to mention it before the officer of the law.

The sheriff, it could easily be seen, believed only two words in ten of what he heard, and was suspicious of the rest. However, facing Rowan's hard smile and imperturbable calm, he did not pry.

The funerals were the next hurdle to be met. The black bombazine and broadcloth and armbands sewn on the bias were brought out, aired, pressed, and donned. The black-bordered notices were posted in town and at every crossroad. Handkerchiefs hemmed in black were laid ready. Hair locks were cut for remembrance. The condolence calls began, some sincere, some mere excuses for morbid curiosity and for measuring the household's grief.

Musetta slept heavily, dosed with laudanum and mulled wine. She woke often to hysterical weeping. Crying, always crying for her brother, never for her husband. Katrine slept not at all, nor did she cry.

An odd numbness seemed to have settled upon her. She held endless conferences with herself, trying to feel some grief, some pain, even some relief. There was nothing. She moved through the hours hardly knowing whether it was dark or light. She spoke, she made decisions, considered arrangements, was a conscientious hostess. She smiled and was as gracious as she could manage.

Inside, there was a waiting stillness. It had, in some slight way, a familiarity about it. If forced to put a name to it, she would have said it was fear.

It was only after the funeral, after the ride in the carriage behind the hearse with its black horses and nodding plumes, after the prayers were said and the dirt sifted onto the coffins, after the drive homeward with Musetta sobbing in a corner and Rowan staring blindly out the narrow window, that she knew why she was afraid.

"A moment of your time, Mrs. Castlereagh," the lawyer who had followed their two carriages home from the cemetery said. Bowing with unctuous kindness, he approached them on the steps before he went on. "I thought you would like to be easy in your mind about the arrangements your husband made for your security."

She turned slowly to survey the man with his expansive chest draped by a watch chain and fobs, his shining dome of a head and luxuriant muttonchop whiskers. Behind her, Lewis stopped short, listening. Musetta, clinging to Perry's arm and dabbing under her veiling of crepe, turned back from where she had almost reached the front door. Trailing behind, standing back politely, was Alan. Rowan waited at Katrine's side, his stillness like a command for silence.

The lawyer did not appear to notice anyone other than Katrine. He said, jocular and hearty, "Your husband, ma'am, left his estate in its entirety to you and your issue. There are only two stipulations that go with it. The first is that you continue the stipend he now makes to his nephew, Lewis Castlereagh. The other is that you house and maintain his sister—along with her husband, who is, of course, no longer a concern—in her accustomed manner."

Katrine swayed a little, as if the weight of Arcadia had settled onto her slim shoulders. There was a roaring in her ears that began to recede only when she felt Rowan's hand upon her arm. She said finally, "I must thank you for telling me." She paused, at a loss, then clutching at her duties as hostess for some semblance of normality, she added, "Would—would you care to come inside for refreshment before you go?"

The lawyer glanced at Rowan. He cleared his throat. "Another time, perhaps. I'll be along in a few days with all the papers and legal language. I just thought I'd tell you how the business stands."

"It was very kind of you."

Nodding smartly, the lawyer clapped his hat back on his head and strode toward his carriage. Feeling pressure on her arm, Katrine swung and began to move up the steps once more.

Inside the house, Lewis spoke. "So we are your pensioners, my dear Katrine, Musetta and I. How delightful."

"I would have preferred," she said tiredly, "that you were not."

"You seem to have no choice; it was Giles's wish." His words were sharp.

She gave him a level look. "I meant to say that I would rather Giles had left you an independent sum. I can't imagine why he did not."

A rueful smile came and went on the young man's face. "Because he knew I should spend it forthwith, I imagine. Never mind. I won't be any more unpleasant about it than I must."

"For myself, I'm glad," Musetta said. "I never want to leave Arcadia, and I prefer not to have the worry of paying my own accounts."

"Never?" Perry said, trying to see her face through her veil.

"Not for a very long time," the other girl said in soft tones. Patting Perry's arm, she released him and drifted away from him up the stairs.

"I think," Alan said, "that a drink would not be out of order."

Cato, appearing at that moment from the back regions of the house, spoke up. "In the library, sirs, all set out and ready."

Katrine was left alone with Rowan. She could feel his gaze on her face. She reached up to untie her bonnet strings and pull the bit of black felt and dyed cock's plumes from her hair. Holding it in her hand, she moved into the parlor.

He came after her, his steps lithe, easy, soundless. Moving to a tray of sherry left on a side table, he poured two glasses and brought one of them to her. She set her bonnet aside. Steadying her hands with an act of will, she accepted the glass of golden-brown liquid.

"Responsibilities," he said, "can be abdicated. For adults."

She had allowed him to come too close to her. Or perhaps

allowed was not the word. He had gained, with the communion of purified emotion, the ability to step into her mind. Their thoughts shifted like a soft wind between them. She understood his resistance, his doubts, and also the honor that would not let him press her. He knew the steel cage of obligation that had closed around her.

You and your issue—

"Do I owe Giles nothing?" she said softly.

"Will you allow your life to be dictated by guilt?"

"It isn't guilt, but rather responsibility. You know about its demands."

"Oh, yes," he said in stringent agreement. "Do you owe his memory a child?"

"Can I deny the only thing he asked of me?" She looked at Rowan, her heart turning inside her as she saw the bandaging above his eye, where he had, once more, been injured for her sake. Her gaze deep, unguarded, she added, "Stay."

"In another man's house, on another man's lands, where you will always be another man's wife?"

"You could make everything yours."

"I would rather give you the world instead. And if our babe is inside you, I would rather it be a child of the wide, revolving earth than a sweet, human cord to bind you to Arcadia."

"Or you to me," she whispered. Then, reading the quality of his silence, she said, "No. That was unworthy of either of us. I would not hold you with that binding."

Compassion and honor might be enough to keep him beside her, but it would not be enough to make him happy. There in Giles's bedchamber he had spoken such glorious vows of loving, but they had been made to save her life. How, then, could she trust them? What was left if they had been no more than a gallant but expedient gesture?

"How can you prevent it?"

As he spoke she remembered too well his reluctance to leave

a child behind at Arcadia, or to be held by the prospect of one. She said, "Perhaps the choice won't have to be made."

"The coward's constant chant. Will you choose, Katrine, or shall I?"

To go or stay, that was the question. Her choice would be between love and duty, his between love and honor. Where would the least damage lie, where the least pain?

"I don't know," she said, staring at the pattern in the carpet.

He stood for long moments with his gaze resting on her lowered lashes. "I would make the decision," he said, "but the temptation to weight the odds in my favor might be too strong to resist. And I prefer not to require an eternal pledge of forgiveness."

"You could have it, I expect," she said, and closed her eyes, sighing.

His gaze was unfocused for long moments, then he looked at his sherry as if surprised to find it in his hand. Drinking the wine in a single swallow, he closed his hand tightly on the fragile glassware. "Don't tear yourself to pieces," he said. "There is another way."

"How can there be?"

He did not answer. Placing his glass carefully on the table beside him, he walked away from it out of the parlor.

CHAPTER TWENTY

"Question."

It was Rowan who spoke that single word into a
small island of silence in the midst of the after-dinner gathering
in the double parlor.

Somber as newly confirmed novices, those few of the house
party who were left were gathered about the fire under the marble mantel. They talked to be courteous, and to pass the time before some excuse could be found for bed. They hardly looked at
each other, touched on no subject that could lead by any pathway to the events of the last days. Their civility and consideration were faultless. Beneath the layers of carefully applied
manners, however, there was ample room for vagrant thoughts.

Katrine's gown was black and high to the throat, unrelieved
by a jewel or even a scrap of lace. The stiff, shining fabric spread
around her was a barrier to touch, a reproach to thoughts of other
intimacies. Pale, composed, she was the most polite of them all.

Her gaze upon Rowan was wide and shadowed with swift-
moving speculation, but she said nothing. It was Musetta, angel-
ically fair in her black, who answered him.

"You are convening the Court of Love? But the tournament
is over."

"Indulge me, if you please," he said. "There is a case left unfinished."

Musetta glanced around at the others, her eyes resting an instant on Katrine. Lifting a hand to play with a shining blond curl lying on her shoulders, she returned her attention to Rowan. With irony in her smile, she said, "I see no one objecting."

Rowan inclined his head in appreciation, then got to his feet. He moved to stand with his back to the fire and his hands clasped behind him. A faint sheen of perspiration appeared across his forehead that had nothing to do with the mild heat behind him. His chest rose and fell as he took a deep breath and let it out again. The waiting silence stretched. His voice was deep and feathered with roughness when he finally began.

"We have discussed a number of questions in the days past. We have decided that the duty of the knight toward his lady-mistress is protection in all its forms, that the duty from wife to husband and from husband to wife is companionship, trust, and respect. But there is one question we have not pursued. It is this: What is the duty of the lady-mistress to the man who has vowed love and protection?"

"That is easy," Musetta said at once. "Fidelity is the answer."

"Constancy, rather," Alan said. "There is a slight difference."

"Oh, dear," Lewis said with a lifted brow. "Not only to be faithful, but to be faithful forever?"

Perry sent them a tight, unseeing smile before he sat forward with his hands between his knees. "I think," he said, "that the true answer is honesty. The lady should never say she loves unless it is so, never speak of tomorrow unless she will be there to share it, never give a kiss where she knows she will never give her heart."

"Why, Perry," Musetta said with unease in her face. She

picked up a green velvet pillow fringed in gold and began to toy with it.

"Yes," Rowan mused, "you are on the right path."

"Perhaps," Katrine said, staring at the high polish on Rowan's boots, "what she owes the man is release from his duty to her, the boon of being free to choose how and where he will love, without obligation."

Rowan tilted his head. "But suppose he prefers his bonds? What sacrifice does he have the right to expect for the sake of his love? What measures does he have permission to use to have his lady at his side?"

"Measures?" Katrine said, alertness rising in her eyes, driving out the apathy there.

Alan, his gaze keen on Rowan's face, frowned. "We are supposing, of course, that the lady wishes to be where the man wants her?"

"Yes," Rowan said, turning to the other man, "always supposing that."

"And that the only obstacles are material considerations, or else duties self-imposed?" At Rowan's nod, Alan went on. "Well, then, it seems to me that any means acceptable to the tenets of chivalry could be justified."

Rowan raised a hand to rub his chin. "The tenets of chivalry; that might be an insurmountable restriction."

"Not," Alan said simply, "to a man of imagination."

Katrine sat watching Rowan for long moments with the firelight flickering in her eyes. She opened her lips to speak, closed them, then began again. "If you are suggesting . . ."

He shook his head so that the light dipped and played in the black waves of his hair. His gaze as innocent as an unfledged dove, as studious as a monk testing miracles, he said, "I was only clarifying a point of honor."

She didn't trust that sound in his voice or the tender edge

in his smile. He had used them to breach her defenses before. It would be as well, she thought, if she was on her guard.

Alan, his voice a little loud, said, "If we have settled it, I should tell everyone that I am leaving, finally, in the morning."

Perry also would be going, or so it seemed. He gave the news with defiance. Musetta received it with her lashes shadowing her cheeks and color under her thin skin. Though she made no comment, the fringe of the velvet pillow came loose in her hands.

"If we have many more tournaments," Lewis said, "the house will want new furnishings."

"There may never be another, now that Giles is gone," Musetta said. She placed the pillow to one side as tears pooled clear and tremulous in her eyes. She looked at Perry, as if expecting some gesture of comfort, but he only sat staring at his hands.

"That may be just as well," Alan said.

No one contradicted him.

It seemed the house party for the tournament was, finally, over. Conversation dwindled away to nothing except strain and discomfort. Katrine made an excuse, a short time later, to retire for the night, leaving the others to do the same at their leisure.

Rowan had not said what his intentions were; not this time. That knowledge went with her as she made her way toward the great, curving central stair in the back hall. She was not certain what that meant, whether he had no intention of departing just yet, or if he had not yet made up his mind when he would go.

She knew what he had said on the subject, but the circumstances had changed. She was no longer in danger, nor was she safely married. A handsome man staying in her house must occasion the kind of gossip that any respectable woman would need to avoid. She was not sure how respectable she could claim to be now, but she thought it might make a difference to Rowan.

Someone left the parlor after her; she heard the door open

and close again. As footsteps sounded, approaching behind her, she paused on the second step of the stairs to glance back.

It was Lewis. He came toward her with a lounging stride. His hands were pushed into his pockets and there was an abstracted frown on his face.

Seeing her turn, he said, "A moment of your time, Madam Katrine, if I may." He did not speak again until he stood just below her. He shifted his shoulders self-consciously as he went on then, "This is not, possibly, the best time to bring up this subject, but it's one of some importance to me."

"If it's about money . . ." she began.

"Well, yes, it always is, isn't it, for some of us." His mouth took on a self-deprecating twist. "I wonder if you would advance me my allowance for a year, as an accumulation of funds, to return to England and settle myself there. If you will, I can promise there will be no further drain on your purse."

She had expected any number of requests, from a plea for payment of gambling debts to a request for a new carriage, but never this. "You want to leave Arcadia?"

"It isn't that I want to leave so much as a simple preference for being my own man. When I came here, I had some idea of making myself useful to Uncle Giles. He wouldn't allow it. It's my belief that Brantley advised him against it, afraid I might usurp his place. Also, Uncle Giles kept me at loose ends to have someone to play off against Brantley when he became too sure of himself."

"I didn't realize," Katrine said, though perhaps she should have.

"It was a small matter between my uncle and myself. Uncle Giles, I think, liked having me around; I amused him. Above and beyond that, he had the intention, laudable but difficult, of turning me into a gentleman."

"I thought you were one already."

"Did you? How kind. But my mother was the daughter of

a wool merchant, you know, not nearly high-toned enough for Uncle Giles, once he had built Arcadia. The estate went to my older brother when my father died, and my mother sent me here in the expectation that Uncle Giles might do something handsome for one of the few male relatives in his line."

Katrine said quietly, "I spoiled that for you, didn't I?"

"Oh, I don't blame you; it was quite my own fault. Idleness is supremely boring, and boredom brings out the worst in me. I am not, basically, a kind person." He paused, then went on in colorless tones. "Uncle Giles always refused passage home when I asked; I thought you might be more amenable. It seems best—that I take myself off before I do more damage than I have already."

Katrine watched the spasm of pain, instantly erased, that crossed Lewis's thin face. She said, "You are blaming yourself for Charlotte's death."

His gaze was stark as it met hers. "Shouldn't I? I exposed her. Out of ennui and pure, jealous spite, I gave Brantley the key he needed to be rid of her. It's the way I am. I can't help it."

She had learned a great deal of late about the pain of self-blame. She said, "If it's occupation that you need, there will be much work to be done here now, with Giles and Brantley gone."

His eyes widened. "You mean it? You would not mock me?"

"You understand that I would not give up all control to you."

Eagerness leaped into his face. "I would gladly be Arcadia's factotum only. That is, if you could bring yourself to trust me." He made a wry face. "I have a mercenary soul along with my other faults. But I am not avaricious."

"A mercenary bent would not be bad in a factotum," Katrine said, smiling. "You could try the position and see if it suits."

He caught her hand and kissed it with fervor. "You'll not be sorry."

She shook her head. "Oh, I expect I shall, from time to time. Both of us being human, there are bound to be clashes, but perhaps we can learn to work together."

He gave her a sly glance from under his lashes. "There could be fewer than you think, if you are elsewhere."

"Why should I be?" she asked. But he had already bowed and was walking back toward the parlor.

She watched his retreating back for a few moments before she turned and began to mount the stairs. She moved slowly, like a woman twice her age. She should have felt that some of the burden of seeing after Arcadia and its people had been lifted from her with the recruitment of Lewis. Instead it seemed that she had accepted the responsibility of yet another person's well-being.

She was capable of bearing it. She would learn, she would prevail, and Arcadia would prosper. The only question was, at what cost? What price would she have to pay to be the chatelaine and mainstay of Giles's dreams?

She knew, oh, she knew full well.

The price was love.

Lewis thought differently; she could see that much. He didn't understand.

She could, if she wished, and if she were less proud, hold Rowan to the words he had spoken in the face of death. How like him it had been to attempt to give them to her then, to leave them ringing in her ears as life left her, if need be. The generosity of the impulse was exactly what might have been expected of someone who had given so much of himself for her needs already.

She would treasure them. She would listen to them singing quietly in her mind her life long, and might, if she were lucky, have them as a soft sweet dirge when in some distant year she finally surrendered to death's beckoning.

Rowan, being strict in his notions of honor, felt himself bound by his spoken word. She had tried to release him. He had not yet accepted that he was free, she thought, but he would, soon, and then she would be alone.

Delphia was waiting for her in her bedchamber. The maid had laid out Katrine's nightclothes and sat ready to undress her and take down her hair. Her face was puffy from weeping and her eyes were red. She kept her eyes downcast as she got to her feet and went about her duties with silent competence.

There had been little time to speak to Delphia in the rushed and confused hours since Giles and Brantley had died. She was not sure how to approach the gulf that had opened between the two of them; still, it could not be put off any longer. It was she who must take the first step, since it was unlikely that Delphia would speak from dread of the consequences.

"Are you all right?" she asked, her gaze on the maid's swollen face. As she received a nod of confirmation she went on, "They are treating you well in the quarters?"

"There are some who say terrible things—" Delphia choked to a stop, then went on. "It doesn't matter."

"I'm sorry if you have been abused. Perhaps if I ask Cato to speak for you?"

"No, no! It—it will pass."

Katrine was silent a moment while she allowed Delphia to lift the black gown she had unbuttoned over her head and put it aside. As the maid began to unfasten her hoops and petticoats, she said, "I know the temptations that caused you to become involved with Brantley, but I can't help wondering if you loved him?"

The girl swallowed. "I was flattered, and prideful, when he chose me. He gave me so many pretty things, and made such promises. I felt sorry for him, married to Madam Musetta, who didn't care about anything except herself."

Katrine stepped out of the petticoats and put her arms into the dressing gown Delphia held for her. Moving to the dressing table where an oil lamp burned, she seated herself. Her voice even, she said, "And did you know he was going to try to kill me—and Rowan—while we were in the tower?"

The ivory hair brush Delphia had just picked up clattered as it dropped from her hand to the floor. "Oh, no, Madam Katrine, dear heaven, no! I couldn't believe it when I saw the tower burning. I nearly went crazy."

"Yet you gave Brantley the note form Charlotte."

"He took it from me, really he did. I was bringing it here, to you, where I thought Master Rowan would be. But Master Brantley caught me in the hall. He threatened to say that I helped him all along if I complained—the arsenic for Mr. Giles and everything. It was a lie—but I couldn't tell you. I just—couldn't."

"I must have been a bad mistress if you couldn't trust me to believe you."

Delphia knelt to pick up the brush, then stood turning it in her hand, staring at it. "It wasn't that. I didn't want you to know I had been such a fool. I let him use me, I was ignorant enough to think he loved me because he said so. I didn't want you to think so bad of me."

"Because of it, Charlotte died." Katrine's voice carried unavoidable censure.

"I didn't know what he meant to do, never dreamed what he had done. I thought that young man, Mr. Rowan's brother, killed himself over Madam Musetta's heartless ways. I didn't know what really happened, I didn't know."

"That may be, but how could you side with Giles, keep me in the tower, after all the years we have been together?" It was, Katrine discovered, that point which hurt the most.

"You could have gotten out, I know you could. You did it, later." Delphia looked as puzzled as she was upset.

"But by helping Giles, you decided that I needed to bear a child for him."

Delphia shook her head. "It wasn't the baby in my mind, but the man. I watched Master Rowan, and it seemed to me he was different. I thought he had loving in him, loving that you needed."

"You should not have chosen for me," Katrine said, looking away, her voice subdued.

Tears rose in the maid's eyes and she choked on a sob. "I was not a good judge of men for myself; I don't know how I could think I could choose for you. If I was wrong, I'm sorry for it. Still, I have to know what you're going to do with me. Will you—send me away? Or will you take me with you when you go?"

"Go? Why should I go?" Katrine said in irritation.

Delphia looked at her in wondering sadness before she shook her head. "But Madam Katrine, why should you stay?"

There was no easy answer to that question, and Katrine did not have the energy to explain the hard one. Instead she sought to reassure Delphia that she would not be handing her over to either the sheriff or the whipping post.

There was no malice in Delphia; she had been caught in something beyond her ken or control. Duped and manipulated by Brantley for his purposes, used to soothe his bruised ego, she would always bear the scars of that entrapment, always live with her share of guilt for the deaths at Arcadia. It was punishment enough.

They talked for a little longer, then Katrine sent the girl away. She had had enough of worrying and wondering over other people for one day. All she wanted now was rest.

It would not come. She was haunted by the endless roll of her own thoughts, and by words and phrases too well remembered.

Why should you stay?
—if you are elsewhere—
—the due of a husband from a wife.
When love is not present—
I love you in my fashion—

The last words had been spoken by Giles. It almost seemed, as she sat there leaning on the dressing table with her head propped on her hand, that she had been used by her husband in a way that was not too different from how Delphia had been used by Brantley. Giles had married her, not for love or companionship, but to camouflage an incestuous passion, to get a child on her for his own glory as well as to cheat death and his brother-in-law's evil designs. He must surely have known that her life was in danger after the carriage accident, yet he had not warned her, had done nothing to protect her. What he had done instead was hurry his plans to force upon her a father for the child he wanted. He had threatened her with degrading, forcible impregnation, and had drugged her and left her to the mercy of a man who, for all he knew of him, might have taken her without kindness or pity. And finally he had tried to bind her to himself and his name in death with the weight of riches and responsibilities.

What was his remorse, or the fact that he had died to save her life, against these things?

But had he really tried to save her, or had he only been intent on avenging his own injuries? It was impossible to know.

What is the duty of a lady-mistress to the man who has vowed love and protection?

What force does the knight have permission to use—?

Was it possible that she had been wrong about Rowan? How could she be? And yet, he was not an easy man to know. The convoluted turnings of his reason left plenty of room for doubt, as did the constant exercise of his excessive notions of honor. He had been armored by his quest for justice for his brother, and by the varied and provocative experiences of his nomad's life. He had begun by despising her and ended by desiring her, but there had been little enough in between to offer her comfort now, or hope.

And yet, and yet. There lingered in her mind the rich enchantment of words spoken in longing, in repletion, in promise.

Katrine rose from the dressing table and blew out the lamp. She stood for long moments in the dark, fighting the urge to go flying from the room and down the hall to Rowan's bedchamber. What she would say to him when she got there, she didn't know, but it seemed that anything would be better than enduring the rack of doubt in her head.

Suppose he prefers his bonds?

She began walking almost without volition, crossing the darkened room to the hall door, pulling it open, and stepping into the long, dim corridor. She moved with ghostlike quietness down the hall, with her dressing gown billowing around her from its pearl closure between her breasts and her hair lifting and wavering down her back. At the door of the bedchamber at the end of the hall, the one Rowan had been given, she lifted a hand and knocked.

There was no answer. She caught her lip between her teeth, then, with sudden determination, gripped the silver knob and turned.

He was not there. Everything was dark and still. The bed was empty. The chimneys of the lamps sitting here and there were cool; it had been some time since anyone was in the room.

Katrine moved to the armoire and threw the door open. Her questing hand, as she reached inside, found only emptiness. His clothing had been removed down to the last linen shirt and pair of boots.

He was gone. He had left without saying good-bye. Or perhaps he had taken her words of release to be their farewell. Either way, she would never see him again, never stand in the encompassing warmth of his smile, never feel his arms around her, or watch the darkness of his eyes grow deeper just before he pressed his lips to hers.

It was what she had intended, of course. She had known it must come. She had just not realized how she would feel, as if someone had torn out half her heart, as if they had raked her brain with razor-edged talons and clamped her chest in a vise. It was agony to breathe, to think, to feel. She stood there with her hands clamped over her mouth, shuddering uncontrollably while tears started from her eyes.

The door opened behind her. She started to turn, though her vision was so blurred she could not see. The tall shape of a man was outlined in the faint light, then the image was cut off as the door closed.

She blinked rapidly and lowered her hands. She wasn't sure what she had seen, or who. The figure in the doorway had been so broad, so tall. Was it Rowan? Had he gone away, thinking the room was empty because there was no light? If not, if he had stepped inside, why didn't he speak?

She parted her lips, listening. In a moment she would say something herself, as soon as she thought she could make a sound through her tight throat.

There came a fluttering movement, and abruptly she was enfolded in thick, soft cloth. It wrapped her head and shoulders and bound her arms to her sides. Inhaling in shock and outrage, she breathed in fine fibers of napped velvet. A cough caught in her throat, becoming a paroxysm that doubled her nearly in half.

She felt herself lifted, swung high against a chest like hewn stone. Clamped there, racked with coughing, she was carried with swift, jolting steps. She knew when they emerged into the hall, because she caught a faint glint of light through the thickness of cloth. Then she heard the warning creak of the door that gave onto the balcony at the corridor's end.

She screamed, a strangled sound, muffled even to her ears. She tried to kick, but her captor's grasp tightened with casual, bruising force. Greater darkness converged around her. She heard the sound of peeper frogs and felt the freshness of cooler air on her feet and ankles. She was outside.

She drew in her breath to scream again. In that instant she felt herself pushed into emptiness, felt the arms supporting her heft her weight once, twice. Then she was dropped.

The cry that ripped from her throat was raw with terror. Falling, she was falling. She hurtled down and down into darkness with the cloth that enwrapped her flapping around her. Her mind, her body, cringed from the moment when she would strike the ground.

She was snatched from the air, caught in arms of whipcord strength, whirled dizzyingly, held close. At her ear, she heard a soft and explicit oath.

Rowan.

The hood that covered her face fell away. Above her, she saw Omar swinging down from the balcony, using the carving for creaking handholds, wrapping his great legs around the columns, and sliding down like a giant ape Katrine had once seen in a tome on the wilds of the African continent.

"What are you doing?" she said in husky yet dignified demand of the dark figure who held her.

There was no answer. The instant Omar touched the ground, Rowan set off at a run. A carriage stood waiting on the drive. Omar ripped open the door and stood back. Rowan tossed Katrine up inside, then leaped in behind her and slammed the door behind him. Before she could right herself on the seat, they were rolling away from Arcadia, heading toward St. Francisville.

To lunge for the door was purest reflex action; she hardly dared hope that it would succeed. It didn't.

Rowan caught her arm and hauled her back, pressing her into the seat with his fingers biting into her upper arms. "What are you trying to do," he asked with grating exasperation, "get yourself killed?"

"You can't do this," Katrine said through set teeth.

It was a moment before he answered, and then his voice was quiet. "It's done."

"Where are you going? Where are you taking me?" There was such a roiling mixture of anger and hope inside her aligned with the residue of fear that she hardly knew what she was saying.

"To the steamboat to New Orleans, for a start, then possibly to my mother's house near New Orleans. After that, to any place in the wide reaches of the world where they don't mind if I keep a woman against her will."

"I—have no clothes," she said through the tightness in her throat.

"You have a trunk packed by Delphia strapped on back. She's on the box, with Omar."

"I'll tell the boat captain you're kidnapping me." The words were embarrassingly tentative.

"I can, if you force me, pour a bottle of whiskey down your throat before we get there. The captain will understand completely when I tell him you have delusions."

She stared at him in the darkness. Her voice little more than a whisper, she said, "You wouldn't."

"Do you think I will release you from your vow of love as you released me? I am not so accommodating. I want you as I've never wanted anything in my life. You are my home, my hearth, the benchmark of my utmost sail. In you I have my grail, my fleece, my sweet redemption and golden glory. I've searched for the heartsease you give me over countless heaving seas and in a thousand flea-infested towns. I've yearned after you these weeks, and tied my guts in knots trying to control the vicious need to hand your husband's head to him, shriveled and toothless as an African trophy. If you think I will lose you now merely because of some scruple that ties you to a dead man, then you don't know me."

The relief and gladness began somewhere deep inside, spreading upward. She said with pensive consideration, "I think I prefer being—what was it?—your soul's sweet apple. Also, possibly, your wife."

"When?" he demanded, his hold slackening only a fraction.

"How can I tell? As you said, I hardly know you."

"You will, entirely and forever." His voice quieter, yet rich with certainty, he added, "It's a promise."

The song of his declaration ran swift and deep inside her, banishing doubts, soothing fears. It reached her heart in a gentle rush, bringing the sweet rise of joy. She slipped her hands up between them, closing her fingers on the lapels of his coat to hold him near.

Her lips curved in a smile. It was there in her voice as against the smooth surfaces of his mouth she said in her turn, "When?"

The carriage rocked them together, the rhythm picking up as they rolled, their progress unimpeded, toward St. Francisville. Rowan touched her face, smoothed a hand down her back. Holding her to him, fitted against the long length of his body, he leaned back into the seat corner.

"Beginning now," he said.

Jennifer Blake was born near Goldonna, Louisiana, in her grandparents' 120-year-old hand-built cottage. She grew up on an eighty-acre farm in the rolling hills of northern Louisiana. While married and raising her children she became a voracious reader. At last she set out to write a book of her own. That first book was followed by thirty-six more and today they have reached more than nine million copies in print, making Jennifer Blake one of the bestselling romance writers of our time. Her most recent novel is *Wildest Dreams*.

Jennifer and her husband live near Quitman, Louisiana, in a house styled after old Southern planters' cottages.